A KITE ON THE WIND

MENDED HEARTS SERIES

An Anchor on Her Heart
Love Calls Her Home
A Kite on the Wind

A KITE ON THE WIND

MENDED HEARTS SERIES

By
Patricia Lee

Dedication

In special remembrance of Mrs. Hazel Peterson,
former first grade teacher at Thurston Elementary,
who once told this six-year-old first grader to,
"Keep writing, Patty."
I'm glad I listened.

Acknowledgments

Polycystic kidney disease is a genetic disorder that affects people in all walks of life. Many afflicted with the disease don't know they carry the gene until it manifests itself in their late thirties and early forties.

My thanks to Rory Wold who shared his history with PKD and guided me to the national PKD website. There I was able to read blogs written by various patients struggling with the disorder as well as case histories and medical solutions. If this story prompts you to become a kidney donor, please write and let me know. Many victims of the disease could be helped with the gift of one working kidney. You could change a life.

To my patient and enduring family, I say thank you for allowing me the time and the privacy to complete this third novel in the Mended Hearts series. To my husband for encouraging me in my desire to write. To my son, Jonathan, who stepped up to the plate, literally, and cooked many meals while I finished a scene or tweaked a chapter. To my daughter who had to give up her computer time so that Mom could finish "the book."

To Heidi Killion Gaul who volunteered to read and critique the story from its onset and made many helpful and insightful suggestions to better the story.

To Rick Brown and David Hall of the National Oceanic and Atmospheric Administration (NOAA) for guiding me to information on the NOAA website about the workings and procedures of the organization. Thanks to the dedicated scientists who work on the teams that monitor the earth's oceans and who take time from their work to blog about their adventures. I gleaned a wealth of information from the stories that the team shared. Any mistakes are mine.

Thanks to my publisher, Miralee Ferrell, and my publicist, Nikki Wright, for believing in me.

Most of all my thanks go to my Lord and Savior Jesus Christ who gave me the gift of words and taught me how to use them. To Him be all glory and praise.

CHAPTER ONE

THE SLAM OF A DOOR CAUGHT Claire Simpson's attention as she watched snow fall on the small patch of beach barely visible beyond the Yaquina View Elementary breezeway. Even though she stood close to the parking lot, she hadn't heard the pickup drive in. She was surprised by its arrival, since Newport's school officials had cancelled classes earlier to avoid the onset of a severe Pacific storm.

A well-groomed man, his uniform suggesting military personnel, climbed from the truck. Trench coat flapping about his knees as the wind played tag, he opened the doors of the extended cab, and lifted first a girl, then a boy from the back. The little boy ran toward the playground, exuberance oozing from his busy body.

"Kite!" He pointed to the beach, but the blunt sound of an angry voice turned him around. He walked bent over toward the truck, head hanging like a scolded dog.

Claire didn't recognize either child, but perhaps they attended school elsewhere. The man might be here to pick up his wife. She hadn't met all of the staff's spouses. The threesome entered through the main doors and disappeared. She returned her attention to the storm, mesmerized as the churning ocean slapped at the edge of the sand, daring the falling snow to encroach its mighty waters. The waves seemed to laugh as the fragile flakes vaporized in the rush of the wind.

She hadn't grown up on the Oregon coast and assumed the north Pacific was all surf and sand. She'd never have guessed the shore could be covered in white, nor had she seen it this way, even in pictures. Mounds on the beach turned into oversized marshmallows. Driftwood transformed to fanciful fences. Did this happen often? On the sand? In November?

Yet here snow fell—sloppy, fat flakes fluttering down like a curtain of white fairies on a theater's stage opening night. The quiet drift of the airborne dancers made her pulse race, their presence evoking memories from her past—images she'd tried to forget.

A brisk whack of wind chilled her. She turned to the school where for the last two years she'd filled her days as the learning specialist. Except today. The voices of children were missing in light of the unusual snow day. The swings jingled in the breeze, their black seats responding to the swish of cold air driving the storm inland. The silvery slide no longer shone, its curved form home to pockets of wintry slush instead. When the squall landed shortly after nine, the superintendent ordered the buses back. High winds were expected, along with freezing rain, and maybe snow. She glanced down at the little stretch of beach peeking through the housing project surrounding the school. Cross off the maybe. Snow still fell.

She checked her watch. Staff members were free to leave at noon. She should be packing up for the day, as grocery shopping lay ahead. The errand meant she'd brought her car. Any other Monday she'd have walked the short mile from her duplex to the school. But Providence had smiled on her, so she wasn't stuck walking home in the storm.

Claire scooted in through the side entrance and headed to her office. The family she'd seen a few minutes before stood talking with the principal. The man, gesturing with his hands, spoke as if agitated. The children clung to his pant legs. She watched them a few minutes, then realized her gawking might be considered rude and entered her room. She couldn't put a finger on her angst, but something about the scene bothered her. Perhaps the father had had a bad experience elsewhere.

She lifted the stack of files she needed to work through tonight, stuffed the papers into a canvas tote, and set it on the floor near the door. In her position, paperwork never ended. Individual education plans had to be evaluated quarterly. Goals set for the disabled student must be addressed, assessed, and re-addressed. A few students with limited abilities never reached their goals.

Others made the adjustment to school with a measured level of success and goals were met ahead of schedule. When that happened, the process started over and new IEP's were formulated. Claire loved when a student performed above his or her expected level. When they failed, she spent a lot of time praying over a workable solution for that individual child.

Claire appreciated the district's flexible approach to education. Not every child she saw fit the disabled category. The school environment occasionally alienated capable students with sensitive personalities. Those needed a little extra attention to mobilize them to achieve their best.

When she first joined the teaching staff two years before she'd met her first impossible assignment. A young autistic girl had defied every attempt by school personnel to help her fit into the classroom. Finally, her mother, McKenna Taylor, had opted for the district's freedom-to-choose policy to home school her daughter. The choice proved perfect for Sydney, a child whose hypersensitive hearing prevented adaptation to a noisy classroom.

Claire slipped into her coat, buttoned the front, and headed to the door where her tote waited. Grabbing it, she locked her office and followed the red tiles toward the entrance. The man she'd seen earlier still stood talking with the principal. Acknowledging them with a nod, she veered to the left.

"Claire?" The principal's voice caught her by surprise.

She turned and faced the superintendent. The woman's smile was forced as if she were dealing with an obnoxious student. Claire eyed the two children, noting the little girl slumped on a chair by the wall. Sandy blonde hair tumbled over her forehead, hiding her eyes. The little boy, arms folded and a frown on his face, stood beneath his father's hand, the man's fingers firmly planted on the top of the child's head. "Hello."

"Claire, this is Montgomery Chandler. He and his children recently moved to Newport." The principal gestured to the boy. "This is Mason. His sister is Mia."

"Mr. Chandler." She held out her hand. "Claire Simpson. I'm the learning specialist." She smiled at Mason, then Mia.

Mr. Chandler let go of Mason and shook her hand. "Most people call me Monty."

The twins studied her, shy grins on both of their faces. The boy, hair like his sister's, had eyes the color of dried walnuts. The girl looked up, and Claire noticed her eyes were blue. Claire glanced at the father. His clear blue eyes scrutinized her like a bug under a microscope and confirmed who the little sister favored. Her cheeks burned in the intensity of his stare. "Twins?" She never liked to ask that question because people often took offense in the obvious, but since this pair were brother and sister, she decided to risk it.

"Yes." Monty drew the boy back toward him and placed a firm grip on the child's shoulder. "Both of them were doing well in school when we left Seattle."

"It's nice to have you join our community." No mother had been mentioned, but Claire decided this was not the time to ask. She could access the children's files easily enough. "Will they start tomorrow?"

Monty stiffened at the question. "I had hoped they'd start today, but the weather had other ideas."

The principal gestured as she spoke. "Usually these storms are only wind and rain. When snow threatens, we have to think of the safety of our students traveling in buses on slick roads."

"Mia and Mason will arrive by car. My sister will pick them

up."

Claire found the defensiveness in his voice curious. More than ever she wanted to read their file.

The principal pressed her fingers together. "Tomorrow, then?"

"Tomorrow." Monty nodded at Claire. "Nice to have met you, Mrs. Simpson, even though my children will have no need of your services."

Claire stifled the urge to correct the man. He was wrong on two counts. She wasn't married, and his children, of the many she'd met at this school, already seemed likely candidates for her expertise. She hadn't encountered many second-grade girls who still sucked their thumbs, and the little boy's unspent energy threatened to explode from beneath his jacket, despite his father's firm hand. Parts of the family's puzzle appeared to be missing. What those pieces were, Claire didn't know, but to do her job, she needed to find them.

He turned, and with a grip on Mason's coat jacket, extended his other hand to Mia, who shuffled at his side sucking her thumb. The threesome walked to the door, the man's brisk strides making the children hustle. As the door opened, Mia glanced back, her sad eyes searching the hallway. When she found Claire standing where she'd left her, she lifted a pudgy hand and waved.

Time for Claire to fill in the gaps of the puzzle.

Monty slid his two children into the car seats at the back of their crew cab, fastened the seatbelts, and hurried to the driver's side. As the engine warmed, he looked over the little gray building where the twins would attend school. The large red letters naming the structure seemed out of proportion to the building's size. Beyond the long, boxlike exterior, a larger addition rose from the back, a space he guessed to be an auditorium or gymnasium. The playground extended behind, newer looking play structures and sturdy swings filling the fenced recreational area. He glimpsed a limited span of the ocean in the distance, the view obstructed by a housing development that graced the school's perimeter.

"Is that a kite? A kite flying in the snow?" Mason's voice rose from the back, high-pitched and excited. Like a ballerina pirouetting on a stage, the kite lifted into the air, reaching a lofty space and dashing toward the ground again.

"Yes, the person holding the string must either be frozen or nuts to brave this wind and the cold." Monty watched, fascinated by the strange dips and turns of the kite's dance across the beach. He hadn't flown a kite in years. He understood Mason's enthusiasm.

"He might be cold, Dad." Mason leaned as far forward as his seatbelt would allow. "But think of all the fun he's having."

"I hope he doesn't catch pneumonia down there." Monty put the truck in gear and reversed out of the small parking place. "I need to drop by the NOAA headquarters and let them know I've arrived. After that we'll go see if your Aunt Ellen is home yet." He glanced in the rearview mirror for a response. Mason, nose pressed against the glass, sat watching the kite. Mia, thumb stuck in her mouth, had collapsed in the corner of her seat, fast asleep.

He sighed. His sister Ellen had her work cut out for her with these two. Had she known what she was doing when she volunteered? He wondered if he should have accepted her offer. But the transfer from Seattle left him few alternatives. If only Marissa could have beaten her illness last spring, she could have transferred with him. But the illness that raged its war against her claimed its victim, its iron grip on her fragile form silencing the spark within her forever. He couldn't help the painful longing tugging at him. The kids so needed her. He needed her.

Mason shrieked. "It got away, Dad. The kite flew away."

Mia, startled by her brother's scream, awoke and started

crying.

Montgomery fisted the steering wheel and closed his eyes. Why did it feel as if everything they did ended in a crisis? How had Marissa smoothed each squall into an ocean breeze? Calmed every fear with a quiet word? He had no answers. He hadn't been home enough to learn. How would his family survive without her?

Claire shivered as she walked into her apartment. She set the groceries on the kitchen counter, hurrying to start the flame in the front room's standing fireplace. The little electric hearth, with its counterfeit blaze and glowing logs, had been a gift from her mother. The fireside might not contain a real fire grate and burning coals, but in minutes it could heat her kitchen, dining, and front room area to a comfortable seventy degrees. In this coastal climate, with the windy days and rain-filled nights, she welcomed the warmth. The snow today made the device even more appreciated.

By the time the apartment lost its chill, Claire had put away her purchases, made a cup of hot chocolate, and settled down at her desk to study the paperwork she needed to finish. Two of the teachers had registered a complaint against a second-grade girl who continued to sneak cigarettes into the girl's restroom and smoke them before dropping them in the toilet. The girl's foster parents didn't know where she might be getting the packs but considering the child's history of pandering on the streets for her drunken mother, the illegal possession of smokes didn't surprise Claire. Figuring out a way to change the girl's attitude toward what she was doing became the goal. Claire had no clue how to proceed. What eight-year-old had already learned to smoke?

The telephone interrupted her thoughts and she picked it up.

"Hi, Claire." Her mother's voice sounded strong and healthy.

"You must be feeling better." Claire settled deeper in her chair.

"Your flu bug made its exit, I take it?"

"Pretty much. I still have a residual cough." Her mother stopped and cleared her throat. "But I'm on the mend. How was school today? Did I understand the news correctly? You had snowy roads?"

"Yep. I saw snow near the water's edge. I'm used to flurries in the valley, but I've never seen snow falling on sand before." Claire remembered Montgomery Chandler and his two children, the father upset that his son and daughter didn't get to start school today. "The students were sent home because of slick roads."

"Better safe than risking trouble."

Claire listened to her mother ramble for a few more minutes, waiting for the inevitable question she always posed.

Mom didn't disappoint. "I saw Nancy at the grocery store, and she asked about you."

"You two are never giving up on us, are you?" Claire sighed inwardly. Nancy, her mother's best friend, was also the mother of Claire's ex-fiancé, Jamie Duval. The two women often conspired to rematch Claire and Jamie despite repeated pleas to stop.

"You came awfully close to tying the knot, Claire. I haven't forgotten. But I also understand why you wouldn't want to try again."

"He left me three days before we went to the altar. For reasons I find unacceptable. I'm trying to forget."

"I don't blame you, though I thought it was only a misunderstanding at the time." Mom paused. "But you obviously had your mind set. Running away to Pennsylvania sealed the deal."

"What was I supposed to do? Sit around and wait for him to come crawling back?" She sipped her hot chocolate. "Angie and Brennan had space for me. And the teaching program at Penn State was excellent." She set the cup down. "I believe I landed on my feet after Jamie's debacle."

"You did. Quite well." Her mother sighed. "Any new men in your life?"

Claire smiled at her mother's question. Mom's mission, it seemed, centered around getting Claire married. Mom had almost accomplished her goal when she and Jamie Duval, an Olympic hopeful, became engaged. The wedding guests had returned their RSVP's when Jamie sent her a note saying he'd changed his mind. He'd been invited to compete in a slalom at Aspen and couldn't pass up the opportunity. The event might have been his ticket to the next Olympics. She'd never viewed snow the same way since.

Only Claire understood the real reason for his departure. Though betrayed, discovering this side of Jamie before she repeated her vows had been a godsend. He'd dumped her with the wedding expenses, the embarrassment, and a future forever carrying the burden of their past in silence. To save face, she'd opted to live with her married sister, Angela, in Pennsylvania. She spent the year there finishing her degree, earning her teaching credentials and healing from the brokenness Jamie's departure created. Time well spent.

When she returned to teach in Newport, he had the audacity to make a reappearance, pleading with her to forgive him. Once she might have considered his request, but she'd discovered the truth behind his absence. Another woman had caught his attention. That she couldn't forgive.

Her mother still waited for an answer. "No, Mom. This is a coastal town. Single men are usually here for the weekend, looking for a good time before they hurry back to jobs in the valley. Those who are permanent wear rings on their left hand or, so far, haven't interested me when I've had the opportunity to meet someone new." She raised her chin in defiance, as if her mother could see. "But I'm happy in my job, glad to be free of Jamie's spell over me, and enjoying my enduring single status. What Jamie and I had is over. I'm not going back there again. Ever."

"I know. I'm only thinking of your happiness."

"I am happy, Mom. I discovered a new life after Jamie walked out. I found out God loves me as I am. Past mistakes are forgotten in His eyes. My slate has been wiped clean. That in itself made me happy. It has nothing to do with my broken engagement or marital status." She checked the clock. "Anyway, I'm midway through a pile of papers I need to complete before tomorrow. I'll have to say goodbye for now."

"I admire your dedication to your students." Mom sniffed and blew her nose. "You've done well with your education."

"Thanks. Stay healthy. Praying for you."

"Oh, I almost forgot. Angie asked me to have you call her. Apparently Fallyn has been having problems. I think Angie needs a sympathetic ear."

Claire swallowed hard. "I'll call her soon. Thanks for the heads-up."

Fallyn had problems? Her five-year-old niece held a special place in her heart. She'd do anything she could to help the child.

A cold shiver passed over her. *Fallyn …*

CHAPTER TWO

Monty arrived mid-afternoon at his sister's split-level home after checking in at NOAA headquarters. Perched on a hill, the upscale dwelling overlooked much of Newport as well as Yaquina Bay. One thing he'd say for Ellen's in-laws—they knew how to pick a view. That they had gifted Ellen and her husband Kevin with the house when the older couple retired to Florida still amazed Monty. Below them stretched glimpses of the bridge, the science center, and the compound of oceanic government agencies where he worked, creating a network of like-minded scientists all driven by the same purpose. Expanses of beach peeked here and there, the panorama broken by homes scattered on the hill. He parked alongside Ellen's sedan and crawled out of his truck, hoisting Mason onto the pavement, and lifting Mia, once again asleep, to his shoulder.

Mason pointed. "I see a kite."

Monty squinted. "I think you're right. In this wind, though, he may not last long." He closed and locked the truck door and guided Mason ahead of him with one hand as they stepped up to the entry. "You and I will have to wait for a sunny day to fly a kite."

The door opened and Ellen smiled, bending down to give Mason a hug. She stood and rubbed Mia's arm. "So, did you get them enrolled?" She stepped a pace backward, allowing him to enter.

Monty carried Mia to her bedroom. He laid the child on the bed, removed her shoes, and covered her with a light quilt. Backing out of the room, he faced Ellen. "Yes. They are enrolled. You're listed as the authorized contact as well as the principle transportation."

"Does the *principal* know of your employment foibles?" Ellen gestured toward the family room, and he walked beside her. "That I'm the primary guardian in your absence out of town?"

Monty nodded. "I told her my work takes me away for big chunks of time, and she understood. The kids should be in capable hands."

Ellen stopped at the doorway. "Thank you for trusting me to help you with the kids. I know moving from Bellevue has been as hard for you as it has for the twins. But with Marissa gone, and the kids still dealing with their grief, do you think you could have managed?"

"Probably not. But I could have asked for a desk job. You wouldn't have been forced to give up your privacy making room for three wayward refugees."

"You're my brother. I can't think of anyone I'd rather help than you." Ellen's eyes glimmered as if her thoughts had struck a nerve. "Kevin's folks made it possible for us to own this house, and with him temporarily gone, there's more than enough room." She put both hands on his shoulders. "Marissa trusted me to share the rearing of the children. That was one of her final wishes when I visited her in the hospital."

"She knew you'd make a good surrogate mother in her place. But what are you going to do with the ugly, brute of a man she left behind?" He squared his jaw. "Some days I'm not doing so well."

Ellen wrapped her arms around his waist and buried her face against his chest. She drew back and pecked him on the cheek. "I'm praying every day for God to show me how to love you through this."

"Good luck with that." Monty stiffened and stepped away from her. "God isn't listening to me."

"Then I'll have to pray enough for both of us." Ellen headed to the kitchen, calling over her shoulder. "Help me get dinner on the table. I made lasagna in celebration of our new beginning."

"What will you do for encores?" Monty raised an eyebrow. "With your work schedule, you won't be making many homemade meals, I'd wager."

"You'd be surprised at my resourcefulness." Ellen opened the oven and the hot, bubbly smell of melted cheese and oregano wafted out. She slipped the baking dish into a wicker carrier and set it on the table. "Mason, get your hands washed." She sliced the garlic bread and grabbed the tossed salad. "Mason?" Ellen glanced up at Monty, panic creeping into the fine lines around her mouth. "You check?"

He nodded and hurried to the boy's bedroom. Mason's coat, hat, and backpack were missing. Monty strode to the living room and found the front door open. He stepped outside and was met by a blast of icy air and a rush of fresh snowflakes. "Mason?"

Only the hush of a full-fledged snowstorm met his ears. Two small footprints led down the sidewalk, rapidly disappearing in the new layer of white.

Claire sat at her desk, adding to the pile of reports she'd finished since she'd arrived home. The inclement weather had seeped in through the cracks, and she shivered in the chill. She stretched her cold limbs and stood, ambling to the kitchen for a cup of water. Punching *beverage* on her microwave, she waited while the water heated, peeling the wrapper off two beef bouillon cubes. She crumbled two saltines into the watery brew and took a sip. Perfect antidote for a cold night.

She found the remote and pressed her way through a maze of buttons until she had the local news. Snow blowing in the background, a reporter faced the camera. "Local law enforcement officials are asking the public to be on the lookout for seven-year-old Mason Chandler, who disappeared from his home shortly after four this afternoon. The child was last seen wearing brown cargo jeans, a royal blue hoodie, and a red jacket. Chandler is new to the area, having moved here with his family earlier this week. If you have information about the child's whereabouts, please contact the Newport police."

Claire stared at the screen, immobilized by the report. That little boy with the perpetual frown was missing? She glanced at the clock. Not quite six. Though darkness would soon envelop the area, bits of light off the ocean might keep the creeping shadows at bay a few more minutes. She'd chosen her apartment because she could easily walk to the school from here. Mason and his sister must live on this end of town, too, if they were enrolled at the same site. Had the child tried to get back to the playground? She'd seen him point to a kite on the beach before his dad called him back. Had Mason's pre-occupation with the kites this afternoon tempted him to search for more? He'd seemed pretty determined.

She had no idea where the child might have wandered off to, but she grabbed her jacket, a flashlight, and her phone, then headed toward the school. By the time Claire had walked the three blocks to the main highway running through Newport, and crossed to the other side, rain had replaced the drifts of snow she'd first encountered. Three more blocks would take her to the school playground. As she neared the structure, she shaded her eyes from the downpour and allowed the waning light to outline anything that might yet be in the yard. She scanned the stretch of road leading north and found nothing of interest. Claire squinted south to where the school's fence overlooked a small portion of beach that often captivated the students. The rounded form of a small being bent against the wind sat on a log. Claire brought her hand to her throat.

"Mason?" She walked with slow determined steps, hoping her casual approach might not trigger a flight response in the child. "Do you remember me from this afternoon?"

Mason looked up at her, his eyes puffy. "You were in the school?"

Claire bent down to where she could speak close to his face. "So were you. What are you doing out here?"

"I wanted to see the kite again." Mason hiccoughed. "But it's gone. And I got lost in the rain."

"Can I help you get home?" Claire held out her hand and straightened. "I'm sure your dad is worried about you."

"Auntie Ellen will be worried. Not Dad." Mason stood and took her hand. "He's gonna be mad."

"Let me make a phone call and we'll go." She led the boy to the breezeway to get them both out of the downpour before punching in the emergency number she'd seen on the television. "This is Claire Simpson. I'm a teacher at Yaquina View Elementary School. I found Mason Chandler here at the playground." She filled the officer in about where she was. "Hurry. It's cold and he's a very little boy."

She waited in the shelter of the school's walls, holding Mason against her to protect him from the wind. Soon a police car pulled into the parking lot and two individuals left the vehicle. One was unmistakably a uniformed officer, and the other looked to be tall, his trench coat flapping about his body. She'd only seen Montgomery Chandler once, but she remembered the long, lean upper body, the uniform, and the protective trench coat.

"Over here, officer." She stepped into the light and waved, Mason standing at her side. Claire couldn't hear anything above the wind howling off the ocean, but Mason's garbled voice beside her carried a definite fear in its pitch. He trembled, and she didn't want to let him go.

"I'm sorry, Daddy."

The taller man reached her in two strides and lifted the child off the sidewalk. He pulled him toward his torso, wrapping the trench coat about them both. Mason started crying, but the man buried the child's face in his shoulder, and the words she imagined passing between them left her face wet with tears. Montgomery Chandler had every right to be angry with his son's reckless behavior, and the boy understood the degree of his mistake, but from where she stood, the overjoyed man on the sidewalk knew nothing but overwhelming relief.

Monty thought he might be ill, the wave of nausea coursing through his frame threatening to knock him to his knees. Mason! Mason gone. If he'd lost his son, after losing his wife earlier last spring, he'd head out to sea and not look back. Heartache had its limits, and he had nearly reached the breaking point. The little boy in his arms proved he'd not yet arrived there.

His knees wobbled—him, the strong, capable NOAA corps scientist who combed the ocean looking for clues to its mysteries. He could walk the walk, and talk the talk, and wear the smart, dress whites any other day of the week, but give him one little seven-year-old boy missing in a snowstorm, and he turned to jelly. Mason and Mia were all he had left of Marissa, a gift to him from across the chasm between heaven and earth.

"She's nice, Dad." Mason looked up from where he had buried his face against Monty's shoulder.

"Who's nice?" He rubbed his son's back, carrying him to the waiting police car. He pulled a peppermint from his pocket and gave it to Mason.

"The teacher." Mason pointed to the end of the breezeway. "She saw me on the playground and called you to come."

Monty stared after the woman who had pulled up the hood on her jacket and was retreating into the darkness. Had she walked to the school in this storm? Searching for Mason? He had to thank her.

"Mrs. Simpson?"

She turned, her right hand holding her hood together at the chin, her left arm drawing her coat tighter about her small frame. Wet curls ringed her face.

He hurried to where she stood. "Did you come on foot?"

She nodded. "I live across the highway from the school. It's not far."

"Please permit me to take you home. You're drenched." He set Mason down and held his hand, extending his free arm to her. "Your husband will be worried."

"Actually, I'm Miss Simpson. But most people call me Claire." She smiled. "So, no, my husband won't be worried. But I wouldn't mind getting out of this storm."

"Allow me." Monty gestured toward the police car. "Officer Blake, can we drop Claire at her residence?"

"Sure, Mr. Chandler." The officer opened the passenger side door, motioned her into the seat, and turned to Mason. "You ever ride in a police car before?"

Monty grinned at the boy's wide-eyed stare.

"No. Am I in trouble?" Mason cast a worried frown his way. "It looks like a cage, Dad."

"That's to keep criminals from crawling over the seat." He pointed to the back seat. "I'm making sure you don't escape again."

"Oh boy, a police car." All thought of repercussion apparently vanished as Mason crawled into the back of the vehicle. The smell of the candy he'd crunched down wafted through the air. "This is so cool!"

"Don't let this lead you to a life of crime, son." Monty slid in beside the child and pulled the door closed. "Claire, please tell Officer Blake where he needs to go."

A few minutes later, they arrived outside a modest duplex and Claire unhooked her seatbelt. She turned in the seat and spoke to

Mason. "I hope to see you at school tomorrow."

Monty smiled at her. "He will be, if I have to bring him in handcuffs and leg irons."

Claire's face lit up at the teasing, the wet curls clinging to her forehead. She winked. "I have a special spot in my office for boys like him."

"I'll be good, Miss Simpson." Mason's frightened eyes made Monty chuckle. "You won't need any special spot for me."

"That's reassuring, Mason." She shared a conspiratorial smile with Monty. "Good night now." She slid from her seat, closed the car door, and hurried to her entry. After unlocking the door, she turned and waved.

Monty watched her disappear inside, the memory of her kindness to his son making him feel better about uprooting his children and moving to this town. Though his kids wouldn't spend time with Miss Simpson because she was a special education teacher, Monty hoped the rest of the staff had the same caring demeanor as she did.

Claire shuddered as she entered her apartment. She'd left the heat on, for which she was glad, but she needed to get warm soon. She headed for the shower and let the hot water steam around her until she couldn't see the mirror when she stepped out. Wrapping her hair in a fluffy pink towel, she pulled on her robe and stepped into her slippers.

Hunger gnawed at her, a sensation she rarely experienced. But she had worked on papers all afternoon and taken off as soon as she saw the police bulletin on television. Now, nearly eight o'clock, she tried to think of a quick meal that wouldn't keep her awake all night but would quiet the growls within. Opening the refrigerator, she spied the eggs. She grabbed the brick of cheese. An omelet wouldn't take long, wouldn't overfill, and would be hot enough to warm her inside.

A few minutes later she sat down to the plate of eggs smothered in cheese and two slices of toast. She'd poured a glass of orange juice, and it waited near her plate. As she sampled the soft omelet with her tongue, she replayed the evening in her mind.

She'd been surprised to see the father arrive in the police car. Perhaps he had a connection to the agency she didn't know of, which would explain his presence. But where was the mother? If the couple had arrived together in a car behind the police detail, that would have made more sense. But perhaps the little girl—Mia—hadn't been well this afternoon. That would explain her sad, forlorn countenance at the school and her absence tonight. No doubt Mia had stayed home with her mother.

But why did Dad bring the children in today to enroll them and not the mother? In her experience, Claire usually saw the mothers making the arrangements for their children, and she usually met the wife if there were special needs to address. What role did the aunt play in their family structure? Had the father and mother divorced? Perhaps the mother worked a difficult shift which prevented her from attending to her children's school registration. Claire needed to read their transfer file more than ever.

Mason had been afraid of his father's anger. She'd felt him trembling against her while they waited for the police to arrive. When Dad stepped out of the car, Mason hadn't run to him like the lost child he'd been. He waited instead for his father to pick him up. While the senior Chandler appeared overjoyed to be reunited with his son, Mason remained reticent until Dad held him in his arms.

Claire winced at Montgomery Chandler's parting words this afternoon. "Nice to have met you, Mrs. Simpson, even though my children will have no need of your services."

From where she sat, the Chandler children stood in need of her services more than any incoming family she'd met in recent weeks. Convincing Dad might be her biggest hurdle. Where was the chink in his armor?

CHAPTER THREE

THE NEXT DAY PASSED WITHOUT INCIDENT. Most of the flurry had melted, but a well-packed snowman, only a foot tall, sagged against the school wall thawing its way into oblivion.

At the final bell, Claire joined the other teachers as the students prepared to depart. As they stood in line for their rides home, the student faces flushed from exposure. The wind bit its way in and around corners all afternoon. School buses rumbled into position along the breezeway, their drivers ready to transport the chattering children home.

Claire studied the lines of kids waiting to board. She spotted Mia standing quietly to one side, sucking her thumb. She didn't see Mason.

A cluster of boys broke into a scuffle near the wall where the snowman had been. Small snowballs smashed against their targets, coating the usually safe breezeway with slick bits of ice. Two teachers entered the fray, pulling the four boys apart as they tried to smear snow into each other's faces.

Claire winced when one of the boys landed a fist to the midsection of a second-grade teacher trying to contain the boy's struggle. When the man straightened the child and grabbed him by the arms, Mason Chandler's face appeared. Eyes narrowed, and forehead wrinkled in a frown, Mason shouted at the teacher to let him go. He kicked and squirmed with all the force his secondgrader body could produce, but the former college wrestler kept the child in his place.

"I'll tell my dad!" Mason's voice rose about the clatter. "He'll beat you up. You can't hold me here like this!"

Claire walked toward the brawl, surprised that the frightened and humbled child of the night before had vanished in the wake of daylight. "Mason?"

He didn't hear her at first. He continued his threats and stomped on the teacher's toe.

"Mason! Stop this!" Claire's voice grew in pitch and intensity.

Mason stopped and looked at her, bewildered. His reddened cheeks and clenched mouth relaxed as if he were a balloon untied at its end. He wilted, the tears flowing down his face. "They started it."

Claire stepped near the child and placed a hand on his shoulder. "Did they hurt you?"

Mason nodded. "Said Mia should go back to first grade, and I should go back with her." He hiccoughed, a sniff punctuating his words.

Claire squeezed Mason's shoulder, giving him a smile when he glanced up at her. She cocked her head toward the entrance as she made eye contact with the other teacher. "I'll take him inside." The man nodded and pushed Mason toward her with a firm hand. Claire found Mia again and called to her. "Mia, will you come join us?"

Mia stared at the sidewalk as she stumbled through the maze of children. Thumb in her mouth, she scuffed her feet, head hanging from her shoulders like a piece of fruit on a tree ready to fall. When she stood next to Claire, she raised her chubby hand to grasp Claire's fingers.

"Let's go inside."

As the doors closed behind them, their footsteps against the tiled floors shattered the silence of the empty hallways. Claire grabbed Mason's hand and led the pair to her office. She offered Mason a tissue to wipe his face as he sat down. Mia found a chair next to her brother.

When Mason appeared calm, Claire attempted a question. "Do you know why the other boys teased you?"

Mason sniffed again, wiping his nose with the tissue. "They

were making fun of Mia because she sucks her thumb."

"And you stood up for her." Claire ached to hold the boy as he wiggled in his chair, rounded shoulders evident of his distress. "Mia, have you always sucked your thumb?"

Mia shook her head.

Mason spoke for her. "Not until Mommy died."

Claire drew in a sharp breath as the plight of these two little ones shot arrows through her heart. They'd lost their mother. Judging from their behavior the event had been recent. She searched for the right words. "I'm sure you really miss her, don't you?"

Tears ran down Mia's face, her mouth screwing up as she fought the need to cry.

Mason jumped to her side, his arm around Mia's neck. "Don't cry, Mia. Don't cry." The boy's eyes closed as he drew his sister closer, streaks of tears creeping down his cheeks. "We'll make it. Mia, please don't cry."

Claire whispered a quick prayer for wisdom, her own emotions threatening to join the others. She pressed a thumb and forefinger across her nose, tightening her mouth for composure.

A knock at the door interrupted her thoughts. She looked up to see a tall, slender woman staring at the children, forehead lined with a frown, concern etched along the outline of her mouth. She smiled at Claire, a brief warmth that didn't reach her eyes. She opened the door. "May I come in? I'm Ellen Norse. Their aunt. I'm sorry I was late picking them up. I didn't know it would upset them so."

Claire found her voice. "I'm glad you're here. Mason got into a scuffle protecting his sister after school."

"Protecting her?" Ellen's brows rose. "From what?"

Mason stood up and faced his aunt. "Some boys were making fun of Mia for sucking her thumb."

"Ah." Ellen reached out and laid a caress across the back of

Mia's neck. "We're working on that, aren't we?"

Mia peered at Ellen and nodded. "But sometimes I forget."

Ellen focused on Claire. "It's a new thing for her."

Claire chose her words carefully, the professional within her vying with the heartfelt need to nurture this brother and sister. "An emotional response to a recent tragedy, if I were to guess. Might be a coping mechanism that needs time to heal."

Ellen studied her. "They told you?"

"Yes. I'm glad they did. I can be on the watch here for ways to help."

Ellen extended her hand. "Thank you. The death upended Monty, my brother. He isn't himself. He's coping by spending more time at work."

"He moved here for work? What does he do?"

"He's a mammal scientist for NOAA with a specialty in sonar training. He was working seventy-hours a week in Seattle driving a forty-five-minute commute both ways. No time for family."

"I guess not!"

"I suggested Monty transfer here so I could care for the children. He'd stayed in Bellevue when NOAA made the switch to Newport a few years ago. But then Marissa became ill." She covered her mouth. "I'm sorry. I'm rambling on like a distraught teenager."

"Lots of situations to keep track of, I take it?"

"If you only knew." Ellen took each of the twins by the hand. "Shall we go home and make supper now?"

Mason leaned into his aunt, his tear-stained face appearing calm.

Mia, though, looked Claire's way. "'Bye." She raised her pudgy hand and sniffed.

Claire fought the urge to follow her to the car.

The following morning Claire stood unlocking her office door when the other second-grade teacher approached, the expression on her face indicating she'd come to unload. What now? Claire removed the keys from the door with a twist and a jingle, pocketed them, and braced herself for the impact of words coming her direction. "Good morning. Hasn't this week gone fast?"

The teacher blew out what sounded like an exasperated sigh and appeared to count the tiles in the ceiling. "Between the unexpected snow day and the surge of energy the boys found in their day off, I'm not sure I accomplished one thing on my lesson plans. We'll be breaking for Christmas in a month, and my progress reports aren't going to show anything."

"We'll get caught up as the routine returns." Claire understood the frustration of working against an impossible timeline. "Snow days are rare here, I was told."

"But there's no shortage of little rascals." The teacher followed her into her office, waiting as Claire dropped her tote with a thud. "Which is why I'm here."

"Any rascal in particular?" Claire turned and studied the woman.

"That new student, Mason Chandler. Have you reviewed his file?"

"No, they've only officially been here one day." Claire angled her head, encouraging the woman to continue. "Problems?"

"Yes. He's speaking out of turn in the classroom, threatening other students, and doodling when he's supposed to be working on math problems." The teacher clasped her hands together. "I'd hate to see him expelled before he gets started. Is there any previous history?"

"No. But there are reasons for his behavior." Claire's heart broke for the distressed child. "I'm seeking solutions."

"Can't come too soon." The teacher reached for the door. "That child worries me."

"Me, too."

With her room vacant and no students scheduled, Claire exited to the office to retrieve the Chandler children's files. Now that she had a complaint, an official reason to investigate, she decided to probe deeper into Mason and Mia's past. She greeted the secretary and moved toward the file cabinet. Not seeing what she wanted, she turned. "Have you processed the two new students, Mia and Mason Chandler?"

The secretary thumbed through a stack of manila folders, stopping midway to retrieve a file. She handed the packet over.

"Thanks. I won't keep it long."

"Take your time."

Back in her office, Claire read the notes of both files. Nothing stood out. Mason and Mia had regular first grade experiences, their teachers reported them to be bright and quick to grasp new concepts. Mia's reading level dragged behind Mason's, but her overall attention span and ability to learn fell within the higher range of academic achievements. Claire chuckled at Mason's teacher who penciled in at the side. "Mason is all boy!"

Claire would never have guessed. And he likes kites.

The summons came as a surprise and Monty reported to Captain Sam Reynolds, his superior officer, the first thing Friday. "Morning, sir. You wanted to see me?"

"Have a chair, Monty." The man leaned on his desk. "I need a data specialist here at the base. You've signed on as mixed tour, and I wondered if you'd consider shore duty first?"

Staying ashore when his first assignment should have been

aboard a science vessel made Monty eye his superior with a suspicious grin. "This wouldn't have anything to do with my son's nighttime excursion to find a kite in the snow, would it?"

"Your family has been through some rough water." The man tapped his pencil on a notepad. "Your children have suffered a great loss, have changed schools, and are coping with a whole new set of challenges being motherless. And what, they're eight-years-old?"

"Will be January 1." Monty folded his arms across his chest. Mia and Mason weren't the only ones dealing with changes. He missed Marissa so much he struggled to crawl from bed some days. None of them would bounce back anytime soon, but the job forced him to cope, to move forward, despite the heartache. "But we're living with my sister right now, who promised my wife she'd care for the kids."

"She's not Mom." The older man leveled him with a knowing gaze.

"No, but she loves them as if they were hers." Monty swallowed a bitter retort. Mom wasn't coming back—ever. "It's the best I can do at present."

"Your kids need time to heal." His supervisor studied him. "I dare say, if you were honest, you need to mend too."

"I'm taking this one day at a time, sir." Monty couldn't deny the loneliness that plagued him, the long, sleepless nights alone in the bed he'd shared with Marissa for ten years. Or how many times he'd awakened in the last six months to reach for her, only to find an empty pillow where she should have been. "It hasn't been easy for any of us."

Monty grew silent, afraid of saying more for fear the thin veneer behind his smile would crack. If anyone asked, death had claimed his reason to exist. The future stretched like a deserted road. The only magnet drawing him forward was his determination to love his children. Mason and Mia needed him as much as he needed them. Otherwise, living no longer mattered.

"Which is why I'd like to you to consider working onshore." The man smiled. "The ocean's not going anywhere soon. You'll be back onboard chasing the grays in January."

Monty squared his shoulders. "I appreciate you thinking of me, sir."

"Report to Captain Neilson. He'll outline your duties and muscle you into routine in short order."

Monty saluted, spun on his heel, and retreated. At least he wouldn't have to worry about falling overboard from fatigue after staring at the ceiling all night. His sister would appreciate having him home more. He'd already noticed her tendency to shrug certain behavior problems off on him. Handling twins had challenged him and Marissa, and together they had coped with the extra demands set upon them by having two children at once. An aunt with little experience in the kid department became easily bewildered, her ability to cope balanced by desire to shower the twins with all the love she could bestow. For Ellen, having the twins around satisfied an inner longing she'd voiced more than once. For him, Ellen was a lifesaver.

CHAPTER FOUR

With the weekend ahead of her, Claire made a note to call Angie. Ever since she'd talked with her mother and been asked to call her sister, Claire wondered what Angie wanted.

Fallyn turned five in November. She went to pre-school. What kind of problems could a child that age develop that merited input from her?

She still remembered the glow on Angie's face when she and her husband Brennan had signed papers for Fallyn. The couple had unsuccessfully tried to produce a child for five years when the opportunity to adopt came their way. Claire had helped Angie nurture Fallyn in those first few weeks and had developed as great a bond with the child as Angie. When the time came for her to leave, Claire had done so with a heavy heart. Fallyn could never be replaced.

"Hey, Sis." Angie sounded tired, fatigue wobbling the ends of her words. "Glad you called."

"Mom said you asked to talk. What's up?"

"Fallyn needs some testing done. She's been plagued by urinary tract infections. Did you have a problem with those when you were little? I don't think I was ever treated."

"No, I don't remember anything like that. Could be something that's peculiar to her."

"Maybe." Angie paused, then changed the subject. "We're thinking of giving Fallyn a sibling."

"Is there another child available to adopt?"

"We were working with children's services and planned to become licensed foster care parents with the goal of eventually adopting a second child, but then we hit a snag." Angie's voice didn't sound disappointed. Rather she spoke as if she were baiting

Claire. What was going on?

"What kind of snag?" Claire's curiosity piqued at her sister's tone. "Something that can't be undone?"

"Definitely can't be undone." Angie's giggle heightened Claire's growing impatience.

"Are you going to dangle me or tell me?"

"Brennan and I have conceived!"

Claire gasped. "Truly! I was going to say I think giving your daughter a sister or brother would be an excellent move on your part." She expressed her contentment in an exaggerated sigh. "But having your own child, after waiting so long, is nothing short of a miracle. When is it due?"

"May." Angie's words tumbled out like a fast-flowing stream toward a larger river. "I thought I had the flu, but I went to the doctor and discovered I'm pregnant." Angie paused. "You don't think I'm too old, do you?"

"Heavens, Angie." Claire shook her head, glad her sister couldn't see the roll of her eyes. "You married young, spent five years trying to conceive, and then the past five rearing Fallyn." Claire's eyes brimmed with tears of happiness. "If you didn't have Fallyn, you'd have spent the five years waiting. Fallyn benefitted from the gaps in your timeline because she enjoyed your undivided attention, and now she'll benefit from gaining a sibling. You're only twenty-nine, two years my senior, you know, and I still hope to find my real Prince Charming and have a child or two with him."

"Do you think it would be a good idea for Fallyn to have a sibling?"

"Why wouldn't I?" Claire breathed deep. "I'm glad I have you, so I can heartily attest to the value of a sister. Fallyn will love having her own too." If anything, the child's life would be deepened and enriched. Growing up alone had little to offer except loneliness.

"How are things for you?" Angie wouldn't probe like their mother, but she did have her curious side. "Have you met anyone interesting?"

"No. As I told Mom, men who come here for the weekend leave for valley jobs on Monday. The ones who don't leave, already have rings through their noses."

"*Lovely*. You make them sound *so* charming."" Angie sniffed into the phone. "I wish we lived closer to each other."

"Don't forget. If you hadn't been living in Pennsylvania when Jamie pulled his double-cross, I wouldn't have had the courage to walk away from a bad relationship, finish my degree, and begin a new life for myself." Claire drummed her fingers on the counter beside the phone. "My present job still challenges me. I love it. Each child I help is a reminder good can come out of bad circumstances. I tend to forget that truth."

"But. . ."

"I buried my regrets, Angie." Claire swallowed hard. "Let's leave them where they are."

Monty couldn't remember when he'd last worked a Monday through Friday rotation. He rose early Saturday morning, like always, and the new-found freedom bounced about his ankles like a mischievous kitten. Cartoons played on the widescreen in the family room as shower pipes rumbled from Ellen's master bathroom.

He sauntered into his sister's kitchen and pulled open a cabinet door, searching for coffee. He'd figured right. She'd stored the grinder and roasted beans above the coffee maker, her natural bent for organization easy to navigate. Within minutes the brew percolated, and the smell wafted down the hall.

He poured a cup and ventured toward the family room. Mason

lay on his belly, chin propped on his hands, as he watched an animated mouse teach letters from a spelling tree. Mia sat in the rocker, thumb in her mouth, afghan wrapped about her shoulders, as she studied the screen.

"Morning, kids."

Neither child acknowledged him at first, their attention caught in the action unfolding on the television, but Mia broke her attention from the television long enough to raise her hand and wave.

Monty paused at the idyllic scene, surprised by how normal it seemed. Maybe the twins had settled in sooner than he had. Wouldn't surprise him a bit.

"Pancakes today?" He looked from one face to the other. "I'm cooking."

Mason sat up. "Does Auntie Ellen know you cook?"

Monty straightened his shoulders. "I'll have you know I used to help my sister in the kitchen when we both lived at home. And I've had a lot of experience since then."

"I'm sure you have." Ellen walked into the room toweling her hair dry. "But I've got waffle batter in the fridge ready to go." She combed through her short cut, fluffing the ends with her fingers. "Can you eat a waffle instead?"

"Waffles!" Mason pumped his fist. "Waffles, Dad."

Monty shrugged. "Looks like I'm overruled." He hefted his mug. "But the coffee is on me." He took a sip. "And it's not half bad."

Ellen aimed a pointed, if not mischievous, grin his way. "You can do clean-up. I'll get the waffle iron hot."

Monty followed her to the kitchen. "Seriously, Ellen. I don't want all the cooking and cleaning to fall to you. Mason and Mia have had to do chores. I needed their help when I was caring for Marissa. They dump waste cans, sort their laundry, make their beds, and dust. That may not sound like much, but it did make a difference."

Ellen turned from the refrigerator, a covered pitcher in her hand. "I'm sure it did. And as soon as your kids are settled in and feeling better about things, I'll incorporate them into the household routine. But right now, they need to be kids, be pampered a little, and let the pains they've experienced losing Marissa fade. The wounds are fresh and raw, Monty. For all of you."

Monty blinked, the truth of Ellen's words stinging. Though Marissa died in March, he'd postponed the move to Newport for several months, using the children as an excuse. They had to finish school. Summer camps followed. Swimming lessons waited. When he finally decided that leaving Bellevue and the NOAA headquarters in Seattle would be a good change for all of them, the children were already established in school for the new year. Moving them to Newport this late in the fall had not been the best decision he'd ever made.

The mistake was his alone. The thought of walking away from the home he'd shared with his wife hurt too much. Memories he'd made with her still lingered in every corner. Each piece of furniture, the sound of a door opening, even the beating of the rain against the windows triggered a remembrance that included Marissa. When he finally did leave, the loss stung as painful and intense as when he buried his bride in a March rainstorm, laying her to rest in a cold and damp Seattle cemetery. As the dirt sprinkled over the casket, his heart wished he could crawl inside and never leave.

CHAPTER FIVE

After she and her sister had talked on Saturday, Angie's news continually occupied Claire's thoughts. What a wonderful miracle to finally happen to the most deserving woman Claire knew. Angie made a great mother. She'd stepped into the role with Fallyn like she'd been practicing all her life. Another child would only multiply her happiness.

Angie had dreamed of motherhood for as long as Claire could remember. Not a day of her childhood passed without a tea party for her dolls. Every weekend she and Claire would dress up like mothers destined for a shopping trip to town, complete with baby strollers and diaper bags. Angie folded and unfolded doll diapers until they were worn at the creases. When she married at eighteen, all she could think about were the children she and Brennan would have. Infertility never entered her mind. Fallyn's arrival had been a godsend. Now, after ten years of tears while she tried to conceive, Angie's dream was coming true.

Yes, Angie had prepared for this responsibility. Her sister would embrace the changes a second newborn brought like a superwoman trying on new wings. Though Fallyn had only turned five, she was old enough to help Angie care for the little one. Claire marked the last day of school in June and made plans to travel east to meet her new niece or nephew. Seeing Fallyn would complete her happiness. She'd missed the child.

Other dates on the calendar needed her immediate attention. Thanksgiving loomed only two weeks away and she hadn't made plans. Mom usually invited her home to the valley that weekend, but she hadn't mentioned the holiday when they'd talked last week. Had it slipped her mind or had her mother accepted an invitation elsewhere?

Claire didn't like the idea of spending the four days by herself, but she hadn't yet made any close friends in Newport. Restaurants in a coastal town often closed on holidays. Cooking a turkey for one didn't appeal, either. She sighed. Thanksgiving waited like a vacant page in an unfinished novel—leaving Claire to finish the scene.

A knock on her office door jerked Claire from her thoughts. The principal stood in the doorway. "Come on in. I'm waiting on Gina Phillips."

"That's why I'm here." The principal entered and held out a message note. "Her foster mother called to tell us Gina has been transferred back to the valley."

Claire groaned. "I'm sorry to hear that. I had some ideas over the weekend on how to help the child. She's not going back to her mother, is she?"

"No. But a more permanent home situation came available, and her case worker thought she should transfer her."

"Stability is good. Think she'll be able to find cigarettes over there?"

The principal raised her eyebrows. "We can only hope not." She pointed to a chair. "Do you have a few minutes to talk?"

Claire glanced at the clock. "I don't have a reading group until 10:30. Make yourself comfortable."

"Have you given any thought to the newcomers?"

"Mia and Mason Chandler?"

The principal pulled a small notebook from her pocket and read from it. "Mia's teacher reports the girl is terribly withdrawn and spends her time in the corner of the classroom, head down, thumb in her mouth, and if you ask her a question, tears run down her face." The woman shifted in her chair. "She's not coping."

"You knew her mother died last spring?" Claire's heart ached for the child, a little girl who desperately wanted her mother.

"Yes. According to her aunt, Mia turns to her brother for

sympathy. I thought placing them in different classrooms would be best, but Mason acts out his anger unless he's comforting his sister. Mia is too fragile to handle classroom instructions. It's a problem."

"Can they be together?" Claire had witnessed Mason's protective spirit at the school bus loading zone. "Or would Mason disrupt Mia's progress by being too near?"

"I don't know. If Mia gets upset, the aide takes her to a corner to calm down. If Mason were in the room, he might take over and both children would be in the corner."

Claire laid her pencil on the desk. "When is Mia most vulnerable?"

"Almost as soon as she arrives."

"What if she came here for a morning reading session with me? Let her get comfortable, then move her on to the classroom after she gets acclimated."

"And Mason?"

More rambunctious than his sister, the boy could create problems being in the room. But somehow Claire believed he held the key to helping Mia. "We could try them together, then make Mason wait for a turn."

"How soon do you want to begin?"

"Are they still coming with their father? Or Aunt Ellen?"

"Dad drops them here. The aunt picks them up."

"Let's start tomorrow. I'll meet them outside and explain to the father that we have a special reading group for Mia." Claire folded her arms across her chest. "Make it sound like she's getting preferential treatment."

"Why?"

"Because the first day they arrived, he assured me that his children would not need my services." Claire still remembered the way he'd brushed her off. "If we word our proposal carefully, he won't object to her participating in an accelerated class." *And I'll have a chance to prove I was right all along.*

"Talk to the aunt this afternoon. Let her know what we plan. She can ease her brother into accepting our help. Mia is suffering."

She's not the only one. Dad is doing his share of mourning, as well.

Monty phoned Ellen mid-morning to tell her he had a surprise planned for the twins and would pick them up from school. They'd also catch dinner out. "You'll have a night off. Isn't today Kevin's day to call from Kabul?"

"You remembered! Thank you. Our time last week got cut short by interference."

"Then I'd say you were overdue for a private conversation with your husband." Monty missed those intimate exchanges with Marissa, sometimes the pain of loss so acute he took a stab to the gut. He could only guess how lonely his sister was with her husband gone the past six months.

"Monty, you're the best." Her sniff gave her away. "Where are you taking the kids?"

"To see my new headquarters. We'll hit a burger joint on the way home."

"There's one after you cross the bridge and travel north through Newport to the other end. Certainly not out of your way at all, is it?"

"You deserve a break, sis."

"Thanks. I appreciate this."

Monty arrived at the school ten minutes ahead of the final bell. He walked into the office and let the secretary know he'd be picking up his children. She nodded, directing him to their classrooms. As he approached the area, the woman he'd met the night of Mason's unscheduled kite search came out of another room with Mia and Mason in tow. "Is there a problem here?"

She stopped—startled—as if she'd been caught kidnapping. "Uh, no. I was taking them to the loading zone so I could talk with . . ." She fell silent. "Are you picking them up today?"

"I had planned to." Monty fought the urge to laugh. The woman appeared flustered at his presence. "My sister Ellen usually comes by, but I have plans for the kids tonight and decided to pick them up myself. What did you need to talk to Ellen about?"

Her face flushed as if she hadn't prepared for this conversation. She took a deep breath. "We would like to place Mia and Mason in a special reading group first thing in the morning. The curriculum would accelerate their progress and help bridge any gaps caused by their move here." She lifted her chin, the errant curl that had stuck to her forehead in the rainstorm, now dangled above her eyes. "Both of your children are exceptionally bright."

"Sounds good." He watched her a moment, not convinced of her sincerity. "Where do they report?"

"I'll show you." She gestured toward the end of the hall and led them along the corridor. Opening a door with a large window in its middle, she pointed to a neat interior with four small chairs circling a large red table. Stacks of books in a rainbow of colors awaited little hands. "We'll take turns choosing stories to read."

Mason scooted into the room, grabbing a book laying off to the side. "Can we read this one first?" He faced the cover their way. "It's all about kites! Dad! Look! A kite shaped like a dragon."

Monty grinned at his son's enthusiasm. "You'll have to ask your teacher." He turned to look at the woman. "I'm sorry. I've totally spaced out on your name. What should Mason call you?"

"Miss Claire." She smiled. "All the children I see call me Miss Claire."

He looked at Mason. "Got that?"

"Can we read this one first?" Mason's eyes were wide. "Miss

Claire?"

She nodded. "As long as Mia gets to pick one too."

Mason turned to his sister. "Pick one, Mia. You can read yours first."

Monty bit his cheek, the tenderness of the moment making him vulnerable. This stranger didn't need to experience his weakness. Too many others had already witnessed his pain, leaving him feeling exposed. The entire world didn't need to see. Especially not this young woman beside him who studied them all with those huge caramel eyes—eyes rimmed with pools of unshed tears.

The next morning Claire waited in the breezeway for the Chandler family, not sure if she remembered the vehicle she'd seen the father driving the first day he arrived. When the pickup with the crew cab drove up, she smiled. Though she couldn't see the faces of the twins, she saw a little hand waving through the glass.

Lowering the window, Mr. Chandler nodded. "Good morning."

"Morning."

He climbed from the cab and came around the front, opening the door nearest her. He lifted Mason out first, then set Mia beside him. He bent down and gave each child a hug. "Miss Claire has a special time for you today. I want good reports from each of you tonight. Okay?" He straightened and addressed her. "Ellen will pick them up today."

Claire made a note on a pad of paper she pulled from her pocket. "Thank you for telling me."

"We're going to read about kites!" Mason's enthusiasm oozed from every pore. "And Miss Claire, Mia wants to read a book on kitties."

Claire touched the boy on his head. "Let Mia tell me, okay? She talks exactly like you do."

"Not when she's scared." Mason folded his arms like a sergeant on patrol. "She gets all knotted up inside when she's scared and needs me to help her."

Claire's heart beat a little harder. "We'll help her together."

She glanced up to find Monty Chandler studying her. He didn't speak, but his eyes were shuttered, as if he didn't want to acknowledge the truth of her words. She prayed for wisdom. Each member of this family needed a little tender, loving care. But in her official role as teacher, she could only help two of the three.

CHAPTER SIX

STUDYING THE CALENDAR ON ELLEN'S KITCHEN wall, Monty dreaded the upcoming holiday. This would be the first Thanksgiving he and his children would celebrate without Marissa. He wrestled with what details he should remember to include and what traditions he had to let go simply because they were part of Marissa and could never be reproduced the way she would have done. The space on the calendar yawned like an empty chasm, daring him to fill the void.

"Thinking about Thanksgiving?" Ellen entered the kitchen and poured a cup of coffee. "You make great coffee, by the way. How's your turkey prep?"

"I know which end to stuff." Monty refilled his cup. "But I've never made stuffing."

"I make it by the directions on the box." She opened her cupboard and retrieved the stuffing mixture. "This is quite good. And easy." She read the back. "Do your kids eat stuffing?"

"They weren't fans, but they ate it because Marissa told them to. And she covered it with gravy."

"Ah. The great cover-up." Ellen put the mix back on the shelf. "Should I buy a whole bird or pick up a breast and bake it?"

"Mia and Mason each like their own drumstick." Monty set his cup in the sink. "That means an entire bird."

"Sounds like a lot of turkey for the four of us." Ellen opened the cupboard where she stored her pans. "I'm not sure I have a roaster." She pushed them around, pots and lids banging each other, and came up empty-handed. "Should we invite someone to join us?"

"Sure. If you have friends you'd like to entertain, ask them. And don't forget to mention the twins." He hooked his thumbs in his jeans pockets. "I don't know anyone here yet." He stared out the window, his mind drifting to past Thanksgivings. "But if you're worried about leftovers, I do like turkey sandwiches with cranberry sauce. A lot."

"So I should buy a thirty-pound bird?" Ellen cocked her head, a smirk on her face.

"That might be a bit much." He looked up to see her eyes dancing. "Don't turkeys come in fifteen-pound sizes?"

Ellen laughed. "I honestly don't know. Kevin and I usually shared a small turkey breast with mashed potatoes and gravy, a green salad, and lemon pie for dessert."

"No pumpkin pie?"

"This dinner is growing and changing by the minute." Ellen fanned herself with her hands. "Vote for the items I name by order of preference. Turkey. Stuffing. Gravy."

"So far, so good."

"Green salad, fruit mold, pumpkin pie, lemon pie."

"No green salad, just a fruit salad. I can eat lemon pie."

"Don't hurt yourself trying." Ellen touched her chin. "Ice cream for the kiddos?"

"They like cookies better."

"So now it's cookies." Ellen leaned her hip against the counter. "What kind, pray tell."

"Oatmeal with chocolate chunks, walnuts, and coconut."

"Heavens!"

Monty cast her an apologetic smile. "You don't have to make the meal our way. The kids will eat whatever is set in front of them. That's the way Marissa handled Thanksgiving. She's not going to be critical." He stopped and drew a cleansing breath. "Maybe we should skip it altogether."

Ellen came and wrapped an arm about his waist. "No. We'll make new traditions. We have to move forward, Monty." She squeezed him a little tighter. "The past needs to stay where it is. Good memories. Good times. Marissa would be so unhappy if she knew you gave up the holiday because she's not here to prepare it for you."

Monty sighed. "It hurts, Ellen. I thought I'd be better by now but losing her still feels like I'm in a bad dream and can't wake up."

"Time, little brother." Ellen laid her head against his shoulder. "Give it time."

Claire wanted to beat the crowds before holiday shoppers overwhelmed the two grocery stores in Newport. She left early Saturday morning with her list and found the store surprisingly quiet and the shelves well-stocked.

On Thursday, she'd called her mother and discovered Mom had been invited to celebrate with the Duvals. In her clueless exuberance Mom had shared that even Jamie, Claire's ex, would be there. Didn't she want to come? Claire couldn't think of any place she'd rather not be than in a room with her former fiancé. A three-hour drive to endure a three-hour dinner with a three-cent loser. No, thank you.

She'd rather teach through the holiday. Her experiment with Mia and Mason Chandler had already garnered results. Mason grew more focused as he read books about subjects he liked. Mia relaxed in the quiet, controlled environment of Claire's conference room. At least for as long as she was with Claire, she transformed into the normal chatterbox personality of most little girls her age. Returning to the classroom, Mia still withdrew from her peers, but her teacher reported she worked harder on her assignments. Progress enough to motivate Claire.

With the holiday cutting next week short, she decided to celebrate alone at her duplex by taking a long, candlelit bath, and reading a book she hadn't been able to open since she'd started teaching in the fall. Cooking for the holiday would be simple—a prepared turkey plate for one from the deli and a pumpkin pie with whipped cream. She'd make the pie herself. Pumpkin was her specialty.

She pushed her cart toward the deli counter and read the special options the store featured for those not inclined to cook. Dinner for two caught her eye—that would have to suffice. She stepped into line to wait and glanced around the rest of the area where the deli offered everything from barrels of olives to bins of cheeses. Newport might be a small town, but the tastes of its constituents spanned the globe.

"Hi, Miss Claire!"

She turned to the sound of the voice and found Mason Chandler and his sister walking beside their father, who pushed a shopping cart. "Good morning. How is the Chandler family today?"

"Look at our turkey." Mason bounced on excited feet. "See how big it is?"

"Wow." She bent down and examined the bird, noting a twenty-pound tag attached to its leg. "You must like turkey a lot."

"I only like the drumsticks." Mason folded his arms like the authority he was on everything. "Me and Mia get those." He turned to his sister. "Right, Mia?"

"I like dark meat best." Mia peeked up at her, a shy smile gracing her face. "But legs are my favorite."

"Well, then, it's a good thing a turkey has two legs, isn't it?" Claire smiled at their father. "Are you the cook?"

"Maybe. I've only stuffed the bird in the past, but my sister Ellen has never cooked an entire turkey before. She and her husband usually only prepare a small breast." He chuckled, studying his twins. "But turkey breasts don't come with legs, so we're trying our hand at the larger prey this year." He looked up at her. "Should be an interesting experiment."

"Turkeys are easy." She pointed to the tag. "Directions are printed here. Most people mess up when they don't allow enough hours per pound to get the bird done. I have a friend who didn't follow the instructions and almost killed her husband that way."

"You're not giving me confidence here." His raised eyebrow almost made her laugh.

"You won't do what she did." Claire waved her hand, smiled, and hurried to explain, remembering the story. "She cooked the bird for an hour until it was nice and brown on the outside, then served her husband. He was sick for three days."

"Poor guy." Monty made a face. "You sound as if you've done this before. Are you cooking for family?"

Claire shook her head. "I usually go to the valley to see my mother, and we find a nearby restaurant. But this year she's been invited to a friend's house, for which I'm glad. She's alone too much. My sister's in Pennsylvania, so I'm winging it here." She chuckled at her pun. "I'll make a pumpkin pie and call it good."

At the mention of pumpkin pie, Monty's attention seemed to sharpen. "Pumpkin?"

"You can share our turkey." Mia's offer surprised Claire. "That's a lot of white meat for Daddy."

"Good idea, honey." Monty patted his daughter on the head and cast a questioning glance at Claire. "Ellen would love the company and the kids can't quit talking about your reading class. Why don't you join us?"

"Oh, I couldn't impose on you that way."

He grinned. "I have a secret motive. You can be the turkey inspector. Otherwise, we may poison ourselves."

She looked at the twins who gazed at her with hope on their faces. "Only if you let me contribute something to the meal."

"Pumpkin pie sounds perfect." He pulled a notepad from his

pocket and wrote on it. Handing her the paper, he said. "That's our address. Feel free to come early and stay late. We like to eat mid-afternoon, so when should we have this turkey in the oven?"

"Are you stuffing the bird or making the dressing in a separate pan on the side?"

"Does it taste as good cooked outside the bird?"

"I think it does. It's also safer." Claire leaned over and read the tag again. "Stuffed you'll need no fewer than six hours. Unstuffed, you can probably get it done in five."

"Get up at six or get up at seven." He rolled his shoulders and groaned. "What a choice."

"'Fraid so."

"Unstuffed it is." He turned his shopping cart and gestured for his kids to follow. "We'll see you Thursday. And please, call me Monty."

"'Bye, Miss Claire." Mia waved, a smile on her face. "You'll like our turkey."

Claire waved. *If it makes you happy, little girl, I'll eat the entire bird.*

"You invited the teacher?" Ellen's question, coupled with her shocked face, made Monty reconsider his invitation. He'd wondered if he'd been a little brash, but the thought of pumpkin pie had thrown caution to the wind. He couldn't withdraw the invitation now.

"Mia invited her." He shrugged. "The kids saw her at the store and Mia heard her say she was making a pumpkin pie and calling it good, so Mia piped up and said she should share our turkey."

"Mia." Ellen frowned at him. "Seriously? Mia hasn't been willing to say two words without sticking her thumb in her mouth since she arrived in Newport." Ellen tipped her head to the right, a look of suspicion on her face. "You're telling me Mia asked her teacher to dinner."

"She did." Monty folded his arms across his chest, lifting his chin. "The kids haven't stopped talking about the reading class they're doing with Miss Claire since it began four days ago. Mason is over-the-moon sharing what he learned about kites, and Mia is smiling." He rubbed the toe of his shoe on the kitchen tile. "Personally, I think she's good for the kids. Isn't that what we want?"

"Absolutely. I'm surprised is all." Ellen went to the kitchen sink, ran water into it, and reached for the celery. She removed a knife and trimmed several stalks. "As big as it is, we'll have to get the bird thawing by Monday. So I better get the vegetables for the stuffing ready early."

"Claire said it's safer to cook the stuffing outside the bird. Plus, you don't have to start roasting it so early."

"She's giving cooking instructions?" Ellen stared at him, mouth slightly open. "Is she bringing her pumpkin pie?"

"I think so. She wanted to contribute to the meal." He checked his watch, his sister's scrutiny making him uncomfortably warm. "Or she wouldn't have wanted to come."

"Uh-huh." His sister smiled. "Mia is quite the social butterfly, isn't she?"

"'T'would appear so."

"The pumpkin pie will be a nice addition. I'll still make the lemon meringue."

"I bought fruit for the salad, and ready-to-bake rolls."

"Did you remember the roasting pan?"

He slapped his forehead. "I knew there was something else."

"We have time. Relax." She looked up and studied him, a grin on her face. "Maybe Claire has one we can borrow."

"Do you think she might?"

Ellen groaned. "Mr. Oblivious."

Three more mornings with the Chandler twins produced two happy, laughing children. Mason's protective defense of his sister diminished as he became more engrossed in the kite books Claire supplied. *A Kite for the Day*, by Will Hillenbrand, topped his favorite pile, and Claire insisted he read another by the end of the week.

Mia gravitated toward Mercer Mayer's books about Thanksgiving. As far as Mia was concerned *Little Critter* lived life in the fast lane. She picked out four *Little Critter* tales, stories she rotated like hands on a clock.

Claire anticipated each morning with the twins. Seeing them emerge from the hurting, withdrawn children they'd been less than a week before to the excited, invested students poring over their readers warmed her. She remembered again why she'd become a teacher, her desire to make a difference in a young learner a lifelong aim.

As Wednesday wound toward Thursday, she stopped by the market and picked up supplies for the pie she'd promised to take to the Chandler home. The aunt, Ellen Norse, had called, assuring Claire she needn't bring any foodstuffs to the dinner, but Claire had stood her ground. "I feel bad enough that I'm crashing your Thanksgiving, Ellen. The least I can do is bring a pie."

"I understand you're going to monitor the progress of the bird as well." Humor laced Ellen's words, her earnest insistence that Claire join their little party for the holiday genuine. "Since Monty's no cook, and I am a little green when it comes to turkey cuisine, your input may well save the day."

"I think everyone will be happy, as long as Mia and Mason get their drumsticks." Claire smiled into the phone. "We've read about turkey, Thanksgiving, pilgrims, and the Mayflower all week. But the one thing that caps the discussion is the size of the turkey leg they are anticipating eating tomorrow."

"If Mia eats an entire leg, she won't be able to eat anything else."

"It's Thanksgiving. The memory is more important than the meal she consumes."

"Well, I will look forward to seeing you in the morning. Monty informed me that the roaster must land in the oven by seven." Ellen spoke conspiratorially into the phone. "You're in charge."

"Oh, my." Claire resisted a groan. "That's early, even for me. He won't put the turkey in the oven until I get there?"

"I'll see that it's cooking by seven. Our roaster has no top. Should I cover it?"

"A foil tent after it has browned a little."

"See you in the morning."

Claire hurried to make the pie. Mason let it slip that he liked cookies better than pie, so she assembled the ingredients for oatmeal chocolate chip. By the time she had the kitchen cleaned, the duplex smelled delicious, scents of cinnamon and nutmeg wafting through the air like freshly sprayed perfume. This would be a special Thanksgiving, one that promised to take her mind off the burdens of past celebrations that still haunted her. Being alone tomorrow would have triggered the ghosts she chose not to acknowledge. And all because one little girl wanted to share her turkey.

CHAPTER SEVEN

Monty fought the urge to stay in bed Thanksgiving morning. Enduring his first holiday without his wife shrouded the day like a dark cloud that refused to rain. Marissa's wedding portrait still sat on his nightstand. The young, vibrant woman smiling from beneath her bridal veil hid the ugly cancer that would consume her body a mere nine years later. Images of her gray skin and sunken eyes as she shivered in the overheated hospice room surfaced in his mind. He moaned as the memory of her last breath sucker-punched him again. Death had brought peace to his wife as she slipped from his arms into eternity. He still wanted to believe, to acknowledge a loving God who cared, but Marissa's struggle with disease had stripped him to the bare bones of his faith. Finding room for God when his prayers went unanswered wasn't something he had yet managed.

If it weren't for Mia and Mason, he wouldn't darken a church door. Marissa's tearful wish that he continue to take the children to church every Sunday had been her last spoken request. She hadn't known what she asked. God had abandoned him. But in Seattle he dutifully took the kids to keep his promise. Now that he'd moved, he'd yet to look for a church, but her request still niggled at his memory.

"Monty?" Ellen's voice came through the door. "I need your help lifting the bird into the oven. We don't want Claire Simpson to find us neglecting our duties."

"Be right there, Sis." He cleared his thoughts. The teacher didn't need to share his sorrow. She might have her own demons to fight. He stood and headed for a quick shower. "Time for your game face, Chandler."

Ellen had the roaster filled and the bird basted when Monty

wandered into the kitchen ten minutes later. A big piece of foil lay on the counter, folded in half.

"What's that for?" Monty poked at the foil.

"Claire told me to make a foil tent for the turkey once it has browned."

"Oh." Monty lifted the roaster. "Get the oven door for me?"

Ellen pulled the door down while he set the pan inside. "Smells like you already baked something this morning." He straightened. "Kind of an orange smell."

She reached behind her and produced a plate of rolls. "Kevin likes these for breakfast when he's here, so I baked them in his honor. Orange cream-cheese frosting."

"Quite the domestic, aren't you?"

"Having you and the kids here has stirred my nesting urges. With Kevin gone. . ." Ellen drew a shaky breath and didn't finish her sentence.

Monty wrapped an arm around his sister. "How many Thanksgivings has he been deployed since you married?"

"Two." She swiped at her eyes. "And two home. So we're even."

"Will you Skype today?"

"Hope so."

The doorbell rang, and Ellen handed him the plate of pastry. "That's probably Claire. Pour a cup of coffee for her and don't eat all the rolls."

Monty glanced at the clock. "We snuck that critter in the oven in the nick of time, didn't we?"

"It'll be our secret. Cooking a turkey is not rocket science."

Claire couldn't stop staring at the view as she waited for Ellen to answer her bell. Standing at the front door of a home high enough above the city to look out over the trees, she drank in the spectacular view of the ocean that rewarded her thirsty eyes. What kind of income could afford a home like this? Her teacher's salary barely paid the rent on her duplex, and it didn't come with an ocean landscape. Imagine waking every morning to a panorama of breakers on the shore, blue sky, and tumultuous waters. Breathtaking didn't begin to describe it.

When she heard the lock clicking she turned back to the door. Ellen stood in the entryway, smiling as if they'd been friends since birth.

"Welcome, Miss Claire." Ellen reached out with both arms and gave her a quick hug. "I'm so glad you could join us today."

"Thank you for inviting me." Claire held up the containers she carried. "I promised to bring a pumpkin pie, and I did, but Mason couldn't stop talking about the oatmeal cookies his mother used to bake, so I made my version. I hope I'm not overstepping my bounds."

"Not at all. He will be thrilled. Please come in." Ellen stepped back and allowed Claire to enter. The foyer was small, but an oriental rug graced the floor and a potted palm stood in the corner. "Let me take your coat."

She removed her jacket and handed it to Ellen, who opened a nearby door and retrieved a hanger.

"Follow me." Ellen ventured left into a large living room and continued on to a swinging door which led into the dining area. Beyond the claw-foot table, a long counter with tall stools separated the kitchen and dining room.

Monty sat at the counter, sipping from a cup. "Morning, Miss Claire. Pull up a stool and join us for orange rolls and coffee. Ellen made them special for breakfast."

Claire drew closer and set her containers down. "Thank you. That sounds delightful." She pulled out a stool and climbed aboard.

"No Mia or Mason yet today?"

Ellen laughed and pointed to another door. "They're in the family room watching the Macy's parade. If I tell them you're here, you won't have another moment's peace. Enjoy a roll first." She held out a pan and a plate.

Claire helped herself.

Monty passed her a mug and held the carafe aloft. "Coffee? Cream? Sugar?"

"All of the above, thank you." She took a bite of the soft, doughy confection. "Ellen, these are superb."

"Thanks. I buy them for my husband. They keep well in the freezer and go directly to the oven to bake. I can impress guests in less than forty minutes."

"You didn't make these from scratch?" Claire licked a dab of frosting from her fingers. "They taste as if you did."

"I know. That's why I like them." Ellen swirled her coffee. "Kevin, that's my husband, still believes I toil for an hour in the kitchen to make the dough. I haven't the heart to tell him they're store bought."

Claire adjusted her position on the stool. "Your secret is safe with me."

Monty went to the oven. "How often should we check the turkey?"

"How long has it been?" Claire directed her question first to Monty, then to Ellen. Guilty grins graced both their faces. She chuckled. "Put it in just before I rang the doorbell?"

Monty stood straighter and folded his arms. "We weren't that late." He glanced at his sister. "It was shortly after seven."

Claire walked to the oven. "May I?"

Ellen gestured her way. "Be my guest."

She opened the door and peered inside. The turkey had begun to brown, but the legs were still attached by a plastic fastener. She looked up at Ellen. "Did you pull out the giblets?"

"Giblets?" Ellen frowned. "What giblets?"

"The little brown sack the butcher sticks in the breast cavity? Contains the kidneys, heart, and liver."

Monty groaned. "Anything else in there?"

Claire fought a grin, trying to remain serious as she explained the inner workings of a turkey. "Usually there's also a neck piece."

"Oh no." Ellen covered her face with her hands. "Is it ruined?"

Claire shook her head and turned to Monty. "Just lift the roaster out and place it on the cutting board for a minute. If it isn't too hot, I'll check the cavity and remove the extra materials."

Monty took two hot pads and lifted the roaster to the counter.

Claire took the hot pads from him and asked for a fork. She probed the breast opening and the abdominal cavity. Within seconds she had the giblet sack removed. Finding the neck, she tugged. Still partially frozen, it wouldn't budge. She looked at Monty. "Do you think you can pull it out? It's still frozen and needs someone stronger than me to rescue it."

Following her example, Monty reached in and grabbed the neck. With a twist and a grunt, he removed the frozen body part and tossed it in the sink. Looking to her, he said. "Now what?'

"Return it to the oven." Claire opened the oven, and he lifted the bird back into place. As she closed the door, she smiled at the uncomfortable faces of Ellen and Monty. "No reason to be embarrassed. That's probably the most forgotten step in preparing a turkey there is. I'm glad we found it early because the frozen neck would have added at least another hour to the cooking time."

"Thank you." Monty laid the hot pads on the counter. "You deserve an extra roll for your role."

Claire started to respond but before she could the kitchen door swung open and Mason burst through. "Miss Claire! You're here. Mia! Miss Claire is here!"

Mia appeared at the doorway, a shy smile on her face. "Now Daddy won't have to gobble all that turkey."

Monty stared at his daughter and Claire laughed. Mia had made a joke.

The cookies had been a hit. If Mia and Mason hadn't been already enchanted by their teacher's presence at the Thanksgiving table, the cookies she offered them afterwards bonded them to her for life. Monty had one, too, to be polite, only to discover Claire's confection begged a person to eat more. Between the turkey, Ellen's dressing, Claire's pumpkin pie, and the cookies for the kids, Monty had eaten way too much.

He'd enjoyed himself, too. He hadn't given this day much chance of finding joy, but the dinner, the contentment on the faces of his children as they played Chutes and Ladders with Claire and Ellen, and the compulsory game of football they watched on television left Monty feeling more satisfied than he'd been in a long time. If Marissa had been here, she would have called the holiday a perfect day. He couldn't have agreed more—had Marissa actually been here.

As darkness approached, Claire stood and wished them all a special weekend. "I've had a wonderful time."

Monty stood, too, stepping to the hall closet to retrieve the light jacket she'd worn. As he helped her into the coat, he caught a whiff of musk. The fragrance suited her—subtle, settled, and secure. As she flipped her hair over her collar, he noticed the playful little curls that teased his eyes.

He swallowed, curbing his thoughts before they caught a runaway train. Why had he noticed her fragrance? Her curly blonde hair? The smile she freely bestowed on his children? He sucked in a burst of air. He'd not line himself up for another round of heartache.

Marissa had been his woman. His love. His life. No one else would ever come between him and his memories, regardless of how tempted he was. And in that moment, Monty was tempted, whether he wanted to be, or understood it, or not.

Claire Simpson had it together. She symbolized a bastion of hope for his children's futures. She understood their pain and how to help them cope. If that understanding came from personal experience, she covered it well. He doubted much could rattle her foundations. He'd rally to her cause if someone so much as tried. But if Claire had ghosts in her past, she had them well under control.

Claire returned to her duplex, ready for the candlelit bubble bath she'd promised herself. She found her book, the phone, and the fluffiest towel she owned. As the tub filled and the water warmed the room, images of the day melted her inner core. Mia and Mason had stepped out of their grief, at least for a few hours, laughing like the little children they were. Mason stopped exhibiting his over-protective care of his sister. Mia, in turn, found her happy spot, giggling when Claire made a mistake during their game and teasing her aunt about coming in last. When Mia seemed strong enough to take correction, Claire would work on sportsmanship rules. But for now, both children showed signs of becoming well-adjusted students with a promising future.

Aware this was the first Thanksgiving the family had celebrated without their mother, Claire had chosen her words with care, unwilling to resurrect any unpleasant memories. Monty performed the duties of the host well, though behind the polished demeanor he remained reserved. He carved the turkey like a chef, pretending to steal one of the legs for himself. When Mason objected to the move, he laughed and surrendered the drumstick to the boy's waiting plate. Mia folded her arms and studied her father. "Don't get any ideas, Dad. I want my turkey leg, too."

Where had that come from? From the reticent, withdrawn child Mia had been when Claire first met her, the emerging personality promised to be a firestorm of resolve when she got her feet under her. God help them all.

Claire retrieved her silk robe from the dressing table and laid it beside the towel. She lit the candles, the forest pine scent permeating the room. She slipped into the water, the bubbles covering the entire surface, as she allowed each muscle to relax as the warmth of the bath performed its ritualistic dance around her limbs.

She leaned back and got comfortable, lifting her book to a tripod she'd picked up at an art store. The small piece of cast iron served her well. She could enjoy her hot retreat, read the book, and never worry she might drop it if she grew sleepy.

A page and a half later, her phone chimed. She perused the screen. Mom. "Hey, how was your holiday?"

"Oh, the usual. Too much food. Lively debates. Speculation on your future."

"My future?" Claire raised her other arm out of the water and checked to see if her skin had pinked. "Why would anyone at the Duvals want to speculate on my future?"

"Nancy still insists you and Jamie are destined for romance."

"Honestly. Does that woman ever give up?"

"Jamie seemed interested in the subject."

"Mom. Don't do this. I've had a wonderful day with new friends and no regrets. I'm enjoying a long, overdue candlelit bath. Don't ruin the moment with comments about a loser like Jamie." Claire huffed. "Please?"

"But Claire. . ."

"No buts. We canceled our wedding, went our separate ways, and have both found new futures. How many ways do I have to say this? Jamie Duval is one of those episodes from my past that I have archived, and I don't want to unlock the vault."

"Would you mind if he drove me to Newport tomorrow? I haven't seen you or the coast in a long time."

"You can't be serious."

"Well, actually, yes, I am. Jamie said he wants to talk with you. He doesn't mind driving, and I would love to see someone from my family this holiday. You're the closest. You're it."

"I have plans for tomorrow." Claire gritted her teeth, allowing several scenarios for tomorrow to pass through her mind. "I'd be happy to meet you for lunch . . . alone."

"We can't stay long, Claire. We have a three-hour drive over and a three-hour drive back. Surely you can give us an hour. What's the problem?"

"The problem is I don't want to see Jamie. Not tomorrow, not next week, not ever."

"He will be disappointed."

Claire resisted a groan into the phone. Jamie would be disappointed? What about the disappointment she'd experienced when he left her at the altar? Had her mother forgotten the days of tears Claire had shed at his departure? The vigil Angie had held, keeping watch over her to make certain Claire didn't do something stupid? The blackness of the future falling in on her?

Two weeks passed before she'd left her bedroom. Angie and Brennan had only come for the wedding and after a day of consoling her, flew home, encouraging her to come see them. Only Angie's persistent phone calls drew Claire from the depths of despondency in which she'd landed after Jamie's departure.

Now *Jamie* would be disappointed? Too bad.

"Claire?"

"There's lot of beach to visit, Mom. Most of them are free. If you want to come and fill your lungs with fresh salt air, by all means, do so. But I will not make any effort to be here or to see Jamie. Are we clear?"

"Crystal."

CHAPTER EIGHT

FOR MOST OF THE DUTIFULLY EMPLOYED, the day following Thanksgiving was a holiday, but not for Monty. He had readings to assess from the recent voyage along the Strait de Juan de Fuca by the vessel Shimada. Climate change, ocean currents, and migrations all merged together in one colossal dance for survival. Monty enjoyed the small part he played in it, even if all he did was read sonar data.

The dock stood empty when he arrived. Two of the ships were at sea, each on month-long research quests. Two other ships waited for marching orders. He wouldn't have to leave until after Christmas, for which he gave thanks. By then, Mason, Mia, and Ellen would have gotten used to each other, the kids would have celebrated their eighth birthdays New Year's Day, and he could leave with a clear conscience, confident that his children would thrive with their aunt in charge.

By the time he returned in late February, Ellen's husband would be thirty days from coming home from deployment. He and the kids would need to find other quarters in which to live. He'd been watching the papers, but rentals were expensive in this coastal town and buying a home didn't come with any less expense. He might have to consider living in Depot Bay, north of Newport, or looking down the coastal highway toward Waldport and Seal Beach. Rentals there were much more affordable, though just as scarce.

"Chandler." A familiar voice called him from the other end of the dock. Captain Sam Reynolds strode toward him, civilian clothes and bomber jacket making him look like a tourist.

"You working today?" Monty studied the man as he approached. "Or are you officially incognito?"

Sam laughed. "Off duty. I'm glad I caught you. I removed you from the roster for today."

"Sir?"

"Go home. Play with your kids." He looked up at the sky. "Might even be a good day to fly a kite."

"Yes, sir." Monty saluted. "My son's enthusiasm for the sport is growing with every book he reads."

"Encourage him." Captain Reynolds returned the salute. "He might be a NOAA scientist one day."

Monty returned to his vehicle and drove slowly out of the NOAA headquarters. Where could he get a kite today? He'd seen a kite store on the main highway leading through Newport, but he suspected other little shops around town carried them too. Perhaps Ellen would know.

"Kites?" Ellen had been working when he arrived and picked up a business directory from her home office desk. "You know about the kite store downtown, right?"

Monty nodded. "But they seem to specialize in the big stuff. I hoped to find a small one we could assemble together that wouldn't be a great loss if it crashed."

"Any kite you smash is going to cause a firestorm of regret from your son. Whether it be a big fancy extravaganza or a homemade flyer with garden string."

"But if we start with the small one and he learns how to fly it, then the big one will be the one he can enjoy over and over again."

"There's a boutique in the Nye Beach district called *Lady Marie's* that advertises a children's corner. The woman took over for her parents about three years ago and added the children's section to help parents browse the store while their children were engaged." Ellen ran her finger down the page. "Want me to call the store?"

"I think I'll take the kids there. Check out her offerings."

Monty pulled out his wallet and checked his cash. "Do you know the woman's name?"

"McKenna Taylor." Ellen closed the directory. "She's married to one of the personnel at the Aquarium. He used to work for NMFS in Alaska."

"I may have met him, or soon will." He glanced around the room. "Kids?"

Ellen pointed to the family room. "Busy. Reading."

Monty nodded and headed toward the door.

Mason sat in a great chair next to his sister, a book in his lap, reading out loud to Mia. "And the kite went spinning in the sky." He looked up. "Hi, Dad. We're reading about kites."

"Would you like to go shopping with me and look for a real kite?"

Mason slammed the book closed and hopped off the chair. "Can we fly it? Can we?"

"Depends on what we find and how soon we can put it together."

"Mia. We're going to get a kite."

Mia picked up her book and laid it on the table. "Can we also get a kitten? That's what my book is about."

Monty struggled to find a good answer. "Can't do both today, Mia. We'll have to ask Aunt Ellen about a cat."

"She already said maybe."

Monty bit back a chuckle. Mia's progress was obviously going well, maybe a little too well. "Let's start with the kite and see where we go from there."

Parking the truck proved the greatest obstacle to shopping in Nye Beach. With the long holiday weekend, tourists had descended on the coastal town. The weather allowed sun breaks even though the air blew cold, and red-nosed shoppers hurried from store to store. Monty found a spot a block up from the boutique, parking in front of a little diner called Tidewater Takeout. "Hey, kids. After we shop for a kite, we can come back here and have our lunch. Would you like that?"

"What about the turkey sandwiches you promised to eat?" Mia's tone could easily have been Ellen's, had she not been sitting in the truck behind him, next to her brother. "Aunt Ellen is counting on you."

"Don't worry, little sis." Monty opened the door and stepped out, lifting Mia to the ground. "I will not let Aunt Ellen down."

"But even she won't mind us having a milkshake, Mia." Mason hopped on the sidewalk as Monty lifted him down. "That's what I want."

Monty took each of their hands and walked toward the boutique down the street. When he reached the shop, the bell over the door announced their arrival. An attractive young woman with ice-blue eyes walked forward from the back. "Can I help you find something today?"

"I understand you have a large, children's section?"

"My specialty."

"You're the store owner?"

With a nod, she extended her hand. "McKenna Taylor."

"Montgomery Chandler."

"NOAA?" His look of surprise triggered a smile. "Uniform's a dead giveaway."

"Oh, yeah." He'd forgotten he'd dressed for work today. "Can't fool anyone, can I?"

She gestured toward the back of the store and spoke to the twins. "There's a large table back there with building blocks, books, and puzzles just for you."

Mason sputtered. "But I came for a kite."

"Ah." She wiggled her pointer finger. "Follow me. I have a different section for kites."

Monty smiled at Mason's exuberance as he followed behind the store owner, his son and McKenna chatting about his purchase. He remembered Captain Reynolds' words from this morning. "Encourage him. He might become a NOAA scientist one day." Watching the short, wiggly seven-year-old dance his way to the back of the store, Monty could only imagine how the child might mature. They arrived at a wall display of kites with barrels beneath, each container filled with a do-it-yourself kit to match the flyer on the wall.

"Look at these, Dad." He turned to McKenna. "Can we put these together ourselves?"

"With your Dad's help, you'll have a sturdy kite in no time."

Monty glanced up. "Do you have string?"

"I have everything a kite maker needs." She held up a ball of twine, several pieces of basal wood, and assorted spools of cloth specifically designed to be a kite's tail. Colors covered the spectrum of the rainbow.

Mia tugged on his sleeve. "I still want a kitten, Daddy."

McKenna glanced up, her blue eyes sparkling. "Can you have cats where you live?"

Monty shrugged. "We're living with my sister right now. We'll be looking for a housing unit soon. If I rent, pets could be a problem. Any kitty kites?"

Mia's lower lip popped out. "I don't want a kite." She leaned against Monty's leg. "I want a kitten."

McKenna lifted a stuffed kitten from a pile of toys near the kite bins and held it behind Mia. She raised an eyebrow toward Monty.

"Perfect." He reached for the toy and looked at Mia. "How about a stuffed kitten until we can have the real thing?"

Mia grabbed the toy and tucked it against her chin. Her eyes widened. "Daddy, it's purring."

Monty frowned and glanced at McKenna, who nodded. "The latest in kid toys. Stuffed animals that behave like the real thing."

"As long as they don't bite or scratch."

Though she had the day to herself, Claire had sprung from bed later than she'd planned, a little after nine. She'd hurried to dress and find breakfast in the kitchen. The pumpkin pie left from dinner yesterday tempted her. She rationalized having a piece—pumpkin was a healthy, high-fiber vegetable, and the whipped cream was a milk product, fulfilling the dairy and protein requirements. Add coffee and she had as balanced a meal as cereal. Sort of.

She opted for a poached egg on kale with red peppers and onions. No one could chide her for surrendering to temptation. She sat down to breakfast, considering her options for today. She had to go somewhere—anywhere—do something other than sitting home and waiting for the doorbell to ring. She didn't trust her mother's ability to dissuade Jamie from coming. He had a talent for charming people into doing as he wished. She shook her head. Using her mother as bait was low, even for him.

You should tell your mother what really happened. The thought nagged her. She hadn't told her mother the whole story behind her split with Jamie. Knowing her mother, she would have purchased a shotgun and found Jamie for a showdown. The conflict would have created an irreparable rift in her mother's relationship with her best friend. Maybe after Claire found someone new to love—then the entire drama could be revealed.

She rinsed her pan and cup in the sink. Nice thing about poaching an egg in the middle of hot, cooked greens meant little clean-up. More time for planning her excursion. She traipsed to the bathroom, ran a comb through her curls, and applied a bit of blush. Throwing a maroon scarf about her neck, adding ruby-colored dangles to her ears, and slipping on her brown tweed jacket, Claire smiled at the image in the glass. Her slacks hugged her thighs and the cream-colored pullover complemented the jacket. She was ready for whatever adventure life at the coast threw at her.

She grabbed her purse and keys, slamming the door on a ringing phone. Not a moment to spare. She hastened to her car and warmed the engine. She'd escaped in the nick of time—but escape to where? She headed to a group of shops she'd wanted to explore at the other end of the city. The shops were somewhat remote, tucked away in the midst of an older part of the area where business and residences co-existed. Mom would love exploring this area with her if only there were some way to skirt a confrontation with Jamie. But if Mom came to town with Jamie, she'd have to accept that an encounter with Claire would be unlikely. She parked and walked up the sidewalk. Quaint little shops of candles and local artists popped up here and there along the storefronts. She remembered McKenna, the mother she'd met at the school two years before, who ran *Lady Marie's* boutique somewhere in this neighborhood. Her husband had died in a fishing accident and she'd since remarried. In two years, Claire hadn't met anyone she'd consider marriage material. Not that she had time to look.

A crowd of tourists grew on the sidewalk as Claire neared the Tidewater Takeout. People entered and exited at remarkable speed as they headed toward the beach. The little deli must do a landslide business on holidays like today. Come Monday life would return to the slow lane. She crossed to the other side of the street to avoid the commotion.

"Claire?"

Her pulse beat faster as she turned to her name, dreading who might be calling her. Did she not escape her mother and driver? She almost laughed as she spotted the Chandlers waving at her.

Monty stood, arms crossed, as Mason and Mia jumped up and

down at his side, pointing to her. Taking their father's hands, the twins dragged him across the street to where she waited.

"Hi, Miss Claire!" Mason shook a bag at her. "I got a kite to fly!" He pulled open the top. "Wanna see?"

"And I got a kitten." Mia held the little stuffed animal under her chin. "It purrs. Want to hear?"

Claire grinned at the excited pair. She knelt down, peeked in Mason's bag, then touched the furry bundle Mia held. The cat buzzed beneath her fingers, and she jumped. "It really does purr, doesn't it?"

Mia nodded. "Her name is Fluffy. She's my cat until Dad can find the real thing."

Claire glanced at Monty, who stood watching the exchange. "She'll hold you to that, you know."

"She needs something to look forward to." Monty rubbed a spot on the sidewalk with his toe. "We have to find our own house before March."

"Is that when Ellen's husband comes home?"

He nodded and looked down the street. "Somehow I don't think a brother-in-law and his two kids would be a welcome addition to his homecoming."

Claire stood. "Better start looking now. Housing here is not cheap, and it's hard to come by."

Monty grimaced. "Afraid you're right." He glanced at her purse. "I don't see any bags or boxes. Are you shopping or playing the tourist today?"

"I haven't had time to revisit the shops in this neighborhood in a while, so I thought I'd use my free day to roam a little." She gestured toward the street. "Lots of places to explore here."

"We were heading to the diner when we saw you. Want to join us for a snack?"

Claire swallowed the pulse drawing her voice box closed. "I

don't want to impose."

"Wouldn't ask if you were imposing. The kids demanded I come get you."

"And you haven't seen all of my kite yet, either." Mason rattled his bag as high as he could.

"Then I guess we'd better go take a look, hadn't we?" Claire tousled the little boy's hair as Mia took her free hand. Monty's reaction was unreadable, but he'd been the one who asked. She welcomed the company. Anything to avoid running into Mom and Jamie if they'd had the audacity to drive over for the day. These children and their dad were a special treat. She resisted calling them good friends. She wasn't sure how Monty would react to that, although it might be fun to find out.

CHAPTER NINE

Ellen sat at her computer screen, chatting with her husband on Skype when Monty and the twins entered the family room. She held a finger to her lips. Monty grabbed each child's hand and led them to the kitchen.

"I want to show Aunt Ellen my kitten." Mia stomped her foot, a pout on her face. "Fluffy will make her smile."

"I'm sure you're right, Mia, but Aunt Ellen is talking to Uncle Kevin right now on a special line and can't be disturbed. You need to stay in here with Mason and me."

"Can we work on my kite?" Mason had climbed onto a tall stool and unwrapped the kite from its cellophane bag. The ball of string fell off the counter and rolled across the floor.

Monty strode to the corner where the sphere stopped and picked it up. "I've got it." He returned to where Mason waited and pulled out a stool for himself. "Mia, come join us."

Mia shook her head. "I want to read my kitten book to Fluffy."

"Where is it? In the family room?"

At her nod, Monty tiptoed to the swinging door and peered through the crack. His kids laughed as he took exaggerated steps, slinking through the opening as if he were a private eye on stakeout. He made a silly face as he disappeared. When he returned, he held up the book. "I escaped alive!"

Mason giggled. "Dad, you're acting happy today."

Mia took the book from him and snuggled into a winged chair in the living room. "Did Thanksgiving bring your happiness back?"

Monty swallowed. He'd admit the last two days had been cheerful. His mind had only drifted to memories of Marissa twice. Allowing happiness to fill him, he'd realized how severe the cloud of despair was that he'd been living under. The lonely days required more energy than he had to give, while the joyful events with his children empowered him. What had made the difference?

"I think you like Miss Claire." Mia didn't look up from her book, but sat holding her kitten, turning pages, her tone matter-of-fact. "Your face gets all sparkly when she smiles at you."

Monty searched for an appropriate response to Mia's statement. Had his daughter noticed something he'd been oblivious to? Was the blonde schoolteacher with the warm smile invading the wall of protection he'd built around his hurt? As well as healing his children? He thought for a minute. Yes, she'd certainly made a difference in their lives. But as for feelings beyond restoring some semblance of order in the Chandler household, Monty doubted anything would come of it. He hadn't healed from Marissa's death, and relationships with women as friends could be landmines— especially women as attractive as Claire. He'd have to tread carefully. "Miss Claire is good at making you kids feel better. And I think we made her happy today, too." *What a lame response, Chandler.*

After saying goodbye to Monty and his kids as they carried their treasures to their truck, Claire headed down the street. She'd planned to buy a kite for classroom work next week, but Mason already had one he and his father would create. Mia had her kitten. Claire needed to visit the boutique and explore other wares the children would like to assemble. The store owner might have suggestions. The diner's busy lunch hour filled the street air with the smell of hot French fries and grilled burgers. The simple salad she'd ordered with the Chandlers left her stomach craving more, a meager fix to a growing appetite, but the time spent with the family lingered like a rich dessert.

Mia's transformation from one terrified little girl to a bubbly, outgoing second grader still perplexed Claire. The child beamed as she'd eaten her lunch, her new kitten as real to her as the hamburger her father ordered for her from the menu. Would Mia remain as engaged in her surroundings as she was today or would a return to school Monday bring back the behaviors? The decision to have Mia begin her day in a quiet environment certainly seemed to have paid great dividends.

Mason's energy had transferred from protecting his sister to his infatuation with books, kites, and all things mechanical. His sharp mind didn't miss anything and, when directed to something new, engaged the boy with every muscle. If only those changes could continue.

She reached the boutique and entered, recognizing the store's owner, McKenna Taylor, at the rear corner as she helped a customer. A ginger scent tinged the air, making the atmosphere friendly and welcoming. Claire worked her way to the children's table, spying the source of the aroma. A basket of what looked like freshly baked gingerbread men waited alongside an assortment of displays that shouted "kid-friendly". Like soldiers standing at attention, coloring kits, modeling clay, and boxed kits of every variety filled the shelves.

She happened upon a stack of nature books. Picking one from the pile, she opened to the second page. A swallowtail butterfly popped up, the text set amid a beautiful landscape of trees and flowers. Curious, she turned to the next one and found a cricket staring at her from his spot near a watercolor rendition of a log. She explored other pages. In each one a different insect rose from the text, set in its habitat with carefully written copy about the creature and how it lived.

"Isn't that an incredible book?" McKenna stood beside her, her ice-blue eyes twinkling, long black hair framing her face. "I have an entire series of the stories, each one focused on a different part of the animal kingdom."

"I'm amazed at the artwork and thought that went into these pages." Claire flipped to the back. "Spendy, but for something of this quality, certainly worth the asking price."

"You're from the elementary school, aren't you?" McKenna's quizzical frown soon turned to a face of recognition. "Claire Simpson, right?"

"Good memory." She extended her hand. "How's Sydney?"

McKenna nodded toward the children's table. "She's back there reading one of these. They're her favorites."

Claire looked to where McKenna had indicated. A young girl of about eight sat reading aloud at the book table. "You've succeeded where many others have failed."

"No accolades for me, yet. Sydney is still autistic, and we continue to struggle on a daily basis."

"But she's progressing, that's what's important." Claire returned the book to the shelf and selected another one on sea mammals. Whales, dolphins, and turtles sprang from their habitats. "Do you have one on domestic animals, like cats and dogs?"

"We should have one, unless we sold our last copy." McKenna thumbed through the stack and stopped near the bottom. "Here it is. *A Trip to the Farm*."

Claire took the book and glanced inside. "This is perfect for what I need. I teach a little girl who is having trouble adjusting to her new school, but she's excited about cats. We're exploring animal books."

"Have you read *Patches, the Unloved Kitten*?" McKenna stepped to another aisle and pulled a small, thin paperback from the shelf. "It's about a kitten who lives on the streets and no one will give it a home."

"Sounds sad."

"A little, but it has a happy ending." McKenna opened the last page. "A little girl with a great big heart promised she and Patches would never be apart."

"Perfect." Claire held out her hand for the book, thinking of Mia's love for her stuffed kitten, Fluffy. "I'll take both of these. Thank you."

A few minutes later Claire exited the boutique and headed to where she'd parked the car. The sidewalk had grown busier while she shopped, and she darted in and out of sightseers strolling the street seeking treasures. Once she reached her car she withdrew keys from a jacket pocket and inserted the door key. A voice from behind made her jaw lock.

"Hello, Claire."

She drew a deep breath and turned. Jamie stood a few feet away, smiling as if he'd won the lottery. He stepped toward her, but she held up her hand, key ring dangling from her fingers. "I have nothing to say to you. When we parted five years ago, the split was for good. I have no idea why you're here, but I don't want to find out."

Jamie's hazel eyes narrowed as his lips straight-lined. "I wanted to talk to you, is all."

"All? With you, it's never *all*."

"Claire, I know I'm not worth your time. I left, leaving you with all the responsibility. I need to apologize."

She studied the man she'd once loved, this guy who'd made promises he'd never kept. He'd aged. Perhaps the rigors of his unsettled life had taken their toll. His clothes still shouted natty dresser—expensive jackets and shined shoes. He wore his hair longer, a stylish cut giving him a rakish look. His eyes, dark hazel and deep, had not lost their ability to stare through her, as if they could read her soul. Yes, he was still the Jamie she'd known, confident and flirtatious, collecting the gawks of women like athletes collect medals. Something he failed to do. She found her voice. "So you're sorry?"

"Very." He stood straighter, as if her words gave him hope.

"Good. I accept your apology. Have a nice trip home." She turned the key and unlocked her car.

He jumped to her side. "Claire, wait, please. I need to know more. Were you able to take care of everything?"

"What?" She held up her fingers as she named off each responsibility he'd left her. "The wedding expenses? Check. Cancel the photographer? Check. Call the guests? Check. Return the gifts? Done." Claire's pulse raced as she revisited those awful days of exposing her pain to the rest of the world. "Yes, Jamie, no thanks to you."

"That's not what I mean."

"As I said, I took care of everything. You don't have to worry. You can live your life without any shadows waiting for you in the wings."

"And you're okay? No lasting problems?"

"If you mean, am I physically okay? Yes. Emotionally? I'm getting there. Am I able to trust and love again? That will take time. But it's been almost five years. Those kinds of hurts go deep and resurrecting what you did to me only lets the pain resurface. Now, are we through?"

"I wish we weren't." Jamie's eyes looked genuinely remorseful.

Seriously? Did he really think she could find feelings for him again?

"I've thought of you every day since we parted. I made the biggest mistake of my life when I left you."

"It's a little late for regrets, Jamie." *That was an understatement.*

"But is it too late to start over?"

"Start over? Us? You and me?" Claire wished someone would

wake her, she was having a nightmare. "You can't be serious."

"But I am. We'd have a fresh start. There'd be nothing hanging over us. We could learn to love again."

Claire clenched her fist and punched the top of the car. She turned and faced him. "You and I will never have a fresh start. I have memories that will not die from the first go-around with you. My time with my sister in Pennsylvania helped. I found a church that taught me about Christ's love and forgiveness. I have forgiven you, just as Christ has forgiven me. He picked up the pieces of my broken heart and put them back together. Thanks to that gift, I once again have a normal life. But that life does not, nor will it ever, include you. Now go fetch my mother, wherever you left her, and turn east and drive. Don't ever look back."

She climbed into the car and started the ignition. Putting the gear in reverse she backed out and headed down the street. In her rearview mirror, she saw Jamie still standing where she'd left him, watching her drive away. *Please, God, make him go home.*

CHAPTER TEN

BY THE TIME MONTY AND HIS children finished assembling the kite and knotting the tail, most of the afternoon had vanished. He didn't want to disappoint Mason, who couldn't stand still, the anticipation of flying his masterpiece oozing from his toes. But sending the kite up this late in the afternoon meant a short time in the air.

"Can we go fly it now, Dad?" Mason's expectant face beamed, waiting on his answer.

"We have two options." Monty picked up his phone and checked the weather forecast. "If we go down to the beach now, we'll maybe get the kite up for an hour before we have to come home."

"An hour isn't very long, is it?"

"No." Monty closed his phone. "But the weather tomorrow is calling for sun spots and we could head to the beach early and probably get the kite up for a longer time."

"Let's go tomorrow." Mason turned to his sister. "Mia, do you want to fly the kite tomorrow?"

Monty suppressed his grin. The determination on his son's face would dare anyone to say no. Monty waited as Mia processed her brother's question.

Mia stroked her stuffed kitten. "Can Miss Claire come and help us?"

Like a splash of cold water Mia's request blindsided Monty. He swallowed, not sure Mia's query was as innocent as it sounded. "Miss Claire probably has things she needs to do to get ready for school Monday. Maybe Aunt Ellen would like to fly the kite with us."

Mia stuck her thumb in her mouth, his answer obviously not making the grade.

Mason piped up, bouncing on his toes. "Aunt Ellen and Miss Claire are friends. Maybe they'd both like to come. We could have a picnic on the beach with Aunt Ellen's turkey sandwiches and Miss Claire's chocolate chunk cookies. Doesn't that sound perfect?"

Monty stuffed his tongue in a corner of his cheek, stifling the laugh he couldn't express. These two were so cute, and he believed their motives to be pure, but what they suggested equaled all the trappings of a dating service. He searched for the right words. "I think we should keep our first flight simple. Just you, Mia, and me. We have to learn how to get the kite up before we invite an audience."

"Won't be as much fun without a picnic." Mason's lower lip could have tripped him if he were walking across the floor.

Ellen entered the kitchen, catching Mason's last words. She looked at him. "You want to go on a picnic?"

Monty widened his eyes and cast his sister a broad grin, shaking his head with vigor.

Ellen frowned, apparently confused by his goofy face. "No picnic?"

Monty spoke in pig Latin. "*Ixnay* on the *icnicpay.*" Did she get it?

Mason frowned at his father and spoke to his aunt. "Dad says we need to fly the kite without you and Miss Claire along. I thought we could make a picnic and have more fun."

Ellen brightened and touched her nephew's nose. "That sounds like a wonderful way to spend a day." She glanced at Monty, a twinkle in her eye. "I'll call Miss Claire and we'll plan the lunch." She studied him. "What time shall I say we'll go?"

Monty resisted rolling his eyes. Trapped by the antics of two little matchmakers and his in-love-with-love sister, he'd have to spend another day with a woman whose company he enjoyed. He didn't regret she'd entered their lives without warning, that her motives were driven by concern for his children, and she appeared clueless about the effect she had on him. He wasn't ready to run the relational marathon that having a fascinating woman nearby might trigger. But if fate kept throwing them together like it had lately, he'd better find his training shoes.

Ellen still waited for his answer.

"I'd like to hit the beach by ten. Unless it's raining, of course."

Ellen picked up the phone. "I have a beach umbrella."

Terrific.

"Mom, how could you do that to me?" Claire fought to keep the anger from her voice, but Jamie's appearance earlier spoke volumes. Her mother's interference had to stop. She'd made the phone call the minute she walked into her duplex and slammed the door. Mom had no right to thrust Jamie back into her life, nor did she have enough information to know what she was doing. "I told you I didn't want to see him."

Her mother's voice was calm. "I assume you're talking about Jamie?"

"Of course, I'm talking about Jamie. And I distinctly remember asking you not to bring him to Newport." Claire paused, the bang of her heart against her breastbone shortening her breath. "Yet you brought him anyway."

"I told him not to come." Her mother's sigh resonated in the phone. "I wasn't there, Claire. I respect you and your feelings enough to know you don't want to go back to where you were."

"You didn't come to Newport today?" Claire's stomach lurched as the comment sucker-punched her in the ribs. She'd assumed wrong. Her mother hadn't interfered.

"No." Her mother coughed. "I still have some of that virus

lingering in my lungs, and I didn't want to risk coastal weather exacerbating my condition. I told Jamie last night, but he seemed very determined."

"Apparently, he was." Claire swallowed her pride. "I'm so sorry. I jumped to conclusions. The only thing I could think when I saw him was that you had encouraged him. Just having him near makes me crazy."

"You are my child. He hurt you deeply. If it weren't for my friendship with his mother, I wouldn't give him the time of day. But Nancy insists something is there, so I play along."

"Thanks, Mom. That means a lot." Her mother's friendships were limited and handpicked. Claire wouldn't ask her to drop a friend like Nancy because her son refused to face the reality of their relationship.

"Did you send him home?" Mom sounded eager to know the details.

"I left him standing on the street with his hands in his pockets." Claire giggled, remembering the surprised look on his face as she drove away. "He seemed miffed."

"Good." Her mother stifled another cough. "Plans for tomorrow?"

"No. But I'll find something to do." Claire's laundry basket overflowed, and her stack of reports sat on the table unfinished. She wouldn't have to look far.

"Of that I'm sure. Make it fun, will you?"

She fudged her answer. "I'll try." *As if that's going to happen.*

Claire punched off her phone and headed to the kitchen for something to eat, the embarrassment of wrongly accusing her mother still haunting her. She should have remained calm after confronting Jamie, but the man had a gift for upending her life.

A growl brought her back to reality. She hadn't had anything to eat since breakfast except the salad and the pretzel she'd shared with Mia at the diner. Her middle now conversed with her backbone. The growls grew louder with each step. She opened the refrigerator and stared. More eggs? No. A piece of pumpkin pie? Maybe.

She spotted Ellen's wrapped gift of leftover turkey. A turkey sandwich with pickles, mayo, and cranberry sauce sounded heavenly. She made the sandwich, cut a piece of the pie, and carried them to her table. She punched the beverage button on her microwave and dropped an herbal tea bag in the hot water when the dinger sounded. "Thank you, Lord. This has been a memorable day."

She bit into the sandwich with gusto, chewing slowly to savor all the flavors. She slid her fork into the pie and popped a bite in her mouth. The rich cinnamon and nutmeg tingled her taste buds. The food made her feel better, the day's problems disappearing like her sandwich. The books she'd picked up at *Lady Marie's* sat in their bag. She removed them and opened the story about the kitten. *"Once upon a time, a kitten lost its mother."*

She paused, thinking about Mia's loss. Maybe this book wasn't right for the little girl. Emotions still ran raw in that family. The opening sentence might trigger a response she didn't mean to ignite.

She read on. The author captured the feelings of the little cat, noting that Patches had no one to care for her. She needed a new mommy. She was wet, cold, and couldn't find food. Those conditions were different than the ones Mia faced. The girl had a loving father, brother, and aunt, and she was well cared for. The new mommy would be something her father would have to figure out.

Finally, the story arrived at a happy conclusion. A little girl picked up the bedraggled kitten and wrapped it in her coat, carrying it home to a warm house and a dish full of food. Patches had a new mommy. Not the same as her original mommy, but someone who could care for her all the same.

Claire savored another bite of the pie. The happy ending would give Mia hope, and the kitten's fate would make her happy. Knowing how much she loved her stuffed kitten, perhaps this story would suffice to bridge the gap of the loss of her mother with the new life she now shared with her aunt. Claire still had her mother, and most days she considered that a good thing, but she couldn't imagine life without the woman. She thought of her adopted niece, Fallyn, who was growing up in the care of her sister, Angie, and her husband. Her life, too, faced a happy ending. Yes, the book met the criteria Claire had hoped for, helping a little girl rise out of the ashes of her grief.

She took another bite of pie and reached for the other book. A buzz sounded on her phone, and she lifted it out, reading the screen. *Ellen Chandler Norse.*

Hmm. Had she forgotten something when she left yesterday? She answered.

"Hi, Claire?" The voice sounded warm and cordial, something Claire had come to expect from this newfound friend. "Am I interrupting?"

"No. Actually, I'm sitting here enjoying a leftover turkey sandwich with cranberry sauce and pickles. Thanks to you." Claire swallowed the pie piece. "And yes, I'm having pie."

"Nothing better than that."

"What's up?" Claire guessed Ellen already knew of the snack date Mia and Mason had dragged her to this afternoon. The twins were not quiet about their adventures. The conversation had been lively, Mason pointing out all the marine touches on the walls of the Tidewater Takeout. He'd especially liked the ship's wheel mounted over his table. Mia had counted the sea stars above the eatery's counter. Monty hadn't said much, his kids dominating the conversation.

"Mia and Mason didn't get to fly their kite today." Ellen paused, a small voice in the background proclaiming his disappointment. "Mason thought it would be fun to take a picnic lunch to the beach tomorrow while he and Monty attempt to fly their new contraption. Mia asked if you could join us."

Claire resisted the need to sputter. This might be getting a little too friendly. Mia and Mason were clever kids, and she suspected more lay behind their innocent request than the adults gave them credit for. If she played along, she could well be walking into a carefully laid trap, conjured up by two active imaginations. But saying no would appear unfriendly. She had enjoyed her time at their home yesterday. This Thanksgiving had become a holiday she'd want to remember.

"What time?" She snapped her mouth closed, surprised she'd answered yes. "I'll need to save some afternoon time for laundry and school lesson plans."

"Monty thought if we hit the beach by ten, we could fly the kite and have our lunch."

"Is the weather expected to cooperate?" Cold, rainy beaches made for a less than pleasant day. She'd had enough rain the night she'd ventured out to look for Mason at the school. "I'm a fair-weather flyer."

"Monty says it's iffy. But his weather buddies at NOAA assure him the sun should shine part of the time."

Claire surrendered. "Sure. I'll give it a go. What shall I bring?"

When the call ended, Claire had a macaroni salad to make. She grabbed her jacket. She'd run out of cucumbers and the last tomato waited in her sandwich. What else might she need for tomorrow? Besides courage.

Maybe she should hope for rain.

CHAPTER ELEVEN

UNABLE TO SLEEP, CLAIRE HAD ALREADY been up for an hour when her alarm sounded. She sipped a cup of cocoa, watching the rays poke through the blinds and zero in on her empty pillow. The bright beams promised beautiful weather—her favorite conditions at the beach.

Newport often had unexpected breaks in the climate. The sporadic patterns of storms, wind, and rain that usually marked a coastal town this far north visited Newport with regular frequency. But following the inclement conditions often came a day, sometimes two, of warm sun.

"And, of course, today is one of those." Claire set down her cup and headed to the shower. "Make the best of it, Simpson."

She dressed in layers. The sun at Newport didn't always mean warmth came with it, especially if the wind picked up from the ocean. She considered capris, but opted for her skinny jeans, sliding them over a pair of sleek-fitting thermals. The mirror told her the jeans fit snugger than she usually wore them, but still had space inside to keep the warmth next to her skin so she stayed with her choice. She layered the top with a tank, a short-sleeved sweater, and a hoodie over that. Her jacket would insulate her if the wind played bully.

Ellen said Monty chose a place called *Jump-off Joe*, located just off 11th Street in the Nye Beach district. Claire hadn't explored the beach area on that side of town, so she drove with caution, not sure where she'd wind up. She spotted the Chandler truck in a parking lot to the right and drove in beside it. She climbed out and studied the stretch of shoreline below. She spotted two little figures dancing in the sand as their adult companions laid out a large blanket and erected an umbrella. Claire grabbed her basket of lunch offerings, her jacket and bag, and slogged through the highs and lows of sand toward the picnic spot. The wind blew in a steady, brisk blast off the ocean, and she shivered. She stopped, put on her jacket, and continued.

"Miss Claire!" Mason romped through the sand like he had cleats on his shoes, meeting her halfway up the rise.

Mia followed her brother, stumbling as she trudged up the soft beach toward her. Her shoes sank in the dry mounds as she scrambled to keep up.

Claire hurried to join the twins, her enthusiasm for the outing growing as her feet touched the wetter sand, making walking easier.

"Ready to fly your kite?" Claire grinned as his inner sunshiny personality spread across Mason's cheeks. No need to guess his answer.

Mason beamed. "It's got a dragon's face and a really long tail!"

"Wow! That should be something to see."

They turned and hobbled together toward the spot where the umbrella quivered in the wind, its stays popping up and down with each gust. Beyond it, Monty knelt in the sand, fiddling with a kite covered in orange and green.

Ellen waved, hands in her pockets and shoulders hunched.

Claire huffed as she joined her friend. "Great day for a picnic. Think the bursts of air will give us a break?"

"Monty says it will make the kite flying easier." Ellen tugged the front of her raincoat closed, popping the hood over her hair. "But I wonder if the kids can get the front aimed right so the wind can carry it."

"We'll soon find out." Claire added her basket to the two containers already sitting on the blanket. Beyond her, Monty stood and tested the kite, the fragile frame crackling in the drafts of air, its knotted tail flopping up and down.

A few minutes passed, the gusts continuing their playful

advance. Monty tested the kite again and the force of the air tugged at it, daring the flyer to release the string. "Mason, let's see if we can fly this thing."

Mason bounded to his dad's side. "What do I do?"

"Take the twine." Monty handed the ball to the boy. "Hold that in your left hand and hold this single strand in your right. Like this."

"Okay." Mason's tongue poked out between his teeth as he concentrated on the task. Once he held it correctly, Monty showed him how to let the string out in a slow, smooth manner and the kite would pull away from him. "Okay."

Monty held the kite and nodded at Mason. "Try it. Let the string out slowly so you always feel a tug."

Mason unwound the string and Monty held the kite higher. Soon the wind grabbed it and lifted the diamond shape above Monty's head. "Let the string out, Mason. Keep it going. That's it. Your dragon wants to fly."

Mason smiled as the kite tugged away from him and rose almost twelve feet in the air. "It's flying! It's flying!" His short-lived joy disappeared when a downdraft caught the kite and sent it plunging into the sand. "Oh, no! Dad. What did I do?"

Monty jogged over to where the kite had landed. He picked it up and checked the pieces of the wood frame for damage. "It's okay. The structure is still intact. A slight tear in the dragon's face. Ellen, do we have any tape?"

Claire reached for her bag. "I brought cellophane tape. Will that work?"

"Should." Monty brought the forlorn-looking dragon to where she stood. "How is it you have tape in your bag?"

"I'm a teacher." She grinned at his open-mouthed stare. "You'd be surprised what you'll find in my bag."

He laughed, tossing the tape in his right hand like a juggler.

"I'm sure I would be. Probably something for every emergency a kid can create, right?"

"Absolutely. Like Boy Scouts, we teachers have to be prepared."

He studied her a moment, a mischievous grin on his lips, then patched the torn spot and handed back the tape. "Thanks. You might start looking for balsa wood. Another crash and this frame will be toast."

"No balsa wood, I'm afraid. Even I have my limits."

"Well, there's always lunch." He looked at Ellen. "Be prepared in case this next lift-off goes sour."

Ellen nodded and knelt by the baskets. She opened the largest one and retrieved plates. She tucked the napkins in the hinge of the basket to keep them from blowing away. A plastic tub of sandwiches followed, along with a container of cut-up vegetables and a bag of chips.

Claire opened her basket and handed Ellen the bowl of macaroni salad and a spoon. She pulled out a carton filled with the oatmeal and chocolate chunk cookies she'd made for Thanksgiving. "Why is this place called Jump-Off Joe?"

"Used to be a promontory of sandstone sticking out that people would jump from. Looked like a boot, I understand." Ellen reached into the second basket and lifted out bottled water and juice. "Eroded over time, but the beach never lost its nickname." She rocked back on her heels and stood. "That looks like a healthy meal."

"At least we're ready to cheer the launch." Claire smiled at her friend as they arranged the food offerings in a circle in the middle of the blanket. They joined Mia, who stood watching her father and brother discuss the finer points of flying.

A dubious stare filled Mason's eyes. "Why don't you fly it first, and I'll watch?"

"I have to man the kite." Monty held up the dragon that shuddered with each passing gust. He glanced at Claire and his sister. "Would either of you like to help Mason?"

Ellen raised her hands and shook her head. "I never was good at this."

Claire zipped her jacket tighter and rolled the cuffs up. "I'll give it a go. Come on, Mason, let's get your kite in the sky."

He held out the string to her.

"No, I want you to let out the string. Just let it slip through your hands but keep a tight tug on the kite. I'll monitor the ball of string. Do you know how to run backward?"

Mason nodded.

"Good. If we run backward, we'll always have our eye on the kite, telling us what to do." She unrolled enough twine to give her a three-foot lead. "Okay, Mason. Ready?"

They started backward, creating a tight line to the kite. Monty let go when the kite lifted to six feet and slipped from his fingertips.

"Okay, Mason, start moving faster." She let the string unravel on her arm and slide into Mason's hand. "Keep it going." She trotted faster, and Mason struggled to keep up. "Let go of the string, and the kite will lift higher."

Mason stared as the kite caught a cross-breeze and flew twenty feet into the air.

Claire kept releasing string as the dragon flipped right and left, its tail waving in a wild flutter behind it. When the kite had soared to a speck in the sky, she handed the ball of string to Mason. "Feel that tug?"

"Uh-huh."

"If you feel the twine go slack or limp, back up real fast until it tightens. The secret to keeping your dragon flying is a hard tug on the string. Understand?"

"I think so." Mason glanced up at the dragon, now barely

visible. "Will we ever get it back down?"

Claire knelt and gave the little boy a squeeze. "When you are tired of flying it, we'll roll the string in slowly and pull the dragon down."

"Mia needs to fly it, too."

Claire looked to where Mia stood. "Mia, Mason wants you to come help him."

Mia shook her head.

"Come on, you need a turn."

The little girl crept toward them, her eyes wide. "I don't know how."

Claire held out her arm. "I'll show you." She took the ball of string from Mason and loosened enough to give Mia a length of her own. "Mason is monitoring the big string, and you can help by unwinding smaller lengths and holding the ball, like this." She showed Mia how to unwind the twine. "When you want to quit, call me and I'll come help you. But don't let go of the string."

She stood and left the twins giggling as the dragon above them yanked their arms, sometimes hard enough to make one of them take a step. She turned to the picnic spot and caught Monty staring at her. "Your turn is next."

"I don't think they need my help." Monty folded his arms, and stared up at the kite, but not before casting a cursory glance her way.

The look on his face made Claire uncomfortable. She'd not had the attention of a male friend since Jamie left, but she hadn't forgotten the way a man's appraisal of her could make her feel as if she'd forgotten an important piece of clothing. His approval showed, perhaps a little too much. As a teacher, involving herself with the father of two of her students wouldn't appear professional. Yet she couldn't deny the fondness she'd developed for the children, and the ache she carried for their circumstances. Had she become too concerned? Perhaps she should cut this afternoon short and bow out gracefully. She found her voice. "If Mason stays out there too long, you'll have to reel the dragon in. I have to finish lesson plans today."

Ellen pointed to where the children stood. "I think Mia's had enough already."

Claire glanced up, and the little girl was waving the ball of string like a distress signal. She hurried out to rescue the child. "Tired?"

"Gotta go potty." Mia stared up at her like doom had taken residence on her heels.

"Go tell your Aunt Ellen and I'll help Mason." She took the string and Mia scooted off to the picnic blanket. Soon Ellen and Mia were climbing the berm to the rest area.

Monty strode across the sand.

"Want a turn?" She held out the string.

"Nah, keeping you tethered gives me a chance to thank you." He grinned. "Without your assistance I'm not sure I could have gotten the kite airborne. I could tell I couldn't handle both ends. Telling Mason how to do it wasn't working."

"Glad to help."

"You've done more than help." Monty dug his heel into the sand. "Adjusting to this new life the kids and I have been thrust into hasn't been easy for any of us. I thought I was going to lose Mia. She'd always been a special spark in our lives, and Marissa's death changed Mia into this crying, forlorn child I didn't know."

"Your children have endured a tragedy few adults manage well." Claire guarded her words. "They are doing better than many."

"People keep telling me that, but they don't see us at home, away from public scrutiny. Nights are hard without Mommy." His line of vision raised to study her face. "But what you're doing at the school made a marked difference the first day. Thank you."

"We simply gave Mia a different entry point into her school day." Claire shrugged. "Coming into a full classroom of children she didn't know was more than she could handle. Her thimble was already full. I'm glad we could be of service to your family."

"Miss Claire?" Worry laced Mason's question. "I'm getting hungry. Can we bring the kite down?"

Monty smiled. "I'll do it. Ellen and Mia are coming back. You ladies can get the lunch."

He turned and strode to his son's side. Claire watched, fighting the happy tears that threatened to undo her calm. *Thank you, Lord, that I could make a difference.*

As soon as lunch had been served and the twins had consumed all the cookies she'd brought with her, Claire stood, brushed the sand from her jeans, and excused herself from the picnic. "Mason and Mia seem occupied with the surf, so I think this is a good time for me to leave."

Ellen looked to where she pointed. The twins were taking turns jumping into the bubbles as each wave scurried up the shore to tickle their toes. Monty stood watching, his calls to the twins reminding them to stay on the sand and not wander into the ocean. Saying goodbye became a mere formality for closing the afternoon.

Ellen helped clear the blanket, stashing her picnic items into the waiting baskets. She handed Claire the bowl that had held the macaroni salad. "Great salad. Will you share the recipe?"

Claire shrugged. "It's so easy, there isn't one. But I can write down the ingredients I used and get it to you. It's a mix of cucumber, tomato, mayonnaise and Dijon mustard with the cooked pasta."

"That's all there is to it?" Ellen's eyes widened. "It tasted exotic, as if it had some special ingredients."

"The mustard gives it that extra tang." Claire tucked the empty bowl in her basket. "But I'm flattered you think it had gourmet beginnings."

Ellen folded the umbrella and set it on top of her baskets. "Monty can help me with the blanket when we're ready to go." She opened her arms, inviting Claire for a hug. "When will we see you again?"

Claire returned the embrace, warmed by the woman's acceptance of her into their little group. "I imagine I'll see you Monday when you pick up the children after school."

Ellen aimed a playful swat at her. "You know what I mean. Really see you for a function or dinner or something." She studied her a moment. "I'm hoping we can become better friends."

"I'd enjoy that." Ellen represented a safe person in whom she could confide most things. "You and I could meet for a Saturday lunch."

"Monty leaves in January for his first sea tour since he moved south. I'll have the twins all by myself. I'm sure I'll go stir-crazy if I don't have some adult interaction."

Claire paused, surprised by Ellen's declaration. "Monty has to leave his kids?"

Ellen nodded. "His contract with NOAA is for a mixed tour— part on land and part on sea. His research takes him to the ocean a lot."

"How long?"

"This first tour will be six weeks. My husband returns home the first of March, so Monty needs to get back to Newport, find a place to live, and help his children settle by then. I'm praying his house in Seattle sells so he can buy here."

"Newport's prices are not cheap." Claire had considered owning property but couldn't find anything she could afford.

"Renting is almost impossible."

"All the more reason for his house to sell."

Claire nodded, grabbing her picnic basket by the handle. "Things have a way of working out. This will, too." Claire waved at Mason and Mia, her heart fully engaged for the two little kids. *Lord, make it so.*

CHAPTER TWELVE

MONTY CAUGHT A GLIMPSE OF CLAIRE as she crossed the highway and popped the trunk of her car. She'd added a special spark to their outing today, and he regretted seeing her leave. As she unlocked her door, a stranger appeared from the parking lot, his hand grabbing the top of Claire's car door. Monty became alarmed and called to Ellen. "Can you take over here?" He pointed toward the parking lot.

As they watched, Claire put her hands on her hips and faced the man. Monty's sense of danger kicked in, even though the pair appeared to know each other. The guy's stance had all the earmarks of a standoff. Why had he waited until Claire left their picnic to approach her? When Claire shook her head, and turned to her car, Monty shouted over his shoulder. "Claire needs help. Be right back."

He trudged through the deeper sand at the top of the beach, his eyes on the scene above him. Claire had her hands up as though warning the man to keep his distance. She shook her head and folded her arms across her chest. When she thrust her arm out, pointing down the road, Monty leaped into rescue mode. As he reached the edge of the parking lot, he heard a car door slam. Claire backed out and squealed her tires as she hit the pavement and sped up the quiet beach road. The stranger had disappeared.

Monty studied the parking lot, searching for a vehicle that might be leaving. At the other end, a silver Lexus pulled forward, its hood pointed down the road toward him, away from where Claire had gone. As the car passed, all Monty could see of the driver were sunglasses and a polo shirt, but his mouth was set in a straight line as if he chewed on his lip. What did this guy have to do with Claire?

Claire forced herself to breathe as she drove away from Jamie—slow, steady breaths to calm her racing heart. He'd frightened her today, waiting in the parking lot while she enjoyed her afternoon with the Chandlers. Her heart stopped when he'd darted out from the lineup of parked cars as she reached her vehicle, reaching her side as she popped the trunk.

"You looked like you were having a great time." Jamie's crooked smile matched the sarcasm in his voice. "New friends?"

"What do you want?" Heart still pounding, Claire eyed him with suspicion, glancing around for others to whom she might turn for help. "Forget your way back to the valley?"

"No, I had some properties here I needed to check out. Prime coastal lots." He narrowed his eyes, penetrating and dark, the hazel irises burrowing through her. "Didn't my mother tell you I'm now a realtor?"

"No, she failed to mention that fact." Claire ignored the war in her stomach, butterflies dancing around the edges seeking escape. "Gave up on the Olympics, did you?"

"Not entirely, but bills needed to be paid, and I lost my sponsor."

"Sorry to hear that." Claire closed the trunk of her car and moved to the driver's side. Jamie followed. She turned and faced him, holding up her palms. "I don't have time to stop and chat. I have lesson plans to finish for Monday, so I must be going."

"You spent the afternoon with them." Jamie nodded toward the beach. "You don't have time for coffee with your former fiancé?"

"I don't have time for someone who is spying on me. Are you adding stalker to your list of accomplishments?"

"I want to talk with you, alone."

"We did talk the last time you were here. There's nothing more to discuss. Our relationship ended five years ago. Or don't you remember?" Claire yanked open her car door. "You closed the chapters between us by jumping into another story. I know about the affair between you and Shelly."

"It wasn't what you think." Jamie rested his hands on her car door.

"Actually, that's good." Claire slid into the seat. "Because what I think might burn the hide off your face." She reached for the door handle. "Goodbye. And don't bother me again." She slammed the door closed, started the engine, and threw the car into reverse. As she gunned the motor, the tires squealed. She'd never done that before.

She glanced in her rearview mirror. Jamie had moved to a car at the other end of the parking lot. He stood watching her drive away. For the second time in two days she'd left this man standing alone. Maybe this time he'd get the point.

Another figure stepped into the space she'd vacated. She gasped. Was that Monty Chandler? Had he seen the exchange? Would he confront Jamie? She resisted turning the car around to prevent the two men from meeting. No. She couldn't risk discovery. Going back could fuel an already explosive situation. But if Jamie and Monty met. . .

Heat rushed up her cheeks, her breathing erratic. She'd closed the door on her past, the history she'd buried safely hidden. She didn't intend for anyone to pry the lock. Not even a nice guy like Monty Chandler. She prayed Jamie had left the scene.

Monty ambled back down the slope to where Ellen stood waiting with Mia and Mason.

"What happened?" Ellen's eyes held worry, her gaze searching his. "Is Claire okay?"

Monty nodded. "She had the situation under control. It just looked different from down here. I shouldn't have thought about interfering."

Ellen didn't appear to be convinced, but she held out a basket to him. "I think the twins have had enough sand and surf. Mia is practically falling asleep on her feet."

Monty set the basket down and held his arms out to Mia. "Come here, pumpkin. Let Daddy carry you."

She stepped into his embrace and wrapped her arms about his neck. He lifted her off the ground, grabbing the handle of the basket as he stood. "Mason, are you doing okay?"

Mason squinted up at him, the sun shining on his face. "I'm really tired. But I had the bestest time ever, Dad. Thank you for flying kites with us today."

"We'll do it again, Son. I promise." Monty gestured toward the parking lot. "Let's head for Auntie Ellen's house, shall we?"

Mia had already fallen asleep by the time they reached the pickup. Monty unlocked the crew cab and set the girl in her booster seat, buckling the harness. He strode around to the other side and opened the doors, first for Ellen, then for Mason. He hefted his son to his spot, the little boy leaning back against the cushion and yawning. He closed the door, reaching for Ellen's door next. "I think we'll have sleeping kids all the way home."

Ellen stifled a yawn and smiled. "I'm not far behind them. What is it about wind and surf that makes us so tired?"

He smiled. "It was all the fun we had. We didn't realize how much energy we were expending. We'll have to get these two to bed early if we're to make Sunday school in the morning."

Ellen's eyes widened. "You've decided to go?"

"Promised Marissa." He winked and shut her door. *And a promise is made to be kept.* The only one who heard him was the One who heard all things, but Monty wouldn't turn back now. He pictured Marissa standing beside her Lord, waiting for him to keep his word. He couldn't fail her. He promised.

Rain pattered the roof of the duplex the next morning as Claire sat at her kitchen table sipping a cup of tea, wrestling with her decision to attend church. No one would know if she skipped today. She wasn't teaching a class, nor was she singing in the choir. Her absence would leave a small hole in a large congregation.

God knows.

The little voice she called her conscience spoke loud in her ear. She'd tried to tame that talking monster over the years, but when she asked Christ to be her Savior in Pennsylvania, the voice had not been silent since.

"Okay, okay." She muttered under her breath as she grabbed her robe and headed to the shower. The hot water would help her wake and warm at the same time. She let the spray beat on her back a few extra minutes before stepping into the steamy room and toweling dry. Donning her robe, she walked barefoot to the kitchen, stopping to ignite the electric fireplace. She pulled open the refrigerator and reached for the carton of yogurt. Blueberries, yogurt and cold cereal sounded like what she needed today.

Her phone buzzed, and she eyed the screen. Angie.

"What? No church today for the O'Brien's?" She glanced at the clock. Church should be ready to commence in Pennsylvania. "Don't tell me you're playing hooky?"

Angie's voice wavered. "Had to. Fallyn's in the hospital."

"What? Why?" Claire fought the lump in her throat.

"That urinary tract infection turned out to be something a little more serious. One of her kidneys isn't functioning."

Claire shivered as she processed Angie's words. A kidney not functioning had to be life-threatening. But in a child of five. . .

"Will she recover?"

"The doctor thinks so." Angie's voice sounded as if she was on the brink of tears.

"What does that mean in the long run for her health?" Claire's heart raced as she thought of the little girl facing serious illness. "Can her kidney be treated?"

"Yes, they are trying to stem the infection. The danger is if the infection spreads to the other kidney." Angie sniffed, her tender heart revealing itself. "If the treatment fails, she could go into renal failure."

"Oh, Angie. I wish I was there." Angie needed a hug, and Claire was too far away to give one. "Is Brennan holding up?"

"He's worried like I am."

"What's the prognosis?"

"If she responds to the antibiotic and the infection clears, she'll be sent home." Angie drew a cleansing breath. "But she'll be monitored after that. If the infection doesn't clear, the worst-case scenario is the kidneys could fail. Then she's looking at dialysis, maybe even a transplant. But right now, that's a long way down the road."

"A transplant? Seriously?" Claire gasped. "But the waiting list. . ."

"Is long." Angie grew bolder. "Want to put yourself in the registry?"

"Absolutely. Tell me where to go."

Bereft, Claire bid Angie goodbye with instructions on how to put herself on the donor list along with a promise to pray for the sick child. Fallyn had only turned five three weeks ago. Why should someone so small face such big problems? This wasn't fair. She considered foregoing church altogether, but of all the days she might have skipped, today wouldn't be one. Fallyn needed her prayers and those of the prayer chain.

She finished dressing, grabbed her Bible and car keys, and headed out the door. After yesterday's windy, but dry day, today the rain returned full force. She pulled the hood of her jacket up over her head and hurried to the car. Fallyn's future depended on people beseeching an Almighty God for mercy. She wouldn't be the one who let her down.

CHAPTER THIRTEEN

MONTY DROVE THE TWINS TO SCHOOL Monday, anticipating an encounter with Claire. The teacher had made such a difference in Mia's outlook, helping the child move beyond her grief and anticipate life ahead, the child practically bounced in her seat. Mason had lost his feisty, protective spirit—the need to pick fights and challenge the world, gone. Both kids were behaving like the children they'd been, finding joy in family and security in their new school situation. The teacher had removed the barriers that frightened them and channeled them into a satisfying school experience.

Ellen helped, taking on the role of mother and nurturer like she'd been born to it, and for that he'd be forever grateful. Monty dreaded the day when he and the children would move to their own home again and leave Ellen behind, acting only as afterschool monitor and taxi driver for the twins. When Kevin returned from overseas, they deserved to be left alone. The couple needed to find common ground and rediscover the course of their marriage after a long absence. Little kids underfoot would not facilitate that kind of bonding.

Monty drove up to the drop-off and stopped. He jumped out of the pickup and hurried to unload Mia and Mason from the passenger side. He glanced around for Claire but didn't see her. "Do you know where to go from here?"

Mason nodded. "We go to Miss Claire's office."

"Which direction is that?" Monty followed the point of Mason's finger to a set of double doors a few feet away.

As if on cue, Claire appeared and waved. She smiled, but the expression did not meet her eyes. A look of wariness—or was it worry—covered her face.

Mason and Mia took off to where she stood, both competing for an opportunity to speak first. Monty followed the short distance, his own need to speak with the woman directing his steps. As Mia and Mason chattered about their Sunday, Monty stepped into the fray. "Good morning. I hope we didn't wear you out too much Saturday."

Claire slipped into professional mode. "Not at all. It was so nice to be invited to share your family holiday. I appreciated the invitation."

Monty sensed her hesitation and decided not to ask about the encounter with the stranger after she left. Whoever the man was, she'd handled the situation. Yet something about her reserved manner made him curious. This conversation felt awkward. Perhaps she feared he'd witnessed the exchange and felt uncomfortable.

"How was your Sunday?" Changing the subject might help the vacuum lingering between them. He waited, surprised as she pressed her lips together and closed her eyes for a second. When she looked at him again, he saw a hint of tears. "Miss Claire?"

"My niece had to be admitted to the hospital. She has a serious kidney infection." Claire's smile returned, brief, but genuine. "I'm worried about her."

"How old is she?"

"Just turned five. She lives in Pennsylvania."

"So not exactly close enough to visit." Monty studied Claire's sad face a minute. "The doctors will know what to do. Kids usually bounce back."

Claire glanced at Mia and Mason before fixing her gaze on him. "I hope you're right. She's my sister's only child so far, and she's adopted." She stretched her hands to the twins. "Well, we better get started or the school bell will find us out here and not in our seats." Holding his children's hands, she nodded his way. "Hope your day goes well. Goodbye." The threesome turned and disappeared into the building.

Monty returned to his truck, Claire's revelation weighing on his mind. She projected confidence when she interacted with people, but beneath the surface a gentle spirit carried its own supply of hurts. The two of them were more alike than he'd first realized.

Monty reported to his team leader, Dr. Richard Neilson, after he left the school. The marine mammal institute had received another memo from the eastern seaboard citing the deaths of two more humpback whales on the Virginia coast. "How many whales does this make?"

"Forty-one." The man's face appeared stricken. "This is considered an unusual mortality event, and no one knows why." He leaned forward on his elbows. "Ten of the deaths were by blunt force trauma."

"They ran into a ship?"

"Or its propellers." The man gazed up at him. "But none of the deaths were due to disease."

Monty frowned. The gray whales he would follow in January when his ship left port hadn't had those kind of problems. Migration from Alaska would begin in a couple of weeks and continue through January as the whales swam to their breeding grounds near Baja California, Mexico. Warm lagoons provided nurseries for expectant mothers. Beginning in March, the whales returned north, the males and the non-pregnant females leading the way. Sometimes the early birds would pass the slow pokes still heading south. In May the mothers and their young made the journey.

Keeping track of which whales were going where comprised the work of Monty's team. Counting the whales with young helped determine numbers of the species. Some whales didn't make the trip back to Alaska but stayed instead near the coast off Oregon. The resident killer whale population also swam these waters and sightings of killer whales harassing the grays had made recent reports. Most of the encounters seemed to be non-malicious attempts to mess with the gray whales, like teenage bullies looking for something to pester, but the incidents had to be monitored.

He enjoyed the work. Working with his science team challenged his expertise in mammal biology. Leaving his kids for six weeks while he sailed the ocean tugged at his heart. He thanked God again for his sister's willingness to step in while he worked. If only Marissa hadn't died. He fought the emotion strangling him and refocused on Dr. Neilson.

"Is there any evidence of that problem on this coast?" He took the chair Dr. Neilson offered.

"Not yet." Dr. Neilson leaned back in his chair. "But we are finding dead zones along the coast where nothing has survived. That alone could cause a shift in feeding patterns and draw the whales into shipping lanes they didn't frequent before."

"And we could be mounting our own mortality numbers." Monty glanced at a map on the wall. Populations of whales were sensitive to feeding ground changes as well as water temperature variances. Every whale that died for no reason threatened the health of the entire pod.

"Killer whales suffered severe losses a few years before when polychlorinated biphenyls and DDT polluted the waters of Puget Sound." Dr. Neilson pointed at the map. "Hydraulic equipment had been dumped in the waters and left to decay at the bottom, polluting the sea floor where plants drew their nourishment."

"I remember. I was on one of the teams out of Seattle." Monty shifted in his chair. "The fish populations ingested the poisons lurking in their food sources. Seals fed on the fish and killer whales ate the seals. The pollutants got into the whale's blubber and tainted the milk of the whale mothers. Their young died."

At Dr. Neilson's nod, he added his thoughts. "If we continue monitoring the whales, like the southern killer whale population has been tracked and followed in recent years, we can probably prevent a mortality event of this magnitude."

Dr. Neilson stood and extended his hand. "I like the way you think. I'm glad you transferred to our team, Chandler."

"Thanks. I'm glad I made the change, sir." *For my children's sake.*

Claire hurried through dinner later that evening, fixing a final turkey sandwich and eating the last of her pumpkin pie. She'd called Angie when she got home but got no answer, and her sister had not yet returned her call. Where was she?

Not knowing how Fallyn fared worried Claire all day. She gathered strength watching Mia and Mason play like happy children on the playground, clinging to the hope that Fallyn would make as much progress as the twins had made since she'd started bringing their problems into her prayers. Her entreaties yesterday resembled furtive cries more than audible petitions, but God was in the business of translation, so she laid her burden in His hands.

Finally, her phone buzzed. She checked the screen. Angie.

"How's Fallyn?"

"Better." Her sister sounded tired. "Her kidneys are responding to the treatment. The kidney they thought had quit functioning is actually working. Just needed to be medicated."

"That's good news, isn't it?"

"Yes." Angie's voice wobbled. "Oh, Claire, I was so scared. You can blame pregnancy hormones, but I love Fallyn like she's always been mine. Seeing her suffer made me feel like I had let her down. All I could think of was, bad mother."

"Angie, you're a natural at mothering. This wasn't your fault. These things happen. As Fallyn's aunt, I love her, too. But I'm too far away to be of any help."

"You are never too far away." Angie sniffed. "As Fallyn's aunt and godmother, I think of you every day. Your picture is on her dresser. If something were to happen to me, I want her to know who you are."

Claire paused, drawing a breath as Angie's words warmed her. "I'm glad you've made certain she knows who I am. It's nice to be included. But nothing's going to happen to you. Fallyn calls you her mother. She's never known anything different. This new baby will be her own sibling."

"She will have to be told the truth one day." Angie sounded resolved. "Brennan and I decided to wait a while, but we want her to know her beginnings."

"When that day comes, we'll all have to weigh in on the decision you made to adopt her." Claire shuddered at what the reaction might be when Fallyn learned of her roots. Would she feel betrayed? Cast away? "Fallyn needs to know she was cherished and most wanted from the time she was conceived, but the circumstances surrounding her birth weren't the right environment to give her a stable home." Claire swallowed. "You and Brennan made that happen."

"She's brought more into our lives than we have ever given." Angie sniffed again. "I can't imagine my life without her."

"She's blessed to call you mama."

Angie changed the subject. "Have you thought about Christmas?"

"What do you mean?" Claire glanced at the calendar. Thanksgiving had been early compared to other years when the fourth Thursday fell on the last week of November. That made an additional four weeks for shoppers to complete their Christmas lists. "I haven't started shopping, if that's what you're hinting."

"No. I thought you might hop a plane and come see us."

"That's a wonderful invitation, but I hate to ditch Mom at Christmas. I already bailed out of Thanksgiving." Her mother wouldn't spend both holidays with Jamie's family, would she?

"You did? Any particular reason?"

"Mom was invited to the Duval home and dropped the bomb that Jamie would be among the guests." She wasn't convinced that the invitation had been an innocent one, or that her mother was as clueless as she wanted Claire to believe. She understood the friendship between Jamie's mother and hers, but the scheming behind her back felt like betrayal.

"No wonder."

"But, get this. Jamie showed up here in Newport the day after Thanksgiving and then found me again on Saturday. He stalked me while I was on a beach outing with friends." Claire smiled as she remembered the forlorn look on the man's face when she got in her car, slammed the door, and drove away.

"You can't be serious."

"Girl Scout's honor. I told him in no uncertain terms that I would never again consider him as a life partner." Other than his handsome face and ability to charm anyone he met, she still wondered what about him had attracted her in the first place. She'd been young, inexperienced, and starry-eyed. She'd paid for her stupidity.

"Good for you. You'd think he'd know that, after what he did."

"He's trying to rid himself of guilt. Even asked how I handled everything when he walked out and left me holding the bag."

"Did you tell him?"

"I told him I took care of all the arrangements. I didn't elaborate. The less need for him to grovel, the better." She glanced again at the calendar, seeking a change of subject. "I'll call Mom and see if she has Christmas plans. If she doesn't, I might try to get two tickets to Pennsylvania. Considering how late it is, I probably won't be able to afford them, but Mom might spring for her own ticket. It's easier to convince her with bait."

"We would love to have you. We haven't shared Christmas in five years."

She blinked at the moisture rimming her eyes. "I'll get back to you, sis. Take care of Fallyn for me."

After she ended the phone call, Claire checked for tickets online. School wouldn't dismiss until the Friday before Christmas. Driving to the valley to pick up her mother before they drove to the Portland airport meant they'd leave Saturday or Sunday, Christmas Eve. Connections involved layovers on almost all the flights, turning what should be a seven or eight-hour trip into a grueling marathon of long delays. Couple that with the weather Angie's part of the country often experienced, she and her mother could be stranded well beyond Christmas.

She didn't want to disappoint Angie, but her mother didn't do well when delayed or inconvenienced. Traveling this time of year might not be the best choice for any of them. Claire typed in June dates, thinking the trip might be better planned if centered around the birth of Angie's baby and not the Christmas holiday. In June she and her mother could fly to Washington, D.C. non-stop and drive the ninety-three miles to Harrisburg. The weather should be better, and she could show her mother all the places she'd visited when she attended school while living with her sister.

Her phone buzzed, and she glanced at the screen. Mom. Good timing. "Hey. What's up?"

"Nancy just called me and said you brushed Jamie off like a bug on your shoe." Her mother's tone sounded tense, which surprised her after Mom had assured her she respected Claire's decision less than a week ago. "You could be civil to the man. You were going to marry him, remember?"

"Trust me, I haven't forgotten." She counted to three, inhaling deep to control her response. "He doesn't seem to understand that what he did finished any relationship we could have had, forever. You, of all people, should know that." Was her mother having trouble thinking? This wasn't like her. The upbeat, down again flipside of her nature lately wasn't something Claire remembered in the woman's personality. Had she always been this way? Or had Claire grown wiser and more in tune with people's quirks since Jamie's betrayal. "Angie wants us to come for Christmas."

"Can't go." Mom's angst had subsided as suddenly as it appeared. Another flip-flop in less than ten minutes. "I'm spending Christmas at Sun River with friends from church."

"Sun River?" She didn't think her mother enjoyed winter resort outings.

"Six of us went together and rented a condo. We're all friends and we're all widows. I volunteered to bring decorations for a Christmas tree." Mom giggled like a teenager planning a sleepover. "Want to join us?"

"Let me get back to you. I still have Angie's invitation to consider."

"Pennsylvania will be cold."

"I lived there for almost two years, remember?" She thought of how much easier it would be to see her sister without Mom along, but the idea overwhelmed her with guilt. Her mother could be difficult, but she always stood by her in a crisis. Traveling without her would make things much simpler. She smiled, and the guilt fled. Mom had given her a hall pass. She pulled reservations back up and chose her day. Angie would be pleased. She couldn't wait to see Fallyn again.

CHAPTER FOURTEEN

"DID YOU BRING YOUR DECORATIONS FROM Seattle?" Ellen's question jarred Monty as he glanced at the calendar. Christmas waited two weeks away. After surviving Thanksgiving, he'd dragged his feet getting ready for the holiday. This would be another first for him and his kids without Marissa. He'd struggled at Thanksgiving to keep a positive attitude in front of Mia and Mason, and with Claire Simpson in the picture he'd managed better than he'd hoped. Repeating that act for his children at Christmas seemed impossible. He couldn't do it. His heart hadn't climbed onboard. Nor did he expect it to.

"I saved the ornaments Marissa gave the kids each Christmas. She had stockings made with their names on them, and there are a couple of holiday scenes she set up on the mantle and in the foyer. I disposed of the rest."

"Are they in storage?" Ellen sat at the kitchen breakfast bar, sipping her coffee. "Or did you stick them in my garage?"

"I think they're in the garage. I'll have to look." He crossed the room to the refrigerator, his stomach growling. He reached for the brick of cheese and cut himself a slice. Returning the snack to the shelf, he closed the door and turned toward his sister. "Truth is, I'm not ready to celebrate the holiday."

Ellen's eyes misted. "I understand. But keeping Christmas for Mia and Mason will help them heal from their loss. Seeing the ornaments they'd received from their mother, hanging the stockings, and putting up a familiar Christmas display will comfort them."

"Who's going to comfort me?" Monty sat on a tall stool beside her. "Decorating for Christmas feels like a punch to the ribs." He bit into the cheese. "Bringing out the ornaments will trigger memories of Marissa, as if she's somewhere in the house wrapping presents."

"Don't give up your memories. You and Marissa shared almost ten happy years together. Her illness robbed you of one." Ellen reached for his free hand. "She wanted you to go on. Trusted you to care for her children."

Monty drew a labored breath, suppressing the sadness. "I know. But, Sis, it hurts."

He stood and returned to the fridge, grabbing a soda from the rack. Popping the top, he took a swig, allowing the bubbles to burn in his throat. His sister's words haunted him, the truth of what she said riddling him with guilt. Being a man wasn't all it was cracked up to be. He needed to grieve as much as his children. "I'll go sort through the boxes. The ornaments should be labeled."

Ellen nodded, carrying her coffee cup to the sink. "I have ornaments, too. I'll dig them out while you look."

He pulled his collar tighter about his neck as he entered the cold garage. Rubbing his hands together to warm them, he studied the shelving where his things were kept. Most of the boxes held household items like pots, pans, and dishes, things he would need when his home sold in Seattle and he bought property here. He searched the labels, seeking the container that said Christmas. At the end of the top shelf, he spied the box he needed. Lifting the ladder from its hook on the far wall, he trudged across the garage. When the box was retrieved, he dragged the ladder back to its spot.

He opened the box and peered inside. The scent of peppermint wafted from the pillar candle laying on top—Marissa's favorite holiday smell. He clenched his fists, eyes squeezed shut, as he fought the gut-wrenching sorrow the memory evoked. He could see her standing by the tree, smiling as she hung the ornaments. Cinnamon buns baked in the oven, lights twinkled from the mantle, the children napped.

Was it only two Christmases ago? She'd fallen ill on New Year's Eve. Her diagnosis came in March. She lived a year. One storm-filled, prescription-heavy, terrible year. *God, it hurts. I'm trying to be strong. I can't seem to climb beyond my grief.*

He clung to the sides of the box for several minutes, his head throbbing, his stomach upside down. He breathed deep, straightened, and carried the decorations into the house. As if he had run a marathon, his body ached from the exertion. Why did remembering the woman for whom he would have done anything have to inflict so much pain?

Ellen had entered the family room and her humming drew him there. She sat in a lounge chair—a box in her lap—lifting holiday mementos from its interior. An intricate ceramic bootie dangled from her fingers. She stuck it back in the box when she saw him.

"Is that a special ornament?" He eyed his sister, searching her face for some sort of clue regarding the small baby sock. "Are you and Kevin planning to add to your ranks when he returns?" He grinned, meaning to tease her, but stopped when her face filled with anguish. Tears pooled in her eyes. "What did I say?"

"You never knew about this chapter of our lives." Ellen spoke, her words halted and broken. "We lost a baby right after we were married."

"Oh, Ellen. How did I not know?" Monty swallowed, his status as worst brother of the year flashing from a billboard in his mind. "Did Marissa know and not tell me?"

"We didn't tell many people. The baby came too early. I was only four months along. I had purchased the bootie at Christmas when I knew I was pregnant, anticipating the arrival of our child in July. Only tragedy got in the way." She raised sad eyes to him. "In July, we were no longer expecting, but I still had the ornament."

Monty sat on the arm of the chair and hugged her. Her shoulders shook as she composed herself, sniffing when she raised her head. "Kevin deployed shortly after that, and so far, we haven't been able to conceive again."

"Does having Mia and Mason here cause you heartache?"

"No. I adore them. They give me hope that Kevin and I can try again when he comes home." She patted his arm. "He is looking forward to the adventure."

"Having the ornament doesn't bother you?"

She shook her head. "A woman never forgets her first child."

When they walked into her classroom Monday, Mia and Mason's animated chatter about their Christmas decorations overshadowed Claire's excitement about her upcoming trip. The Chandlers had apparently decorated their tree over the weekend, and the twins couldn't stop talking about the ornaments.

"My first Christmas ornament was a brown rocking horse with a fluffy tail." Mason grinned from ear to ear. "Mia has one just like mine, but hers is black with a white mane."

"It's nice you both have one." Claire sat at the table with a stack of books on Christmas traditions at her side. "Would you like to read about holiday traditions for children in other countries?"

Mia nodded, adding her own bit of news. "I have a stocking with my name on it. Auntie Ellen says my mother *boidered* it herself." She glanced up at Claire. "What does it mean to *boider*?"

Claire smiled at the little girl. She hadn't seen the child poke her thumb in her mouth in almost two weeks. Mia's personality blossomed more with each new day. "The word is embroider. Your mother liked to stitch and make pretty patterns on things with a needle and thread." She reached for a book on Christmas crafts. "Let's look in here and see if we can find a picture of someone stitching."

"Our stockings both have glittery thread." Mason slid around the table to sit next to Claire. He pointed to the page she had flipped open for Mia. "Our stockings have a border on them like this one."

"Are your stockings red?"

"Mine is pink." Mia touched the page. "Mason's is blue and red and green squares."

"Like a plaid?"

The twins stared at her. "What's a plaid?"

Claire flipped through the book, searching for a sample of plaid. She found a green and gold puppy in the stuffed animals section. "This is a type of plaid. See the lines crisscrossing each other?"

Mia squinted at the picture. "I like Mason's plaid better. His colors are more like Christmas."

"Are you coming to our house again?" Mason's face lit up as he asked the question. "Auntie Ellen is going to serve ham."

Claire closed the book. "That sounds good, but I'm going to ride an airplane to see my sister in Pennsylvania." She reached for a globe, using her finger to show the little boy. "We're here in Oregon and my sister and her family live here."

"How long will it take to fly there?" Mia walked her hand across the span.

"If I don't have any delays, it shouldn't be much more than a few hours. But weather can be bad during the holiday season, and I could be slowed down by snow and ice."

Mason frowned. "We used to have snow in Seattle. When my mommy was alive. Newport never gets snow."

"We had snow the first time you came to our school." Claire remembered how sad both of these children had been that day. "But now you have sand and ocean and kites!"

Mason raised his arms in the air. "Let's go fly a kite!"

Mia nudged her brother. "Silly. We have to do school."

"Speaking of school, it's almost time for you two to get to

class." Claire bit her lip, fighting back the chuckle forming in her throat. Mia and Mason were sounding like the happy children she'd imagined them to be when she first met them. She pictured their dad in her mind, his pain during the holiday season probably nearing the excruciating mark. She understood. She'd been blindsided by depression that first Christmas after Jamie walked out of her wedding. Thank goodness she'd been at Angie's house. Fallyn had arrived the week after Thanksgiving, Angie and Brennan overjoyed to bring their adopted daughter home. Fallyn had transfixed them all, her soft, transparent eyes those of a newborn, glancing around. Her mournful cries filled the house with her presence. Nothing like a baby at Christmas. Claire swallowed the memory, savoring it like a favorite book.

Monty wandered the aisles of children's toys at his local superstore. He didn't know what Christmas gifts to buy for either of his kids. Mia might like another doll for her shelf, but which one? He'd never kept track of the ones she already owned—Marissa had done that. Mason could use a dump truck to go with his assortment of toy machinery.

Ellen said both kids could use a pair of shoes, since they'd outgrown the ones they now wore. He wouldn't guess on that. He'd take the twins out for a shoe shopping trip and turn it into a lunch at the local burger joint. He might even spring for a movie afterwards.

January loomed closer with each passing day, its nearness pressing in on him. First week of the new year he would have to join his science team and head out for six weeks on the Pacific. Spending time with his kids and celebrating their birthday on New Year's Day would have to be his priority until then. Again, he gave thanks for Ellen. Ocean science was his passion, his life's work. His children were his blessing. Though his quiver only held two, he'd safeguard their existence with every fiber of his being. With Marissa gone, his sister helped make that happen.

He turned the corner and found Claire standing next to her shopping cart, examining the dolls on the display before her. She didn't see him, so he walked quietly to where she stood and stopped. "Do you know which dolls an almost eight-year-old girl might like?"

She glanced his way, surprise evident in her eyes. "No, I don't. But I suspect Mia would take every stuffed kitten in the store." She set the doll she'd been examining back on the shelf. "Do you know what dolls she already owns?"

Monty shook his head. "My wife kept track of that sort of thing."

"I know the problem. I'm buying for my niece, and I haven't a clue what she'd like."

"Is she doing better?"

"I'd forgotten I'd told you about her." Claire stepped nearer her shopping cart and gripped the handle. "She responded to the antibiotics and was released from the hospital two days later."

"How old is she?"

"Five last month. I'm going to see her at Christmas." Claire's eyes glittered, the anticipation of her trip lighting her face.

"When did you last see her?"

Claire sobered, the twinkle from a moment before gone. "A year. I go visit my sister every summer if I can. I receive pictures, of course, and Facebook updates, but not as good as the real thing. It's been five years since I shared Christmas with them."

"You'll have lots to catch up on, then."

Claire nodded. "Five years of hit and miss is a long time."

CHAPTER FIFTEEN

CLAIRE'S FLIGHT INVOLVED TWO DELAYS, BUT she managed to land in Harrisburg late on the twenty-third. She looked for Brennan as she disembarked the plane and entered the terminal. Angie assured her one of them would meet her, no matter how late her plane arrived. Glancing around the terminal and seeing no familiar faces, she followed the signs to baggage pickup. The luggage from her flight hadn't yet entered the carousel so she studied the perimeter of the room seeking her sister or brother-in-law.

A young girl dressed in an elf costume, complete with green vest and stocking hat, walked around the carousel toward her carrying a Christmas present. As she came closer, Claire inspected the child's outfit, loving how her hair curled from beneath her hat, and chuckling at the elf shoes that made her shuffle as she walked. She stopped near Claire, her eyes dancing, and held out the gift. "Merry Christmas, Aunt Claire."

"Fallyn? I'd have recognized you anywhere." She marveled that the tiny baby had grown into this sweet little girl. She fought the sudden intrusion of tears threatening to cloud the moment. Angie had taken good care of her. She couldn't spoil this reunion.

The child grinned, one front tooth missing, and pointed behind Claire. She turned and laughed as Angie and Brennan stood watching her, a camera pointed her direction. "Surprise!"

She stepped into her sister's arms and hugged her, noticing the depth of her sibling's torso. "You've thickened a bit since I last saw you." She looked at Brennan and teased. "What have you been feeding her?"

He pursed his lips and lifted his hand, tapping each digit as he went. "Pickles. Peppermint ice cream. Chicken legs. Toast." He stopped on the pinkie finger. "Crackers."

"Drumsticks?" Claire studied her brother-in-law to see if he teased. But he nodded at her, pointing at her sister.

"I couldn't' get enough." Angie laughed. "Maybe this kid is part bird. But I ate chicken by the bagful."

"Bad morning sickness?" Her sister didn't have any extra pounds to shed. Staying well during this pregnancy would take extra vigilance.

Angie's cheeks grew pink. "At first. Not so much now." She pointed to the baggage claim. "Do you see your bag?"

Claire turned and spotted her luggage. "There. The blue one with the wooden handle."

Brennan reached beside her and lifted the suitcase out of the lineup. "Shall we go? It's way past one little girl's bedtime."

"But Daddy, it's almost Christmas. And Aunt Claire is here."

She grinned at her niece, still overwhelmed by how much she'd grown and how beautiful she'd become. The golden blonde hair enhanced her angelic image, and the eyes had taken on a surprising hazel hue. What a treasure of a child to surrender to someone else to raise. Thank God her sister and husband were the blessed recipients. In Claire's book, no one else would have qualified. Just thinking about it made her tremble. If it weren't for the hazel eyes, Fallyn could be anyone's child. But those gold-flecked irises and their solemn stare were unique to someone from the child's lineage, and if compared, would leave no doubt as to whom this little girl once belonged.

Monty plugged in the tree lights early Christmas morning, tiptoeing his way across the family room so as not to wake the children. He and Ellen had stacked the gifts beneath the tree last night and filled the stockings they'd hung on the mantle. He and Marissa had agreed not to make Santa a big part of the holiday, and Ellen understood their reasoning. Instead they explained who the man really was and how the stockings represented a tradition they wanted to keep alive.

Despite images of the jolly fellow everywhere around them—at the store, on television, and at street corners—the twins had yet to adopt the typical childhood behavior of waiting for Santa and his reindeer to visit. Both kids had memorized the second chapter of Luke, thanks to Marissa's tutoring, and together they recited it on Christmas morning. Mia and Mason were happier talking about the shepherds, the wise men, their camels and sheep than they were imagining a fictitious man in a red suit.

Monty lit the gas fireplace to warm the room and crept toward the kitchen to make coffee. Ellen had cinnamon rolls waiting to be baked for breakfast, so he grabbed two mugs and set them on the counter for cocoa later. He glanced around for more to do, his memories nagging at him as he remembered how he and Marissa would share a cup of coffee together while they watched the children empty their stockings. Mouths full of chocolate balls, the twins would sit next to the tree and wait while Monty read the prophecy in Isaiah telling of the Messiah's coming. When he finished, he distributed the gifts and the quiet, spiritual atmosphere disappeared in the wake of wrapping paper, squeals of delight, and babbling children eager to try their new toys.

"Oh, God." Monty breathed in deep and squeezed his eyes shut. "How am I going to navigate this day without falling apart?"

"We'll get through it together." Ellen patted him on the shoulder, stepped to the oven, and set the temperature to bake. "It won't be easy, but I believe you've healed enough to save the day for your children."

"The twins are doing better than I am." He leaned against the counter to watch his sister work. "And I know in part it's due to Claire Simpson's input."

Ellen removed the cinnamon rolls from the refrigerator and put the pan on the range top. "She's definitely made a difference, hasn't she?"

"Did you know Mason invited her to Christmas dinner here?" At her surprised look, he nodded. "She'd made plans to see her sister in Pennsylvania. Otherwise, Mason and Mia would have insisted on her sharing the ham."

"Would you have minded?"

He stopped, unprepared for the question. Giving the query thought, he chuckled. "I don't know how to answer you. If I'm honest, I find Claire attractive, but I don't know if it's because she has such a heart for my kids or if it's something else." He glanced up at his sister. "Admitting that makes me feel guilty, as if I'm betraying Marissa. It's too soon to even think about another woman."

"Marissa wanted you to move on. To give her children a new mother. She told me she feared the kids would never know a mother's love again." Ellen set the pan of rolls in the oven and set the timer. "I'm not a substitute for the real thing."

"But thinking about starting over with someone else makes me queasy."

"Leave the seasickness on the boat next time you're out." Ellen cast him a sideways grin.

"That's just two weeks away, you know." Monty glanced at the calendar.

The kitchen door swung open and Mason peeked in. "Aren't we going to have Christmas? Mia and me have been waiting *forever*!"

Monty laughed and headed toward the family room. "We didn't know you were awake. Let's get this party started."

Claire's heart ached as she packed to go home to Oregon. The week in Pennsylvania with her sister had been amazing—full of museums, ice skating, and time with Fallyn. Her niece hung on every word, holding her hand wherever they went, drawing her into imaginary conversations with her dolls.

"I wish you didn't have to go back." Fallyn held the doll Claire had given her, watching as she packed her things into the rolling tote. "We could have tea parties and make real cookie snacks."

Claire patted the child on the head. "I'm a teacher. I have students who expect me to come back and help them learn."

"Could those kids be friends with me?" Fallyn's curiosity knew no bounds. "I have friends at pre-school."

"If they knew you, they'd love to have you as a friend." She threw the little girl a promise. "Maybe after your little brother or sister is born, you can come and visit me. I'll show you the ocean. Would you like that?" She tilted her head at the little girl's pout. "Fallyn?"

"The baby won't let us go anywhere." Her small face sagged. "He will be little and cry a lot. Mommy will be too tired to travel."

Claire laughed in spite of her need not to. A little sibling rivalry perhaps? She realized Fallyn might be feeling jealous of this impending newcomer, having had Angie and Brennan all to herself for the past five years. "The little one won't always be small, and your Mommy won't always be worn out. Your mother is pregnant and having to work extra hard to do things when she's carrying a baby inside. That's not as easy as it may sound."

Fallyn seemed to consider this, answering Claire's question next. "What is the ocean like?"

"It's big, and blue, sometimes windy, and it has seagulls floating above it like kites in the sky. I flew kites with a family on Thanksgiving." Claire hadn't thought of the Chandlers all week. How had they fared this first Christmas without their mother? What kinds of activities would she have to plan to help the children re-enter school? "We had a dragon with a tail and we sent him high into the clouds."

"I don't like dragons." Fallyn frowned. "They snatch people up and eat them."

"This guy was too busy flying to eat anyone. The wind made him swoop and turn and twist all over the sky." Claire thought of Mason's enthusiasm as the dragon tugged at him, trying to break the string. "The little boy holding on to his tether thought the dragon was going to blow away."

"Where would he go?"

"Higher and higher until he disappeared into the sky."

"That's where I'd like him to go." She picked up her doll. "Dragons are scary."

Claire made a note to ask Angie about Fallyn's fear. Perhaps she'd encountered something frightening while she was in the hospital. Whatever had upset her, it had left an impression.

"Would you rather fly a kite with stripes or flowers?"

Fallyn sighed. "Doesn't matter. I'll never see the ocean."

"Why do you say that?"

Fallyn didn't respond, only shrugged.

Was there more to Fallyn's declaration than an innocent assumption? Had Angie said something? Did Brennan have a distaste for things west of the Mississippi? Claire stashed the information in a corner of her brain, saving it for when she could talk privately with Angie.

She studied her niece, looking for a response that would leave the door open. "Well, I hope you will visit my ocean someday. I think the beach is a perfect place to play."

Again, Fallyn didn't say anything, her attention fixed on her Christmas doll. Claire closed the zipper on her rolling tote, her fondness for Fallyn and a need to embrace the child overwhelming her. She couldn't love a child more. The desire to whisk her away fought with the reality that Fallyn belonged to Angie. Someday Claire would have her own daughter to hug. For now, Claire belonged back in her classroom. Mia and Mason would be waiting.

Monty pulled out his duffle bag and stuffed underwear and socks into the corners. Tomorrow the twins returned to school and he reported for his first tour with the science team since he'd transferred from Seattle last fall. Six weeks of sailing the ocean awaited him, monitoring the migratory habits of the gray whales who headed to the warmer waters of Baja California to birth their young. He was grateful to his skipper for keeping him on shore duty when he first arrived, giving him and the children an opportunity to adjust to their new surroundings. Mia and Mason were now comfortable with their aunt and anticipating the return to school because they would get to see Claire again.

She'd told him she planned to spend the holiday with her sister, and he hoped to have a little time tomorrow to catch up on her travels before he reported for duty. Now that the holiday had passed and he'd lived through it without Marissa, spring beckoned him. Somehow, he associated Claire with the upcoming season. She'd brought hope to his children just like spring promised renewal to a world rising from the sleep of winter. Thinking of her made him want to go on.

Who was he kidding? Thinking of her made him want to know her better. He never thought he'd feel that way again.

"Daddy, will you take Fluffy to the ocean with you?" Mia popped into the room, holding out the stuffed kitten. "She wants to see what sailing is like."

He bent down and wrapped an arm about his sweet daughter. "Kitties don't like the water, Sissy. Fluffy would be unhappy on the ocean."

"But she could tell me stories when she gets back." Mia's lower lip popped out. "And knowing she's with you, I won't be so afraid."

"What are you afraid of?"

"That you won't come back. Mommy's gone and she's not coming back. And now you're going away." Mia looked up at him, her blue eyes misting. "Do you have to go?"

Monty's heart threatened to break in two. He lifted Mia and carried her to the new kitten calendar they'd hung New Year's Day. He pointed. "There's today. Tomorrow you go to school with Mason and get to see Miss Claire." He flipped the page to February. "There's the day I come back. That's not so long, is it?"

"No, I guess not." Mia studied the calendar for a minute. "I forgot Miss Claire would be at school tomorrow."

"She's special to you, isn't she?"

Mia smiled and nodded. She turned her blue eyes on him, poking him in the chest. "And I think she's kind of special to you too."

Monty stared at his daughter. Out of the mouths of babes, or so the saying goes.

Mia continued to watch him, waiting for an answer.

"I'm glad she was here when we moved, helping all of us make Newport our home. She helped you not be afraid of school and. . ." he tickled Mia's tummy, making her giggle, "I haven't seen you suck your thumb in weeks."

Mia's smile turned mischievous. She raised her thumb to her chin. "If I suck it, will that keep you home?"

Monty wrapped a bear hug about the child, pulling her closer and laughing into the mane of curls. "You stinker. Daddy's going to miss you and your brother so much." He choked back the need to moan. "But six weeks will go by fast."

His phone vibrated in his pocket and he hugged Mia once more as he set her down. He checked the display screen. Realtor, Lucas Braeburn.

"Hey, Lucas! I hope you have good news for me. Did we finally get a nibble on the house?" The house in Seattle needed to move if he were to settle here in Newport.

"How about an offer?"

Monty stopped. "No kidding?"

"I'm faxing you some papers to look over. The offer is solid, and the couple have financing."

Monty whisked a hand through his hair. "Can you send it today? I leave tomorrow morning for six weeks on the Pacific."

"Talk about bad timing." Lucas sighed into the phone. "Well, if you like the offer, accept it, and get the document back to me. If you counteroffer, the deal may be gone when you return."

"I'll look at the offer. If I need to counteroffer, I will. That's a risk I have to take. I've already been dockside longer than I usually am. But being home has helped the kids adjust."

"Don't sweat it. Another offer will come along if this one doesn't suit you." The realtor paused. "You needed the extra time with your family."

"Thanks." Monty swallowed at the halt in the other man's voice. Lucas had been a friend before Marissa died. He had walked the journey with Monty—witnessed the pain, shared his grief, and offered comfort. "Get those papers to me."

"Sending them within the hour."

Monty clicked off his phone. House-hunting waited for him when he returned. Though the task was not something he particularly enjoyed doing, he could give his sister her privacy once again. Perhaps Claire would know a realtor here. Even better, maybe she'd go along to help him search.

CHAPTER SIXTEEN

CLAIRE SAW THE TRUCK APPROACH THE school breezeway, two little hands waving wildly through the window as Monty pulled up and parked. He opened his door and stepped down, coming around the front of the vehicle. "Good morning. How was your holiday?"

"Busy." Warmth crept along her jaw. Seeing the man again ratcheted her pulse into a staccato rhythm. *He's the father of two of your students. Have you forgotten?* "Pennsylvania has a lot to see and do."

"No snow?"

"Oh, yes. That's part of it. We went ice skating a couple of times." Claire could still feel the squeeze of Fallyn's hand as they circled the pond. "The temperatures weren't as cold as they sometimes are, and I feared we wouldn't have the opportunity."

"Sounds like fun." Monty opened the passenger door. Mia and Mason were scrunched together at the opening, waiting to get out. He lifted Mia down first, then reached for Mason.

"Hi, Miss Claire!" Mia held up her kitten. "Fluffy missed you. Did you miss us?"

"Yes, I did." Claire bent to hug the little girl. "Are you ready for school?"

Mason beamed. "We had our birthdays on New Year's."

"Oh, that's right! Was it a good birthday?" Claire chided herself for having forgotten.

Mia nodded, then sobered. "Daddy's leaving today." The thumb found its way to her mouth.

Claire glanced at Monty. "Ocean calling you?"

"My tour begins tomorrow morning. I report today for orientation. Six weeks on the Pacific chasing whale tails."

Claire reached for the child's hand and guided it to her side.

"You and Mason will have so much fun while he's gone, the time will pass quickly. Mason will be ready to fly kites when your dad gets back."

Mason came and stood beside his sister. "We have to find a house first. Our old house in Seattle sold."

Claire stood and clasped her hands together. "What a great adventure to anticipate. Searching for a house just for you." She tilted her head at Monty, giving him a knowing nod. "That will make waiting for you to return that much more exciting for them."

"If you know of a local realtor who could help Ellen look while I'm gone, I'd appreciate it. My guy in Seattle won't be much help, so far away."

Claire froze. Jamie now sold real estate, the coast his new territory to prowl. She'd never recommend him to anyone, let alone Monty Chandler. She'd have to be extra zealous in her search for a real estate broker. Otherwise the combination of Jamie and Monty together could spell disaster. She found her voice. "I'll ask around. I haven't needed a realtor myself, but there are others on staff who've purchased homes."

"Thanks, Claire." He turned toward the truck.

She stifled her gasp. He'd called her by her first name, instead of her teacher moniker. She fought the urge to quirk an eyebrow, though she didn't really mind.

Monty must have caught himself, his face registering shock as he quickly turned back. "I mean, Miss Claire."

Claire suppressed the chuckle forming. "You're welcome, Mr. Chandler." His grin made her laugh. "Don't worry about your kids. I picked up some new materials in Pennsylvania to share with them. They'll be fine."

"I know they will. Thanks for taking such an interest in their welfare." He hugged each of his twins one more time and hurried back to the driver's door, climbing in. Mia and Mason called out their goodbyes before turning and taking her hands.

As the truck rumbled out of sight, she watched in wistful silence. Six weeks would be a long wait to see him again. He'd be gone until after Valentine's Day. But she had his kids. Not a bad substitution.

That afternoon Claire stood with the other teachers as the children found their buses and departed for home. She watched for Ellen's car. Mia and Mason stood nearby, their backpacks loaded with new chapter books to read tonight. Mia's interest in reading had doubled in the last few weeks, her fascination with nature drawing her into more animal stories. Mason had become absorbed by books on mechanics, his interest in machinery taking precedent over his love of kites. But he still talked of spring and better weather when he and his dad could return to their stretch of beach and send the dragon soaring again.

Ellen's car pulled up and stopped. She killed the engine and stepped out, waving at Claire. "Nice to see you again. Did you have a happy holiday?"

Claire smiled, extending her hand for a squeeze. "I did. I trust yours was filled with special moments too."

Ellen nodded, wrapping her hands about the children's shoulders. "My husband and I were able to connect several times by telephone and on Skype. I'm anxious to see him again in March."

"That will be a busy month for you, I hear. Monty said his house in Seattle may have sold, and he'll be searching for another when he returns."

Ellen studied her, a pensive smile on her face. "Did he drag you into the house search as well?"

Claire shook her head. "No, he only asked if I knew of a competent realtor. He said you could use the help."

Ellen squeezed the twins. "These two will accompany me on house-hunting excursions. Monty told them to pick a house they'd like to grow up in. He plans to stay in Newport."

"That's good news for you." Claire couldn't blame him, wanting to provide a stable environment for his children. Newport maintained the coastal town feel which had appealed to her. Yet it sat only a little more than a hundred miles away from a major city and an international airport. When Monty lived in Seattle he'd said commuting to work took him almost an hour one way. Not the life he wanted with his kids. She glanced Ellen's way. "Having you nearby is a big draw."

"I urged him to move here when Marissa died. With Kevin deployed, living alone in that house was morbidly lonely. Monty and these two darlings have been a welcome addition. Christmas was actually fun!" Ellen beamed. "Meeting you has been icing on the cake."

"Me?" Claire touched her throat, not certain she'd heard right. "I only rescued you from a turkey disaster."

"Your friendship and your concern for the children has been a Godsend." Ellen's eyes misted. "I was very close to Marissa. Losing her was like losing a childhood friend. I hadn't found anyone else to replace her until I met you."

"Thank you, Ellen. I've enjoyed our times together, too. I moved here to forget some things from my past and became a type of lone wolf doing so. You've been a bright star in a cloudy sky."

Ellen glanced at the children. "I'm taking Mia and Mason out for hamburgers tonight to help ease the stress they feel losing Dad. Want to join us?"

"I have work here to finish up before I can leave." Claire didn't miss Mia's lower lip popping out at her answer.

Neither did Ellen. "Can you make it by six? We'll go to the Chalet. It's next to the supermarket at the north end of town."

"I'd be delighted." Claire's duplex, though cozy, lacked the warmth of human interaction spending time with her new friend and Monty's twins would provide. "Six o'clock it is."

Mia's smile made it all worthwhile.

Monty loved the feel of the ship on the water as the *USS Fort Clackamas* chugged out of Yaquina Bay and headed to the open sea. The two-hundred-foot vessel had been built specifically as an acoustically-quiet stern trawler for NOAA. As one of the most technologically-advanced survey vessels in the world, the ship allowed scientists to track and monitor underwater species behavior without being detected. Through the use of sonar and highly sophisticated equipment, he and his team of scientists worked like ocean spies. Working ashore he'd missed the excursions and basked in the adventures this mission promised. He'd spent the day familiarizing himself with the maze of computers and data-collecting machinery aboard, talking with other shipmates and getting a firm grip on their operation.

The migration of the gray whales had begun. These mammals were no longer listed on the Endangered Species roster, but a competent count of their numbers needed to be amassed. Monty knew how important the tally would be to current statistics. He'd read studies that said the grays were once hunted to near extinction with a population of 2,000 grays in the Eastern North Pacific. An international agreement in 1946 placed them under protection from whalers. The latest figures indicated the species thrived and now more than 26,000 of the small mammals were believed to cruise these waters.

Monty smacked his palm with his fist in a show of satisfaction. Much could be said about hunting bans. Gray whales on the Western Pacific near Sakhalin Island, Russia weren't as lucky. Still unprotected, as few as one hundred fifty mammals remained in those waters. He wished that government showed more interest in the environment.

The gray whale had the longest migration of any of the species which made tracking them arduous. The idea of following the creatures in two directions intrigued him. Preferring the Arctic waters to spend their fall and winter, the pods traveled the entire Pacific coast to Baja California in late December and early January. Traveling that far put them at risk for collision with trawlers or entanglement with fishing lines. Many more whales died from man-made causes than they did from food ingestion or disease.

Captain Neilson joined him on the bridge. "Ready for a sail?"

Monty smiled. "It's great to be back aboard ship."

"Keep your eyes peeled for floaters. Several humpbacks have been spotted along the Canadian shoreline, and we don't know what killed them. We don't think the grays are involved in the problem, but if it *is* the food supply, any mammal could succumb."

"The humpbacks migrate south too, don't they?"

"Yes, but their size usually gets them in trouble with fishing nets and the like."

"Do we have enough divers aboard to perform a rescue?" Monty had been certified to dive and would go when needed. "I'm a diver."

"No, we'd have to call in support. There's too few of us to carry out a rescue." Captain Neilson clapped him on the shoulder. "I can't risk my scientists for that."

Monty nodded his agreement. Though participating in a rescue would be exhilarating, he didn't want to chance injury or worse. His kids couldn't take another loss. He resolved to play it safe. Scanning the horizon, he watched the waves continue to break around them. The roll of the ocean never ended, nor did his appreciation for its power.

His mind drifted to Claire Simpson, and a random thought flitted past. Would she miss him if he were never to return?

The next morning the *USS Fort Clackamas* cruised off the shore of San Francisco. Monty shed his coat in the warmer California weather. A pod of grays had been spotted west of their location, and the ship headed that direction. He scanned the waters, looking for spouts or flukes as the whales surfaced for air.

"Chandler?" The shout came from the bridge. "Whale in trouble reported two miles south."

Monty sprang to the starboard side, a few feet off the bow. He raised binoculars to the dark waters, trying to glimpse signs of debris or other colored floats that might have snagged an unsuspecting whale. Voices behind him made him turn. Other crew members stared and pointed in the direction where the whale had been spotted, all bent on finding the distressed animal.

Captain Neilson came and stood beside him. "Discover anything?"

Monty lowered the glasses and shook his head. "Not so far." He studied the man. "Lots of fishing down here?"

"No. These are San Francisco waters. Crab pots are the biggest culprit. Fishing lines are further out."

"Orange floats?" Monty raised the binoculars. Something flashed in the sun ahead. "Take a look over there." He handed the glasses to his captain.

Captain Neilson surveyed the water for several minutes. "You're right." He raised his arm pointing almost directly south. "Debris of some sort cluttering the water." He stayed there, quiet, for another minute. "Fluke!" He handed back the binoculars. "See it?"

Monty rushed the binoculars back to his eyes. The tip of a tail disappeared into the water. "I saw something. Can't tell if it is a whale in trouble from here. But that was definitely a fluke."

"All hands on deck." Captain Neilson called to those around him, then headed for the bridge. "There be whales out there."

Everyone laughed as the ship steamed due south, their mission now set to save a whale.

CHAPTER SEVENTEEN

THE WHALE'S PLIGHT MADE MONTY CRINGE. Ensnared by the nylon ropes that link crab pots together, the humpback's entire body was covered in the netting. Bobbers and anchors dangled off her sides like ornaments on a Christmas tree. A large float hung near her blowhole, threatening to cut off her air. She swam aimlessly, her fins useless in their confinement. Only her tail remained free, its slap on the water signaling her distress.

Captain Neilson shook his head. "She needs immediate help. One wrong move and that float on her back could drift into her blowhole's range and stop her breathing."

Monty watched the crippled creature bob with the waves, her predicament sure to put divers at risk. A rescuer could be crushed by one wrong move of her tail. "She's not going to make it if something isn't done."

Captain Neilson agreed. "Let me contact the Marine Mammal Center in Marin County. If they can supply two more divers, we can attempt a rescue. Since this is not something we routinely do, we don't have enough personnel to complete the mission."

Monty nodded, a sick feeling in his stomach. Flying two divers out from the mainland might take more time than the whale had. Her obvious signs of distress meant she'd been confined for some time. Watching her die a slow, torturous death revolted him. He conjured up memories from another death he'd recently endured—Marissa's losing battle to the cancer that claimed her. He turned away from the scene below, his heart already bruised enough for two lifetimes, and headed below deck. He couldn't watch the creature's life eek away.

"Chandler!" The shout jolted Monty from his reverie. One of his crewmates, Lenny, stood at the bottom of the stairs. "Captain wants us to suit up for a dive."

"Really?" Monty sprang to his feet. "We're going in for the whale?"

"Captain said we'll join the crew headed out from the NOAA marine mammal center. They'll be dropping divers in the water in about ten minutes." Lenny gave Monty a thumbs-up. "But we get to participate in the rescue, too. What a hoot!"

Monty found his diving gear, suited up, and hurried topside. The crew huddled around the starboard side of the ship, peering into the water below. Captain Neilson gathered the diving team around him.

"This is a dangerous undertaking, but with the three of you and the personnel on their way, we should have enough divers to allow everyone a good measure of safety. When the dispatched team gets here, you'll join them in the water. Stay away from the mammal's tail. Approach her as one unit. Cut the ropes and back away. Once the fins are free she may dive. Watch out for sudden movement."

Monty knew he should pray. Lifelong habits were hard to break. But it seemed that God had quit listening to him when Marissa had been ill. Why would the creator of the universe bother to care about a marine mammal more than his wife? He checked his tanks and prepared to enter the water.

A helicopter could be heard approaching in the distance. The chopper swirled the waters some five-hundred yards away from the boat, four scuba divers dropping from its belly. When they surfaced and waved, Monty and his crew jumped overboard.

When he bobbed back up, he glanced around for the others. The whale languished nearby, her body movement non-existent, as if having seven humans drop in beside her meant nothing to her. Beside her he felt like a flea on a dog's back—she was so massive. One wrong move and the whale could crush him.

He had landed near her right front flipper, and what he saw

made him nauseous. The ropes were wound so tight they immobilized the flipper and were cutting into the flesh. One rope ran across her mouth, locking her jaw closed. She rode so low in the water Monty sank beneath the surface to get a better look. At least a dozen crab pots were trailing her, pulling her down, making it difficult for the animal to keep her blowhole out of the water. The whale lacked any chance of survival if they didn't succeed.

At the signal from the crew leader, Monty raised his knife. They moved in slowly, keeping their heads above water, their voices calm, careful not to panic the ensnared creature. Monty sawed on the rope supporting the crab pots, submerging a couple of times to sever the underside of the rope. Another diver on the animal's far side did the same. The nylon line didn't give up its cargo without a struggle.

After what seemed like an hour the first rope split on his side. The other diver cut through a minute later and half of the crab pots dropped to the ocean floor. The loss of the weight, which easily could have been several hundred pounds, allowed the whale to ride higher in the water. She rolled her eye back toward him, its inky blackness looking through him as he worked. Monty shuddered, realizing how close he was to the creature and how dangerous the situation remained. One bend of her middle and she could disappear on him, the suction of her massive size sucking him deep into the water.

Monty returned to the confined flipper and aimed his knife at the tangled line cutting into the whale's side. Sliding the knife in under the rope without nicking the whale's flesh proved tricky. But he saw a split in the rope just beyond the joint and worked on the weakened fibers. The rope gave way and the whale's flipper moved free. Monty backed away, allowing the animal room if she needed to wiggle. She remained still, her dark eye still watching him as he swam nearer her head.

He slid his knife against the rope holding the whale's mouth closed. The other diver on the opposite side did the same. Together they sawed, the stare of the whale's eye so close, Monty forced himself to focus on the ensnarement and not on the feeling he was watched by a monster.

Finally, the rope around the creature's mouth gave way. The whale, without the weight on her back, lifted to the surface of the water, her blowhole cleared. Monty swam backwards toward the ship as quickly as he could. He glanced around, looking for the other divers. As they bobbed on the surface, distancing themselves from the massive creature, he gazed back at the animal one more time. The whale, free of her encumbrances, dove below them, the fluke of her tail waving as it disappeared into the surf.

Grabbing the ladder, Monty pulled himself up to the deck and unloaded his diving gear. The others followed. One of the men from the mainland pointed over the side. He followed the direction the man indicated and there came the whale, her huge body lifting out of the water as she breached the surface. The splash from her jump sprayed water across the deck. Like a little kid set free from a timeout, she surfaced again, her exuberance exhibiting nothing less than sheer joy.

"That's one happy mammal." Lenny said as he stood by Monty's side. "You guys are to be commended for setting her free."

"How long were we in the water?" Monty frowned at the sun resting low on the horizon. "We were on the surface most of the time, so I didn't use up my tank, but still it seemed like we were there for quite a while."

"Four hours."

Monty shook his head. "That's something for the record books. No one injured?"

Lenny grinned. "Not even the whale."

Mia's loss of her father to his job hovered over the child like a thundercloud after he left, her distress lingering for the better part of two weeks. Claire prodded her out of her depression with new books and activities, but the little girl really missed her daddy.

Mason grew louder than he had been, but he seemed to be coping better than his sister. He held on to the hope and expressed it daily, that he and his dad would fly their kite when Monty returned home. Claire encouraged both children to express their sense of loss, allowing them a voice in their vigilance. Teachers reported their progress remained steady, and Ellen confirmed there were few issues at home. Only Mia's return to routinely sucking her thumb exposed her distress.

For now, all the adults in the kids' lives agreed the twins were adjusting to reality without a mother, handling their new school situation, and marking time as they waited for Monty's return.

Friday, two weeks after Monty had left, Ellen pulled up outside the school and waved a fistful of documents at Claire. "He did it!"

Claire frowned, puzzled at the woman's outburst. "Who did what?"

"The sale of Monty's house finally closed. I faxed him the papers he needed to sign and got them back this morning."

"That's one more responsibility off your shoulders." Claire dreamed of one day owning her own home as well. Sharing it with a husband would be even better. "Now to house-hunting?"

Ellen smiled, a conspiratorial grin on her mouth. "I toured a house this morning that I loved. I'm taking the children there tomorrow afternoon. Want to come?"

"I love looking at homes. Do you have the key?"

"No, the realtor is meeting me there at one." Ellen opened the door for the twins and helped them inside. "I answered his ad in the paper. He sells properties in the valley too."

Claire grew cold, perspiration forming beads on her brow. It couldn't be. She had to ask. "My mother lives in the valley and has connections. I'll ask her if he's reputable. Name?"

Ellen grinned from ear to ear. "Jamie Duval. He once tried out for the Olympics. Can you believe that?"

Claire nodded. "I know who he is." *Life would be better if I didn't.*

Claire didn't know how to avoid Ellen's invitation to see the house she thought Monty might buy, but the last person she wanted to encounter was Jamie. She busied herself Saturday morning, trying to think of a reasonable excuse. Her phone buzzed, and the screen lit, Ellen on the other end.

"What's up?" She scanned her brain, still scrambling for justification that would appear legitimate enough to keep her out of today's excursion. "House-hunting still on your agenda?"

"No." Ellen sighed into the phone. "Mia's running a fever, so I made an appointment at the clinic. She's pretty out of sorts."

"I'm sorry. Anything I can do to help?" An image of Fallyn flashed across her memory, the thought she might fall ill again always a worry to Claire. "I can heat soup."

Ellen laughed. "I'm sure you can. But she says her throat is sore and won't touch anything. I'm hoping it's not strep."

"What time is your appointment?" Claire glanced at the clock. Nine.

"Mia's appointment is at eleven. I cancelled the realtor."
Thank you, Mia.

Claire grinned to herself. "Mia's more important. You can look at the house another day."

"Assuming it hasn't sold. The realtor said houses in this area move really fast."

"Which explains the shortage of properties available."

"Oh well, Monty won't be home for a month, anyway. I'll have to pray something else opens up." Ellen spoke away from the phone, then returned. "Gotta go. Mason's hungry. I hope you'll join us on the next house inspection."

"My mother suggested giving Marilyn Woods a call. She's an experienced realtor." Claire breathed a sigh of relief. As long as Jamie did not join them for the tour, she'd be glad to tag along. "It will be fun to find a place for Monty and his children to live."

"I'm so glad to have him here in Newport. Family is important. He wasn't coping in Seattle. And he's good for me here." Ellen sounded depressed, the woman facing a long afternoon with Mia ill. "My co-workers all have families tying up their free time."

"Tell you what." Claire cherished this newfound friendship. "Why don't I pick up lunch and bring it to your place after you take Mia to the clinic?"

Ellen's gasp didn't miss her ears. "You'd give up a Saturday to watch me play doctor?" She giggled. "You need to get out more."

"No. I'll give up my Saturday to spend time with a friend. We'll tend the sick child together."

"You're the best." Ellen sniffed, telling Claire she'd made the right decision.

"See you around noon."

The wind had picked up after the *USS Fort Clackamas* dropped its guest divers off at the Marine Mammal Center in Sausalito and chugged south again, back on course for tracking the gray whales in migration to Baja, California. Monty zipped a windbreaker to offset the chill of the air. Another few hours and the ship would coast by San Diego, the crew anticipating tomorrow's arrival at their destination.

He hadn't contacted Ellen in a while and wondered how the children fared without him. Mia had been the most noticeably upset, Ellen had said, thumb stuck in her mouth for hours. He should call and talk with each of the twins. Mason would love the story about rescuing the whale. He could tell Mia about the kitten he'd seen when they'd stopped at the Marine Mammal Center. The mother cat had popped up out of a storage unit near the dock, a fat kitten firmly caught in her mouth. She'd waddled the struggling youngster to a spot across the marina and disappeared. Five minutes later the mother re-appeared and headed for the storage unit from which she'd come. She'd no sooner disappeared than she once again stood on the marina carrying a second kitten. Monty waited to see how the adventure would end and wasn't disappointed. Five kittens later the mother vanished into the hidden shadows of the walkway and didn't make another appearance.

"Think we'll hit Baja in the morning?" Lenny, his newest acquaintance since joining the crew, stood beside him.

"Can't imagine why not." Monty faced his crewmate. "Pods have been sighted from the fly bridge."

"Is the acoustics team reporting noise?"

"Clicks and whistles." Monty had been in the lab when the acoustics team picked up the sounds to their starboard side last night. The whales had been tracked for several miles before losing their signal. Echolocation picked them up again this morning. "They were swimming at about 3-4 knots an hour."

"Must be in a hurry to get to their romantic getaway."

Monty snorted. "Yeah, right. Afraid they might miss the free drinks and the rooms with an ocean view." He glanced up at the fly bridge where his team of observers gathered. "Time for me to take over on the observation deck."

"Happy water watching." Lenny saluted and walked away.

Monty headed to the upper deck, making a mental note to call his sister when his shift finished. He didn't want to leave the twins wondering where their dad was any longer than necessary. Maybe Ellen would have word of Claire. Watching her through the eyes of his sister certainly seemed a safe way to observe. His casual responses would keep gossipers quiet. Those who wanted to push him forward would remain at arm's length. Marissa still haunted his nightmares, but Claire had started invading his dreams. What new adventure had she planned for his twins? What story were they reading together? He could imagine her with both twins in her lap, telling them about her visit to Pennsylvania. The thought corralled the loneliness.

CHAPTER EIGHTEEN

CLAIRE KNOCKED ON ELLEN'S DOOR JUST before noon, her arms laden with a sack of groceries and a six-pack of bottled pineapple juice. The lunch she'd put together resembled a picnic more than a lunch date in late January, but Ellen had said Mia wasn't eating and her throat was sore. Claire had depended on pineapple juice mixed with lemon and honey to fix her raw mouth for years. With Ellen's penchant for natural cures, she could only imagine the woman would do the same for her niece.

"You're here." Ellen's wide smile didn't disguise the fatigue in her eyes. "Come in and advise me. Mia's done nothing but sleep since this morning."

She stepped through the entry and followed Ellen to the kitchen. "No test results from the clinic?"

"Strep." Ellen took the juice from her and popped it into the refrigerator. "Which I feared. We'll have to take extra precautions to protect Mason."

"And you." She set the bag of groceries on the counter. "You're not exempt from these bugs, either."

"You're putting yourself at risk too."

"I have to get a flu shot every season because I'm around kids every day. They bring diseases into the classroom on a regular basis. In fact, I brought an effective home remedy with me today."

"I'll try anything to get Mia eating." Ellen peered into the bag. "Hot dogs and lemon juice?"

She laughed. "No. Grab one of those bottles of pineapple juice from the fridge. I'll need a glass." She opened the lemon juice and the honey. Ellen produced the glass and the juice. Claire mixed the three ingredients according to the recipe guidelines she'd brought with her, then stirred in a little ginger. She popped a wiggly straw into the yellow brew and handed it to Ellen. "After she gargles with hot saltwater, offer that to Mia and tell her I have animal crackers to go with it."

Ellen sniffed the mixture, then grabbed a spoon and tasted it. "Not bad."

"The two juices together have healing properties you won't find in cough syrup."

Ellen headed for the hall, mixture in her left hand.

"Don't forget the hot, saltwater gargle."

Ellen did a U-turn and grabbed a mug. "How much salt? A tablespoon?" At her nod, Ellen fixed the cup of hot water and left.

As she waited, Claire pulled out the lunch fixings, laying the kosher wieners on the counter and lining up the other items in readiness.

When Ellen returned, Mia followed on her footsteps. "Hi, Miss Claire. I have a sore throat."

"Did you gargle?"

Mia nodded. "Saltwater is yucky."

Claire bent down to hug the child. "How did you like the juice drink I made for you?"

"Better than the saltwater. Can I have the animal crackers now?"

Claire opened the box and pulled out a kitten. "You can have one and more after you eat your lunch. I brought hot dogs, macaroni salad, and oranges for dessert."

Mason burst through the door. "Hot dogs? I'm hungry too."

"That settles that question."

After the twins had eaten a decent amount of food and Mia drank more of Claire's concoction, Ellen led the girl back to bed. Mason contented himself in the corner with a pile of blocks. Claire cleaned the kitchen and sank into a nearby dining chair.

Ellen returned and joined her. "Tell me about Christmas

vacation."

She recounted the highlights–her outings with Fallyn and Angie, the church service Christmas Eve, and the difference in temperature between Pennsylvania and their part of Oregon.

Ellen listened, smiling and nodding as she described the wonderful two weeks she had spent during the holiday. "Do you have a picture of Fallyn?"

Claire reached for her phone. "I have so many." She held up the screen and Ellen leaned forward.

"She's adopted?"

"Um-hmm. Angie had tried to get pregnant for five years when Fallyn joined their family."

"She looks like she could be your daughter." Ellen gazed up at her, eyes intent upon Claire's face. "Except for the hazel eyes, the likeness is amazing."

"She's a special girl, that's for sure." Claire put the phone back in her purse.

"Why did you pursue your degree half way across the continent? You couldn't get those credentials here?" Ellen's brows drew close together, the look one of someone not convinced by haphazard answers. "Let me guess. You wanted to get away from a boyfriend."

Claire stared at her friend. How much did she know? Or suspect? The room grew uncomfortably warm as she considered her answer. "Has someone said something?" Ellen had met Jamie, but Claire didn't think he knew she and Ellen were friends.

"No. Just curious." Ellen shrugged her shoulders. "When someone chooses to leave home to go halfway across the continent to *finish* her teaching credentials, there's more to the tale." She stood. "Would you like a cup of tea?"

At her nod, Ellen went into the kitchen and set the stainless teapot on to boil. She retrieved cups from the cupboard and reached into a canister for tea bags. When she returned, she placed a tray between them, hot tea steaming from a china pot, two cups, saucers, and cookies on the side.

Claire took one of the teacups, filled it, and let the fragrant Earl Grey waft up to her face. She stared into the brew for a minute, then sighed. "I was engaged."

Ellen's eyes grew wide. "I've wondered why you aren't married. You don't seem like the type to be passed by. What happened? The war?"

"He sent me a note three days before the wedding saying he had changed his mind."

"No!" Ellen leaned forward, pain registering on her face. "Oh, Claire. How awful."

She sipped her tea, the admission of her disgrace somehow freeing. "As soon as I regained my sanity, I cancelled the wedding, returned all the gifts, and paid the bills. I accepted Angie's offer of a place to live, boarded a plane for Pennsylvania, and tried to put the nightmare behind me."

"I don't blame you." Ellen offered her a cookie. "I don't know what I would have done in your place." She chuckled. "Probably bought a loaded gun."

"Don't think I didn't consider it." Claire cradled her teacup, the bittersweet memories nagging at her. "But actually, when I realized how shallow the man's character was, I thanked God for providing roadblocks to the altar. He wasn't husband material. I'd have been locked in an ugly divorce."

"By then, there might have been children involved, too." Ellen set the cup on the tray, studying her. "Seeing Mia and Mason dealing with their loss, I wouldn't intentionally put any child through that trauma. Parents splitting up would be tough on them."

"I see too much of that at the school."

"I'll bet you do." Ellen offered the plate of cookies. "How nice it was for Angie and Brennan to adopt Fallyn while you were there. That gave you better memories to fly home with."

"Except coming home meant I'd eventually have to face my ex again." Claire looked at her friend. "The one thing I wanted to avoid."

"Did he surface?"

"Yes. His dreams of being an Olympic star had vanished." Claire pierced Ellen with her gaze. "He's become a realtor."

Shock covered Ellen's face. "You don't mean. . ."

"I do."

CHAPTER NINETEEN

MONTY'S TOUR DREW TO A CLOSE. As the *USS Fort Clackamas* chugged north to Yaquina Bay, he leaned against the rail, watching the horizon for Newport. He'd enjoyed the experience—being on the ocean again, the camaraderie among his crew members, and the adventure of chasing whales as they migrated to and from their breeding grounds. Foremost in his mind, though, was returning home and holding his children.

Ellen's faithfulness in taking pictures and recording the activities of Mia and Mason kept him informed, most of the material school related. Mia lost another tooth. Mason whined that the fairy didn't like him since his teeth remained intact. Mixed in with the children's adventures were tidbits of Ellen's friendship with Claire, a relationship his sister enjoyed with increasing enthusiasm. He'd learned answers to questions about the teacher he'd not have felt comfortable asking. Claire had been in love, her heart broken, yet hoped to marry one day. She wanted a family of her own. Add her love for his kids to Ellen's information pool, and Monty felt his heartstrings tugged like a tethered kite.

Guilt needled him. The one-year anniversary of Marissa's death loomed ahead. The house they'd shared sold. His first task when he returned would be to buy a home for his family. His eagerness surprised him, considering this would be the final break from his former life and the wonderful years he'd shared with Marissa. But with Claire in the picture, he didn't feel the pain he might have once endured. If anything, knowing her filled him with hope. He couldn't wait to get home.

"Spy hoppers, port side!" An observer on the fly bridge pointed to the west. Like children in a competition, gray whales dotted the horizon, their large heads pointed up out of the water to have a look around. One whale leapt out of the water and landed with a splash as it breached. Not to be outdone, another gray rose up and fell backward, its tail slapping the ocean.

"I wonder if that's one of our pods." Captain Neilson stepped beside him, watching the mammals display their abilities. "I understand the *Shimada* followed killer whales all the way to the mouth of the Columbia. But they reported a group of transient orcas who were hassling the grays."

"The killers don't come this far south?" Monty hadn't tailed the black and white whales.

"Not during the winter months. But the transients were reported to be agitated as if they had just made a kill." Captain Neilson lifted his binoculars. "As excited as these grays are, they might have been pursued."

"We can report this pod in our data. They're headed north so they must have already gone to Baja and headed home."

"Which makes the presence of the orcas that much more disturbing." Captain Neilson lifted his binoculars a second time. "The grays coming behind this pod will have young at their side."

"Making them easy prey."

Captain Neilson gazed out over the water. "Exactly."

Mia and Mason couldn't sit still, their anticipation of Monty's return later today fueling their excitement. Claire tried several different activities to channel their energy in an educational direction, but to no avail. The children missed their father and couldn't wait to see him again.

Claire found her own thoughts wandering to the missing scientist, his clear blue eyes as intent as a cat watching a mouse hole. Perhaps Monty would return early enough to pick up his children from school. She would have an excuse to be there, waiting in the breezeway as all the students departed for the day. She'd heard from Ellen that he'd enjoyed his six-week tour and was anxious to go house-hunting when he returned. Soon he would be permanent in Newport, one of the few single men about town her mother kept asking if she'd found. The competition for his favor might be substantial. Claire didn't allow herself to dwell on that.

"Miss Claire?" Mia's tentative voice startled her back to the task at hand. "Can I draw a picture for my daddy?"

"Of course, you can. That's a great idea. You'll have a gift for him when he returns home." Claire reached for two sheets of art paper nearby. "Mason, would you enjoy making your dad a present?"

Mason grabbed the paper and began folding it.

Claire watched for a moment, trying to figure out what the boy was doing. When the paper turned into a diamond shape, she understood. "A kite reminder?"

Mason grinned. "Yes. I'm making a giant kite card to give Daddy." He folded the bottom end. "He promised to fly kites with me when he gets back."

Claire reached over and flattened a seam. "Let's make sure the shape is a diamond. We don't want him to have to guess what you made him."

Mason handed the paper to her, the odd angles resembling an object headed to recycle. "Can you make it more kite-shaped?"

"Let's fix it together." Claire unfolded parts of the paper and showed Mason where to refold to achieve the diamond look he wanted.

Mia sat quietly, her gaze intent on her picture. The blob of connected circles resembled a distorted computer image, but Claire could see what the little girl had attempted to draw. "Your dad will love your kitten."

"When we buy our house, Aunt Ellen is going to help me talk

Daddy into a kitten of my own." She colored more gray into the tail. "This will remind him."

"I'm sure it will." She looked at the clock. "Finish up. Your second-grade teacher will be waiting."

Claire laughed to herself. She'd make sure she was on the sidewalk this afternoon to witness the homecoming. She'd film it on her phone if she could. It would be a reunion worthy of YouTube if she were free to post. But she wasn't–not something so personal about a student. But seeing Monty's reaction heightened her anticipation, making her wish she could.

Monty strode toward the marina parking lot, duffel bag on his shoulder, sea legs feeling wobbly on the solid ground. He spotted Ellen's sedan parked near the end and headed that direction.

She stepped from the car and hurried toward him, arms outstretched. "Welcome home! We've missed you so much."

He dropped the bag and wrapped her in a bear hug. "Thanks, Sis. It's good to be back on dry land."

She glanced up at him. "Was it a good tour?"

"The best." He grabbed his gear and with an arm about his sister, moved toward the car. She popped the trunk, and he set the luggage inside. "You and the kids doing all right?"

"They can hardly wait to see you." She pulled her phone from her pocket. "School's almost out. Do you want to pick them up or shall we go together?"

"Do we have time to get my rig?"

"Yes. It will be tight, but you can make it."

A few minutes later Monty roared into the school parking lot, stopping behind the last vehicle space, waiting for an opening. Spotting Mia and Mason as they emerged from the school's double doors, he popped the truck into park and stepped onto the sidewalk.

The kids didn't see him right away, their gazes on the swarm of children intent on finding their bus or their ride home. Behind them, Claire came into view, her gaze scanning the vehicle lineup. Her eyes locked with his and she smiled, placing a hand on Mason's shoulder and pointing his direction.

"Daddy!" Mason's shriek could have been heard all the way to the Yaquina Bay Bridge. He ran toward him, a colorful piece of paper flapping in the wake of his path.

Mia hurried behind her brother, tears streaming down her cheeks. "Daddy! You came home. You didn't leave us behind." She hiccoughed and cried more tears. "I was so afraid you wouldn't come home."

Monty's heart broke. He bent down, holding his arms out wide, wrapping both children in a tight hug as they slammed into his body. He kept his eyes down, fighting his own emotions as he greeted his kids. Claire would be watching, and he couldn't let her see how torn up he was reuniting with his twins.

He spoke to each of the children, Mia first, pulling a handkerchief from his pocket and wiping her face. "I promised I would come home." He kissed her, making butterfly kisses on her cheek.

He turned to Mason. "I'm so glad to see you. Aunt Ellen said you were a big help to her while I was gone."

His son beamed.

They stayed there for several minutes, Monty's face close to his children, not willing to risk a glance at Claire. Finally, Mia stopped sniffling and Mason held out his piece of paper. "This is to remind you of your promise to fly kites with me."

"Whoa. Nice kite." He placed a peck on the boy's forehead. "We'll fly a kite soon. Spring vacation is only a month away. If the weather cooperates, we'll have lots of time then."

Monty straightened and faced Claire who had walked closer.

"How have you been?" He placed a hand on each of the twins, touching their shoulders. "Have these two behaved while I was gone?"

She smiled and glanced down at the children. "They are making remarkable progress." She folded her arms. "Was your tour successful?"

"I'm seeing gray whales in my sleep." He looked down at Mia, who had wrapped an arm about his hip. "But I'm glad to be home."

"Well, welcome back. Mia and Mason were beside themselves today, waiting for you." She gazed at the twins again. "I'll see you two tomorrow, okay? Make your daddy feel welcome tonight." She focused again on him. "I'll see you around, I'm sure." With that she turned and walked back into the school.

Monty fought the urge to run after her and ask her out for coffee but stopped himself. Ellen and Claire were now good friends. He would surely run into her soon once his sister felt free to accept new kinds of social invitations. He'd wait and make his move when the time was right. For now, he had children to greet, a house to buy, and plans to make. When those items were fulfilled, he'd consider adding a pretty blonde to his pursuits.

Claire couldn't get Monty's wind-burned face out of her mind that evening. She hadn't realized how much she'd anticipated seeing him again. Nor did she understand the depth of her eagerness. They'd shared only a few encounters since they'd met, yet in her mind the man seemed like a friend she'd known for years. She fixed a light supper and picked at it while she watched the news. Nothing tasted good. Television held no appeal. She dragged herself to the papers she needed to review for tomorrow's school day. The only image filling her mind tonight stood a little over six feet tall, with short, dark hair, a shadowed beard on his chin, and piercing blue eyes.

"You've got it bad, kid." She forced her mind to focus on the papers in front of her. What were the twins telling him tonight? Did Ellen drag him to a house she thought perfect for his family? Was he the type to immediately empty his duffel and shove the dirty laundry in the washer? Or would he sit back and listen to the chatter of his children, reacquainting himself with their tender affection?

She opted for the latter. Monty seemed to be that kind of man. Gentle, loving, unselfish. The type of fella she'd look for if she decided again to marry. Ellen said he struggled with God's involvement in his life after Marissa died, heartbroken that the Creator didn't answer his prayers to heal his wife. But Claire understood that struggle. She'd been at that same point of disappointment with God when Jamie left her shattered. Only the loving congregation in Angie's neighborhood church enabled her to forgive Jamie, and to love again, leaving the bitterness in God's hands. Monty could find that, too. Maybe he already had. He'd seemed at peace today when he returned.

Jamie, though, remained the thistle in her thinking. She'd artfully tiptoed around the subject of house-hunting with Ellen, afraid she'd wind up at a showing where Jamie held the key and instead of a showing, there'd be a showdown. Ellen knew she'd been engaged, that her heart suffered, and that she'd emerged from the trauma whole. Or at least she thought she'd healed.

Now, with Monty returned, she couldn't risk an encounter with her former fiancé. Jamie walked out of her life almost six years ago. If she never spent time with him again, she'd be happy. She prayed God would keep him well away from her and her new friends. But Monty needed a house. Now that Ellen knew the truth, and Mom had provided the name of another realtor, she'd enjoy seeing the Chandlers find their new home.

Monty drove the kids to the local hamburger hangout and treated them to an afternoon snack. Mia ordered her usual strawberry smoothie, and Mason opted for a burger and fries. Monty cherished the moments watching them down their food, keeping his promise to Ellen to get the kid-sized portions. She'd planned a special welcome home dinner for him, and she didn't want to eat it alone.

Mia held up her picture for him to see. "We made these for you in Miss Claire's room today. This is a kitty like the one I want when we move into our new house."

He smiled as he took the picture from her. "Have you found our new house?"

Mason piped up, mouth full of fries. "No, Mia got a sore throat the day we were going to find one with Auntie Ellen and Miss Claire. She brought us hot dogs and chips and a special drink for Mia."

"Special drink?" Monty frowned, not sure what kind of drink would go with hot dogs.

"Hot, salty water. It was yucky." Mia scrunched up her face. "But then I got to have pineapple juice mixed with some other stuff. It made my throat feel a lot better."

"But now that you're here, Daddy, we can go look at that house. Auntie Ellen has a realtor she can call so we can see it."

"I think that's a good idea. I want you kids to have your own home again." Monty swallowed the lump threatening to strangle his words. "We'll be a family like we were before."

Mia puckered up, tears dribbling down her cheeks. "Except for Mommy."

He kissed his daughter's forehead. "I miss her too, sweetheart. But God needed her in heaven. He promised to take care of you when she left. And He has, hasn't He?"

Mason popped the last bite of his burger in his mouth. "Yep. He sent us Miss Claire. Mommy would have liked her a lot."

He stared at his son. At least he wouldn't face objections if anything were to happen between them. If anything, Mason promised a little too much support.

Mia made noise with her straw and giggled. "If Mommy can't come back to us, maybe Miss Claire would like to be our mommy. She likes kitties!"

Monty picked up the trash and stood. "Ready to go kids? It's getting pretty busy in here."

As he followed the twins out the door, he sighed. *And I'm a little warm around the collar.*

CHAPTER TWENTY

ELLEN'S FERVOR FOR THE HOMES SHE'D found compelled Monty to tour the neighborhoods with her and the twins the following Saturday. He liked the first one for its size and its price, a good home tucked into the city.

The second one had no yard, a postage stamp-sized lawn without enough room to toss a football or erect a swing set. His kids needed room to grow, and he needed space to turn around without bumping someone. Mowing grass wasn't his favorite outdoor chore, but if he needed to mow he wanted more than five feet of grass to justify starting the mower.

When they stopped in front of the third house, he stared at the view. Though the house faced into a cul-de-sac, behind it lay a panorama of the Pacific. The circular drive allowed visitors to pull up in front of the door, the portico protecting them from the elements.

"Let's look at the backyard. The gate is open." He climbed from the car and walked to the opened passage. Inside the fenced yard was an adequately sized lawn, a covered patio, and an outbuilding for tools and yard maintenance machines.

Monty loved the split-level design. His children could play behind the house, away from the busy street, always in view of the Pacific. "I want to see inside." He turned to Ellen. "This has three bedrooms?"

"Four. And three baths." Ellen pulled out her phone. "Let me see if the realtor is in town. Or an associate."

A minute later, she hung up. "He's in the valley today. He can meet us tomorrow, if we'd like."

"Why don't we see it in the afternoon?" Monty studied the layout of the lot— rhododendrons and azaleas marking the back border. The view of the ocean made up for a lot of deficits, but what Monty could see pleased him.

"Is this the one you and Claire toured?"

"We planned to, but Mia's strep throat put an end to our trip."

"Maybe she'd like to see it with us." Monty glanced up at the arched windows. "Does she like architecture?"

Ellen dipped her chin and peered at him, an amused grin on her face. "I can certainly ask her. Should we meet her after church to tour the house and then go out to dinner? Or have dinner and then meet her here?"

"Let's eat after the showing." Monty led Mason and Mia toward the car. "Claire can join us for a meal." He noticed Ellen's smirk. "What?"

Ellen flashed him a knowing smile. "Nothing, sweet brother. I'll make the call."

Hearing the tease in Ellen's voice, Monty thought about what he'd said and groaned. He'd have to be more careful or Ellen would have him in hot water. Or walking down an aisle.

Claire had loaded a laundry basket into her trunk when her phone buzzed. She'd spent the morning catching up on the pile of dirty clothes that haunted her bathroom all week. Now her belongings were washed, folded, and ready to transport home. Her screen lit. Ellen waited on the other end. "Hey! What's up?"

"Monty and I have been house-hunting this morning, and he found one he thinks is promising. We're meeting the realtor I mentioned tomorrow after church and then going to dinner. Monty wondered if you'd like to come? He said we'd make an afternoon of it."

Claire froze. Touring the house with Ellen and Monty would be fun. But seeing Jamie would ruin the day. "Did you try to contact the other realtor?"

"I tried. I'm sorry. I don't know what to tell Monty without telling him too much. What should I do?"

Claire had had no more contact with Jamie since he'd sprung himself into her path last Thanksgiving. Having him in the mix with her new friends promised a confrontation. She couldn't let that happen. "Tell Monty that the tour sounds like so much fun, but I've been busy with laundry this morning and tomorrow lesson plans beckon me. I'm snowed under."

"I understand, totally." Ellen sounded apologetic, whispering into the phone. "I tried to get Marilyn to come, but the only one available tomorrow is your ex."

Claire scrambled for words. "Invite me to the open house, okay?"

"You can count on that. Wish you could join us tomorrow."

As she ended the call, she closed the trunk of her car and found the key. If Jamie were here showing houses, she'd do well to stay invisible. She might have to stay home from church tomorrow to stem the argument. She'd do anything to avoid Jamie Duval.

Monty squelched his disappointment at not having Claire join them for a tour of the home he hoped to buy. Somehow, getting her approval for the purchase mattered. He lifted both children from the back of his truck after helping Ellen out of the cab and walked to the front entry. The door opened, and a man in a smart jacket and perfectly pressed trousers smiled at them.

"You must be Mr. Chandler, Ellen's brother." He stuck out his hand, hazel eyes twinkling as he invited them inside. "Jamie Duval. Real Estate agent."

Monty returned the handshake, studying the man's face. "You can call me Monty."

"Then call me Jamie, please."

Inwardly, Monty frowned. Why did Jamie seem so familiar? "Have we met before?"

Jamie studied him. "I don't think we have."

Monty wasn't convinced. "Have you ever visited the marina? Or toured a NOAA ship? Your face reminds me of someone I've encountered at a different place."

"Really?" Jamie seemed surprised. "I'm not in Newport much. Most of my business is conducted in the valley. I think I've only been here a handful of times since I started signing homes last November."

Monty shrugged. "And I've only been here since November."

"Perhaps I just have one of those faces that reminds people of others they've met."

"That's probably it." Monty introduced his children. "My kids and I want to make Newport a permanent place to live."

"This home would be a great place for them. Close to schools. View of the ocean from their bedrooms. All the latest amenities."

"Let's see it." Monty followed the realtor into the front living room. The spacious area featured a gas fireplace and vaulted ceilings. The brickwork of the chimney offered a wraparound hearth that made it the focal point of the room.

When they entered the kitchen, Ellen, who had been unusually quiet, gasped. "Wow. This would be any homemaker's dream come true." She walked around the center island, running her hands across the granite countertops. "Everything speaks convenience."

Jamie spouted details as they climbed the stairs, Monty listening with a half-tuned ear while he worked on placing the man from the past. He'd seen this guy somewhere, of that he was certain.

Ellen had gone into the master bedroom and called him. "Monty, come see this bathroom. Two sinks, a shower, and a jetted tub."

He followed the sound of her voice and stopped at the doorway. "Nice."

"Oh, I wish Claire could have come with us."

"You'd have her twisting my arm to buy this." Monty laughed. "Talk about outnumbered."

"I know how to stack the deck, dear brother." Ellen cast him a wink. "The kids' teacher is on my side."

Jamie turned. "Claire Simpson? How do you know Claire?"

Monty sucked in a quick inhale of breath. Now he remembered where he'd seen this fellow before. This was the man Claire argued with in the parking lot last November. The one from whom she stormed away, leaving tire tracks on the pavement. "She teaches my kids."

"Yes, she is a teacher." Jamie was all smiles. "We were once engaged."

When Ellen blanched, and her sudden intake of air sounded like a growl, Monty's gaze riveted to her face. She glared at the realtor, fire in her eyes. "I think Mia needs a nap, Monty. We probably should be going."

The realtor appeared surprised. "Have you seen enough of the house to make a decision?"

"I *have*." Ellen called to Mia and Mason and headed for the stairs. "Thanks for the tour."

When they reached the truck, Monty studied Ellen as she climbed into the cab and he started the ignition. "What do you know that you aren't telling me?"

Ellen ground her teeth, eyes full of anger. "I'll tell you at home. Right now, I need to leave before I punch someone's lights out."

"You still want dinner?"

A huge sigh escaped Ellen and she nodded. "The kids are

starving." She offered him an apologetic face. "I'm sorry. Claire has shared some of her past with me. That man was part of it. I hoped you wouldn't find out for her sake. It was all I could do to keep quiet while we did the tour. Thanks for leaving so quickly. I might have messed up his tidy house showing if I'd stayed there much longer."

They arrived at a favorite eatery a few minutes later, placed their orders, and waited for their drinks. Monty remained silent as Ellen calmed down. Whatever happened between Duval and Claire obviously raised Ellen's hackles. He'd never seen his sister so worked up over an ex-boyfriend. Many couples broke off their engagements. That Claire broke hers off shouldn't have sparked such a meltdown.

"He left her at the altar." The steel in Ellen's voice punctuated her words. For the next several minutes, Claire's history with the agent tumbled from Ellen, her irritation evident.

"Ouch. Poor Claire." Monty mentally stroked that errant curl on her forehead back into place. He needed to stop thinking about those blonde curls.

"I think there's more she's not telling me." Ellen moved the silverware so the waitress could set her plate down, then helped Mia and Mason with ketchup for their fries. "There's an entire year in Pennsylvania that she's left blank."

"Wasn't she going to school?" Monty frowned. Ellen's perception didn't often fail her. If she sensed something amiss, she was usually right. He cut the kids' burgers with his knife. "Wouldn't that take a year?"

"She was. She had to qualify for her teaching credentials." Ellen toyed with her food.

"Maybe she needed that extra year to avoid him."

"You're right. She certainly doesn't want to see him around here." Ellen sipped her drink. "But she has an unusual attachment to her niece, a girl her sister adopted while she was there."

"She has an unusual attachment to my twins too. She loves children. Why is that suspicious?" He handed Mia a spoon for her milkshake, sticking the straw in the side. "If she were there one or two years, living with the family, she probably grew attached to their child."

Ellen glanced at him. "That makes sense. It's not unusual when you put it like that. But I have a hunch more will come out as I get to know her better." She stuffed a wad of fettuccine into her mouth. "Whatever she's hiding, it haunts her. I want to help."

"I'm glad you two have become friends." He picked up a napkin and wiped Mason's face. "You've entered each other's lives at a time when you both needed a girl companion. Claire will be to you what you were to Marissa. A confidante."

"Those are big words coming from a guy who is trying not to get involved." Ellen's eyes danced. "But you're right. Claire has filled a void left empty when Marissa died."

Monty picked up the check and guided Mia and Mason out of the booth. He couldn't admit what he thought to Ellen, but Claire had begun to fill empty spaces in everyone's hearts with her presence. Including him.

Claire forced herself to concentrate on lesson plans, even though her mind kept running scenarios of what might be happening between the Chandlers and Jamie as Ellen and Monty searched for a home this afternoon. She'd so wanted to join them for the tour and lunch afterwards but explaining her past relationship with Jamie in a positive light would have taken more strength than she possessed. Staying home was the right thing to do.

She finished the stack of evaluations she'd brought home over the weekend. At least she would begin the week caught up. Spring vacation wasn't far off and end-of-the-year reviews with parents would begin. The academic calendar and its responsibilities made time pass in a blur, her interaction with Mia and Mason filling each school day with happy memories. The best part of her teaching time centered around the twins. If she couldn't be near her niece, the twins made a good substitute.

The phone rang, and she hurried to dig it out of her tote. She checked the screen. Ellen.

"How was the house?"

"Gorgeous. But your secret with Duval came out." Ellen sniffed. "I tried to keep it quiet, honest."

"How did he find out you knew me?"

"I made the mistake of mentioning to Monty that I wished you could have gone with us. Jamie heard me and volunteered the information."

"It's all right. I know you did the best you could."

"He was lucky to leave that house alive." Ellen's chuckle confused Claire. "When he revealed to Monty who he was, I had to force myself to leave the showing and not kill him with my own two hands."

"He's not worth prison time." Claire warmed at Ellen's loyalty to their friendship, suppressing a giggle. "Trust me."

Ellen's laugh resonated in the phone. "Still, if I could have gotten away with it, I would have."

"You don't want him on your conscience. He's one of those people you love to forget."

"Have you forgotten him?"

Claire didn't answer. How did she forget a man who had changed her life forever? Who did irreparable damage to her heart? Who thought he could waltz back into her existence with the flash of a smile and a sorry? "No, I haven't forgotten him. I pray someday I will."

CHAPTER TWENTY-ONE

After Ellen's revelation about Jamie Duval, Monty decided to contact Lucas, his agent in Seattle, to help him secure the deal on the house in Newport. Fortunately, the home had been listed with another agency, and he could make his offer through his agent without involving Jamie. Ellen had toured the house the first time, wary of the man because of his connection to Claire. Though she assured him she could handle another meeting, Monty wanted to avoid any future confrontations between his sister and the man. Ellen could be brutal. Lucas offered to drive down and tour the house with him before finalizing the offer.

He pulled into the school parking lot to pick up his children and spotted Claire waiting by the door. He stepped out and waved, striding toward her as he looked around for Mia and Mason.

"Did Ellen find a house you like?" The smile didn't reach her eyes, her demeanor guarded as she waited for his answer. Perhaps Ellen had told her he knew about Jamie and the truth embarrassed her. He didn't blame her.

"Actually, she did. My agent from Seattle will be here in an hour to take me through it again." He studied her expression, noticing relief filled her eyes. Not mentioning Jamie made her visibly relax. "Since you were too busy on Sunday to join us, why don't you come with me and the twins to see it?"

"Really?" Claire's eyes widened. "Ellen said it was spectacular. I was sorry to have missed it."

"Then here's your chance. I'll have Ellen meet us there. She will be *thrilled* to show it to you." Monty narrowed his gaze. "I'll warn you, though, she hasn't stopped talking about the kitchen since we saw it. You may go home with a deaf ear."

Claire laughed. "Kitchens are important to a woman who

cooks. If you're a microwave chef, all the amenities Ellen described won't matter much."

"But they might be the draw for the future Mrs. Chandler." Monty checked himself. What had he just said?

Claire was staring at him, her mouth slightly open, a twinkle in her eye. "Ellen didn't tell me you had a woman on your agenda."

The heat creeping along his neck and spreading across his jaw line suggested Monty would soon be the color of a lobster. "I . . . I . . . don't. But I hope to find someone to spend my life with eventually. My marriage was a happy one, and I promised my former wife I wouldn't remain single forever."

"Your children need a mother to love them like Marissa did." Claire's eyes pooled as she shifted her attention to the twins, who had emerged from the double doors. "That places an even greater responsibility on you."

Monty needed to break the tension. "All the more reason to buy a house with a fabulous kitchen."

A wide grin on her face, Claire shook her head. "You are too much. Let me get my jacket and load my homework." She eyed him, a question on her face. "You won't mind dropping me off at my duplex afterward?"

"Did you walk today?"

"Yes. I'm not very far away."

"I remember." Had he ever thanked her for finding Mason and keeping him safe until the deputy and he arrived at the school? Her quick thinking and her actions probably saved his son from a night out in the cold alone. "You'll have to give me directions again. I wasn't driving the night you rescued Mason."

Lucas waited on the porch when Monty pulled up and parked. He helped Claire from the cab, then lifted the twins to the ground. Mason ran up the sidewalk, making a right turn toward the backyard. "Mason, wait up, buddy."

"I wanted to see the yard again." Mason turned and inched his way back to the front. "Will we get a swing set when we move in?"

Lucas reacted with a belly laugh. "This sounds like an easy sale." He held out his hand to Monty, then offered it to Claire. "Lucas Braeburn."

"Claire Simpson."

Monty stepped to her side. "Forgive my manners. Claire is a teacher at the school where the twins are enrolled. She's also a friend of Ellen's."

At the mention of his sister's name, Ellen drove into the cul-de-sac. She stepped from her car and waved.

Monty pursed his lips in an amused grin and gazed at Lucas. "Stand back and watch Ellen sell this house. She hasn't stopped talking about it since we toured it last Sunday."

When Ellen joined them at the front entrance, Lucas pulled a key from his pocket and held it up. "I've got the drop box key. Shall we go inside?"

Claire followed Ellen into the kitchen, her friend's enthusiasm for the room gushing forth like a spring. The expanse surprised her. One wall boasted floor-to-ceiling cabinets with a granite counter gracing the middle, while its opposite side housed the appliances. The island in the center had a small sink and faucet as well as a generous area for food preparation. A larger sink filled the counter space beneath an end-of-the-room window that allowed a glimpse of the Pacific.

She stepped through a door to her right and discovered a dining area, complete with patio doors that accessed the back yard. A glass-fronted china cabinet formed one wall.

She glanced Ellen's way. "This is certainly designed for a family or for someone who entertains a lot."

"I knew you'd love it." Ellen's eyes twinkled. "Doesn't it feel like a queen's royal kitchen?"

"If you mean, can I see servants in here? Yes." Claire narrowed her gaze. "What will Monty do with all this? He's not a cook, is he?"

"I'm hoping he will marry someone who cooks. It would be a shame to waste a kitchen like this." Ellen gestured for Claire to follow. "Come see the bedrooms."

The home lived up to all of Ellen's previous proclamations. Claire couldn't find fault with any feature, other than the house was massive. She could envision Mia and Mason getting lost in the space at first. But what a great place to play hide and seek. If Monty married, his new wife might give him more children and fill the extra bedroom. She followed Ellen back downstairs and out to the patio where Lucas and Monty talked.

"So, what did you think of the house?" Monty directed his question to her. "Has Ellen sold you?"

Claire formed her response with care. "This should serve you and your family well for many years." She risked teasing him. "And that new Mrs. Chandler you mentioned at the school will be one lucky woman."

Ellen gasped. "What new Mrs. Chandler?" She glanced from Claire to Monty. "Are you keeping something from me?"

"No." Monty blushed. "I mentioned how much you liked the kitchen, and Claire agreed it would make a great place for a woman to practice her culinary skills. That's all."

Ellen studied both of them, amusement in her eyes. "I'm glad you two agree. The kitchen is definitely a plus in this house."

Lucas, who had watched the exchange in silence, broke the conversation with a piece of paper. "Want to make an offer, Monty?"

"Yes." He looked at his sister. "You sure you don't want this place?"

"I'm quite satisfied with what I have." Ellen gestured for Claire to follow her. "We'll be in the backyard with the twins."

Claire sneaked a glance at Monty as she passed through the open patio doors and regretted it. He stood with his hands on his hips, watching her every move. Something intent registered in his eyes, a look that made her tremble. She'd seen that expression before, only in the eyes of someone not as honorable as she believed Monty to be. Was she ready to navigate those waters again? For the first time since she'd come to tour the house, she questioned her presence.

Monty and Lucas worked out a deal that allowed room for a counter offer if the owners didn't like what he proposed. He didn't want to take on too much debt, but the sale of his home in Seattle had netted him a nice equity, one that made payments on this property affordable.

"I'll present this before I leave town in the morning." Lucas stood and shook his hand. "I'm confident we'll get a good price for you and the kids."

"If anyone can seal the deal, you can." Monty glanced at his watch. "Wow. It's almost dinnertime. I'll need to take the kids out somewhere to celebrate. Want to join us?"

"No, I'm meeting a former associate in Lincoln City. Thanks, anyway." Lucas narrowed his gaze. "That little blonde number is a keeper. You making moves on her?"

Monty shook his head. "No. The kids have adopted her since they started school here. She's gone the extra mile to see they've settled in." Monty couldn't contain his grin. "But she definitely has possibilities."

Lucas nodded. "Don't let her get away."

"Time, my friend. All in good time." Who was Monty trying to kid? He merely bided his time. When the moment was right, he planned to move.

Claire agreed to join the Chandlers for dinner, listening with amusement to Ellen's ongoing praise of the house they'd toured. "I'm wondering if you shouldn't move into it and let Monty and the twins live at your old place."

Ellen laughed. "Don't think I haven't entertained the idea. If Kevin were home, I'd show him the house, but he'd never go for a change. His parents owned our house as a vacation getaway and when we bought it, they gave us a great deal. Kevin would consider it betrayal if we ventured elsewhere."

"And so he should." Monty hailed a waitress to bring more ketchup for the children's fries. "You have a view of the city and the ocean that's to die for. I can only imagine what price a skyline home with a view of the ocean and the city would bring."

Ellen reached for the salt. "Trust me, it's not cheap. We're very fortunate to live where we do."

Claire sipped her soda, images of her cute little duplex competing with the home she'd toured. "Well, if either of you are feeling lost in all that space, I'd be happy to rent you my spare bedroom for a week, so you can feel cramped." She winked at Mason, who'd stopped chewing to stare at her. "But it's going to cost you a mint."

"Can I, Daddy? Can I rent Miss Claire's spare room?" The child's eyes were as round as saucers. "She could take me to school in the morning."

Monty appeared amused, as if the idea were one he'd consider. "I'm not sure how long Miss Claire would put up with you, Mason. You'd have to pick up your clothes,"

"Oh, I would. I would." Mason glanced at her. "I promise."

Ellen gazed at her, one eyebrow arched and a twisted smile puckering her lips. She glanced at her brother before looking again at Claire. Whatever she thought, the idea amused her. Claire stuck a fork in her mashed potatoes and swirled the gravy, uncomfortable in the woman's scrutiny. Ellen wasn't playing matchmaker, was she?

They finished their dinner and Monty guided the children to the truck. He opened the passenger door for her as Ellen brought up the rear. "Monty, I'd be happy to take Claire home."

Monty shook his head. "No. I talked her into coming and promised I'd take her back. I'm a man of my word."

"Uh, huh." Ellen emphasized the last syllable before patting Claire on the shoulder. "I'll see you soon, girlfriend."

"Loved your choice of houses. That one is going to be great for the kids."

Ellen grinned. "Glad you liked it. Probably a good thing, don't you think?"

Claire swallowed. What was Ellen saying? Before she could respond, Ellen sidestepped her and squeezing the fob, unlocked her car. Claire faced Monty and forced a smile. "Time for me to hit the books."

Monty gestured for her to climb in, closing the door behind her. He strode around to the driver side and glanced over the seat. "You kids ready to go home?"

Mia piped up. "Can we go to Miss Claire's house?"

"Yep. I promised to take her home." He turned the key and the engine roared to life. "Next stop, Miss Claire's duplex."

Claire filled the silence with light conversation. "You're going to enjoy being in your own space again. Thanks for letting me see it."

"I'm glad you liked it." When they pulled into her drive, Claire reached for the door latch, but Monty stopped her. "Let me help you with that tote of books you brought home."

She started to protest, but he hopped from the cab and came around to her door before she could utter a peep. He helped her down and reached behind the seat for her bag. Carrying it to the door, he waited while she fumbled for her key. At last she inserted the device in her door and opened it, her fingers trembling as the moment turned into something more. She glanced up to say goodbye and found Monty studying her, those clear blue eyes intent.

"Claire, would you consider seeing me outside of the classroom?" He handed over the tote. "Like for a movie, or a sail on the Bay?"

She gulped. "The children would love an outing like that."

"I wouldn't bring the kids. It'd be just you and me."

"Oh." She lowered her gaze, suddenly shy standing next to the man. Could she do this? Did it break any rules? Shoving the excuses aside, she found her voice. "Sure. I haven't seen a movie at this theater since I moved here."

Monty grinned. "Then I'd say you're long overdue." He stepped back a pace. "I'll call you."

She nodded, afraid of saying something stupid. He turned, walked back to the truck, and climbed in. With a wave, he put the vehicle in gear and headed down the road. Only then did her heart stop pounding. She gasped for air. A movie date shouldn't leave her breathless, so it must have been the man asking her to join him. *I'm in serious trouble here.*

CHAPTER TWENTY-TWO

Claire tried on three different outfits before deciding to wear a simple cashmere sweater with a pair of matching slacks. Going to a movie didn't require more formal attire, did it? After all, she wasn't trying to impress anyone. Monty wanted to get better acquainted. That could mean they'd be better friends. She'd know his children more intimately. Or grow closer to Ellen. Or fall in love.

She drew a comb through her hair, pulling hard at the tangles. She didn't know what it meant to be in love. She thought she'd loved Jamie, but knew now she'd been infatuated, falling victim to his charms, believing his false sincerity. He'd led her down an enticing path of deception, promising things he didn't intend to produce, making her believe that he held her in the highest esteem. Until someone else came along who had a cheerier smile and found his arms easy to climb into. It hadn't mattered that she and Jamie had been planning a wedding for six months, that the guests were days away from showing up, the cake ordered, the deposit on the flowers paid, the wedding dress. . .

She stopped. Dredging up all the bitterness wouldn't change anything. Jamie's betrayal had set her free. Because of him, she'd found faith in a loving heavenly Father. She'd discovered forgiveness at its deepest level. Though Jamie had ripped her apart, Christ had restored her. That Monty showed interest in her proved she'd healed without too many scars. Four years ago all she would have given him were sarcastic putdowns. She'd sworn off men back then. Now her heart ached to find one perfect love. Sitting home rehashing Jamie's offenses wouldn't produce the results she longed to find. Spending time with Monty might.

She glanced at the clock. Monty would be here in half an hour.

He'd chosen a movie that released last week, and he'd heard she'd need tissue to get through it. Afterwards, they'd go for a late supper. Sounded like fun.

She brushed her teeth and retouched her makeup—a dab of lipstick and a swipe of powder. Slipping on shoes, she stood before the mirror and opted for an emerald green, diamond-shaped pendant. The single stone suspended in a gold setting lay gently against her breastbone. Perfect accessory for her honey-colored sweater, the weight of it hid the wild beating of her heart beneath.

Monty helped Claire from the truck and guided her up the sidewalk to the retro café he'd chosen for their supper. The movie had lasted longer than he'd thought it would, making this repast a welcome attraction. His stomach had growled twice already. Claire's smile said she'd heard it protest as well. But she hadn't reacted, merely agreed with him on his choice of a place to dine.

As they entered, seventies music played from a jukebox, two couples dancing to the rhythm in the open area between tables. The checkerboard tiles amplified the red of the upholstered chairs lining both walls. A handful of couples occupied tables. He directed Claire to one in the back corner. A fire-engine red tablecloth beneath a glass top held a carrier of mustard, ketchup, and mayonnaise packets in its center.

"This is definitely before our time." Claire smiled as she sat down and opened her menu. "Those songs came straight off an oldies radio playlist."

"You like something more from today? Like reggae rock or a little hip-hop?" He grinned from behind his menu, guessing Claire preferred classical pieces to music that made others wiggle.

"Actually, I like to listen to Beethoven, Brahms, and Chopin." Her mouth twisted in a pucker. She couldn't hide the twinkle in her eyes. "Ever heard of them?"

"Definitely not on my playlist." He nodded at the waitress who'd brought them glasses of water. As she questioned them about drinks, he took his lead from Claire, who ordered a chocolate soda. "I'd like a root beer float."

"Are you ready to order?"

"Cheeseburger basket for me, please." She pointed to something on the menu. "That's a substitute?" The server nodded.

"Monster burger basket." He handed the waitress his menu. When she left, his curiosity got the best of him. "What did you substitute?"

"Salad for the fries."

"No greasy foods for you?"

"Not if I want to sleep tonight." Claire made a face. "Heartburn is not fun at three in the morning."

"How did you like the movie?" He'd found it rather dull, the action scenes missing the momentum car chases usually flashed across the screen.

"I enjoyed most of it. I've not had time for a movie in a long time, so this was a treat. The actors made their attraction for each other believable."

"You've got me there."

"How are the twins adjusting to the idea of moving into your new home?" Claire studied him, the warmth of her caramel eyes melting him into a puddle of shyness. She always seemed as if she understood what he was thinking, as if she had a special insight into his head.

"I think they're going to make the adjustment well." He chuckled, thinking of Mason's incessant nagging for outdoor play equipment. "If I provide a swing set, Mason will be thrilled. If I adopt a kitten, Mia will purr like one."

"How soon does Kevin return home?"

"He's due back the end of next month, after spring vacation." He tapped the calendar app on his phone.

"Ellen seems anxious to see him."

"They've been apart more than they've been together since they married." He leaned back in his chair. "Hopefully, this was his last tour and he can put the military behind him."

"I hope so too. Ellen wants a family."

Her statement surprised him. "After the twins I thought maybe she'd opt out."

"If anything, helping with the twins made her longing more acute." Claire's attention swept the restaurant. "Many women anticipate raising a family."

He noticed how she skirted the room, as if looking for someone. Was she fearful of running into her former fiancé? What had that man done? "See anyone you know?"

Claire jumped. "No. Thought I did. Sorry." She leaned back in her chair as the waitress brought their dinners. "Will you be into your new house in time for Kevin's return?"

"We close on the fifteenth. The following week we move in. All I own is in storage. One big truck should get us into the house before Kevin arrives and boots us out onto the street." He made a face. "He's not as keen on a pair of little ones underfoot."

"His loss." She sipped her soda. "Your children are a delight."

Did his kids make Claire long for children as well? He'd have to ask that question when they knew each other better. Of course, his new house could support a couple more. Maybe that's why he chose it.

After Claire bid Monty goodnight, she slipped into her duplex and snapped on a lamp. Her phone had buzzed three times during their dinner, and she'd not taken time to see who had called. Now as she scrolled up the messages, she saw Angie's name in the queue. A peek at the clock said bedtime in Pennsylvania had probably come and gone, making it too late to call, but as she opened the texts from her sister, panic flooded her. She punched in Angie's number.

"Where have you been?" Angie sounded irritated or tired, Claire couldn't decide which. "I'm an absolute wreck."

"I went out to dinner and a movie with a friend."

"And you couldn't answer your phone?" Angie's tone changed, her mind no doubt zipping through all the reasons why Claire didn't return her calls. "Is he cute?"

"No." Claire lied, remembered the way a dimple indented his left cheek when he smiled. "He's ruggedly handsome, recently lost his wife, and is father to a set of twins."

"So he's available?" Angie's incredulity rose in pitch with each syllable. "At last!"

"Angie. Did you hear me? He lost his wife a year ago."

"Oh, I heard you, or rather the excuse you are going to use to keep him at arm's length."

"I'm not, it's not, oh, forget it." She didn't want to talk about Monty now. Maybe later. "What's wrong with Fallyn?"

"Her kidney infection returned." Angie paused, a heavy sigh resonating in the phone. "And it's worse than before."

"I had my blood type checked for a match. Specified Fallyn's doctor."

"You weren't a match." The tremor in Angie's words worried Claire. What was her sister not saying? "I'm not either."

"Is Fallyn in danger?" Her stomach rolled over as she thought of her niece facing such huge medical problems.

"She will be, if this doesn't clear up." Angie's sob made Claire shudder. "Pray for her like you've never prayed before."

"You know I will." She attempted to change the subject. Angie's stress level couldn't be good for her condition. "How's your pregnancy?"

The question made Angie laugh. "I'm bulging like I swallowed a watermelon." Her chuckle warmed Claire. The tension had left her sister's voice. "Brennan said he doesn't know me when I waddle. And I've got eight weeks left."

"Do you know yet what you're having?"

"A baby, of course." Angie's no-nonsense declaration was followed by giggles. "We decided not to know. We want to be surprised."

"You won't make it easy on me, so I can buy you some well-deserved baby clothes?"

"I want you here when the baby comes." Angie's voice wobbled. "I don't think Brennan or Mom, oh perish the thought, could handle a birth. I'm going to need someone level-headed to help me."

"Ha! And you think that person is me?" She appreciated Angie's confidence in her, but Brennan should be by her side, not Claire. "Brennan will do fine. Give him a chance."

"You will stay with Fallyn? She's excited, but this kidney infection has left her fragile."

"A lot can happen in eight weeks, Sis. Modern medicine can do wonders. Trust God to heal your daughter and see you through labor." Claire closed her eyes and prayed. "I couldn't survive if I lost either of you."

Monty thought about his time with Claire as he drove to his sister's home. The pretty blonde teacher made him smile, lingering in his memory like a flower's fragrance. Though quiet, she answered his questions with care, her responses sensible and composed. Her reserved demeanor made him think she wasn't ready to open up to him yet. That was okay. He knew of her past and could only imagine how hurt she'd been when her fiancé left her three days before the wedding. How a guy could do that to a woman as pretty and special as Claire baffled him.

The man needed a brain change. He'd confronted Claire in the parking lot last November. Her body language shouted she wasn't happy. Her tire-squealing departure confirmed what Monty had witnessed. She'd opted out of Monty's first new home tour because she'd known who the agent would be. She didn't want the man in her life. Apparently, the guy didn't get it.

But Monty did. Knowing she no longer held feelings for her former love gave Monty the courage to keep pursuing her. He'd only lost Marissa a year ago, but she'd made him promise he'd move on, find someone new to love, give their children another mother. Claire had walked into his life as if she'd been pre-arranged. Peeling away the memories haunting her from an unhealthy past relationship might prove as daunting as removing old wallpaper, but in the end a fresh new surface would appear, and Claire would shine again.

He should have asked her if she sailed. One way to find out.

CHAPTER TWENTY-THREE

THE WIND WAXED AND WANED AS Monty guided the sloop across Yaquina Bay, the mainsail billowing as the boat headed upwind. Uncommon for an Oregon coast day in early March, the sun beamed warm and inviting, making the water sparkle as the breeze blowing in off the ocean powered the sails. Monty kept his hand on the tiller and a watchful eye on the boom as he tacked the turbulent air which swirled around them.

He hadn't sailed in what seemed like decades. Sailing with Marissa had drawn them together early in their relationship. Many dates happened on the water. They'd enjoyed Seattle's nearby lakes and ocean waters after they married too, but when the twins arrived, time for sailing took flight with the winds. He'd feared his skills would be rusty with disuse, but this boat he'd borrowed from a friend at work maneuvered like a well-trained horse. Guiding the sloop along the coast proved much simpler than he'd first imagined.

Claire relaxed near the bow, leaning back into the padded seat of the open cabin. Her legs stretched in front of her, fingers dangling over the side. Head aimed toward the sky, her blonde curls fluttered beneath a straw hat tied at the chin. Sunglasses covered those warm, caramel eyes. Spray from the impact of the bow against a breaker misted her from time to time, but she took it all in stride, smiling as the saltwater beaded her skin. From the expression on her face, the experience enraptured her.

"Let me know when you're feeling hungry." Monty swung the boom forty-five degrees to keep the sail full, turning the tiller to match the direction the wind pushed them. They'd been on the water at least an hour, competition for the Bay's playground growing more acute as other sailors and boats sampled the sunshine-filled day. Too many vessels to steer around made him nervous. He didn't want to risk an incident.

Claire lifted her wrist, angling the watch strapped to it as if to block out the sun, and peered at him through the dark glasses. "It's almost noon."

"I figured we were getting close." Monty checked his mainsail, now sloughing as the breeze let up. "The sun is directly overhead, and the traffic is growing."

"Traffic?" Claire's frown spoke volumes. "Like congestion?"

"Yep. Too many vessels make for a less than satisfactory experience." He made a face. "Some sailors tend to be careless and create collisions."

She settled back, fingers clasped at her midriff, apparently undaunted by the prospect of other boats getting in their way. "I'm good, so whenever you'd like to picnic, head to shore."

He brought the boat about, catching a slight wind that let them approach the marina at a lower speed. Lowering the sails, he engaged the engine, its hum barely audible over the sounds of the ocean beyond, and aimed the bow for the mooring, inching the sloop into its slip. When they'd come to a stop, he hopped onto the slatted walkway and tied the vessel up at the ring. Claire helped him secure the craft, putting the canvas cover in place over the cabin area and tying up the sails. When he was satisfied the locked boat would remain protected, he offered her a hand to the dock. "Let's go tackle that picnic lunch you brought."

They drove to the Yaquina Bay Natural Area and found a free table. Claire opened her basket and placed a tablecloth across the surface of the wooden slab. She set two places—plastic plates, silverware, and mugs—on opposite sides from each other. A bowl of fruit salad and a stack of sandwiches found space in the center.

"Bottled water or iced tea?" She held up the containers.

"Tea for me." Monty slipped onto the bench seat and sat. "Couldn't have asked for a more beautiful day."

"Considering this is March, I'd say we drew the lucky straw." A sea gull shrieked above them, emphasizing her assessment. Claire handed Monty his bottle of tea and pushed the plate of sandwiches toward him. "Turkey and Swiss on rye."

"Health nuts, are we?" He grinned at her as he put a sandwich on his plate. "That fruit looks wonderful." He scooped a spoonful beside the triangular-shaped bread. "Won't be long before we can get fresh berries."

"I'll probably go to the valley and pick strawberries with my mother." Claire stabbed a piece of pear. "She likes to get a few every year. We always make jam together."

"Are you close to your mother?" He took a swig of the tea.

"Not as much as we once were." Claire stared out at the ocean, as if lost in thought. A wave crashed in the distance, the splash sounding like a waterfall. "Life has a way of skewing things sometimes."

"What distanced you?" He caught himself. "If I'm being too nosy, stop me."

"No, not really." Claire cast him a rueful smile. "Like your sister pushes you, my mother thinks I should work harder at getting married. And she's all too willing to help me find someone."

Monty stopped chewing. "And you disagree?"

"I'm sure Ellen told you about Jamie?" Claire pinned him with her gaze. At his nod, she continued. "Mom thinks it was merely a misunderstanding, that I ran off to Pennsylvania too quickly before Jamie had a chance to explain himself."

"Didn't he pull out of the wedding?"

"Yes. He feared marriage would get in the way of his career hopes." Claire's face turned wistful, the shadow of a smile on her lips. "I knew if I stuck around here to finish my degree, I ran the risk of running into him." She lowered her chin as if the memories hurt. "His departure devastated me. He left to chase his dreams only to shatter mine. I couldn't be here." Claire glanced up. "But my mother doesn't get that."

Monty took her hand. "Well, I get it. It's my hope that you can put Jamie behind you and make room for me. If you haven't noticed, I'm attracted to you."

"That explains the movie, the dinners, and the sailboat ride." She pursed her lips, teasing in her eyes.

"Smart girl." He lifted her chin and studied her face, suddenly shy in his revelation. "You've done miracles for my kids. You've befriended my sister. You've filled a void I thought would never heal. Maybe it's too soon for me to replace Marissa, but the emptiness I feel without her keeps me awake at night. She made me promise I'd find a new love, another mother for Mia and Mason. She'd be the first to tell me to go for it." He gave her a squeeze. "And she'd love you."

Claire's face softened. "I wish I could have known her."

Monty reached for his tea. "You'd have been best friends."

Claire sat up straighter. "She'd have had an instant babysitter."

He laughed, then sobered. "Will you give us a chance? See where this, whatever it is between us, goes?"

She grew silent, staring out at the ocean, her face reflecting a thousand thoughts. Her mouth pressed in a straight line, brows moving with the feelings that must have besieged her. Remorse lingered in her eyes, the slight hint of moisture at her lids testifying to the hurt she carried, sorrow which had embedded itself deep in her soul. He wished he knew her well enough to hold her in his arms and kiss away the tears. With time, he might.

After several minutes her shoulders lifted, then fell, as she sighed and brought her attention back to him. "Yes, Monty. I'm willing to explore what we have. But you may not like how long you have to wait."

"I'm not going anywhere."

"Well, I am." She faced him, that tease again in her eyes. "Spring break is ahead, and I've decided to visit my sister again. My niece is seriously ill, and Angie is almost eight months pregnant. I thought I'd visit and offer my help."

"That sounds like something you'd do." He took her hand, small and soft, in his, and squeezed it. "You're always giving of yourself to help another." He gazed at her. "Is your niece seeing a doctor?"

Claire's eyes clouded. "Yes. She's had recurring kidney infections this past winter. The anti-biotic works for a while, but still the problems reoccur without warning."

"That's pretty serious."

"I think there's a lot my sister isn't telling me. I'll know more if I go." Claire shuddered. "That's why I want to spend as much time as I can supporting her."

"Your sister will appreciate your input, especially the respite time you provide so she can rest."

"I hope so." Claire bit her lip. "Angie married young and has been unable to have a child. This baby is a special gift." She stared at her hands now in her lap. "Too much stress can't be good for her."

"You'll be gone the entire week?"

"Actually, I fly out late the Friday before and return late Sunday night. I'm giving new meaning to red eye flights."

"You must be."

"But doing it this way gives me most of nine days."

"Well, when you return from your trip, I'll take you to see NOAA headquarters where I work." He spread his arms wide. "Our ships make the sloop we sailed this morning look like a dinghy."

"Probably have a lot of electronic paraphernalia, too."

"That, my dear teacher, is what you'd call an understatement."

"Did you get enough to eat?" She pointed at his half-eaten

sandwich.

He looked at his plate. Two yellow jackets were feasting on the leftover meat, and a crow squawked nearby, waiting to make off with the bread. "I think I may have to toss this first helping and start over."

"Ditch your plate." Claire reached in the basket and pulled out a fresh one. "There's another sandwich and more fruit in the container."

"Sorry to waste that first one." He stood and carried the plate to the trashcan. The crow hopped up beside him, beady eyes on the uneaten food. He dropped the sandwich to the ground. "Have at it, fella." The bird wasted no time zeroing in on his treasure. "Didn't waste it after all." He returned to the table.

"You ate most of it before the critters discovered it." She loaded the second plate. "But be careful as you eat. These bees have been known to land on food just as it's being bitten into. That will hurt."

"Thanks for the warning." He examined the new sandwich and finding nothing in or around its edges, took a big bite. "The turkey and Swiss are really good together, just like you and Ellen."

"We've had a lot of fun becoming friends."

He swallowed the bite he'd chewed, took a swig of tea, and cast her a big grin. "So which are you? The turkey or the Swiss?"

She tossed a grape and hit him squarely on the nose.

"Must be Swiss. Turkeys have very bad aim." He dodged a second grape. "Do you need a ride to the airport?"

CHAPTER TWENTY-FOUR

THE AIRPORT TEEMED WITH TRAVELERS EITHER hurrying to catch flights or with those disembarking, people intent upon their search for loved ones in the crowd. Claire studied the faces around her, hoping to catch a glimpse of Brennan or Angie waving. This spring break seemed to inspire traveling, passengers hustling in every direction.

"Claire!"

She glanced in the direction of the male voice that hailed her. Brennan waved and pushed through the crowd, arriving at her side in a couple of strides. He carried his suit coat over one arm, his tie askew as he struggled to give her a hug.

"Sorry I'm late." He kissed her on the forehead. "Angie's on bed rest and so I had to ask our neighbor to watch Fallyn while I came to get you."

"Is Angie okay?" Claire's pulse quickened. "It's too early for labor."

"No labor, just some problems with blood pressure and fatigue. She's been worrying too much about Fallyn's kidney infections and not taking care of herself."

"I'm glad I came today, then. That will give me nine days before I fly home."

Brennan gestured toward the baggage area. "She's going to wear you out. Prepare to assume the role of chief slave."

"It will be my pleasure."

They neared the carousel and Claire spotted her bag dropping to the belt. She pointed, and Brennan strode to meet the luggage. He pulled it out, nodding for her to follow him to the car. Depositing the bag in the trunk, he opened the passenger door before hurrying to the driver side. She buckled her seatbelt, sensing urgency in her brother-in-law. As Brennan wove through town, rounding corners like a roller coaster, Claire's tension grew. Had Angie's pregnancy taken a turn for the worse? What wasn't Brennan telling her?

The house smelled of lavender, Angie's candle preference lending its scent to the rooms. Brennan walked straight back to the bedroom, Claire on his heels. Opening the door, he gestured for her to enter. "Look who I found wandering around the airport."

Fallyn sat on a chair by the bed, a woman Claire guessed to be the neighbor beside her. When she saw Claire, the child jumped off her perch and ran to her side. Claire bent down and hugged the tiny girl. "Hello, sweetie."

"Auntie Claire!" Fallyn wrapped her arms about Claire's neck. "You came."

"Of course I did." She glanced at her sister. "You awake, Sis?"

Angie's puffy face sagged, cheeks drained of color, dark circles beneath her eyes. Fatigue draped her like a heavy blanket. A slight smile graced her lips. "I'm as awake as I can be. Doctor sent me to bed earlier, and I haven't done anything but sleep since. Fallyn is out of school for a week, so I'm grateful you're here to provide a diversion." She nodded toward the other woman. "This is Mrs. Thornton. She lives across the street."

"Nice to meet you." Claire winked at Fallyn, who still clung to her. "Fallyn and I can get into mischief, you know."

"I'm sure." Angie pushed against the pillows and slid to a more upright sitting position. She rotated her neck side to side. "So stiff."

Brennan stepped to the side of the bed and sat on the mattress edge. "Need a massage?"

Angie nodded, turning slightly so Brennan could reach her neck, a move that revealed her expanded girth.

Claire couldn't contain her surprise. "Has the doctor said anything about your due date?"

"What do you mean?" Angie leaned back against Brennan's

hands, eyes closed as her husband's fingers relaxed her stiff muscles. "Other than I'm bigger than a house." Angie grinned. "Didn't think I could expand like this, did you?"

"I thought the doctor might have moved your date." Claire lifted an eyebrow. "He hasn't?"

"No. But there is an explanation for my size." Angie cast her a crooked smile, and Claire caught her meaning.

"You're not!" Claire gasped. "Tell me it's not two."

"Okay, I won't." Angie glanced over her shoulder at Brennan, who winked at his wife. "You can be surprised when I call you with the news."

"Angie." Claire needed to sit. She found a chair against the wall and sank into it. Fallyn crawled onto her lap. "Are you serious? Two babies?"

"Um, no." Angie leaned back against the pillows as Brennan lifted the covers to her chin. "We've hired Mrs. Thornton to help me when the babies arrive." Angie narrowed her eyes, a tease spreading across her face. "Remember when I told you we decided not to know? The doctor saw me this week and insisted we get an ultrasound. That confirmed the doctor's suspicions. I'm carrying triplets."

Claire's mouth dropped, the intake of air loud in the silent room, her surprise wordless. "Three babies?" At Angie's nod, she squealed. "Well, you're certainly making up for lost time, aren't you?"

Brennan laughed. "So it would appear. But Angie has to have complete bed rest from now until the babies arrive. Her swollen feet and ankles indicate she's retaining water. Her blood pressure has also been high."

"Signs of pre-eclampsia, then." Claire bit her lip. She'd heard some women had problems toward the end of their pregnancies. But they weren't carrying triplets. "Will you deliver normally?"

"Doubt it." Angie's words sounded out of breath. "If I can make it to thirty-seven weeks, I'll probably wind up with a caesarean section."

"What week is this?"

"Thirty-four." Angie emitted a low groan. She glanced at Brennan. "Another cramp, honey."

He picked up a notebook on the night table, wrote in it, and flashed it Claire's direction. "Doctor's log. Keeping track of all pains." He replaced the notebook and blew his wife a kiss.

Angie smiled before focusing back on her. "The babies are pretty small yet. But carrying three to term is probably not going to happen."

Claire shook her head. "Carrying three anywhere is going to be a challenge." She hugged Fallyn who still sat quietly on her lap. "Daughter number one is too little to push a stroller for three."

Angie grew quiet. "We'll figure this out."

The words sounded ominous to Claire's ears. Where would Fallyn fit in the flurry of care for three tiny newborns? Would she have to take a number to get her needs met? "Does Mom know?"

"No. Once the babies are born and we bring them home, we'll fall into a routine. I'll invite Mom to come meet her newest grandchildren." Angie's eyes closed again. "Maybe she'll stay a month and help us get caught up."

"I can come when school is out." Claire ruffled Fallyn's hair. "But by then the babies will be half grown."

"Bring your new boyfriend while you're at it." Angie's cheesy grin suggested she knew more than she did. "I want to see if he's good father material."

Claire remained silent. She hadn't claimed Monty yet.

With the twins out of school on spring break, Monty made

arrangements to be off work twice during the coming week. Oregon's coast weather could be tumultuous in March, and he crossed his fingers that the days he'd chosen would break sunny and warm. Today proved to be one of those blustery days, but because it was Saturday he still hoped for a break in the clouds in the near future. The rain beyond the patio of his new home, where he assembled swing set parts, fell in torrents.

Mason checked on him every ten minutes. "Swing set yet, Dad?"

"Working on it."

Once Monty finished the monstrosity, the kids would play while he worked on getting the house ready for move-in. Ellen's husband, Kevin, would arrive the last day of the month and Monty was determined to be out of the way of his brother-in-law by then.

He picked up the instructions, remembering Marissa's teasing about how the words, *some assembly required,* struck terror in the hearts of parents. He laughed at the memory. They'd worked together on more things needing construction than he cared to count. Marissa made the work fun. He ordered his breathing to slow from its fast, choppy pace, missing her once again.

If Claire were here, she'd bring life to the task. Like Marissa, her sense of fun colored everything she did. She'd refused his offer of a ride to the airport, reminding him she'd need a ride back as well, and wouldn't he need the time to set up the house? He appreciated her thinking ahead—the two-hour trip both ways would have eaten away at his vacation. But if she'd been here, he'd have sought advice on furniture placement. She might have handed him a screwdriver. She'd have entertained the twins while he worked. To be truthful, he liked having her around. Though they both deemed their relationship as one between friends, Monty sensed his commitment growing steadily stronger the more time he spent with the lovely woman.

"Dad?" Mason called from the stairs where he and his sister sat watching the painters slather fresh color on the upstairs hallway.

He stuck his head in the doorway. "Not done yet."

"Will we fly kites this week?"

"We might take a day and do that, Son." Not smelling any lingering smell, he grew curious. This brand of paint he'd chosen boasted a low VOC which meant the odor would be minimal. "How's the work coming?"

"My room is going to be pretty, Daddy." Mia clapped her hands, twisting on the stairs to tell him. "You should see it."

"I'll be up soon." Mia's room would be a shade of hot pink Monty feared would shine across Yaquina Bay. Mason had chosen sky blue with a paper border of kites near the ceiling. Ellen had helped find the kite-themed motif as well as delighting Mia with a border of kittens. Both wallpapers had bedding to match. The children would live in rooms filled with their favorite things, thanks to his sister's sleuthing. Monty would look like a hero.

He returned to the set-up guidelines for the swing set and laid out more pieces on the patio. Rain still fell, making him nervous about plans for the coming week, but a warm air mass could improve conditions overnight. For that he prayed.

He had bolted one of the support posts when he heard a car approach out front. Two doors slammed, and voices floated around to the back where he listened.

"Monty?" Whoever had arrived had entered the yard.

"Back here on the patio." He straightened and walked to the edge of the cement where he could see. Two of his tour mates, Lenny, who dove with him, and Corbin, a man who tracked radar aboard ship, came across the grass, slipping in under the roof where it was dry. "What brings you guys here?"

"We came to offer our muscles." Lenny grinned and flexed. "Do you know what day you'll be moving?"

"Seriously?" Monty had wondered how many movers he would have to hire to get his belongings from the storage unit to his home. At their nods, he replied. "The first day the sun shows up."

Lenny chortled. "Let's go, then. Monty won't need us until next year."

Monty ignored the banter, picking up a screw. "I hope to move in this week. Whatever the painters don't accomplish today, they'll finish on Monday. The carpet is scheduled Tuesday morning. I've taken two days off from work with the stipulation they will be on days that are sunny. Can I call you?"

Lenny nodded, giving Corbin a chance to also agree. "But we haven't taken days off because all the family men will be gone, what with spring break and all."

"Saturday would be better for you?"

"Or after work. A couple of hours a night would save our backs." Lenny fingered the swing supports. "You want any help assembling this?"

"Sure. It would go a lot faster." Monty handed the directions to Lenny. "Holding the posts at the same time as I try to secure them has proven a challenge."

Corbin took the instruction sheet. "I used to assemble swings sets when I worked at a home improvement store during college. We can have this up in no time if we work together."

Monty handed him a screwdriver and Lenny a wrench. "Have at it. I've got to check my kids." Mason and Mia had disappeared from the landing where they'd been earlier. "Mischief comes in small packages around here."

Lenny picked up the support post Monty had been working on. "We'll have this done by the time you get back, Mr. Slowpoke."

"I guess I'll take the long way around, then. Wouldn't want to impede the march of industry."

He entered the house through the patio doors, took the stairs where the kids had been, and arrived on the second floor. A slight paint odor hovered in the hallway, and he heard voices coming from Mia's room. He poked his head through that doorway first. Mia and Mason sat in the middle of the room, the paint crew applying the bright pink color to the walls. "Wow, Mia, I'm going to need sunglasses to kiss you goodnight."

"Oh, Daddy, no, you won't." Mia's giggle sounded progressively more like the little girl she'd been before Marissa died. Or did the memories of her mother reflect the miniature she'd become? Her next sentence sealed the assessment. "Don't you know Auntie Ellen and I will break up the color with curtains, bedspreads, and furniture?" She crossed her arms in Marissa style. "Dad. Nobody wants a room *all* pink!" She shook her head. "It's simply not done."

Monty swallowed his chuckle, his daughter's perfect imitation of her mother a delight. Marissa might be gone, but she'd left her mark on their daughter. He breathed deep, forcing himself to find joy in the moment, rather than sorrow. How wonderful Mia remembered the mannerisms of her missing parent. When they moved in, he'd dig out the family pictures and spread them around the house. The memories promised healing for all of them. Claire's influence softened the edges of their hurts. No doubt the mental healthiness of his children came as a result of her input. A stab of emptiness poked him in her absence. He anticipated her return. Couldn't come soon enough.

CHAPTER TWENTY-FIVE

CLAIRE WAITED WITH FALLYN IN THE doctor's office, nerves shaky as the test results of her niece's kidney infection were evaluated. Angie, now bedridden, sent Brennan and Claire to the follow-up appointment, only to have Fallyn beg Claire to take her into the examination room while Brennan remained outside. Claire disagreed, telling Fallyn her daddy should hear the lab reports, too. The child didn't argue, only saying that her mommy usually saw the doctor. Claire lifted Fallyn to the waiting table, amazed at the amount of trust the child placed in her, holding on to her arm as if she feared to let go.

The doctor entered and smiled, ruffling Fallyn's head which brought a smile. "Good to see you again." He raised his gaze to Claire. "I understand from Mr. O'Brien you are the appointed stand-in for a very pregnant woman."

"Claire Simpson. Angie's sister." She extended her hand.

"Dr. Blackwell." He gestured toward a chair for Claire before he pulled up a rolling stool and sat beside Fallyn. "I have the lab work we ran on Fallyn a week ago."

"Is she better?"

"Yes and no." He gave Fallyn a reassuring smile. "The infection has cleared, which is good, but her kidneys are not functioning as they should. Another infection could occur at any time."

"Why is that?"

"It's too early to draw a conclusion, but my professional guess is that it's a congenital defect known as polycystic kidney disease. Because she's adopted, and Mrs. O'Brien said a history of kidney disease wasn't listed on the papers that came with Fallyn, we can only assume it's genetic." The doctor ran his finger down the form in front of him. "Her medical records show she has repeated tract infections. Her red blood cell count is low, suggesting anemia, and there's protein in the urine. Sometimes, in little girls, the urethra is blocked and in need of treatment. In Fallyn's case, we believe there's more to the problem than that. We've caught the infection soon enough each time to clear it, but continued infections threaten damage to the kidney."

"What's the prognosis?" Claire fought the lump in her throat. "Can she go on as she is?"

"She has developed a few cysts in her kidneys. Some people can live with cysts for years without any further problems. Then somewhere in their thirties or forties, the cysts start to cause trouble." The doctor lifted his attention from the chart in front of him to Claire. "Fallyn, though, is already showing signs of organ distress. The kidneys are losing their ability to function. If she suffers a series of future infections, she could be a candidate for dialysis." He turned to Fallyn, listening to her heart and lungs, probing her neck, most likely looking for swollen glands. He patted her shoulder. "Today though, she's out of danger. Let's hope she stays that way."

"What will another infection mean?"

"Let's pray her kidneys stay healthier than they have been, but PKD is progressive." He closed Fallyn's chart. "Any future infection could push her into the next level of treatment."

"Isn't dialysis done several times a week?"

"Hemodialysis is. And she won't feel good while she's being treated." The doctor peered over his glasses. "That process cleans her kidneys by a machine outside the body that filters out the toxins."

"Is there an alternative?"

"Peritoneal dialysis uses the lining of the abdomen to act as a filter. A catheter is inserted into the tissue and dialysate is pumped into the body. It is a mixture of water, minerals, and sucrose that filters the blood. After a few hours the liquid is drained."

"How long can that treatment sustain her?"

"Nothing's permanent." The doctor folded his arms, Fallyn's chart in his hands. "Transplant is the only long-lasting cure."

"A transplant?" Claire's world spun around her. How could this young child be in line for a donor kidney? "Angie and Brennan aren't wealthy people."

"Here in Philadelphia we have several organizations who will help parents fund their child's treatments. Brennan's insurance will top out, I'm sure, but additional funding is available."

Claire's meager savings account would amount to an ink spot on a white wall compared to the cost of the life-altering procedure. She'd take out loans to help the child. Fallyn had stolen her heart, and she wouldn't let the little girl suffer.

"Funding isn't really the issue." The doctor set the folder on the examination table. "Locating a kidney will be the primary problem."

"I offered mine, but Angie said I wasn't a match." Claire's mind raced with the names of people she might approach, friends for whom she'd once done a favor. *Hi, remember that paper I helped you ace in college? Well, I need your help. Would you consider donating a kidney to my niece?* Even in the seriousness of the moment, the idea sounded ludicrous. But she was determined to try. "I live and work in Oregon. I can ask people there that I know. Perhaps that would expand the donor pool."

"Anything helps." The doctor stood to go, giving Fallyn a hug. He turned to Brennan. "Keep a close eye on any sign of infection. Low-grade fever. Overly tired. Loss of appetite. Any of those are indicators that another infection is lurking." He extended his hand. "Avoid salty foods, which, in our culture is almost impossible. Plenty of water can do more good than a lab full of medicine, but it's not a cure-all." He nodded to Claire. "It's nice to have met you."

"Thank you, doctor." Claire had a last-minute thought. "Can Fallyn travel?"

"As long as she doesn't have to sit for long hours." He grinned. "But I doubt you drove here from Oregon, right?"

"Didn't have the time."

"Should Fallyn come to visit you, the good news is there's a dialysis lab in Newport." He winked at the child. "She'd be protected if she needed help."

Claire frowned. Had Angie said something to the doctor? Or Brennan? Why else would the doctor have mentioned that? The idea, though, set Claire's mind spinning. With triplets, Angie might welcome a summer of fun at the beach for Fallyn. Claire could think of nothing she'd rather do.

Brennan dropped Claire and Fallyn off at the house after the doctor's appointment. Angie slept in the recliner when they entered, the television murmuring in the corner. Claire took her niece's hand and led her back to the front door. "Want to walk to the corner convenience store and get a small ice cream cone?" She opened the door, noticing how cold the blast of air felt. The child's shiver didn't escape her attention. "Or would you be too cold?"

"Chocolate peanut butter?" Fallyn's eyes twinkled, ignoring the question.

"Is that your favorite?"

"Uh-huh." Fallyn glanced behind her, checking on Angie who still slept. "Don't tell Mommy."

"Are you not supposed to have ice cream?"

Angie's voice sounded from the other side of the room. "She'd be better off with something protein. Nothing salty."

"Mommy. A little one, please?"

"Let's go see what else they have, Fallyn. You want to stay healthy." Claire hurried to re-button the child's coat. Fallyn's pale skin and deep circles beneath her eyes contrasted with the bright red wool she wore. The sparkle in the hazel irises masked the truth of her condition.

Claire wrapped her own jacket tighter around her. Spring hadn't yet broken here, the wind's bite deep and mean. She opened the door and Fallyn reached for her fingers. As they ambled down the sidewalk, Fallyn chattered about the trees along the street and the barking dog behind a fence. Claire could think of nothing better than listening to the child's ramblings. Despite her health concerns, Fallyn acted like a happy little girl, one who had been loved and nurtured. Claire prayed Angie would have the energy to continue that level of care when the triplets arrived.

They found a small, round table by the shop's door where they could sit and enjoy their treat. Claire chose a hot unsalted pretzel first, then ordered a tiny, baby cone.

Fallyn ate with caution, licking at the drips as they occurred, but not in a hurry to make the cone disappear. She stared around her, remarking on the variety of snacks waiting against the wall. A soda machine at the end of the counter caught her attention. "Have you ever tasted soda, Aunt Claire?"

"Yes." What kind of question was that? "I like the grape-flavored ones."

"They have grape?" Fallyn's eyes grew wide. "I always thought the orange ones looked good."

"Have you tasted soda?" Claire understood Angie's pre-occupation with healthful habits for her daughter, but did soda hold some hidden danger for the child? She remembered the doctor's words, "Plenty of water will do wonders." Angie had always been one to take every word literally. This might be one of those times.

Surely soda, though it wasn't water, could be permitted once in a while?

"No. Mommy says it's bad for my kidneys."

Claire's heart sank. She couldn't disobey Angie's wishes, but part of her wanted to buy a huge grape soda and give Fallyn a sip. She reached for the napkins instead, offering one to Fallyn whose chin sported melted chocolate. "Maybe we can taste grape soda together one day. Would you like that?"

Fallyn's eyes twinkled as if Claire had promised her the moon. She took another lick of her cone and handed it to Claire. "I can't eat anymore. My tummy feels too cold."

Claire stared at the uneaten portion. Fallyn had barely touched the frozen confection, and there'd been less than a quarter cup to begin with. How sick was this child? The melting ice cream in Claire's palm made worry trickle down her spine. Fallyn needed a lot more than a drink of grape soda. The child might soon need a miracle.

Tuesday broke bright and sunny. Monty gave thanks he'd chosen the day as one of his shore leaves. Ellen packed him a picnic lunch and left it on the counter with a note telling him to be sure and grab the drinks from the refrigerator when he left.

He placed the drink pack on top of the basket and called Mia and Mason to follow him to the truck.

"Where are we going today, Dad?"

"I know a stretch of beach down the road where we can have a picnic and fly our kite."

"Will Miss Claire come too?" Mia bounced forward, peeking over the passenger seat. "She liked flying kites last time."

"No, Miss Claire is spending spring break in Pennsylvania with her sister." Monty tweaked Mia's upturned nose. "Put your seatbelt on."

"I wish Miss Claire was coming." Mason plunked himself against the bench seat and snapped his seatbelt. "She helped me hold the string when the wind got too strong."

"I can help you." Monty frowned. Did his kids think he couldn't function without Claire's help? Sure, she'd made it easier, but he wasn't without resources. "Ready for our adventure?"

"Can we go by our new house and swing when we get done?" Mia had enjoyed Lenny and Corbin's efforts to finish the swing set last Saturday. But by the time they had the play set upright and secured, darkness had almost settled over the yard. The kids climbed on their new equipment for little more than ten minutes before it was time to leave. They'd been disappointed, but once assured the swings would remain to entertain them when moving day came later in the week, the twins agreed to return to Ellen's.

"Yes, we'll drop by the house. I want to see how much carpet the installers laid today." Monty winked at Mia in the rearview mirror. "But I'm wearing sunglasses when I go into your room."

Mia giggled. "Daddy. You need to get used to it. I like pink!"

"And kittens." Mason drummed his fingers on the window. "Don't forget Mia likes kitties."

The sound of two small hands meeting for a high-five smack in the back uncovered the twins' conspiracy. The little rascals. *How could I forget?*

Monty headed toward Beachside State Park. The bright day promised warmth, assuring the kids a fun experience as they discovered the nice stretch of beach where they could run. The wind blew strong from the ocean, catching his truck in pockets of roadway where the trees didn't provide a breaker. If the gusts were too great, the kite would be difficult to control. He prayed the strength of the breeze would relax a little by the time he arrived.

He parked in the Day Use area. The wind gusted against the

truck, rocking it. One person walked the beach, bent over, holding his coat as he struggled in the wind.

Monty sighed. The twins would never manage the blasts of air coming off the ocean. What could he do to salvage their day together? He turned and looked at them, expectation written on their faces. "Kids. The wind is too strong here. People can't even walk along the water's edge."

"We can't fly our kite, can we?" The disappointment in Mason's voice matched his sagging brows.

"No, we can't. But I'm going to drive down the highway a ways and see what I can find to do that would be fun." Monty started the engine and drove out of the parking lot, heading south on Highway 101.

Within minutes, a community called Seal Rock emerged. On the east side of the highway were quaint shops offering everything from a bear carved by a chainsaw to a fudge shop. On the ocean side, Monty spotted a sign for the Seal Rock Wayside, a small pull-off beckoning him to stop. Parking, picnicking, and the promise of whale watching all waited on the visitor directory.

"This looks like a fun place to have our lunch." Monty parked and hopped to the asphalt. He helped the children from their seats. Mason took charge of the picnic basket and Mia carried the drink cooler. Monty grabbed the blanket and towels.

They followed a paved walkway through a thicket of undergrowth, rhododendrons, and other coastal plants. A small brown rabbit jumped from the low-lying bushes, wiggling his nose before hopping back into the brush. Monty spotted an empty picnic table and led the kids to the opening. Beyond them the ocean roared, the huge rock formations breaking the bite of the wind.

"Can we go down there, Dad?" Mason stood on the bench seat of the table, pointing to the rocky shoreline surrounding the larger rocks. "We can take our basket with us."

"It will be colder."

"But there are rocks to climb on and stuff." Mason spoke as if nothing else mattered. "Can we take our shoes off?"

Monty laughed and picked up the basket. He led the twins to the paved walkway again and they descended down the trail to a square landing that allowed viewing of the ocean in every direction. Monty gazed out over the water, looking for water spouts on the horizon. The migration of the grays north continued, and he'd love to show his kids a whale tail slapping the water. "Look! Look over there where the water is smoother."

Mason and Mia hopped up on the bench and leaned against the railing surrounding the wooden landing. They stared where he had pointed, their foreheads wrinkling in concentration. Suddenly Mia gasped. "I saw a water fountain." She pushed her chubby hand toward the water. "Like the sprinklers that shoot water up at that place we used to visit in the summer. When Mommy took us there to play."

Monty gulped at the comparison, then regained his composure. "That's a whale spouting." He put his hands on their shoulders, his head between theirs. "Watch where you saw the spray, Mia. You might see a tail."

Mason shouted and jumped. "I see it. I see a tail." He pointed to the left. "It's already gone, Daddy."

"They don't stay up long. Keep looking." Monty wished he had brought the binoculars. He'd no sooner thought of the glasses than a small whale breached quite a distance from shore.

Mia's mouth popped open. "It jumped, Daddy! It jumped out of the water!"

Mason had seen it, too. "Will they do it again?"

Monty smiled at his kids. "They might, but they are moving up the coast to a place where they spend most of their year. The water will be colder and the food more plentiful. Then late next December they'll migrate back down again. That's what I was doing on the ship. Tracking the migration of these whales."

"You get paid to watch whales?" Mason's face beamed. "That would be a job I'd like to do."

Monty remembered the words of his superior. *"Encourage the boy. He might one day be a NOAA scientist."* Watching Mason's enthusiasm, Monty could easily see that happening. "Let's go find some rocks to climb."

They left the landing and picked their way to the beach. Monty found a circle of rocks that the kids could sit on, and he set the basket on one. Opening the container, he distributed the food, the roar of the ocean keeping harmony with the call of the gulls behind him. The tide was in, and the waves blasted the rocks as they pushed through the narrow canyon between the high, rounded rock domes. The wind howled as it raced through the crowded passageway.

"After we eat, we'll explore the tide pools and see if we can find a crab or a starfish."

"Can we take one home, if we find something?"

Monty offered Mia a napkin, pointing to the mayonnaise on her chin, and watched as she cleaned her mouth. "Neither a crab or a starfish would be happy going home with us, Mia. They prefer to stay here where the water is always available and the ocean not far away."

"Do you think the kite would fly here, Dad?" Mason spoke between bites. "The kite is tough."

"No, the wind is too strong." Monty smiled at the boy's belief in his flyer. "The kite is only a toy in its power."

"And the kite gives in, doesn't it?"

"Yes, it yields to the force against it, causing it to soar higher. But by doing so it preserves itself. Otherwise it could snap in two." Monty spotted a gull soaring in the wind, bouncing as the gusts knocked it during flight. "See that seagull? He's riding the wind right now, giving in to its power. Letting the wind carry him helps the bird achieve greater success."

"Are we like seagulls, Dad?"

Monty wished Claire had joined them. Mason's questions made him think too much, as if God used his child's curiosity to probe his own soul. An inner voice poked at him, repeating Mason's question. Wasn't he, like a kite, resisting the power of the Almighty God? When he surrendered, God took him places he'd like to be, didn't He? Monty had said yes to the move to Newport, a change that gave him more time to spend with his family.

He chose his words with care. "We are like the kite when we resist hearing God's voice and obeying him. We flounder in the same way the kite spins and dips and doesn't go anywhere. Sometimes we even crash. When we surrender ourselves to His will like the seagull is doing, God takes us places we never would have known, just like the bird gives in to the wind and flies higher."

"That's cool, Dad." Mason craned his neck as if seeking the bird above him. "I want to soar like the seagull."

"Learn to listen for God's voice, Son."

Monty closed his eyes and gave thanks. A simple question from his second grader had reached into the depths of his soul, making him face the reality of his situation. He'd said yes to his sister's offer to care for the children, enabling him to accept NOAA's invitation to relocate. Staying in Seattle, he would have further plummeted into despair. He now had a new home where different memories could be made. As if he were tethered by an unseen force, he had ascended in the power of God's divine will.

Coming south he'd met Claire, an undeserved gift from a generous God. Thinking about her made him feel as if he could fly to the moon. Should their relationship continue, he might find love again. He'd fulfill his promise to Marissa—their children would have a new mother. Mia and Mason wouldn't be her biological children, but he knew Claire's heart welcomed and returned the twins' love.

He lifted his gaze to the heavens. *I'm still listening, Lord. In your time, make it so.*

CHAPTER TWENTY-SIX

WHY DID THE NINE DAYS HAVE to pass so quickly? Claire's flight back to Oregon tomorrow left little time for any meaningful activities with her niece. She'd taxi to the airport while Brennan took Fallyn to Sunday school and Angie stayed in bed. Her brother-in-law offered to drive her, but saying good-bye to Fallyn promised to be emotional, and Claire preferred her tears be shed among friends. If Fallyn waved as she walked to her gate, Claire feared she'd race back to the child, missing her flight.

Instead, she'd hugged Fallyn goodbye tonight, kissing her on the forehead, and reading a bedtime story. Tucking the little girl under the covers, she'd whispered a prayer over her, and tiptoed out. She'd returned to the guest room to pack her bag. A soft knock sounded. "Come in."

Brennan stuck his head in the door. "Fallyn's asleep. Angie wants to talk with you a minute."

Claire frowned inwardly. Angie had been quiet at dinner, her breathing difficult. Today completed week thirty-five. Seven days closer to Angie's due date, seven days that could mean the difference between strong triplets able to come home and hold their own, or babies destined for an extended stay in the intensive care unit. Claire prayed the babies would wait for their debut so Angie could be home with them and with Fallyn. She could easily shortchange her eldest daughter in the flurry of activity surrounding three small and needy newborns.

"Hi, Sis." Claire entered the room and sat on the edge of the mattress. "Brennan said you wanted to talk?"

Angie's face reflected no smile, eyes shuttered, jaw tight. "We need to discuss Fallyn's future."

Claire wrinkled her nose. "What? High School? College? Give

me a clue, please."

"Immediate future." Angie sank against the pillows and sighed, the bulge of her abdomen forming a dome under the blankets.

"You mean her health?" Claire picked at a thread on the comforter, tracing the pattern of a yellow rose with her finger. "I know she's facing huge challenges."

"You and I both know she's going to need a kidney sooner or later." Angie stared at the ceiling, blinking as though she fought tears. "I'm going to have my hands full with three babies. I don't know how I'll be able to get her to multiple treatments, should they arise."

"Isn't that why you hired Mrs. Thornton? To help you with three newborns?"

"Yes. But it's more than that." Angie narrowed her eyes. "Fallyn needs more from me than I'm going to be able to give. She's enamored with you."

"For that I am grateful." Claire patted Angie's knee. "You kept me in the loop."

Angie twisted the comforter in her fingers. "I'd like to send her home with you. She wants to see the ocean. She could finish the school year in Oregon. That's only ten more weeks.""

"Ten weeks to a five-year-old could seem like forever." Claire's mind whirred as she weighed the possibilities. "And I work full-time."

"Most teachers do. Even those with families." Angie leaned forward, grunting as her middle got in the way of the effort. "Fallyn is school-age now. While you work, she can spend her day in school there as well as she can attend kindergarten here."

"Don't you think this is kind of sudden?" Claire stood, the need to pace the room overwhelming. Then she stopped and turned. "Dr. Blackwell told me we have a dialysis clinic in Newport. I wondered why he said that." She looked at her sister. "You've already broached the subject with him, haven't you?"

Angie nodded, her mouth downturned, her eyes squeezed shut. "Guilty."

"A little pre-mature, aren't you?"

"Brennan packed her bags yesterday." Angie leaned back against the pillow. "He agreed we need your help. These next few weeks are going to be touch and go for us. We may face a crisis without warning. Please consider doing this for Fallyn, if not for me."

"Have you told her?"

"Brennan asked her what she thought." Angie's eyes pooled. "She cried and wanted to know if I was going to be all right." Her voice faltered. "She said the doctor should give me antibiotics like he gave her."

"What a sweetheart."

"I know. This is going to be hard on all of us." Angie sniffed. "But Brennan promised her time at the ocean if she went. She asked if she could stay the entire summer and feel the breezes."

Claire couldn't believe her next words. "I'll see that she has a great summer."

Angie groaned, holding her side. Her eyes closed, she lay still, the wrinkles across her brow deep and face pain-filled. She took a breath and blew it out. "Thank you. Fallyn needs someone she can rely on. A person with whom she can share her triumphs. I'm out of commission at the moment."

"You'll be back on your feet and ready to mother her in no time." Claire went to the head of the bed and kissed her sister. "I need to book a flight for Fallyn."

"Brennan has her school records ready, the legal papers giving you authority to seek treatment for her, and the medical records." Angie gave her a wistful smile. "We already booked the flight."

"Am I that predictable?"

"Your love for Fallyn wouldn't let you do anything else."

Monty grunted as he shoved Mia's dresser into place. Lenny stood behind him, holding the empty drawers. Corbin sat on the floor, cordless drill in hand, screwing the headboard and footboard of the bed to the rails. The mattress and box springs waited against the wall.

Mia stood in the doorway with Ellen, chattering about the curtains the pair wanted to hang on the windows once the men were finished. "Do you think the walls are too pink, Auntie Ellen?" Mia held the sheer curtains against the fresh, painted wall beside her. "Daddy said he's going to need sunglasses to come in here."

Ellen laughed. "Look how your white furniture breaks the pink into smaller sections, Mia. With those curtains your room will be the showiest one on the block. Maybe Dad will let you have a sleepover."

"Will you come?" Mia's brow wrinkled. "I don't think Daddy can handle a room full of girls."

Ellen looked at him, her mouth pursed, and eyes twinkling as she fought the laugh he saw there. "I'd be delighted to come. We'll make taffy."

"Oh, taffy!" Mia jumped up and down. "I can't wait."

Monty leveled what he hoped Ellen caught as a panicked stare. A slumber party? With little girls? Ellen better keep her promise. Or send a recruit. A certain woman with blonde curls and caramel eyes came to mind. Maybe coming encounters would provide the environment in which she could help. Otherwise, Mia faced huge disappointment.

"Monty, is the bed where you want it?" Corbin stood, holding the supports for the mattress. "We can put the mattress in place."

Monty glanced at Ellen. "What do you think?"

"I think Mia will sleep better if the bed sits alongside the dresser and points into the room."

Lenny and Corbin swung the bed around, placed the supports across the rails, and lowered the box spring and mattress into place.

"Perfect." Ellen grabbed the bag of bedding she'd ordered for Mia's room and, with the child beside her, went to work making the bed. "I have sheets and comforters for Mason's room as well."

Monty nodded at Lenny and Corbin, and both men rolled their heads in a circle, lifting their shoulders as if their muscles were tight before following him to Mason's room. With their help today, the job of setting the furniture in place had moved as smoothly as the hands on a clock. Only his room and the odd-shaped corner room on the second floor remained. Ellen thought it should be a guest room. He and the children would sleep in their new home tonight.

Ellen called after them. "Dinner will be served in about half an hour."

"I can already smell it cooking, ma'am." Lenny breathed in deep, the aroma of oregano and sage wafting up the stairs from the kitchen. "Spaghetti?"

"Good guess." Ellen had taken the children shopping for groceries and returned with bags of goods to stock the refrigerator and fill the cupboards. While Mia put pots and pans in place, Mason lined wastebaskets and garbage containers and carried them to their rightful rooms. Ellen had filled the Crockpot with homemade spaghetti sauce. The children kept busy, enjoying their roles as helpers. Once dinner cooked, Ellen directed the children to fill the silverware trays while she lifted the tableware to their waiting shelves.

He couldn't have asked for a more efficient job of organizing his kitchen if he'd brought in a consultant. He'd miss Ellen's input as he and the children navigated the uncharted waters of living in their new home. Kevin had arrived in San Diego yesterday. Tomorrow she'd meet her husband at the Portland airport for a long-awaited reunion. Monty doubted he'd see the couple in Newport before mid-week. He swallowed the pain that surfaced every time he thought of the joy married couples found in each other, his heart still tender over losing Marissa.

They finished Mason's room a short while later. Monty had saved a spot on the wall for the dragon kite to hang between outings. He placed a hook above Mason's bed and fastened the frame securely to it. Lenny helped fix the tail in place, and Corbin made a spot for the ball of string to stay.

Mason came into the room and gasped.

Monty chuckled at his son's astonished face. "You like it above your bed?"

"Does this mean we can't fly it anymore?" The child's crestfallen face spoke volumes.

"No, the kite will soar again. But it needs somewhere to sleep between beach outings. I thought your room would be the best place for it."

"All right!" Mason raised both hands as if he'd scored a touchdown. He pulled out the bedcovers Ellen had left. "Did you see my stuff, Daddy?" The sheets tumbled from the bag, falling on top of the comforter. Kites of all sizes, colors, and shapes composed the pattern that filled the blue background, their tails winsome renditions of the kite's own on the wall.

"Whoa!" Lenny's eyes widened. "When you said he likes kites, you weren't kidding."

Monty shook out the bedding, handing the sheets to Lenny and Corbin. They helped Mason tuck the layers in around the corners. Monty floated the comforter over the top and tossed the pillow to its spot. "I think this will be a great room for you, sport."

"I love it." Mason danced around the room, touching his

dresser, checking his closet, and peering into his toy box. "I'm glad to have my own room."

"Dinner!" Ellen's voice carried up the stairs.

Monty gestured for Lenny and Corbin to precede him as they bounded down the stairs.

Fallyn couldn't contain her enthusiasm. Claire gave the child the window seat, telling her what to look for on the ground below. "I see mountains!"

"Snow on them?"

"Um-hmm." Fallyn pressed her nose to the glass. "Two little airplanes are flying down there. Above a lot of trees." She pointed. "Now there's clouds. How do they know where to fly?"

"Planes come with navigation systems that tell them how high they are and which direction they need to go."

"What's a nabigation system?"

"Navigation." Claire touched the child's hair. "Your daddy's car has lighted circles on the dashboard?"

"Yes." Fallyn frowned. "Mommy's always telling him to watch his speed."

Claire grinned at the child's revelation about Brennan. Fallyn didn't miss much. "Planes have indicators like those, too. Only the gauges tell how fast the wind is, or how strong, things like that. The pilot flies the plane based on that information."

"Will we see the ocean from up here?"

"Not if there are clouds." Claire tried to remember if she could see much when she landed in Portland before. "I'm not sure. It will depend on the approach the pilot uses, and the amount of daylight left." She squeezed Fallyn's shoulder. "Don't worry. If we can't see it from up here, we will when we drive home to my house."

"Your house is on the ocean?" Fallyn's eyes widened.

"Not far." Claire leaned back against the headrest. "You can see the ocean from your school playground."

"I can't wait." Fallyn grew quiet, sitting straighter in her seat. "I think I need a nap."

Claire wrapped an arm about the child, drawing her closer. Fallyn's eyes fluttered closed and little soft snores soon filled the immediate space around them. Claire stroked the wispy hair curling about the child's forehead, fearful of the sunken eyes and dark circles beneath.

Fallyn murmured in her sleep. "Mommy."

Her heart broke for the little girl who'd had to leave her family behind. What would she do if Fallyn grew critical in her care? The little body tucked next to her heart threatened to steal it. But if Claire were honest, she'd already given it away a long time ago. Fallyn had always been special.

CHAPTER TWENTY-SEVEN

"CLAIRE?" SHE TURNED TO THE SOUND of her name as she and Fallyn headed toward the baggage claim. Ellen Norse quick-stepped her direction, waving her hand.

"What brings you here?" Claire couldn't believe her good fortune, finding her newest and dearest friend waiting at the same airport where she and her niece had landed. "I'm in shock."

"Kevin's flight is due any minute." Ellen's enthusiasm oozed from her, the twinkle in her eyes conveying the happiness she felt. "He's finally home."

"I'm so happy for you." Claire hugged her and stepped back. "Did you get Monty out of the house on time?"

"Yes. He and the twins moved into their own home this week. Spent the night yesterday." Ellen's gaze drifted to Fallyn, who peeked from Claire's side at the stranger. "Who is your delightful little sidekick?"

"This is my niece, Fallyn O'Brien. She's come to stay with me for a while." Claire gave Fallyn a squeeze on the shoulder. "My sister is having triplets and is on total bed rest until the babies make their appearance. So Fallyn came home with me."

Ellen studied the child, a look of surprise written on her face. "This is Angie's little girl?"

"Yes. Fallyn stole all our hearts and keeps them locked away." Claire winked at her niece, the child's shy smile lighting up her face. "She wants to see the ocean."

"Plenty of that here." Ellen held out her hand and Fallyn took it. "I'm so glad you've come to stay with Claire. My niece and nephew are eight, and I know they will want to meet you. They have a new swing set to play on. Would you enjoy that?"

Fallyn nodded, still clinging to Claire's side.

"Thanks, Ellen. Fallyn will be at school tomorrow. Perhaps she can meet Mia and Mason then."

"I hope she can." Ellen grew quiet, her voice conspiratorial. "Kevin and I are spending some time in Portland before we come home."

"I'm so glad." Claire gave her friend a wide smile. "I'll look forward to meeting him when you return."

Ellen stepped back, twisting her watch to check the time. "Kevin's plane is probably ready to unload its passengers. I'd better go." She gave Fallyn one last smile. "I hope to see you again soon, Fallyn."

Claire took Fallyn's hand. "I see our luggage is on the carousel. Enjoy your time with your husband." She turned and hurried toward the baggage claim, Ellen's demeanor lingering.

Her reaction to Fallyn had almost seemed too businesslike. Maybe meeting Fallyn and knowing she was adopted had struck a chord with her friend, a reminder that Ellen hadn't conceived and if she didn't, adoption remained an option. If nothing else, Fallyn's presence should have given Ellen hope of being a mother. Angie's journey had not been lost on her.

Fallyn stared wide-eyed as she followed Claire into the homey duplex. Though Claire enjoyed the cozy space, having Fallyn share the area shrank the place by half. Would Fallyn find the home cramped after living in Brennan and Angie's spacious craftsman?

"Is this my bedroom?" Fallyn had found the door to the room Claire reserved for her office and also doubled as space for guests. She'd need to move the large office desk out. The twin bed, with its floral print, and short chest of drawers left space to accommodate a smaller table for Fallyn's play area and schoolwork, should she have any sent home from kindergarten. Claire doubted she'd have much. "Auntie Claire?"

"Yes. We'll go shopping for a new comforter and matching sheets as soon as I can find a spare moment." Claire carried the travel bag into the room, searching the child's face for signs of disappointment. She found none. "Try the bed and see if you like the mattress."

Fallyn flopped on the bed, kid-style, and turned over, facing the ceiling. "It's just my size." She sat up and grinned. "Like Goldilocks and Baby Bear's bed."

Claire laughed, and clapped her hands, delighted at the child's analogy. "Do you feel like you are Goldilocks sneaking into the bears' home?"

"No. I came in the front door with you." Fallyn bounced on the mattress. "The bed is perfect because it's in your house." She fluffed the pillow. "I've always wanted to see where you live. Sometimes I visit my Aunt Morgan, Daddy's sister."

Claire fought the tears threatening to intrude. "I'm glad you're happy." She reached for the suitcase still sitting on the floor and lifted it beside Fallyn. "Let's see what kind of clothes your Dad packed for you. We may need to go shopping for those too. This isn't Pennsylvania."

"You mean I don't have to dress like a polar bear?" Fallyn's wide grin lit her face as she teased. How did a five-year-old come up with such sophisticated phrases? "That's what you said I looked like when we went ice skating at Christmas."

"That's right. I did. What a memory." She pulled a pair of pajamas from the bag's interior. Flannel and pink. Panties. Pink. Socks. Pink. Corduroy jumper. Pink. Pink-flowered blouse. "Fallyn, is your favorite color pink?"

"Mommy said pink turns me into an angel, and I don't look so sick when I'm wearing it." Fallyn studied her shoes. "But I also like blue." She covered her mouth with her hands. "I shouldn't have said that. I could hurt Mommy's feelings."

"It won't hurt *my* feelings. If you like blue, we'll find you something new in blue."

"Even a comforter?" Fallyn touched the floral cover on the bed. "I mean this is pretty, but I've seen blue ones in the store."

Poor child. Swamped in pink at every turn. She understood Angie's fashion sense, having always dressed her girl dolls in frilly pink frocks, but to force that on a living child made Claire cringe. Yes, pink quite possibly would make Fallyn look healthier, but wearing a color she loved could brighten her outlook, too. Claire always chose russets, forest greens, and beiges for her clothes because her coloring needed fall hues. Fallyn's hazel eyes would shine in something sky blue. "You shall have a blue comforter and a blue outfit as soon as we can make it possible."

Fallyn jumped up and hugged Claire as tight as her arms would allow. "Oh, thank you. I knew visiting you would be fun."

Claire stroked the child's blonde tresses. "We'll have a great summer together."

"Lots of ocean." Fallyn grew sober. "How long is a summer?"

"June, July and August."

"I'll miss Mommy and Daddy."

"I know you will. When you return home, you'll have two new little brothers and another sister." She squeezed Fallyn's shoulders and turned the child to face her. "You'll be the big sister."

"But you'll be left without anybody." Fallyn's hazel eyes peeked up at her. "If I stayed here, you wouldn't be lonely."

Claire bit her lip and closed her eyes. If only.

Monty hurried the twins into the truck, anxious to get them to school on time. His right shoulder ached from lifting heavy pieces of furniture yesterday, and his left leg burned from climbing the stairs one too many times. Though Lenny and Corbin worked alongside him all day, they hadn't complained. He wasn't that much older than they were, was he? He owed them a huge favor. Maybe he could take them to lunch one day when they were all working the same schedule. He gave thanks the worst part of the moving had finished.

"Will Miss Claire be back from her trip?" Mason hooked his own seat belt while Monty tossed his backpack on the front seat. "I want her to see my new room."

"She should be." Monty lifted Mia to the seat, planning his invitation for her to see their new house—with them in it.

"Can I tell her we're getting a kitten?" Mia's eyes danced at the possibility. "You said you'd think about it."

"I *am* thinking about it." Monty growled at Mia, drawing close enough to rub foreheads and make goofy eyeballs with her. She giggled. He lifted her backpack and set it next to Mason's. "Be patient. Hook your seatbelt."

"Daddy! Please!"

"What is our rule about whining?"

Mia grew quiet and settled into her seat. "Sorry."

He drove into the school loading zone, scanning the sidewalk for Claire. Her absence this past week had troubled him. He'd missed her bright smile, the way she loved on his kids, her wholesome no-nonsense approach to life. Without even trying, she'd wiggled her way into a space in his heart he'd thought would forever be vacant. The hurt left there following Marissa's death had been slowly pushed to the back of his heart, like the furniture he'd stored when he moved, and hope had arrived, bringing with it the joy he and the kids had found in their new home. He wanted Claire to see his digs, now occupied, the kid rooms, now painted, and the kitchen, fully stocked, thanks to Ellen. Who was he fooling? He wanted Claire to see herself in his new house. Her opinion mattered to him, probably more than it should.

He killed the engine and stepped out, moving to the other side where he could help Mason and Mia from their seats. No Claire. Did she miss her flight home?

"Isn't Miss Claire going to meet us, Daddy?" Mia's thumb flew to her mouth as she frowned at the vacant spot where Claire usually waited.

"She'll be here, sweetie." Monty reached into the cab for the backpacks and helped the children shrug into them. He handed the twins their lunches. He took the hand of each and led them to the door where they began their school day, Mia's palm damp from the sucked thumb earlier. "She won't miss work."

"Monty!" He swiveled to the sound of Claire's voice behind him, surprised she led a small child beside her. Face flushed, she smiled, waving at Mason and Mia. "Hi, kids."

"We thought you weren't coming." Mia's discouraged face reflected how relieved she was to see her teacher. "You need to see my new room!"

"We tried to fly kites last week." Mason raised his arms above his head, making a pulling motion with his hands. "But the wind was too strong. So we played in tide pools."

"But we found a crab!" Mia bounced on her toes. "And saw a whale's tail!"

"Sounds like you had a wonderful spring vacation." She tugged the girl beside her forward. "I'd like you to meet my niece, Fallyn O'Brien. She's come to live with me for a while because her Mommy is having triplets and needed bed rest."

"Triplets?" Monty forced his jaw to close, remembering the shock of Marissa conceiving twins. "That's going to be a lot of work for her and her husband." He focused his attention on the child, kneeling down to her level, his muscles reminding him of how much furniture he'd moved over the weekend. "I'm happy to meet you, Fallyn. Sometime maybe you can come and play with Mia and Mason at our new house."

Fallyn cast him a shy smile. "Okay."

Monty looked from Fallyn to Claire. "She certainly carries a family resemblance."

"You think so?" Claire's cheeks grew red, the blush creeping along her neck and up her jaw. Was it something he'd said? But he was right. The child's blonde curls and deep-set eyes, except for their color, could have passed for Claire's facial features without anyone giving them a second thought. Claire drew the child in front of her, arms wrapped about Fallyn's neck. "I'll take her any way she comes. Ellen invited her to meet Mia and Mason."

"When did you see Ellen?" Monty tried to figure out the time of Ellen's departure for Portland and Claire's arrival. "Did you meet at the airport?"

"Yes." Claire knelt before the twins. "Are you two ready for school?"

"Yes!" They hugged her in unison.

Fallyn stood there staring, a faint smile on her lips. Monty winked at her. "My kids really like your Auntie Claire."

"I do, too."

Mason glanced her way. "Do you like to fly kites?"

Fallyn shrugged. "I don't know."

"We fly them over the ocean." Mason spread his hands wide.

Fallyn's eyes lit up. "Auntie Claire promised to take me to the ocean."

Monty grinned at the little girl. "I work on the ocean, so I know you're going to like it a lot."

"He swims with whales." Mia smiled at Fallyn's gasp. Without a breath she spoke again. "Do you like dolls?"

Fallyn nodded and looked at her aunt, her face unreadable.

"We'll have to work out a play date later." Claire held out her hand. "It's time for class, kids." She turned, Fallyn on her right and Mia on her left. Mason fell in behind. She called over her shoulder. "See you after school."

Monty stood motionless, watching the three children disappear into the building. Like the Pied Piper of Hamlin, Claire worked her magic with the kids, each of them happy to be with her today. He returned to his truck, climbed in the cab, and started the engine. Only then did he notice the rain beginning to fall. He turned on his wipers, the squeak of one reminding him he needed a new blade.

As he pulled out of the parking lot, Monty thought of Ellen and Kevin, who planned to come home later this week, leaving him to pick up the twins today. The inconvenience made him smile from ear to ear.

CHAPTER TWENTY-EIGHT

"CHANDLER? CAPTAIN REYNOLDS IS LOOKING FOR you." Monty nodded at the messenger and strode across the grounds to NOAA headquarters. He entered the building, traipsed down the hall to his supervisor's office, and stepped into the doorway. "You wanted to see me, sir?"

"Ah, Monty, come in, please." Reynolds gestured to a nearby chair. "Have a seat."

Monty did as requested, his curiosity piqued at the man's summons.

"I know you only returned from sea assignment a month ago, but I've got an urgent request for personnel with underwater expertise to form a team headed to the Bering Sea."

"Alaska?" His experience dealt mainly with underwater sea life in warm waters, not the frozen north. He'd never tested his wetsuit in that environment. Let alone his abilities.

"Further than that. A crabbing boat with a crew of six has gone missing in the upper northern waters near St. George Island in the Pribilofs. It seems to have disappeared without a trace. We need people with underwater sonar skills as well as diving training to search."

"What kind of time frame?" Monty didn't want to put his kids on hold any more than necessary. They'd already endured one six-week-absence this year. "My family moved into our new home yesterday. I haven't unpacked everything. Leaving so soon would churn the waters."

"I know. That's why I offered your services for only a week." His supervisor leaned on his chin. "You'd leave Wednesday and return next week."

"Wednesday?" Monty worked to keep his mouth from hanging

open, but he couldn't stop the gasp. "My sister is the one who watches the children while I'm gone. Her husband returned from overseas deployment yesterday, so they've taken a little time away." He shook his head, thinking. "I don't know anyone I could ask to take her place." Sometimes his job demanded more than he, and now Ellen, could give. His sister deserved this time with Kevin. Captain Reynolds needed to find someone else. "I'm sorry."

"Could you think about it for twenty-four hours?" His boss leaned across the desk. "Surely someone could fill in for you. I'm desperate for an officer with your expertise to make this mission."

Monty stood and offered his hand. "Twenty-four hours. But right now I'm coming up empty." He turned to go. "Promise me you'll look elsewhere."

His boss looked grim. "Promise me you'll try."

Monty exited the office and headed toward his work area heavy-hearted. Mason and Mia hadn't had time to adjust to sleeping in their new rooms or exploring their new house. He couldn't just bundle them up and ship them off to another place so soon. They'd endured enough trauma in their lives. Ellen would take them if she were here, but he wouldn't attempt to find her. She and her husband needed time to get re-acquainted. Fall back in love. Make a baby. Captain Reynolds asked too much.

Claire stood with Mia and Mason as they waited after school for Monty to pick them up. She'd asked Fallyn's teacher to keep her niece in the classroom until she could come. Tonight they were going to buy bedding for Fallyn's room. But first she'd keep her promise to Fallyn and drive to Yaquina Bay for a glimpse of the Pacific Ocean.

The child couldn't stop talking about the air here. "Why does it smell so crisp?"

"Crisp?"

"Like it's clean or something."

Claire assured her that what she smelled was ocean air—a fresh, salty scent that blew in non-stop from the west. Once Fallyn witnessed the size of the waters that stretched to the horizon, she'd understand the enormity of the force that bore her *crisp* air. Claire could only imagine the questions to follow.

Monty's truck circled the parking lot and drew to a stop near the loading zone. He stepped from the cab and approached them. "Hey."

"Daddy!" The twins trotted toward their father, arms outstretched.

He bent down and waited, his smile not meeting his eyes. "How was your first day back?"

Mia and Mason broke into excited chatter, each with their own story to tell. Mia had seen a stray kitten wandering near the playground she was certain was hungry and lonely. Mason flashed a new book he'd picked up at the library about early flying machines. Monty listened for a moment then led the children to the truck, lifted them to their seats, and shut the door. He turned toward her.

Claire studied the scene, a niggling sense at the back of her mind that something bothered the man. She resisted the urge to pry. "Looks like you've got this under control. Enjoy your evening."

"Claire, wait." Monty came to where she stood. "I've got a problem."

She frowned. "What? Has something happened? It's not Ellen, is it?"

"No." He shuffled his feet as if he were about to unload a bomb at her doorstep. "A vessel disappeared off the coast of Alaska last week, and I've been asked to join the search team. One of their sonar technicians is on a leave of absence."

"Is that good?"

"Ellen and Kevin are on a second honeymoon." Monty's voice dropped to a whisper. "I know this is probably against school policy, but would you consider living at my house with the twins for a week?"

Claire gasped. "Me? Remember, I'm now caring for Fallyn."

"I set up a guest room with two twin beds. It's that spare room Ellen and I couldn't decide what use it would serve." Monty glanced around, as if searching for listening ears. "You could share it with Fallyn and be close to the twins."

"How soon do you need to know?"

"Tomorrow?" Monty inhaled and made a face. "I know. It's a crazy request. Borders on impropriety. But I'm desperate. And the kids would have no problem with you."

"Let me think on it tonight." Claire resisted the urge to touch him. "I'll give you an answer in the morning."

"Thanks. I have to leave Wednesday." Monty took her hand. "If you say yes, I'll set the booster seats in your car that morning."

Claire nodded. "And I'll take them home."

He grinned. "I wanted you to see our new house with its furniture set up. This is definitely going to be an intimate look at how we live."

"I prefer calling it an insider's eye view."

"Works for me."

As the truck drove off the school grounds, Claire let the breath she'd been holding whoosh away. What was he thinking? Stay at his house? Even the thought made her blush.

"Claire?"

She spun on her heel and her heart dropped to her toes. The kindergarten teacher stood holding Fallyn's hand, tears trickling down the child's cheeks. Claire rushed to Fallyn's side and knelt before her, cupping the child's sad little face in her hands. "Oh, sweetie. Did you think I wasn't coming?"

Fallyn nodded and her sobs grew louder. "I thought you forgot me."

Claire wrapped her arms about the small, shaking body. "I will never, ever, forget you. You are more important to me than any other person on earth." She drew back and held Fallyn by the shoulders. "Mia and Mason's dad needed to talk to me a minute. I'm sorry I was late."

Fallyn hiccoughed. "I miss my Mommy and Daddy." She sniffed, wiping the tears from her cheeks with the back of her hand.

Claire reached in her pocket for a tissue and pulled it out. She held it to Fallyn's nose. "Blow." When the child complied, she dabbed the tip of the little nose with the tissue. "I'm sorry I made you cry. Shall we go find some ocean for you to see?"

"I can see it today?" Fallyn's eyes grew wide, tears subsiding as her excitement grew. "Oh, yes. Let's go see the ocean!"

Claire spoke to the teacher who waited. "Thanks for taking care of her for me."

"She's pretty fragile." The teacher frowned. "It doesn't take much to upset her. If she remains this insecure, she might need intervention."

"She's left her parents and flown halfway across the country, changed schools, and her living arrangement." Claire folded her arms across her chest. "That's a lot for a five-year-old to take in. I'll need to work harder to uphold my end of the deal."

The teacher graced her with a look meant to tame a grizzly bear. Claire accepted the censure, fully aware she'd left Fallyn without thinking. Acting as a mother should would mean adopting new habits. Claire refused to believe she'd grown set in her ways. She'd adjust to anything to lessen her niece's struggle. She took Fallyn's hand. "Let's go see that ocean."

Claire hugged Fallyn close to her, shielding the child from the force of the wind greeting them at Beachside State Park. She waited, allowing Fallyn to stare at the immense body of water that spread from where she stood to the horizon where the world appeared to drop off its edge. Her little mouth had popped open at the first glimpse of the massive waves rolling toward the sand, eyes wide, blonde curls flipping in the breeze coming off the breakers. She shivered.

"Are you cold?" Claire had carried jackets from the car, knowing within minutes the gusts could become intense. She offered Fallyn her coat and helped zip the front. "That better?" A smile rewarded her efforts.

"It's so big!" Fallyn turned away and faced the water again. "But I thought the ocean was blue." She looked up at Claire. "Isn't it supposed to be blue?"

"On a sunny day it will be blue. But we have clouds in the sky today and the ocean reflects the color above it. The wind ruffles the water and gives it those little ridges of white you see coming toward us. They are called whitecaps."

"Like ruffles on a petticoat."

"Where did you hear about petticoats?"

"I read a picture book about girls who used to wear long dresses and layers of petticoats under them." Fallyn raised her fingers to her forehead, shading her eyes. "Lots and lots of petticoats out there."

Claire laughed, squeezing Fallyn's shoulders. "You'll be seeing petticoats every time you come here. I guarantee it."

"I hope we come a lot. It smells so good here. Makes me hungry."

"And what would you like to eat, Miss Fallyn O'Brien?"

"Hamburger with fries?" Fallyn sneaked a peek her way, searching her face. "With grape soda?"

Claire took her hand. "What would your mother say to that?"

"She's not here, and you are." Fallyn scrunched up her face and wrinkled her nose. "You can decide. Can I? Please?"

"Let's go find a hamburger, but no fries."

"Okay. that's better than nothing."

Fallyn skipped ahead of her toward the car, her squeal of delight carried away by the growing force of the wind. Claire laughed at the child's enthusiasm. It took so little to make her happy. Remembering the tearful scene at the school, it also took little to make her sad.

The restaurant teemed with patrons as she and Fallyn entered the retro diner and found a table. Fallyn's curiosity knew no bounds. She pointed at the black and white checkerboard floor and exclaimed over the red tables with upholstered chairs the same color. Sitting down, she wanted to play the miniature jukebox on their table. Claire gave her a quarter for the machine and soon Elvis crooned from the small speaker. Fallyn sat captivated by the music, her face barely registering when her grape soda arrived with a straw and a napkin. The song ended, and the child stared up at Claire in awe. "Can I push another one?"

The waitress appeared beside them. "Hamburger basket with salad?"

"Me, me, me!" Fallyn raised her hand. "Oh, my grape soda is here too."

"Fish and salad?" The waitress slid the other basket in front of her.

Claire nodded her thanks, taking the ketchup bottle the waitress offered. "Fallyn, let's say thanks for our food."

Fallyn smacked her hands together and closed her eyes. "God, thank you for oceans, and hamburgers, and grape sodas. And for Auntie Claire. And help Mommy and Daddy get those new babies born. Amen."

Claire resisted the urge to laugh, handing Fallyn an extra napkin. "Looks good?""

Fallyn placed the napkin at her chin, took the hamburger, and bit into it. "Cut it, please?" While Claire divided the sandwich, Fallyn picked up a carrot stick and popped it in her mouth. "Umm. I love carrots."

Claire fingered a piece of fish and dipped it in the tartar sauce, taking a small bite. "You must be part rabbit."

Fallyn giggled, spearing her salad as if she'd not eat again for a week. The sad child with the tearful face at the school had disappeared, and a happy five-year-old had emerged. Claire forgave herself for having caused stress on Fallyn's first day here.

She forked a bite of salad to her mouth, her thoughts on Monty's dilemma. And what a quandary it was! He needed an answer tomorrow. She found the prospect of living in his home, even though the arrangement was purely innocent in its nature, a little jarring. Her reputation, especially in a town this small, could be permanently damaged if the facts were distorted. She did a mental inventory of her duplex. The sofa wasn't large, but it did make into a bed big enough for two small children. Mia and Fallyn could sleep together there. Mason could have the twin. She'd have to go back and forth to get enough clothing for the days Monty would be gone. He'd already offered the food, so feeding three children wouldn't be a problem.

Ellen would return before the weekend and, knowing the woman as she did, would offer to help. Claire anticipated meeting Kevin and sharing Ellen's joy at the return of her husband, but she would work extra hard to make sure Ellen didn't feel burdened with the twins in Monty's absence. Ellen needed to bond again with her husband. She'd waited too long.

Fallyn had stopped eating. Her smile sagged, and her eyes narrowed beneath her frown.

"What's the matter?" Claire became alarmed as the child rubbed her tummy. "Are you sick?"

Fallyn shook her head. "Full. To the brim." She looked as if she might cry. "I can't eat it all."

"It's okay, honey. We'll take the leftovers home. Did you like the grape soda?"

"The best I ever tasted."

"Let's go get you some new sheets and a comforter."

"I think I'd rather go home." Fallyn's eyes pooled. "I miss my Mommy."

Claire stood and gathered up the remnants of their dinner, taking Fallyn by the hand. Worried that she'd overindulged the child by giving her too much too soon, she led Fallyn to the car on shaking legs. She wasn't the natural at mothering that Angie was. She might need to get a few pointers from someone who knew better. If only Ellen were here.

CHAPTER TWENTY-NINE

MONTY CARRIED BACKPACKS FILLED WITH EXTRA clothing changes into Claire's duplex Tuesday night, relieved the twins had a place to stay while he was out of town. Order reigned in the small space—books on shelves, pillows on the sofa, dishes in their cupboards. After caring for his kids for a week, Claire might regret her decision to help him. Mason and Mia had learned how to perform chores early on but staying with Ellen had relaxed his grip on their responsibilities, and he was no longer certain they'd prove the reliable help he'd come to depend upon during Marissa's illness.

Claire showed Mason where the twin bed was and directed Mia to put her backpack next to the sofa. "You and Fallyn can share the hide-a-bed. Mason will have his own."

Monty held out the list he'd made—the pediatrician who cared for the children, people to call at work if she had an emergency, and Ellen's cell phone. Ellen would break speed records to get here if one of the twins fell into harm's way, but he didn't want her time with Kevin disturbed if it could be avoided. "Thanks for doing this. I won't be available by phone, so pass any messages on to my supervisor. He can reach me."

"Your house key?" Claire tacked the phone list to a bulletin board by the kitchen window. "I'm sure we'll run out of clothes, or toys, or some such thing before you return."

He fumbled in his pocket and pulled out the spare, placing it in her palm. Her soft hand radiated warmth as he brushed her fingers. He caught himself before he clasped her hand and squeezed. That would be the exact response she'd hoped to avoid. He knelt before the twins. "Mia, Mason, remember this is Miss Claire's home, and you need to respect it. Put your toys away when you're finished playing with them and keep your clothes in their packs. I'll see you when I return next Wednesday." He held out his arms. "Hugs?"

Mia embraced him first, her shampooed hair smelling like baby powder. He gave her an extra squeeze, kissing her on the forehead as he let go. Mason came next, his face unreadable, something Monty had learned meant the boy hid his feelings. He wouldn't cry in front of others, resolved to act like the man he wanted to be someday.

Monty stood to go but felt a hand on his waist. Below him Fallyn held out her arms, smile hopeful. He leaned over and lifted the petite girl off the floor. "What are you made of, little Miss Fallyn? Fairy dust?"

Fallyn giggled. "No. Hamburgers!"

"Hamburgers?" He poked her in the tummy. "You are light as a feather. You can't have eaten many burgers."

Claire reached for her niece. "We went to the Retro Diner after school yesterday, and she downed a jumbo sandwich. She was so full I feared she'd be sick today."

"Nah. Fallyn's stronger than that, aren't you, pretty girl?" He rubbed her shoulder. "You and Mia are going to be great friends. I know it."

Claire set the girl on the floor. "We'll be fine. Don't worry about us. Ellen will call me when she returns and probably steal your kids back."

"No! I want to stay with Miss Claire." Mason raised a fist in the air. "Miss Claire! Miss Claire! Miss Claire!"

Monty held up a hand. "Okay, okay. Calm down. Mason, remember what I said about respecting Miss Claire's home."

"Goodbye, Daddy." Mia turned away and carried her backpack to the sofa, holding Fallyn's hand. "I brought extra dolls for you to share with me. And a tea set."

Fallyn dropped to the floor beside Mia's pack. "Show me."

Monty backed away as he found the door. "Thanks again for

doing this."

"We'll have fun." Claire followed him out the doorway. "Ellen will call me when she returns."

"She'll be anxious to see the twins and spend time with Fallyn." Monty forced himself to leave. Sometimes his job pushed him to think about other careers. Leaving his children like this was one of those times. But in Claire's capable care, the twins would thrive. Perhaps he should think more about making her a permanent part of the landscape and less about changing careers. The idea certainly had its merits for everyone involved, including him.

Claire had cereal bowls ready and toast on a plate when she roused the children for school the next morning. They awakened, each at his or her own pace, and took turns using the single bathroom. Mason grumbled that the girls could be in there together which made their time longer, but when he sat down to breakfast, he had dressed, combed his hair, and wore a smile. Claire suspected he wanted to outshine Mia for Fallyn's attention, but she kept her amusement to herself.

"Can we all fit in your car, Miss Claire?" Mason munched a piece of toast as he spoke around the mouthful. He reached for the box of cereal, the little circles tinkling as they filled his bowl.

Claire handed him a napkin. She poured three glasses of milk. "If the weather stays nice, we can walk to school."

"Walk?" The twins repeated in unison.

Mia spoke first, her spoon clattering against the side of her empty dish. "Daddy never made us walk before."

"Maybe your last school was too far away." Claire stirred milk into her mug. "Walking is a nice way to start the day."

"Not in a snowstorm, it isn't." Mason chomped another bite of his toast. "I thought I'd be lost forever when I walked to the school in the snow."

"God was watching out for you." Claire sipped her coffee, the memory of that night still vivid. "He knew where you were and made sure you were found."

"I didn't think Daddy believed in God anymore." Mia's sober eyes matched the frown on her forehead. "When Mommy died, Daddy stopped taking us to church."

Claire's heart hurt for the little girl. How could she explain the pain Monty endured when Marissa died? How disappointed with God he probably was? Or how angry? Claire knew that kind of heartache—the devastating sense of loss when losing someone you loved, or who you thought you loved, that overwhelms you in your weakest moments. She searched Mia's face as she sought the right words. "Your daddy will find room for God again when he stops hurting."

Mason piped up. "Auntie Ellen is making him keep his promise to our mommy."

"What promise is that?" Claire waited for his answer with cautious anticipation. One never knew what Mason might say.

"She makes Daddy take us to church." Mason's beaming grin reflected victory. "I heard her remind him of what he promised to do."

"I like church, too." Fallyn handed her a hairbrush. "Will we go to church here?"

Her niece's hopeful eagerness touched Claire, reminding her of yet another motherly task she must perform. As she straightened the curly blonde locks and fastened them with a clip, she made a mental note to check out her church's weekly calendar. She liked the worship service where she'd been attending, now even more so as she remembered all the programs for children the church offered. She looked at Fallyn, expectancy written on her face, and smiled. "I think you'll like the church I attend."

Mason stood and carried his bowl to the sink, rinsing it under the faucet. Mia followed him, stacking her breakfast dishes on top of his. Fallyn watched the twins for a minute, then transported her half-eaten portion to the garbage can and scraped out the leftovers. Apparently inspired by the example set by the twins, she washed her bowl out and laid it on top of the other two.

"Good job, kids. Let's get our backpacks and head for school."

"Are we really going to walk?' Mia stood rigid, as if she couldn't believe what Claire asked of her.

"Yes. We are *really* going to walk."

Monty shivered as he stepped from the plane in Kodiak. Though spring had shown signs of its arrival at home, snow still lay in heavy drifts here. He'd brought his thermals, flannel shirts, and parka, not sure he'd need them. A brisk surge of air raced by him, leaving no doubt.

"Chandler?" A man dressed in the NOAA officers' dress whites hailed him.

Monty waved, picking up his duffel as he walked toward the waiting vehicle. "Captain Burnside?" He extended his hand and the other man returned his gesture. "Did someone forget to ask spring to join us?"

Burnside laughed and opened the car door. "March and April are typically warmer, but winter temperatures persist. We won't melt until late May."

Monty climbed into the passenger side as the captain moved around to the driver seat. "How does that affect the temperature of the water for your diving team?"

"Dry suits help protect them." Burnside stuck a key in the ignition, and the engine purred to life. "You've worked a NOAA vessel before. The weather doesn't stop us."

Monty fastened his seatbelt and leaned back against the headrest. "I've been aboard when the elements did their best to undermine our research, though." He scanned the landscape around him. "Tell me about this mission."

"A fishing vessel disappeared two weeks ago. No distress signal was sent, nor did we find debris. The disappearance was a complete mystery until a life preserver was spotted on the coast of St. Paul Island."

"Have you probed the area yet?"

"No, that's why we sent for you. Our sonar technician had to take a leave of absence. Something about becoming a new father." The captain glanced his way. "You'd think it was his first."

Monty chuckled. "I only got one first time at becoming a father because my wife produced a set of twins. But I can relate. I wouldn't have missed the birth of my kids for anything."

"Not even for a sunken fishing boat?" The captain laughed as he steered the car down the highway. "No need to answer that." He sobered and continued explaining the mission's scope. "We put out the alert for a volunteer, but when we saw you're not only a sonar tech, but a diver too, we asked for your services."

"Glad to be onboard." Monty hadn't worked the Bering Sea before. This assignment would be another notch, in the growing number of experiences, on the gun of his career. Though he had to be gone a week, the kids would love hearing about Alaska. Unless they had so much fun with their teacher, they didn't miss him. Would a certain blonde enjoy the adventure story as well? He could only hope.

Claire heard whimpering coming from the sofa. She stood, grabbed her robe about her, and tiptoed into the living area. She expected the distress to be Fallyn's, the new school and living arrangements so different from what the child enjoyed in her everyday routine. But when she reached the arm of the hide-a-bed she found Mia sitting up, her sobs coming from somewhere deep within her. Claire snapped on a night light and sat beside the trembling child.

"Mia? What is it, sweetie?" She wrapped an arm around the shaking body, pulling Mia's wet face against her in an effort not to wake Fallyn, who still lay sleeping.

"I miss my mommy." Mia's cries grew louder, and the tears soaked Claire's thin robe. "She's never coming back."

Claire closed her eyes and prayed for wisdom. Mia had come so far in the few months she'd known her, Claire never suspected she still had night terrors over her mother's death. Her father's absences, her changing from one home to another, then to another, and now her arrival at the home of her teacher, probably left the child feeling upended, forgotten, and displaced, triggering this response. She pulled the girl into her lap and hugged her as she rocked her in her arms. "Hush, little one. Your mommy can't be here, but I can."

"Can you be here forever?" Mia lifted her chin toward her. Though the light was dim the unmistakable red and puffiness from crying was clearly visible. "Nobody ever stays. Mommy's gone. Daddy's gone. Auntie Ellen's gone." Mia's tears started to flow again.

Claire reached in the pocket of her robe and produced a tissue. She kissed Mia on the forehead and wiped her cheeks. "I'm here, Mia. I can't be your mommy, but I can be your friend."

Mia grew quiet. "If you married my daddy, you could be my mommy."

Claire resisted the gasp she felt within, concentrating instead on the child's angst. What would Monty say if he knew of this conversation? How on earth could she report the incident to the children's father and still wear a straight face? She drew Mia closer, resting her chin on the girl's head. She'd have to be careful not to get the child's hopes up. Not to mention keeping a tight rein on her own feelings. She sensed Mia probed her for an answer. "Your daddy will find you a new mommy, Mia. Give him time."

"He's found you. He smiles now. He didn't before." Mia hiccoughed, taking the tissue from Claire to wipe her nose. "You've made him happy again."

Claire didn't respond. Children often sensed things before adults understood what was happening. Mia's assessment of her father might be nothing more than wishful thinking on her part. Claire wouldn't fight the attraction she felt, but she wouldn't seek it either. Monty needed to come to terms with his grief over his wife's death. She needed to learn to trust again. Both of their roads to happiness stretched long and distant. Time would, indeed, have to heal all wounds.

"I want you to be my other mommy." Fallyn's sleepy voice sounded from the other side of the bed, surprising Claire as the child sat up and moved toward her. "When Mommy's having babies."

"Are you missing her?"

"Uh-huh. And Daddy." Fallyn leaned against her shoulder. "But I'm glad I've got you too."

Mia made room for Fallyn. "We could be sisters."

Claire closed her eyes, glad for the shadows the night light afforded her. If she wasn't careful, her desires might cloud the reality she lived in. The wishes of these girls only made that reality more difficult to accept. God knew her heart. And maybe Monty, or someone else God had planned, would fulfill her innermost longing. God sometimes took a while to answer, but He was never late.

"Getting any readings, Chandler?" Burnside stood beside him as the technicians worked together to probe the depths of the dark water below the ship.

"So far, nothing has shown on the screen, sir." Monty sensed the frustration of the crew as they worked to find the remains of the downed vessel. He'd caught the disappointment himself, having always been sent out to find mammals—alive.

In the last three days they'd circled Otter and Walrus Islands without success, as well as Saint Paul Island, where the life preserver had washed ashore. With three of the four islands that formed the Pribilofs not shedding any light on their investigation, Monty worried this final sounding around St. George would not produce results. Families of the missing crewmen would be devastated, the wait for news keeping them all suspended until they knew the truth. Monty could only imagine how anxious relatives were for closure, for an official report they could claim as their own.

He returned his attention to the screen as the other men worked to get a reading on the objects below them. The Bering Sea wasn't as deep as other oceans, but a lost vessel in its waters remained no easier to find.

"Chandler!" Another crewman looked up from his station. "Got something."

Monty peered into the screen, watching as the shadowy objects danced like watery ghosts in front of him. A darker, larger object entered the picture and the undeniable shape of a ship appeared. "Burnside, we have a ship!"

Laying portside down in the water, the unmistakable outline of a fishing trawler rested on the ocean floor. Monty exhaled, unaware he'd been holding his breath. Though he'd rather be looking for whales and other living creatures, he congratulated himself for having participated in this search, knowing grieving people would now be able to move on with their lives. Personal experience had taught him how healthy that action could be.

CHAPTER THIRTY

Claire drove the children to the Chandler home Sunday morning after they'd attended her church's early services. She couldn't remember where Ellen said they regularly attended, but Mia and Mason adapted to the change, glad Fallyn could also be in their class.

Mia and Mason packed their toys to exchange for different ones. She'd visited on Friday to pick up the groceries Monty had said she should use, and the children had opted for a new bag of playthings then. Claire found it strange to enter Monty's home, rummage around in the kitchen for food staples, and enter the bedrooms in search of clothes. She didn't live here, yet she acted as if she did. She could only hope the neighbors weren't spying on her.

Mia disappeared up the stairs to her pink wonderland, Fallyn following her every step. Giggles wafted from the two conspirators. The plunk of the pack as it hit the floor fueled Claire's curiosity. After a brief stop in his room, Mason hurried to the backyard to check on his swing.

Claire had brought the dirty laundry and planned to do a load. She set the washer and returned to the kitchen, opening the refrigerator to find the rest of the fresh produce she'd left behind on Friday. Three hungry mouths required frequent restocking of her kitchen supplies. She didn't want Monty to come home and find his stores spoiled when he'd asked her to use them. The sound of tires outside interrupted her as she made a third sandwich. Leaving the turkey and rye on a plate she hurried to the front entry to see who had arrived.

Looking worn and sleep-deprived, Monty descended from his truck, steps calculated as he approached the door. A squeal from upstairs, followed by footsteps clambering down the carpeted steps, stopped Claire as she reached the door. Instead, Mia raced by her, flung open the door, and leaped into her father's arms. "Daddy!"

"Whoa!" Monty stepped back a pace, knocked off balance by the force of Mia's embrace, and caught himself on the porch rail. "Careful, baby, or we'll both be on the ground."

"Dad?" Mason came from the backyard, his feet barely touching the ground as he rushed to join his sister. "Why are you home so soon?"

Claire joined the threesome on the front porch, Fallyn's hand in her own.

Monty set Mia down and faced her as he answered his son's question. "We found the sunken vessel early yesterday, so I opted for a flight home." Dark circles underscored his eyes, and his smile drooped. "The families of those fishermen can now say goodbye."

"That must have been a satisfying feeling." Claire could only guess how relieved the loved ones of the missing crewmen must feel, even though their worst fears were confirmed.

"The tragedy cannot be undone, but the wives and mothers now know the fate of their fishermen, and don't have to spend their days and nights wondering where their guys disappeared to." Monty inhaled, the slope of his shoulders testimony to his fatigue. "Closure is important."

Claire couldn't have agreed more. She'd needed closure when Jamie deserted her, freedom to surge ahead into the remainder of her life. Without it, she'd still be stuck in the what-ifs and whys of her failed relationship. "I've made sandwiches for the kids. Would you like one?"

"That would be great." He looked down at his disheveled clothes. "First, though, I think I'll shower and get cleaned up." He rubbed Mason on the head. "Did you kids have fun?"

"We ran out of toys, so we came home to get more."

Mia put her hands on her hips. "Mason, we went to school. That was fun."

"Oh, yeah. We went to school, Dad." Mason's lopsided grin revealed what he thought of Mia's idea of fun. "I'm going back to my swing."

"Come on, Fallyn, we've got to finish our tea party." The two girls held hands as they clomped back up the stairs.

"Everything okay here?" Monty's gaze skirted the perimeter of the porch before following her inside.

"Your kids were fine." Claire continued on into the kitchen. "I'll clean up here and go home. The laundry will be in the dryer."

He touched her arm. "Claire, stay. I'm dead tired and in no shape to deal with a thousand questions from curious little minds." He studied her face. "Please?"

"Okay. Go take your shower and if you need a nap, take one." Claire picked up a sponge from the sink and wiped her spills. "I'll finish the laundry I started and keep the kids busy until you're ready." She rinsed out the sponge and left it on the counter.

"I'll shower and eat with the twins. Then I'll nap."

How comfortable this setting seemed, so familiar, as if she and Monty had spent the last ten years discussing naps and showers and the condition of the kids. Her heart tugged at her, desire playing havoc with her thoughts. She forced herself to reality. "But I have to work on lesson plans later today. Fallyn will need a nap too."

"Has she adjusted to coming west?" Monty's question was interrupted by a rush of laughter upstairs, giggles and squeals wafting down the hall.

"That answer your question?"

"Yep." He winked, his hand catching a yawn as it escaped. "See you soon."

Claire turned and forced herself to finish cleaning. As the girls upstairs shrieked and giggled as they played, their chatter wafting down the stairs, making working alongside the man who lived here feel too much like playing house. She needed to keep busy or her imagination might run wild.

She'd looked so natural on the front porch, as if she were meant to be there. Monty couldn't remove Claire from his mind as he stripped off his sea-going clothes and climbed in the shower. He scrubbed his skin and washed his hair, thinking about the quiet, gentle woman downstairs.

The kids adored her. She took to mothering like a natural. Marissa and she would have been fast friends, so alike in their ways he needed to pinch himself. He couldn't believe he'd found another woman around whom he felt comfortable. Marissa had been spunkier, more sass, but Claire had an inner quality that sparkled from her heart. While she was more reserved than Marissa, she operated from what seemed a well of wisdom, a past that guided her in her future. Is that what a broken relationship did to someone? Or had the pain of what she'd endured taught her lessons from which she drew?

He didn't know. What he did know was he wanted more time with her. Not as a teacher to his children. But as a woman he wanted to learn to love.

"Time to move, Chandler." He stepped from the shower and dried his hair. He shaved his whiskered face and patted aftershave on his cheeks, hoping the scent wasn't too strong. He'd left Kodiak so quickly he hadn't thought about what he might look like. He hadn't noticed passengers staring on the flight home, but maybe he'd been so engrossed in getting here, he'd not bothered to pay attention. None of that mattered now. The person he wanted to impress was downstairs making him a sandwich. For her, he would take pains to appear presentable. She wanted to go home soon. He needed to hurry. In more ways than one.

After sending the children to the bathroom on the main floor to wash their hands, Claire called them to the table, setting a sandwich at each place. She'd found fruit to serve and some juice packs for their thirst. She hoped Monty would join them soon. She'd made him a bigger sandwich, adding layers of tomato, onion and lettuce that she'd learned he liked when they went sailing. The coffee pot neared completion of a brewing cycle, the smell permeating the kitchen and no doubt drifting up the stairs.

Footsteps sounded on the stairway and soon Monty appeared, nose tilted up sniffing the air. "Coffee smells wonderful. Great way to lure a man from his cave." He rolled his eyes at the kids and growled, making Mia shriek as her dad mimicked a bear before he sat down.

Mason simply shook his head. "Dad."

Claire laughed at his silly face, enjoying a side of Monty she'd only seen glimpses of. She set his sandwich in front of him, returning to the kitchen for a mug of coffee. She picked up the salad she'd made for herself and carried the coffee to the comical character waiting in the next room.

"Thanks." Monty stood and helped with her chair before returning to his seat. "Let's say thanks."

Claire sat dumbfounded. For a man who had only recently struggled with acknowledging God in his life, Monty had made remarkable progress. Had the trip north rekindled the fire that burned in his soul? Had Ellen connected with his hunger for spiritual comfort? Whatever had triggered this outward display of reliance on God, Claire welcomed the change. She'd assumed certain things with Jamie only to discover his trust lay in himself and not in God. That assumption had cost her several years of heartache. She had no desire to travel that road again. But this path on which she found herself with Monty certainly held promise.

Monty carried his plate to the kitchen and rinsed it, setting it in the dishwasher. Claire followed, the children's plates stacked in her hands. "Good sandwich. Thanks for including me in your lunch fixings."

Claire set the plates down. "Wouldn't seem right to leave you out since I made the lunches with your groceries, now would it?"

"But late arrivals deserve the leftovers." Monty took the plates she'd carried and deposited each one in the dishwasher. "The food really helped boost my energy."

"Take your nap." Claire added a plate to the dishwasher. "I can stay that long."

"Are you sure?" Monty leaned against the counter. "I've already imposed on you more than I should have."

"You nap. I'll finish the laundry."

"No, I'll get that later."

"I've got a few clothing articles still at home too." Claire looked thoughtful. "I'll try to remember to put them in a bag and give it to you at school in the morning."

"That sounds like a—"

"Miss Claire?" Mason burst into the kitchen holding her phone. "Your phone pinged."

"Thanks, buddy." Claire glanced at the screen and blanched.

"What is it?" Monty grew alarmed, as the color of her skin turned pasty white.

"A text from my sister." She lifted a hand and walked away to the patio, pressing in numbers. As she reached the door, Monty heard her connect. "Angie? What's up?"

He handed Mason a dishrag. "Thanks for bringing her phone in here. Can you wipe the table for me?"

"Sure, Dad." Mason went back the way he had come, twirling the rag in his fingers, slinging drips behind him.

Monty grabbed another towel and followed his son, mopping up the sprinkles as fast as Mason made more. Entering the dining room, he directed Fallyn and Mia to straighten the chairs, glad he could keep the children busy. Monty wanted to allow Claire the privacy she needed, the look on her face telling him the phone conversation had taken a serious turn.

Claire rejoined them a few minutes later, her frown creased in worry lines above the bridge of her nose, lips pressed into a straight line. "Fallyn? Your mommy is on the phone and wants to talk to you."

Fallyn spoke into the phone. "Hi Mommy." She listened for a minute, her eyes growing wide and her smile spreading across her face. "Wow!" A frown followed. "Mommy wants to talk to you again."

Claire turned her back on him and spoke in low tones. She ended the call and faced him, her eyes a mixture of worry and surprise.

"Bad news?" Monty gripped the back of one of the chairs, uncertain what he should do if she faced an emergency.

Claire snapped to attention and shook her head. "Sorry. Not really bad news. The triplets were born this morning and are thriving, though they're small."

"Mommy had her babies!" Fallyn hopped to her side. "Can we go see them?"

"Yes, you are now a big sister to Katy, Patrick, and Sean." Claire knelt in front of her niece. "But we can't go see them for a while. They were born almost five weeks early, which makes them too little for visitors. They are living in a special crib to keep them warm. Let's give them a little time and then you, me, and Grandma

Simpson can go see them."

"Mommy won't be so tired, then, right?"

"With three babies, she'll probably still be tired, but she will be glad to see you."

"Will I get to come back?"

"I hope so."

Fallyn beamed, all smiles as she looked at Mia. "That's perfect!"

Mia raised her hand and the girls swapped a high five.

Monty grew suspicious. What master-minded scheme had these two cooked up? He could only guess. He returned his focus to Claire. "How much did they weigh?" Monty assumed the triplets were in the neo-natal unit. The twins had needed a day there after they were born because they'd only weighed four pounds at birth, arriving two weeks early.

"Patrick and Sean were three pounds. Katy tipped the scales at three pounds, one ounce. Sean and Katy are breathing on their own. Patrick is struggling." Claire studied her phone screen. "I need to get home."

"Let me get those booster seats." Monty tossed the towels to Mason. "Put these in the laundry room, please. Mia, come check the car for toys." He led the way to the driveway where Claire's car was parked. She and Fallyn followed, opening the car doors as Monty angled the seats out of the back. Once Fallyn was belted in, Claire headed to the driver's side and slid behind the wheel. Monty came to her window. "Thanks for doing this for me. If you need anything, I'll return the favor."

Claire's smile wavered. "I might take you up on that, Mr. Chandler."

He grinned, tickled at the way she played the formality card, keeping him at a proper distance. "See you tomorrow, Miss Claire." He stepped back as she turned the key and drove away, wishing with all his being he could find some reason to make her stay.

CHAPTER THIRTY-ONE

HER CONCENTRATION SAGGING AS SHE UPDATED reports for school, Claire checked on Fallyn, who napped on the twin bed she'd reclaimed once Mason went home. The child's cheeks were flushed, and her sleep time had stretched to almost three hours. Was this normal for her or had the morning excitement worn her out? When Angie had called to tell Fallyn about the triplets, she'd asked how Fallyn was doing. Claire had told her Fallyn seemed to be fine. But she didn't know the child's habits yet, the care needed still a learning curve in Claire's mind. Especially the extra details Fallyn required, who'd come to her already fragile. She touched Fallyn's forehead, her hand coming back damp, the skin surprisingly hot. Alarm swept her as Fallyn awoke to her touch.

"Hi, big sister." Claire knelt on the edge of the mattress, stroking the errant curls away from Fallyn's eyes. "You were tired."

"I don't feel good." Fallyn sat up and leaned against her, head resting at her shoulder.

"Tummy ache?" Claire prayed for wisdom. She wrapped her arms about Fallyn, drawing her close. She'd put the pediatrician's medical records in a safe spot in case of an emergency. She hadn't had time to call the clinic yet and establish Fallyn as a patient. She mentally scolded herself.

"I'm hot. All over." Fallyn held her stomach. "My stomach feels sick."

Claire frowned. She needed to call her sister. If Angie wasn't available, Brennan could tell her. Did Fallyn's kidneys malfunction and give her flu-like symptoms? "Do you need to use the bathroom?"

Fallyn stood and wobbled to the toilet. "Oh!"

"What's wrong, honey?" Claire hurried to her side.

"I'm sorry, Auntie Claire." She burst into sobs. "I didn't make it in time."

"Sweetie, it's okay." She hugged the crying child. "Take off your panties, and we'll get you cleaned up."

A few minutes later, Fallyn had taken a quick bath under the tub faucet. Wrapped in a warm towel, Claire helped her dry off and put on clean clothes. Together they walked back to the bedroom and Fallyn sat on the bed. "I want to lie down."

Confidence sagging, Claire kissed the top of Fallyn's head and pulled the covers over her. "Stay quiet, Fallyn, while I read the medical papers your mother sent with you." She pulled the medical file and sifted through the forms her sister had meticulously filed. One doctor report stood out. *Patient came in with fever and an upset stomach. Urine output almost non-existent. Puffiness in the eyes and stiffness in the ankles.*

Claire prayed for her niece as she put the medical forms back in the pouch and returned to Fallyn's side. "What do you want for dinner?"

"I'm not hungry. I need my Mommy." Fallyn rolled over and went back to sleep, the circles beneath her eyes reflecting a purplish hue.

Claire opened her phone and called her sister. As she waited for one of them to pick up, she found the number for the clinic. She prayed this wasn't an emergency.

With Claire gone, Monty finished the laundry she'd started, taking care to hang out the garments she'd said should be allowed to air dry for less wrinkling. He'd never paid attention to that kind of thing. Marissa hadn't bothered to show him, taking care of those details herself and Ellen, apparently, had followed suit. Only Claire had thought it important enough for him to know, things a dad on his own might need help figuring out. He appreciated the way she anticipated what information he might lack and took the time to explain. She'd only been gone an hour and he already missed her.

"Dad?" Mason came into the laundry room carrying a book under his arm. "I got a new book this week. It's about flying machines." He held it out. "Want to look?"

"Let me finish these shirts first." Monty reached for a hanger. He handed Mason a pile of folded underwear. "Take these to your dresser and put them away. Then bring your book back to the family room."

"Okay." Mason hurried away, the stack of clothing tottering in his hands.

Monty held his breath, wondering if the neat piles he'd made would remain as tidy in the boy's drawers. Probably not. He'd check later.

He carried a fistful of hangers up the stairs to Mia's room. She sat cross-legged on her bed, talking to two dolls sitting on her knees. She looked up at him. "Hi, Dad."

"How's Mia today?"

"I miss Fallyn." Mia set the dolls to one side and stuck her legs over the edge of the mattress. "She's really fun to play with."

"You like her a lot, huh?"

"Yes." Mia's expression turned thoughtful. "She's not happy about her new brothers and sister."

Monty sank on the mattress beside his daughter. "Why is that?"

"These babies are from her mommy's tummy—her real babies. Fallyn is adopted." Mia lifted a sad face to him. "She says her mommy won't like her as much because she came from some other place."

Monty touched his daughter's nose. "I don't know Miss Claire's sister. But if she loves her half as much as Miss Claire does, I don't think Fallyn needs to worry. Miss Claire thinks the world of that little girl."

Mia picked up her doll and put it on her shoulder. "Fallyn wants Miss Claire to be her second mommy so she can live here during the summers." Patting the toy with her hand, she kicked her legs and rocked. "Do you think that could be possible?"

Monty hugged his girl. "Possible, maybe, but probably not something that's going to happen. Fallyn has a Mommy and a Daddy in Pennsylvania." He bit back the chuckle threatening to spoil the moment. "Miss Claire will probably get married and have her own babies to love."

"You mean I'd have another brother or sister?"

Monty frowned. "What do you mean?"

Mia hopped down from the bed. "Oh, Daddy, you are so clueless. Anybody can see you and Miss Claire are in love. So if Miss Claire has a baby, it will be my new sister." She laid her doll in its bed. "I'm going downstairs. 'Bye."

Monty stared after the giggling girl. *What just happened?*

The pediatrician on duty at the clinic pored over the paperwork Claire had brought in, turning each page as if tomorrow would never come, the minutes dragging by as he studied the chart notes. When he finished, he set the file down and leaned back in his chair. "Fallyn's history indicates this kidney problem is chronic."

Claire nodded, squeezing Fallyn's hand to reassure her.

"Does kidney disease run in the family?"

Claire shrugged. "Fallyn is adopted."

"Really? She looks enough like you to be your child." The pediatrician leaned forward in his chair.

"The adoption agency works to pair children with parents who have similar coloring and other details."

"They are obviously good at what they do. Except there should be medical information on her. I'm surprised there isn't."

"I was present at the adoption." Claire winked at Fallyn. "As far as I know, there was no kidney disease in either biological parent."

He picked up the file. "I want to run some tests to check the albumin levels in her blood and I want an ultrasound of her kidneys."

"Do you think she's getting worse?" Claire's pulse soared. Angie would never forgive her if Fallyn grew sicker on her watch. "If she is, I need to call her parents back. We talked once this morning already."

"Her kidneys are not filtering as they should, haven't been for awhile. In three months' time, she's had as many infections. Her physician in Pennsylvania already checked out our dialysis center here in Newport. That alone tells me he feared the worst. Fallyn is facing dialysis if we can't clear these infections. Maybe even a transplant if we find what her physician in Pennsylvania and I both suspect is causing this problem."

"Polycystic kidney disease." Claire stared at her hands, her heart doing a flip in her chest. "He said it was a possibility. I don't know much about it."

"Cysts in her kidneys. They are taking up space that the kidneys need to function." The physician looked grim. "That's why I asked if there was polycystic kidney disease in the family." He wrote on a clipboard. "This condition is often genetic."

Claire's fluttering heart plummeted to her toes. Dear, sweet, Fallyn. How could such a young child face so complicated a future? Opening Fallyn's birth records promised to reveal all sorts of information many might not want uncovered. She wondered how certain parties would respond to the investigation—a secret they thought hidden—suddenly laid bare. To open the past and confront the issues considered long ago buried could produce trouble. For

Fallyn, Claire would go to any lengths. Even that.

Late that afternoon, the doorbell chimed as Monty sat reading a favorite book to Mason and Mia. The twins each claimed a knee as he filled the great chair near the fireplace. The gas flame sent cheery bits of light around the room, the glow warm, peaceful, and welcoming.

"I'll get it." Mason hopped out of his lap and hurried to the door, Mia not far behind.   Monty stood and stretched, the weight of the kids on his legs leaving them semi-asleep. He thanked God his jaunt to Kodiak had ended so quickly, even if his findings proved five fishermen had lost their lives to a freak storm. Families of the men could move forward, and Monty's work was done. The task granted him new appreciation for his surroundings, his homecoming, and the promise of an onshore work environment for at least the next six months. He picked up the pace as he heard the door swing open and Mason's excited voice. "Auntie Ellen!"

Monty smiled as his sister and her husband entered, Kevin's civilian clothes smacking of a recent shopping trip. Ellen bent down and hugged each of the twins as Kevin stepped toward him. Monty pointed to his clothes. "Hey, dude. I haven't seen you looking so sharp since your wedding."

Kevin cocked his head, an amused smile on his lips. "Ellen turned our getaway into an excuse to explore every menswear store in greater Portland." He extended his hand. "Glad to see you again."

Monty gripped his hand, pulling the man into a bear hug. "I'm relieved to see you safe and sound." He stepped back and looked into Kevin's eyes. "Though she won't admit it, Ellen has had her share of sleepless nights."

"Every military wife worries about her husband when he's

deployed." Ellen's face beamed, her happiness at the return of her husband evident. "Things go smoothly here?"

"Daddy had to fly to Alaska." Mia tugged on her aunt's fingers. "We stayed with Miss Claire."

"Oh, really?" Ellen's gaze met his, an eyebrow raised. "Did she stay here?"

"We stayed at her house." Mason puffed his chest. "I got the twin bed and Mia slept on the couch with Fallyn."

"She brought the kids here for new toys and food supplies, but they spent their time there when they weren't in school."

Ellen shot him a crooked smile. "She knows what tongues in a small town can do."

"So she said." He gestured toward the family room. "Want to join us? I might even rustle up something to snack on."

Kevin went first. "Ellen said you'd bought a spectacular house. If this is an indication of the rest of it, I'd say she was right."

Monty followed, the twins and Ellen behind him. "Well, so far, we're excited. I haven't been here enough to discover its hidden mysteries."

Ellen found a chair and sank into it. "I'll ask Claire. She'll know."

Monty ground his teeth, pinning a glare on Ellen he hoped would silence her. "What can I offer you to drink?"

"Truth serum?" Ellen giggled at her joke. "Water will be fine."

"Soda for me, if you have it." Kevin sat on the ottoman near Ellen.

"Be right back." Monty headed for the kitchen, praying the kids wouldn't interpret Ellen's words and spill them tomorrow at school. Claire valued her reputation, and this kind of banter could be misconstrued. The strange part in all of this was that Ellen should know better and yet she did it anyway. Sisters!

Claire stopped by the pharmacy on the way home, Fallyn's need of a new prescription uppermost in her mind. This doctor's assessment of the child's condition—the second one she'd heard—frightened her, but the prospect of opening Fallyn's birth records scared her more.

The doctor had offered hope. "I would suggest you make inquiries of people you know to be tested for a kidney match." He had tapped his pencil on his chart notes. "Should Fallyn reach the point where she needs a transplant, there's a possibility you may already have found a donor. Waiting on a list for a donated organ can take years and often the patient doesn't have that kind of time."

"Can you tell me how to do that?" Claire had listened to every word, optimism fueling her interest. Time could be on her side if she acted now. She'd left the clinic, clinging to the instructions, intent on pursuing every angle she could. Fallyn needed her. She would not let her down.

Fed and medicated, Fallyn climbed into bed and fell asleep almost immediately. Claire covered her with a light quilt and tucked her favorite teddy bear in alongside her. A ping on her phone interrupted the bedtime ritual, but satisfied Fallyn slept, Claire tiptoed from the room and checked her screen. Ellen.

"So you're back?" Claire spoke quietly, careful to walk away from the bedroom.

"Yes. I heard you had an extraordinary week."

"Pretty routine, actually." Claire smiled to herself. "Except for my miniature visitors."

"I thought that was pretty clever, getting him to bring the kids to you."

"What else could I do?" Claire sank onto a nearby chair. "He suggested I live there!"

"Smart lady." Ellen chuckled. "Other than that, how was your week?"

"Fallyn's sick. I took her to the clinic this afternoon." Claire's eyes pooled as she thought of how weak Fallyn had seemed on the way home.

Her hand shook as she spoke into the phone. "Would you be willing to be tested as a kidney donor?"

After Ellen's call, Claire checked on Fallyn one last time before preparing for tomorrow. A cool forehead met her fingers and gentle, rhythmic snores filled the quiet room. She watched the sleeping child for several minutes, appreciating her delicate features. Her blonde curls wisped about her face, hiding the eyes and accenting the graceful curve of her pixie nose and the dainty curve of her lips. Fallyn would grow to be a beauty—if her kidneys didn't fail her.

The vibration of the phone inside her shirt pocket interrupted the trail of her thoughts and she backed out of the room, taking care not to make a sound. Closing the door with a soft click, she dug the phone from its hiding place and touched the screen. Mom. No doubt excited about the arrival of Angie's latest.

"Hey, Mom. I'm guessing you heard the news?" Claire kept walking as she talked, ending up in a chair at the kitchen table. She'd left a cup of tea there, forgotten in the flurry of phone calls and school papers, and lifted the cup to her lips. Cold, but decent. She waited for her mother's exuberance to dance out of the phone lines like a chorus girl on Broadway.

"Triplets!" Her mother sounded aghast. "Neither of you rascals told me Angie carried three babies."

"Sorry, Mom." Claire shoved the guilty feeling to the back of her mind. "I assumed Angie told you. I only learned of the multiple births when I visited her spring break—" She squinted at the calendar on the wall, counting backwards. "—a mere ten days ago." She sipped the tea. "I haven't known much longer than you."

"Should we fly back there and help?" Her mother's voice rose in pitch, a sure sign she was rattled. "One of the boys is struggling."

"No, that's not necessary." Claire tapped the table, counting to ten to make sure she didn't spill Angie's plans to keep her mother away until the babies were stable. "When I was there, Angie had hired a woman to come in and help once the babies were born. I met her. She's quite capable." Claire waited, but her mother didn't push a trip to Pennsylvania, for which she was glad. "I think we'd be better help going back when school is out."

"But will the woman take care of Fallyn, too?"

"I've got Fallyn, Mom. Angie thought she'd be better off with me during this time."

"Will that work with your job?" Mom thought of everything.

"So far, it's not been a problem. She goes to school with me, spends her day in kindergarten, and we come home."

"You girls were always more efficient than I could ever hope to be." The sigh that resonated in Claire's ear sounded deflated. "I doubt I do anything well anymore."

"You're good on the phone. Want to make a few phone calls?"

"For what?" Claire smiled as her mother's enthusiasm rose with her voice.

"A transplant volunteer." Claire listened to the silence on the other end. "Fallyn may be headed toward kidney failure."

CHAPTER THIRTY-TWO

MONTY'S HOPES TO FURTHER HIS RELATIONSHIP with Claire after the emergency trip to Kodiak seemed to stall, every attempt–thwarted by the woman herself. Had he done something to offend her? He didn't think he had, but other than her cheery greetings at school, Claire kept her distance. Didn't answer his texts. Always busy with something for Fallyn when he called. Six weeks had passed. Confused, Monty struggled to find the reasons why.

"She's responsible for Fallyn," Ellen said one afternoon when their discussion had turned to his frustration. He'd left work early to pick up his children from his sister's and she'd invited him in for coffee. "The child became quite ill after your Alaska jaunt, and Claire has spent a lot of time taking her to the doctor. She's suffering from a condition that affects her kidneys."

"Is it serious?" Monty couldn't hide his alarm. He understood how much Fallyn meant to her aunt. He pulled out a chair from the kitchen table and sat. "Claire would do anything for her niece."

"Apparently so. She's searching for kidney donors." Ellen reached for mugs in the cupboard.

"Why didn't she tell me?" Monty thought of all the young men and women he saw every day in his work. He could be looking for a candidate as well. "I would help."

"She probably didn't want to burden you with her problems. She has her mother calling friends in the valley. I've asked in my circles, too." Ellen filled a plate with cookies and set them near him. "I baked these this morning."

"When will Fallyn need the transplant?"

Ellen poured him a cup of coffee and reached for the other mug. "That's just it. Fallyn isn't there yet. The pediatrician suggested Claire line up potential donors ahead of time, so Fallyn doesn't wind up on a waiting list." She carried the mugs to the table and joined Monty in the other chair.

"Is her sister involved?"

Ellen sipped her coffee, jerking back as the liquid touched her lips. "Hot!" She set the mug down and reached for a napkin. "Angie has enough on her plate with newborn triplets. She's relying on Claire to help."

Monty could hear the walls of his heart crumbling inward. Fallyn's needs overshadowed his own desires. He should face the truth. "She's not ever going to have time for me if Fallyn's health continues to deteriorate, is she?"

Ellen rubbed her finger along the rim of her mug. "I think she will. School will be out in two weeks. Her responsibilities as a teacher will end. I know she's accompanying her mother to Pennsylvania the third week of June to see the babies. Fallyn will also go. She may not come back."

He pulled out his phone and tapped in the calendar app. School ended mid-June. The following week would be the one Ellen said Claire planned to be gone. "Not much time for a kite party at the beach." Monty cast her a frown. "Mason promised Fallyn we'd go kite-flying."

"I'll mention it to Claire when I see her next week." Ellen rose and set her cup in the sink.

"How is it you can get time with her and I can't?"

"Because you're at work when she's free." Ellen cast him what looked to be a sympathetic smile. "We meet after school and take the kids to the beach, or a park, or something fun before I bring the twins to you and Kevin gets home from work. Mia and Fallyn are close friends."

"And you were going to tell me this, when?" Having returned to the coffee maker, Monty stopped, crossed his arms, and assumed an annoyed stance. "How often have you been doing this?"

Ellen waved him off. "We've managed to get together at least once a week since Kevin and I returned home. She and I discuss all kinds of things while the kids play." She winked. "Even you."

"Great." He refilled his cup and added cream. "I thought we were making good progress until spring break." He returned to the table. "Did I ruin things by asking her to watch the kids while I was gone?"

"No." Ellen reached out her hand and laid it on his wrist. "She's quite taken with you. But distancing herself after that seemed like a wise decision." Ellen tugged on his hand, making him look at her. "Did you know the family on the corner of your cul-de-sac is the superintendent's son?"

Monty could feel the blood rushing from his face. "No! Seriously?"

Ellen let go of his hand and leaned back in her chair, nodding. "Let school get out. Claire will have more time after she takes Fallyn home and will be waiting for your call."

Monty laughed at his own stupidity, running a hand over his chin as he thought how reluctant he was to take time to meet the neighbors. That had always been Marissa's strongpoint. She thought knowing the neighbors made for a stronger neighborhood. Pointing a finger at his chest, she'd quoted the Bible where it said to love your neighbor. He made a note to do better. Soon.

As the time to accompany her mother to Pennsylvania neared, Claire grew more and more anxious. She had hoped, as Angie had hoped at the beginning, to postpone the trip until the end of August, but Claire's mother decided they needed to go and help Angie sooner. Nothing could dissuade her.

"I can't get her to wait." Claire had poured out her irritation to Angie over the phone. "She calls continually, asking for updates."

"Just come, Claire." Angie sounded tired. "Mom will keep busy changing diapers and you and I can discuss Fallyn's health. I'm anxious to see her." Her voice wobbled. "Any luck finding a donor?"

"Not so far." Claire sucked in a sigh. "Those who are willing have not matched."

"Now you understand why the pediatrician urged you to start early."

"It didn't help when Mom told me Jamie's mother said the condition runs in the Duval family." Claire growled into the phone. "I may be desperate, but confronting Jamie is not something I want to do.

"You may not have a choice." Angie's tone sounded defensive. "One kidney is worth the encounter."

"I'll pray we find another donor first so it doesn't come to that." Angie's words still haunting her, Claire said goodbye, hung up the phone, and smiled at her niece. "Shall we go get some dinner?"

Fallyn shrugged, as if she'd suggested an outing to the school parking lot. "Mommy's forgotten who I am."

"No, sweetheart." Claire hurried to hug the distraught little girl. "You and I and Grandma Simpson are all going to see your new brothers and sister." Claire gathered Fallyn in her arms. "We'll help change diapers, give your Mommy a break, and explore the city." She kissed Fallyn on the forehead. "Are you excited?"

Fallyn's eyes searched hers. "I didn't get to play with Mia and Mason at the beach. Mason wanted to fly kites with me."

"I'll do everything within my power to see that you get to fly your kite." Claire kissed the child on the cheek and set her down. "But you can't fly a kite if you don't eat. Let's go get our fish and salads."

Fallyn found a table by the window as Claire ordered their meals. The restaurant, built out over the sand, featured large picture windows to view the ocean waves breaking about a hundred yards beyond the beach beneath them. Claire had met a couple of storm watchers since she'd come to Newport. Experiencing the fury of the wind as it battered the breakers from behind a glassed enclosure appealed to her. If she didn't live so near to the ocean, she might have considered booking a night with a room overlooking the sea. She carried the baskets to the table where Fallyn pressed her nose against the window. Fascination with the swells appeared to have stolen her imagination and stifled her appetite. "Time for food, sweet girl."

Fallyn turned her attention to the salad, picking at a lettuce leaf as if it contained a worm.

Claire angled her face as she considered Fallyn's lack of interest in her food. "No appetite? Or you don't like the fish?"

All traces of her earlier distress disappeared and Fallyn shrugged. "I like salad, but I'm tired of it. I'd really like some fries." She poked at her fish portion." What's this white stuff beside the bigger lumps?"

Claire laughed and handed her a fork. "The bigger lumps are the fish cooked in batter and the white stuff is tartar sauce to dip the fish in."

"What's tartar sauce?"

"A mixture of pickles, onions, and mayonnaise." Claire dipped her piece of fish. "Want to taste?" She held out her fork. "If you don't like it, you can eat the fish plain."

Fallyn stuck out a tentative tongue and tasted the mixture. She grew silent for a moment, her face an unreadable mask. "Too gooey." She stabbed her fish. "Still want fries."

"I wish you could have them." Claire patted her hand. "But the salt is not good for you."

"It's not fair." Fallyn stuck a piece of fish in her mouth. "But this is good."

"Hello, Claire."

The voice jolted Claire to attention, as a figure appeared at her shoulder making her jump.

Jamie stood beside her, his gaze riveted on Fallyn.

Claire grew cold inside, the adversary in her nightmares too close for comfort. She forced a smile. "Hello, Jamie. Have you met Angie's daughter, Fallyn?"

"Nice name." He refocused on Claire, eyes narrowed and lips pressed in a straight line. "I heard about her through my mother. She said you're looking for a kidney donor."

"Yes."

"Not many people probably willing to do that." He angled his face as though asking a question, a twisted smirk on his lips. "Are there?"

"Not so far." Claire passed a napkin to Fallyn. "Corner of your mouth, right here." She touched her lips where Fallyn's mouth sported a slurp of salad dressing. She turned her attention back to Jamie, praying he would leave. "But we aren't in an emergency situation, so we've got time."

Jamie snorted, his curt smile forced. "My uncle died waiting for a kidney. I hope you find one in time."

How dare he say that in front of Fallyn! Claire bit back the retort she wanted to deliver. No reason to rile the man intentionally, even if he deserved it. She spoke with calm. "I'm praying I do. God knows the right person to ask."

Jamie squirmed, his stance shouting his impatience to leave. "I don't share your confidence in a *Being* we can't see, but I respect your right to your beliefs." He nodded at Fallyn. "Nice to meet you,

Fallyn. I hope you enjoy your visit to Newport."

As he walked away, Claire exhaled, having held her breath until he reached the other side of the restaurant. He'd been a part of her past, but he certainly held no place in her future. She prayed she'd never have to make an exception.

"Why don't you like that man?"

Claire startled at Fallyn's comment. Was she that transparent? She searched for words the child would understand. "He and I were once engaged, but we decided not to get married."

Fallyn's eyes grew round. "Didn't you want to get married?"

Claire laid her hand on Fallyn's shoulder. "Yes. I wanted to get married. Just not to him."

Appearing deep in thought, Fallyn dunked a piece of fish in her salad dressing. "Mr. Chandler is cuter."

Every day he dropped his kids off at school and left them in Claire's capable hands, Monty prayed he'd find an opening to ask her out again. He'd talked to her, knew Fallyn occupied a lot of her free time, and end-of-the-school-year paperwork kept her buried in extra hours at home. He also understood her reluctance after babysitting his children while he flew to Kodiak. Being seen in his house with his kids could have fueled some unsavory stories from those looking to make trouble, but the incident had passed more than two months ago, and he doubted anyone now cared. If he didn't act soon, Claire would leave for Pennsylvania, and he would once again be forced to wait. Absence did make the heart grow fonder. He was living proof.

This morning he pulled his truck into the parking lot a few minutes earlier than usual and scanned the sidewalk for signs of her. He parked and ambled to the passenger side where Mia and Mason waited to unload. He lifted them down, treating them like they were fragile glass, taking extra time to scout the area around him. Still no sign of Claire.

He handed backpacks to the twins, kissed each one on the cheek, and closed the pickup door. He smacked his fist into his palm when she didn't show in time today and prepared to leave when he heard Mia behind him. "Fallyn!"

He turned to find Mia and Fallyn jumping up and down as they grabbed hands, Claire gesturing the girls into the school. She put out her hand for Mason to join her.

"Miss Claire!" Monty made a beeline for the teacher. "I need to talk to you."

Claire waited, eyes wide and smile wavering, as he strode to her side. "Good morning, Mr. Chandler. Mason and Mia seem well today."

"But Mr. Chandler is not." He swallowed his grin as Claire frowned, eyes narrowing. A worried smile replaced the amused one she'd worn before.

He blurted out his question. "I want to see you again. Is that possible?"

Claire looked over her shoulder both directions, stepping closer so she could whisper. "That can be arranged." She smiled at him. "But not here."

"Got it." He stood straighter. "Shall I call you?"

"Ellen's taking Fallyn to see a movie with the twins tonight. Why don't you drop by?"

Monty's heart sprouted wings. "Is it safe?"

"That depends. Will you knock or ring the bell?" Claire's eye's twinkled, that errant curl dangling an inch above her eyebrow.

"I'll beat down the door if that's what it takes."

Her hand went to her throat. "Gracious. That's not necessary."

"See you around seven." He turned and headed to his truck, whistling loud enough to be heard at the water's edge. She'd said yes.

CHAPTER THIRTY-THREE

With Monty's arrival imminent, Claire brewed a pot of tea and popped a box of frozen cookies in the microwave for a quick thaw. Grateful Ellen had volunteered to take the children tonight so she could focus on end-of-the-year evaluations, Claire leaned back in her great chair and marveled at the turn this evening had taken. An encounter with Monty! She regretted she'd had to put him off for so long, but Fallyn's needs and her own work demands had taken almost all of her time. She'd purchased tickets to Pennsylvania, her departure the day after school ended. Seeing him might be nothing more than a date for coffee in the time that remained. *More would be wonderful.*

Fallyn had accepted the idea of returning home, as long as Claire kept her promise she could return. Claire stayed vigilant watching the child's health, whisking her to the clinic at any sign of fatigue or grumpiness. Fallyn continued to avoid any new infections, her energy level rising with her depth of happiness. Having a friend like Mia close, with tea parties, doll dress-ups, and a sleepover or two, Fallyn seemed to come alive. Why hadn't Angie taken time to make those kinds of arrangements? Had Fallyn been so sick Angie didn't think she could handle them? Seeing the happiness Fallyn experienced at those outings made Claire more determined to ensure they continued.

The knock on the door startled her, the rhythm one she'd heard long ago—shave and a haircut, six bits. Giggling as she hurried to greet her visitor, she opened the door to a bouquet of flowers, a pair of hands holding them out to her, and a grinning Monty peeking around the side.

"They're beautiful." Claire gestured for him to come in. "But really, I don't need flowers for you to visit." She pointed to the table. "Care for some tea and crumpets?"

"Are you English?" Monty stepped into the room, handed her the bouquet, and donned an accent. "I rather thought you Irish."

She imitated his brogue. "A bit of both, it would seem." Chuckling at his nonsense, she ushered him to the compact kitchen and offered him a chair. "My mother's French. My father was a blend of several backgrounds which included English and Irish." She reached in the cupboard below the sink and retrieved a vase for the flowers. Setting the centerpiece on the table, she lifted the plate of cookies and the pot of tea and carried them to where two cups and saucers waited. "This is Earl Grey. Do you take sugar?" She poured a cup and slid it toward him.

Monty took a sip. "No, this is fine." He fingered a cookie. "These look like those mint cookies the Girl Scouts sell in the spring."

"They are." Claire bit into one. "I buy several boxes when they are available and freeze them. Handy to have when you have visitors coming and no time to bake."

"My favorite." Monty chewed his cookie as he looked around her kitchen. "You've certainly done a lot with so little space." He reached for another cookie. "I noticed how organized the kitchen was when I left the kids in your care." He cast her a crooked grin. "But I didn't know leaving them here would close the door on the relationship we'd kindled."

"The door didn't close." Claire blinked, choosing her words with care. "But jumping from a sailboat ride to keeping the twins overnight seemed too fast, at least to me. Call me old-fashioned but I prefer to fan the embers and build a relationship to a slow burn. If the flames start to flicker and the fire crackles, then all the world can see. Jamie pushed, claiming he loved me, but in the end proved he didn't know me at all." She focused on Monty. "People knew we were dating, planned to attend our wedding. Jamie's departure stripped me of my dignity. I felt exposed—as if standing naked before the world." She made a fist and punctuated her sentence with a knock on the table. "I promised myself I wouldn't fall into that trap again."

"I won't do that, Claire." Monty reached across the table and touched her hand. "I want to spend time with you. See where we're going. I want to know you."

"Thank you." Claire poured another cup of tea. "I'll be back the last week of June. I still may have Fallyn, so you'll have to share my time with her."

"When will she return home?"

"In time for school, supposedly. But she's missing her parents." Claire didn't want to think about parting with the delightful little girl. "She hasn't had her kite-flying excursion with Mason yet, and she's determined."

Monty laughed. "Let's set the date for the Fourth of July. That way we can all look forward to the outing."

"Fourth of July it is."

The front door creaked open and Fallyn appeared in the entry. Behind her stood Mia and Mason with their Aunt Ellen, all of them laughing over a shared joke. "Aunt Claire."

"Did you have a good time?" She stood and went to hug her niece. "Monty has something he wants to tell you."

Fallyn stared at Monty, her eyes as big as gumballs, grip tight on Claire's fingers. "What?"

"When you and your Aunt Claire return from Pennsylvania, I'm taking you to the beach for a day of kite-flying." He tilted his head and raised his brows. "Fourth of July sound good?"

"It's perfect!" Fallyn released Claire's hand, sprang across the floor, and leaped into Monty's lap. "Thank you!"

Monty hugged the child, his gaze on Claire. "You're most welcome."

Claire couldn't swallow, the knot in her throat too big.

Claire took Fallyn's hand as she and her mother disembarked the plane and entered the terminal in search of Brennan. She doubted Angie would come to the airport to greet them, but her mother's anxiety over Angie's triplets, the plane ride, and the need to see her other daughter made Claire wish Angie would show. To her surprise, she heard a shout and saw a waving hand as Angie and Brennan hurried across the airport to their gate.

"Fallyn! Mom! Claire!" Angie opened her arms wide and hugged each of them in turn, holding Fallyn longer than the rest. "I'm so glad you're here."

"Where are your babies?"

Claire smiled at her mother's question, the woman's eyes round and mouth agape. Mom had come to rescue the troops—the sooner, the better. She winked at Angie.

"The triplets are safe in the care of Mrs. Thornton, our helper." Angie wrapped an arm about Fallyn. "But one of my babies is right here."

"I'm not a baby." Fallyn folded her arms and lifted her chin. "I go to school."

"You'll always be my first baby." Angie tapped her daughter on her head, gazing at Claire through shuttered eyes.

Claire couldn't read her sister's thoughts, but in her look a message waited, and not necessarily one she'd be glad to receive. "I'm so glad to see you."

"I'm going home with Aunt Claire to visit one more time. I have to fly kites with Mason."

"You and Mason have become good friends?" Angie studied her daughter, the radiance on Fallyn's face stunning. A pensive smile graced Angie's lips, but in her eyes, Claire saw a storm.

What did she see that had her on edge?

"Let's get your bags and go see all the babies, then you can talk." Brennan gestured toward the baggage claim. "I only parked in a short-term parking area."

A short ride later Claire helped her mother out of the car and followed Fallyn as she skipped ahead to the front door of the O'Brien home.

Angie hurried to catch up, calling over her shoulder. "What did you feed that child? She acts like she's high on caffeine!"

"Ocean air and fresh fish."

"Must agree with her." Angie zipped to the front door. "She's not the same girl I sent west with you." She followed Fallyn into the house as Claire helped her mother bring up the rear.

After introductions were made and Claire's mother finished holding the last of the triplets, Angie took the baby and stood. "He needs a bottle. Do you want to feed him, Mom?" At her nod, Angie returned the little boy to her mother's waiting arms. Mrs. Thornton gestured for Mom to follow her.

Angie pointed toward the living room. "Let's go sit where we can talk."

The uneasiness she'd sensed in Angie at the airport still lingered. Claire only hoped Angie wouldn't fail Fallyn, showing preference for the newborns over the daughter she'd been given. At the door of the room, Claire listened for sounds of Fallyn. "Where did Fallyn run off to?"

"Her room, probably." Angie called down the hall. "Fallyn, are you nearby?"

Fallyn popped out of her room, holding a stuffed bear, an annoyed expression on her face. "I was having a tea party with Mr. Teddy. He's been very lonely with me gone."

Angie raised her palms as if trying to calm the child. "We won't disturb you, dear. Finish your tea party. But you'll let me know if you get hungry, won't you?"

"Yes." Fallyn tucked the bear in her arm and retreated from the room, leaving Claire and Angie alone.

"I can't thank you enough for taking Fallyn with you." Angie crossed the room and offered Claire one of the wing chairs facing the fireplace. They sat down together, the cold hearth an eerie third party, as if it listened to their conversation. "It got pretty crazy here when the triplets made their appearance. Fallyn would have gotten lost in the confusion."

"We've had a good time." Images of their outings played across Claire's memory. "I discovered I don't know as much about motherhood as I should."

"From the looks of her, you've done a splendid job." Angie relaxed into the backrest, her arms limp over the sides. Fatigue rode her forehead like a tiara. "No one would guess she has congenital kidney problems. Have you found a donor?"

"I've had two or three willing to be tested, but no matches yet." Claire slumped into the chair, lifting her chin toward the ceiling. "I keep praying Fallyn won't need the procedure, but the pediatrician at the Newport clinic seems to think it's only a matter of time."

"That's what Fallyn's physician here said." Angie glanced at her hands. "You live near Stanford, one of the best transplant hospitals in the country."

Claire studied her sister. "But Fallyn probably won't be living in Newport when she needs the kidney." She bit back the sting of loss she felt saying those words. "She wants to go home with me, did she tell you?"

"I'm not surprised. She's obviously quite enthused with the ocean." Angie's attention shifted to the row of framed portraits sitting on the mantel. "Her health has improved in your care."

"How do you feel about her leaving again?"

"I hope you'll take her the rest of the summer, even though it's hard to have her gone. Caring for three babies is exhausting for Mrs. Thornton and me. Fallyn would be bored to death. She'll have a better summer with you."

"Unless she has another crisis." Claire couldn't hide her angst. "She wants you when she's sick."

"I know, but knowing you are there to stand in has made things here so much easier."

"Still, I'm not you."

Angie didn't respond, a light in her eyes made Claire suspect there was more she wasn't saying. "She needs you."

"Mom approached Jamie's mother about the kidney." Angie picked at a thread in the arm of the wing chair. "Have you thought of asking Jamie?"

"He's the last person I'd ask." Claire didn't like the direction this conversation headed. "I saw him not long ago when Fallyn and I went out to dinner. He'd heard I was searching. . ." Claire made quotation marks with her fingers, ". . . for a kidney."

Angie sat up straighter. "No kidding? What did he say?"

"He wished me good luck. Said not many people would want to be a donor. His uncle died waiting for a kidney." Claire resisted the urge to stand and pace, opting instead to rap her knuckles on the chair cushion. "I won't go begging anything from him."

"Not even to save Fallyn's life?" Angie leaned forward and grasped Claire's wrist. "What will it hurt to add one more person to your possible donors list?

"Do you think that selfish rat of a man would undergo surgery and convalescence to help a little girl in need? Have you forgotten what he did to me?" Claire clenched her fists, her heart racing like a frightened horse. She drew long, sustained breaths, containing her fury for her sister's sake. "Angie, you can't be serious."

"People change." Angie pushed herself from the chair. "He might want to redeem himself in your eyes."

Claire tightened her jaw, gazing Angie's direction, but her sister's stare unnerved her. "I don't want to ask him, to give him the upper hand over me again." Claire looked away, folding her arms across her chest. "In the first place, his selfishness would prevent participation in a deed as heroic as giving up a kidney, and in the second, the donor suffers the most trauma and the longer recovery. Can you honestly see him making such a sacrifice?" Claire laughed, the sound of it bitter in the silence that separated them. "That's not the Jamie I knew."

Angie's voice had grown soft. "You might be surprised what could happen, given the truth."

Claire stood. What Angie suggested would take a miracle. "I think I'll go check on our kidney candidate. She's awfully quiet."

"So you'll take Fallyn with you." Angie stated the question rather than asking it, sounding fearful of her answer. "I'd appreciate it if you would."

"In a heartbeat." Claire walked on air as she left the room. Dreams do come true.

CHAPTER THIRTY-FOUR

The Fourth of July arrived with sunshine and gentle breezes. Whitecaps licked the tops of the waves, and the beach Monty chose for their outing stretched long and inviting. Claire held Fallyn's hand as they maneuvered around driftwood and rises of sand. Monty pitched an umbrella to stake out their picnic spot. Ellen and Kevin dug a fire pit and rimmed it with rocks from the shoreline. Mia and Mason were setting up folding chairs around the circle.

"Did you remember the wieners?" Ellen shaded her eyes with her palm as she grinned at Claire's approach.

"Buns, too." Claire set her basket next to Ellen's. "Fallyn's got the iced tea thermos."

Fallyn dropped the container and ran to join Mia, who had abandoned the folding chairs and was digging in the sand.

"Monty hiked back to the car to bring the kite and his offerings."

"Is he contributing to the lunch?" Claire raised an eyebrow. "Does he cook?"

"Coleslaw from the deli up the highway." Ellen pointed over her shoulder. "Kevin asked me to make potato salad."

"No shortage of side dishes." Claire laughed as she reached in her basket. "I brought macaroni salad as well."

"We'll have to roll out of here." Ellen puffed out her cheeks.

"Hey, Claire. Fallyn." Monty's panting competed with his words as he approached them. He had a basket in one hand, a round table he rolled along the sand with the other, and a kite that bounced in the spurts of wind behind him. The string came over his shoulder and ended in the ball he'd tucked in his shirt.

"Multi-tasking, I see." Claire marveled at the man's ingenuity as he added the items to the growing picnic spot. Where did he get the energy to move all that at once?

"I thought the kite was going to lift off and fly me down here a couple of times." Monty handed the ball of string to Kevin before he popped the legs on the table and set it upright. "Tie it off to a leg and the kite will stay put."

"You could have asked for help, you know." Ellen made a face at her brother. "You might have torn the kite."

"Is that Mason's dragon?" Fallyn's eyes were wide with wonder.

Mason strutted to where his uncle had tied the kite. "Yep. This is it. Best dragon in the sky when we get it up."

"Wow!" To Claire's ear Fallyn sounded impressed. Could a five-year-old have a crush on someone? She supposed it to be puppy love, but she'd keep a close eye on their attraction. Mason had been vying for Fallyn's attention ever since Mia stole her away to play dolls. She'd now entered Mason's territory, and he seemed determined to prove his superiority.

"You want to try your hand at flying the kite?" Monty finished laying out the tablecloth, holding it down as Ellen set their baskets around the table's rim to secure the flimsy piece of plastic. He reached for the ball of string and handed it to Claire. "We could get it up before we eat and then take turns monitoring its flight while we munch on hot dogs."

"Can we?" Fallyn's expectant face searched hers, anticipation lurking in every feature.

"You can help me feed the string while Mason and Monty run the kite."

Mason swaggered to where his kite bobbed on its short tether. "Watch us, Fallyn. Me and Dad will have the dragon flying in no time."

Monty's gaze met hers and from the looks of his mouth, he fought a grin at his son's declaration. Claire pushed her own chuckle down, refusing to laugh at the little boy's boast. More likely Monty would get the kite flying while Mason ran alongside, and then she would dole out the string as they'd done before. Fallyn, as small as she was, would hold the string and not much else. Still the fun waited in sharing the experience with friends. Fallyn needed that.

"Let's do it." Claire held up her ball of string. "Untangle me, please."

A glimmer flashed across Monty's eyes, and Claire's cheeks grew warm. He removed the kite from the table leg and led the way to the longest stretch of flat sand. Handing the kite to her, he took the ball of string and fed several feet of line as he walked backwards.

Fallyn's head whipped back and forth as her rapt attention swiveled between the two of them, caught up in the scene of flying the kite.

Mason jumped up and down, pumping his fists, shouting encouragement to the rustling piece of plastic at the end of the string. "Fly, Mr. Dragon, fly!"

Claire ran as fast as she could down the straight stretch, letting the string out as the kite took flight. Monty came running from behind. When he caught up, she'd run out of lead line. He handed her the ball of string, wrapping his arm about her waist as they backed away from the kite. His breath came in puffs against her neck, the strength of his body solid against her shoulders. They slowed to a standstill, neither one speaking as she fed string to the ever-widening space between them and the dragon soaring overhead. Claire's awareness of Monty competed with her attention to the kite. His woodsy aftershave tantalized her nose, like a romp in the forest might. Both of their breaths grew erratic—short, raspy, halting. But what she noticed most was the pounding of his heart against her back, its beat rivaling her own—the noise of both together strong enough to vibrate across the waves.

Neither of them had escaped the attraction nearness to the other had ignited. What Claire most needed here on this beach of wind, waves, and endless sand was air—something that shouldn't be in short supply, but it was. She forced her lungs to work.

"Dad?" Mason stumbled across the sand toward them. "Can Fallyn and I have a turn holding the kite?"

"Think we should let them?" Monty's whisper at the base of her neck sent shivers down her spine.

She turned slowly toward him, meeting his gaze, the hunger in his eyes causing a catch in her throat, her breathing staccato and shallow, as if her lungs had stopped working and her heart faltered in her chest. "Fallyn . . . will be disappointed . . . if she doesn't get a turn."

He smiled, a dimple in his cheek deepening. He stood so close she could see the shadow of his whiskers threatening to darken his jaw. For a minute, she thought he might kiss her, his head angled as if he'd considered the idea. "We don't want to disappoint Fallyn, do we?"

She shook her head slowly from side to side, eyes riveted to the tease across his mouth, and handed him the ball of string. "She's pretty lightweight. The kite's pull might be too strong."

He stepped back a pace, the movement breaking the spell she'd sensed between them. "Fallyn, let me show you how to hold the string."

Fallyn bounced across the sand to where they stood, Mason on her heels. "I get to hold it?"

Claire smiled at the wonderment on the child's face. Even though her health had improved, Fallyn remained small. A hearty gust of ocean air could send her toppling.

Monty knelt beside Fallyn, his hand protective against her back, bracing her as she grabbed the string. The kite's tug jerked her arms in a playful give and take with the wind. Fallyn giggled as the kite rocked her, a comical sway from her heels to her tiptoes.

Claire pressed her lips together, memorizing the tender scene before her. Monty treated Fallyn with the same gentle strength he gave his own children, sensing her needs and guiding her hands as she flew the kite. No matter where their relationship went from here, Monty's kindness and consideration for the child would remain embedded in her memory. Claire breathed deeply. Her heart had taken flight.

Monty could feel the tickle of Claire's curls against his cheek long after they drew apart and Fallyn, with his help, assumed the flying of the kite. The woman's hand fit in his like a softball in a mitt, her small frame tucked against his torso like pieces formed together in a woodshop project. He hadn't experienced this kind of nearness to another since he'd lost Marissa, and the sensation rocketed his senses. He'd fought to breathe, his awareness of her so close, it heightened his need for her presence in his life.

When Mason insisted on a turn, Fallyn had relinquished her hold on the string and joined Claire at the water's edge. Seeing Mia digging in the sand, Fallyn left Claire wading in the surf. He'd called Kevin to take over and found his way back to the picnic table. Pulling out the two-pronged forks he'd packed to cook the wieners and his container of coleslaw, he closed the cooler and set both on the table. Ellen had grouped the condiments in the middle and stacked plastic plates to the side, her potato salad and Claire's macaroni dish occupying space with the glasses.

"You two do well together." Ellen placed spoons in the salads, her gaze on his face. "A passerby would think you'd rehearsed your plan to fly the kite, the way you both worked in tandem getting it in the air."

"Pure coincidence." Monty kept his attention on the table and placed the roasting forks near the packages of wieners, ignoring his sister's keen insight. "Is the fire hot enough to cook the hot dogs?"

"Probably." Ellen's smile matched the twinkle in her eyes. "If you fan the flames of her heart, that fire will crackle too."

Monty made a face at his sister, hoping to silence her before Claire returned and heard them. "Mia, Fallyn, do you girls want a hot dog?"

The pair sprang from their spots on the sand and hurried to the table. Mia reached for a pronged fork. "Can I roast mine?"

Monty placed a wiener on the end. "Be careful to keep the handle back from the pit and only let the hot dog sit above the fire. Want some help?"

Fallyn nodded, as did Mia.

Monty gave Fallyn her own fork and knelt between the two girls in front of the blaze, helping them balance the forks over the flames. When both wieners were sizzling, he pulled them back and directed the girls to where Ellen had prepared buns on plates. He squatted in front of the fire, poking at the logs to stir the embers a little hotter.

Claire had left the water and stood watching Mason and Kevin fly the kite, her attention on their conversation.

"Claire." She turned at his call and stepped toward him. "Why don't you cook a wiener now before Mason and Kevin get tired of flying, then you can take over for them?"

"Sure." She picked up a roasting fork and held her wiener over the pit. "The fire feels good in this wind."

"Did you bring jackets for you and Fallyn?" Monty checked his hot dog. "By the time the fireworks start, the wind off the ocean will have grown colder. We were here last week for the hot air balloon exhibition, and the wind turned mean."

"I have coats in the car." Claire's smile faded as fast as it came. "Fallyn told me she's getting tired." She bit her lip, frown lines forming across her brow. "I hope she's not getting sick again."

Monty sensed the tension behind her words. "Can it come on that fast?"

"In children, it's almost a constant worry." Claire's face reflected a deep-seated concern riding the tide of her emotions.

"We'll get her out of here in a hurry if she worsens."

"Thanks."

Claire tried to persuade Fallyn to leave for home, convinced the child's health had taken a turn in the excitement of the afternoon activities, but the girl insisted she wanted to watch the fireworks over Yaquina Bay. Circles beneath her eyes had deepened and a persistent yawn plagued her as she put on a brave face and struggled to keep up with Mia and Mason. A knot in Claire's stomach grew tighter as the evening wore on.

Though she had never attended the event here, Claire had heard these fireworks were some of the noisiest in the nation. After the first explosion, she needed no more convincing. The sound reverberated against the hills surrounding the Bay, magnifying the original blast at least two-fold. Fallyn visibly wilted before her, covering her ears, and shrinking into her coat, the hood pulled up over her head.

"Too loud?" Claire wrapped her forearm around Fallyn's neck, pulling her into the hem of her own jacket, providing an extra layer of sound-proofing.

"Scary." The muted reply was spoken into Claire's side as Fallyn pressed her small self against Claire's thighs. Fallyn looked up. "Colors are pretty."

"Lots of sparkly reds, greens, and blues."

Beside her, Monty kept vigil over Mia whose reaction to the

noise mimicked Fallyn's. Mason, though, jumped up and down at every explosion, shouting his delight at the bursts of color streaming across the sky. The reflection on the water only doubled his pleasure. Monty glanced her way and lifted his shoulders, a shake of his head confirming what he thought of Mason's glee. "All boy."

Claire chuckled, agreeing to the statement with a nod. She'd never doubted Mason's male approach to life, from his love of kites to his need to investigate. He had a thirst for learning no one could quench, his insatiable hunger for knowledge driving him beyond his years. She wondered what would become of the eager child as he grew.

Fallyn shuddered at her side, a moan doubling her over before she lost her lunch on the ground beside them. "Mommy!" Claire knelt over her as she continued to convulse, reaching in her pocket for a tissue to wipe Fallyn's tears and clean her mouth. "I'm sorry, Auntie Claire. I'm sick."

Monty pushed Mia and Mason toward Ellen before he came to her rescue, but not before Mason declared his disgust. "Eww."

"Mason." Monty's tone forbade any comment. "Fallyn's sick."

He wrapped an arm about Fallyn's back and looked at Claire as she finished wiping Fallyn's face. "Want me to carry her to the car?"

"No." No sooner had Claire shaken her head and told him Fallyn could walk than the child let out a cry and fell against his shoulder. Her body went limp and her legs sagged. Claire gasped, her hand across her mouth as her niece passed out. "Oh no!"

Monty scooped her up in his arms and stood, barking orders to Mason and Mia. "Aunt Ellen will take you home to her house. I'll pick you up there after we get Fallyn home." He turned his attention to Ellen, a raise of his eyebrows asking her if that would work. She nodded at him and said to Claire, "I'll be praying."

Claire touched her friend's shoulder in a show of thanks and followed Monty to the parking lot, stumbling over the rises of sand and around the driftwood that had been easier to see in the daylight. When they reached Claire's car, Monty slid Fallyn into her booster seat and locked the straps in place. He straightened and turned to her. "She's burning up."

Alarmed, Claire leaned in and felt Fallyn's face and arms. Hot skin and beads of sweat met her fingers. She stepped back and closed the car door, Monty's eyes on her as she fought the urge to cry. "I'm taking her straight to the emergency room." She blinked back the moisture threatening to spill down her cheeks. "I'm frightened."

Monty stroked her cheek and pulled her into a hug. "I'll follow you there, to be sure you make it."

"That's not necessary." Claire drew away from his shoulder. "Your children need you."

"I either follow you, or I drive. Take your pick."

Surprised by his tone, she stared into his eyes. His expression broached no argument. He intended to oversee her safety. In that moment her independent spirit, the one force that had propelled her through the hills and valleys of life, wrestled with a longing she'd never acknowledged, a need for a man's strength and protection. No one had ever cared enough to take charge over her, to allow her to be helpless, and yet secure, within the cloak of his power. The sensation, though strange, brought with it a blanket of comfort she'd not before experienced.

"You drive." Claire handed him the keys. "I don't trust myself to stay on the road."

Monty fingered the key ring, holding her hand an extra second. When she lifted her gaze he smiled, leaned in, and kissed her. In that instant a rupture of light sparkled in her mind, and it had nothing to do with the ongoing celebration bursting around them.

CHAPTER THIRTY-FIVE

THE EMERGENCY ROOM TEEMED WITH PEOPLE waiting their turn in triage or for a call from the doctor. Monty carried Fallyn in his arms, taking a chair near the door while Claire sought assistance. She waited, a calm, but urgent expression on her face, her body at attention. Though the surge of the storm within her must be raging, she remained stalwart on the outside.

Monty appreciated her reserve, the ability to handle stress, even in the toughest situations. He swallowed. The pretty blonde woman with the tantalizing curls had found a chink in his armor, the weakness leaving his heart vulnerable and exposed. Enamored by her beauty and inner strength, he had no power to fight it. He glanced around the clinic.

One little boy held his reddened arm, a sparkler burn on his flesh raw above the elbow. Another fellow had come in on crutches, his left leg bearing the brunt of a dune buggy rollover. The crush of people shrank the small space, time slowing to a stop as the holiday claimed its victims. Even the air seemed in short supply.

As Claire filled out paperwork and explained Fallyn's condition to the overwhelmed receptionist, Monty held the child on his lap. He prayed as she breathed, the pallor of her skin resurrecting memories of those last days he'd shared with Marissa. Fallyn couldn't be that ill, could she? The change baffled him, remembering her laughter today as she'd tugged the kite down after flying it for more than an hour. Except for an occasional moan or a gasp for air, her mirth had vanished, her joy silent. He'd not prayed like this since Marissa's diagnosis, the need pressing him like an old friend.

"Monty?" Claire motioned for him to follow her. They were ushered to the back, down a narrow hall, and into a room filled with medical equipment. Monty laid Fallyn on the bed, stroking her sweaty forehead, the damp curls windblown around her face. "She got sunburned today."

Claire caressed Fallyn's face, her fingers doing an assessment of each feature as if to assure her the child didn't suffer from something else. "Maybe the warmth we feel is sunburn and not inner temperature."

Monty wanted to agree, but before he could utter a word, a doctor dressed in hospital whites with a stethoscope around his neck entered, picked up a chart, and stepped to the bed. "She's been well since I last saw you?"

Claire took a deep breath and nodded. "She's acted so healthy, and this collapse came as a shock." Her words were dogged with gulps of air, as if speaking required more of her than she had to give, but she pressed the physician. "Can her condition turn this quickly?"

"If she's gone from a stable state to an acute one, yes, it can." He looked at Monty. "Are you here in an official capacity?"

"I carried her in." Monty didn't want to leave Claire. Though she was strong, the incident had left her fragile, struggling with emotions riding her sleeve. "I'm here to bolster Claire."

"You're not on the documents regarding Fallyn, so I'll have to ask you to wait in the lobby."

Monty fought the impulse to argue, instead addressing Claire. "Will you be all right?"

"I think so. Thank you for bringing her here." She held out her hand and he took it, giving it a squeeze. "Go home and hug Mia and Mason for me."

"I'll call Ellen to come and get me. Call me, no matter what time it is, and let me know what's happening." He kissed her knuckles, winking at her as he made his exit. Each step dragged, his need to stay with Claire weighing heavily on his shoulders. He found his phone and called Ellen.

"Is she going to be okay?" His sister sounded as worried as he felt. "Do you know anything?"

"No." Monty struggled to answer. "She's in with the doctor now. Can you or Kevin come get me and take me back to my truck?"

"Kevin can be there in ten minutes." As though she were trying to be strong, Ellen's words wobbled in the phone. "I'm at your house and have put the kids to bed." She paused a minute, speaking to someone in the room. "Kevin says you can stay with Claire if you need to, and I'll stay here with the twins tonight."

"What would I do without you two?" Monty exhaled, the many instances Ellen had come to his aid marching across the memories of his mind. "Claire needs someone to support her. Fallyn's condition may have changed to critical today."

"I'll call the prayer team and have her covered in prayer. I know that's hard for you—"

"—No, Ellen, it's not. You'd be proud of me. I spent the last hour in the waiting room praying for her myself. Once I retrieve my truck, I'll be back here, praying."

"This *is* a day of miracles, isn't it?"

Claire's mind spun as she considered what might have caused Fallyn to collapse. The doctor had whisked the child away to the imaging section of the medical facility and blood tests had been done. When Fallyn returned, she was attached to a monitor that checked her blood pressure, pulse, and oxygen levels as well as a bag that measured her urine output and performed other tasks Claire didn't understand. Still unconscious, she lay on the bed, her skin as white as the sheet beneath her. *Oh God, where are you?*

The doctor returned, his face stoic, schooled to be unreadable.

What felt like an eternity passed before he stopped flipping pages and looked up. "I have the test results from her last visit here. I'm comparing those to what we are seeing now. Apparently, the infection was worse before than we originally thought. The ultrasound showed a cyst ballooning in her right kidney. That cyst has burst, probably today, and is bleeding. We've found blood in her urine. We need to airlift her to Eugene or Portland." He looked up from his clipboard. "Do you have a preference?"

"My mother lives in Eugene. It would be easier for me to get around." Claire laid a hand on her throat. "What will happen there?"

"River Bend is a regional hospital with more sophisticated equipment to monitor Fallyn's progress. Have you found a kidney donor yet?" The doctor's face reflected skepticism—he understood the reality.

"I only have possible volunteers. None have been tested yet." Claire tried to sound confident. "But some of them are in Eugene."

"When you get to Eugene, get on the phone and start contacting those you've considered. Fallyn may completely recover from this incident. She could well be healthy again for a time. But with this disease the prospect is she will have recurring episodes the rest of her life. Eventually she will be looking at hemi-dialysis three times a week. She won't feel good. She won't be able to play like other children do. The doctor may send her home with a dialysis machine once she's stable, but that's hard on a child. A kidney could stop this disease in its tracks."

"Can't the new kidney become infected?"

"No. The new kidney will come without disease and function as it was meant to." The doctor offered her a smile. "She could be happy again within a relatively short time."

As his words registered with her brain, Claire nodded. "I'll start calling immediately."

The doctor scheduled the life flight within the hour. Claire made as many arrangements as she could by phone, alerting her mother to the emergency, and calling Ellen.

"Eugene?" Ellen sounded shocked. "How will you get home?"

"I'll fret about that when Fallyn can travel with me." Claire fought the trembling within her, the nagging worry that she had somehow let her niece down. Aware of the lateness of the hour, she'd have to call Angie first thing in the morning. "Ellen, pray for us. I'm so afraid I'm going to lose her."

"The doctor sounds competent. Fallyn's young. The combination should make for a happy ending. Don't surrender to your fears."

"Tell Monty thanks, too."

"Isn't he there?" Ellen spoke to someone in the room with her. "Kevin dropped Monty at his truck. He planned to come back to the clinic and wait for you."

Claire glanced at the clock. The poor man had been waiting all this time? She hadn't even known. "He must be out in the lobby. I haven't seen him since the doctor asked him to remain outside." Claire made a fist with her free hand. "He wasn't on the paperwork, so he wasn't allowed to stay."

"By now he's asleep in his chair." Ellen chuckled, her voice low into the phone. "After a day of kite-flying, picnicking, and fireworks, he's probably out cold. Better check to make sure they didn't admit him to the ward."

Claire started walking up the hall as she finished the call. "I'm going there now. Talk to you soon."

Only one couple remained in the lobby area. The man sat holding a towel to his head. His friend filled out the clipboard in front of her. Monty wasn't anywhere to be found. Claire turned to the receptionist. "I think I have a friend waiting in the parking lot, but my niece is in the emergency room. Can I get back in if I go check on him?"

"Put a chair in the door." The nurse stacked files on a corner counter. "Usually we are closed by now, but this being a holiday forced us open a little longer than usual." The nurse gave her a sympathetic smile. "I'll wait while you check. Just knock if you get locked out."

"Thanks. I'll hurry." Claire scooted out the entrance, leaving a rock against the casing so the door wouldn't close. She glanced around the parking lot and spotted the truck parked next to her car. She hurried to the driver's side and peeked in. Asleep in the seat, Monty's head was propped against the open window frame, his mouth open enough that the noise of his breathing competed with the rush of the waves in the distance. Claire touched his cheek, careful not to startle him. "Monty?" He didn't stir. She brushed his hair back from his forehead, the intimacy of the act setting her heart to dancing. "Monty?"

He opened one eye and grinned at her. "Want to brush the other cheek while you're at it?" He sat up, depressed the handle, and slid to the ground in front of her.

Claire thanked the night for darkness, her cheeks burning as she stepped back to give him room. "I didn't know you were out here. Ellen told me."

"How long have I been here?" He stretched and yawned. "Are they planning to keep you all night?"

"Lifeflight is taking Fallyn and me to Eugene." Claire's voice faltered as she fought tears. She didn't want to cry in front of him. She had to remain strong. "If you know anyone who might have an extra kidney lying around, send them our way."

"Has it come to that?" Though she couldn't see his features well in the dark, Monty's voice held concern. "She seemed healthy."

"Or so we thought." Claire looked at the clinic door. "I've got to get back in there before they lock me out." She handed him her keys. "Do you think you could get my car back to my duplex?"

Monty's hand folded over hers, the warmth of his palm shooting tremors up her arm. "I'll make it happen." He leaned toward her, drawing her close. "Claire, I know this isn't the time or the place, but I'm falling in love with you." He kissed her on the forehead, then let his lips brush her cheek. He found her mouth and sealed his statement with intensity. Drawing back, he looked into her eyes. "Hurry back."

Rattled by his kiss, Claire shook in his arms. "I will." She touched his face. "Thank you for caring about us. But before we go any further, there's much you don't know about me. I need to tell you the whole story. If you still feel the same way after that, we'll talk."

A frown crossed Monty's forehead, as he measured her words, followed by a smile. "Whatever your story is, I will be waiting to hear it."

"Miss?" The nurse from the clinic stood at the entrance. "I need to close up here."

"Coming." Claire placed a peck on Monty's cheek and ran for the door.

Monty whistled as he drove home. His revelation to Claire had surprised him as well as her. But it was true. He'd fallen for the quiet and efficient schoolteacher. He wasn't sure when it happened, but she'd had his attention that first day when she'd rescued Mason from the snow. Marissa would urge him to follow his heart. Knowing she would give her blessing, if she could, only made him long for Claire more.

He pulled into the drive, thankful lights still burned downstairs. Ellen, and maybe Kevin with her, waited. He entered with quiet steps, tiptoeing through the entry to the living room. The television played to a silent screen, the sound muted. Kevin and Ellen sat in the loveseat, arms wrapped about each other, hushed murmurs passing between them. As he approached an armchair, Kevin landed a kiss on Ellen's cheek.

"Sorry to break up your party." His whispered words made them sit up. "Claire sent me home."

"Are you going to follow her to Eugene?" Ellen's eyes were wide, cheeks flushed as if she'd been crying.

"Her mother lives there and has already been alerted she's coming. Claire will stay with her when she'd not at the hospital."

"We've got to help search for a kidney." Ellen gripped Kevin's hand like a lifeline. "I didn't know Fallyn had that kind of kidney disease."

Monty leaned forward, using his elbows as props against his knees. "Apparently her kidneys weren't functioning as well as they thought." He straightened and studied his sister. "I'm putting out a plea at work when I return on Monday."

Kevin held up his phone. "I sent a message to the men in my unit, asking them for help."

Monty smiled. "You two have been busy while I slept."

Ellen smiled. "You might say that." She glanced at Kevin, laying an arm over his shoulder. "We did a home pregnancy test yesterday. We're going to be parents, ourselves."

"What an ending to a very full day." Monty stood and shook Kevin's hand. "Congratulations, Dad."

"Thanks, Monty. I only pray it's not twins." Kevin rolled his eyes. "One set is all we need in this family."

CHAPTER THIRTY-SIX

After the emergency flight to Eugene, Fallyn was stabilized and resting comfortably at the regional hospital, so as morning broke Claire wasted no time calling potential donors. Since cell phone usage was not allowed inside she took residence on a bench near the main entrance. The tower clock above her chimed ten. A cascade of ripples tumbled over a nearby man-made waterfall, the sound of the burbling pool threading its way across the courtyard. Claire welcomed the calm, a muted and soothing alternative to the bustle of cars and buses on the thoroughfare beyond.

Having lived in Newport the past two years, the valley heat surprised her. The temperature already soared, promising a blistering afternoon. She scooted to the other end of the bench, seeking the shade of a small maple tree. The peaceful landscape quieted her weary heart, though her thoughts remained on Fallyn. The attending nurse promised to call when Fallyn awoke, aware of the urgency of Claire's mission.

Angie was called first.

"I was afraid this would happen." Her sister sounded resolute, as if the events of the past twenty-four hours were something she could have foreseen. "I wish I could travel, but the triplets are still too much work to leave. I know she's in good hands with you there."

"She needs you." Claire could oversee the child's illness, but to others Angie's absence might seem strange. What mother would not come with her child so desperately ill? Angie was not thinking clearly. "You can leave the triplets for a couple of days."

"I'll try." Fatigue punctuated Angie's words, a condition Claire was beginning to understand. Her sister sounded more troubled by Claire's misery, worried when she told her of the overwhelming guilt she carried, believing she had failed Fallyn somehow. She'd missed the signs of a deadly illness while the child remained in her care. Angie was quick to respond. "I'll come, not just for Fallyn, but to be with you."

"I'm stronger than I sound. I'm feeling guilty, is all."

"You're not to blame." Angie's words were balm to Claire's heart. "Fallyn has had enough urinary tract infections to fill a clinic file with chart notes." Angie's resolve reassured Claire as her sister detailed Fallyn's medical history, facts Claire hadn't known before. "She's been increasingly ill, each bout with a urinary tract infection worse than the last. I didn't call you before because I didn't want you to worry. But Brennan and I have known her kidneys were not good since she was two."

"I wish I had known." Claire thought of the anguish Angie and Brennan had suffered caring for their daughter. "I could have offered support."

"What could you have done? We've had the best doctors, who always insisted she was going to be fine." The exasperation in Angie's voice silenced Claire's objections. "Nothing could have prevented this from happening. The doctors couldn't remake her kidneys."

As Claire continued listening, the situation became clear. For whatever reason, Fallyn had been plagued with two malfunctioning vital organs. Finding a good kidney for the child was the only thing that could give her a better life.

"I've alerted several people here to ask their friends." Claire didn't know who might be willing to help a small child, but if Fallyn were to thrive, someone had to be found. Surely there was a match out there and a willing donor to go along with it. She'd prayed like never before, beseeching God to bring her to the man or woman who'd save Fallyn's life.

"I know someone you haven't asked." Angie's tone broached

no argument. "Give me Jamie's number. Do you have it?"

"Angie, no." Claire's pulse raced. "There's got to be another way." She closed her eyes, remembering the encounter in Newport. "He almost sneered when I ran into him at a restaurant not long ago."

"I want to save Fallyn." Angie's voice had lost its compassion, her tone flat and unfeeling. "Surely you can shove your hurt and your pride aside to ask the man to help our child."

Claire remembered his lack of concern when they'd broken their engagement. His feeble excuses for his behavior. Could five years have changed him enough to rise to the occasion? Claire sighed. "I don't have his number. But Mom can get it from Nancy. Fallyn's life is far too important to ignore Jamie as a possible donor." Claire closed her fist to control her growing animosity. "I'll make the call."

"Thank you. I know this is causing you personal pain."

"I'll survive. I have before. But don't be surprised if nothing comes of this."

"People change." Angie's voice grew soft. "He might surprise you if he were given all the facts."

"I'll pray to that end." Claire ended the call.

The sun had climbed to the top of the sky when the tower clock chimed twelve. Claire finished contacting those on her list of possible donors. She checked for messages, but the nurse hadn't yet left a page. *Was Fallyn still sleeping?*

She hurried to the pediatric ward, fearing the worst. In the corridor near Fallyn's room her mother leaned against a chair, engaged in conversation with one of the medical staff. "Mom?"

Mom turned and aimed an exasperated pout her way. "Where have you been?" She pointed to a pair of armchairs in the corner. "Come sit down where we can talk."

Claire balked, waving her mother off. "I want to check on

Fallyn first. I've been making calls to potential donors."

"That's why I'm here." Mom's voice had an edge in it, each word rising in pitch. "With donor information."

"Give me a second. Okay?" Claire spun on her heel and entered Fallyn's room. The silence bounced off the walls, the only sounds those of the monitors tracking Fallyn's progress. An attendant on duty checked readings on the machinery. "Is she still sleeping?"

The attendant nodded. "The pain meds will keep her out for a while."

Claire returned to where her mother waited. "No change." She sank into one of the lounge chairs, the fatigue of several night's lost sleep threatening to win the battle she fought with her tired mind. She drew in a deep breath, hoping to clear her head.

Mom sat watching her, a knowing look in her eyes. How many hours had her mother waited in a hospital, a lobby, or a parking lot keeping tabs on Claire or her sister? Before Fallyn, Claire had never understood the sacrifices a mother made, the decisions that demanded her time, the anxiety some situations thrust upon her. Thousands of them during a child's upbringing. Even now Claire sensed she waited, assessing the situation, deciding how best she could help. Mom spoke. "How is your search for donors going?"

"This morning I alerted everyone who said they might consider it." Claire let her attention drift to the window, the green lawns and meandering paths below beckoning her to come and explore. Anything would be a welcome change from where she presently sat. The circumstances in which she found herself threatened to smother her. Claire's spirit begged for release. "I have three friends in Newport asking acquaintances." She blinked, fighting the ache in her heart. "Angie will try to fly in tomorrow."

Her mother sniffed. "With us here, it seems a shame to drag Angie across the country."

"Fallyn is her daughter."

"Which is why I'm here." Her mother pulled out a piece of paper. "Nancy asked me to give you this. She wants to help."

Claire stared at the numbers on the note. "What is this?"

"Jamie's phone number." Her mother sat back, a hesitant smile on her face. "I know you don't want this, but Nancy is a dear friend, and she allowed herself to be tested for a kidney match. Turns out she is not a candidate, but there was some sort of marker for a filial connection which made her think Jamie might be a better fit."

"Thank Nancy for this." Claire's heart beat as if it contained lead. "I promised Angie I'd add Jamie to my donor list."

"You make it sound like a death sentence." Her mother's words stung. "You didn't consider him so bad five years ago."

"Five years ago, I planned to marry the man." Claire studied her mother. "Now I'm glad he's gone."

"Are you still carrying a grudge?"

"No. I forgave Jamie a long time ago, Mom. I just don't want him back in my life."

Monty paced the floor, waiting for Kevin and Ellen to arrive. He planned to drive to Eugene today to see Claire and find out how Fallyn fared. Mia and Mason would remain with his sister. Watching the helicopter lift off had been heartrending, knowing it carried the woman with whom he was falling in love, and a child he'd grown to adore.

Fallyn had been crying when they transported her to the waiting chopper. Her pale face frightened him, so changed from the radiant child she'd been yesterday at the beach. Claire said something burst inside her, like a balloon they hadn't known existed, lurking in her kidneys. She'd bled internally.

He prayed again, an act that had grown foreign to him in the past year. In the crisis of the moment his need to pray returned, as familiar as the bicycle he used to ride. He hadn't forgotten how. *Fallyn needs a miracle. Claire needs a friend. Make me a vessel of your love to them both.*

The sound of tires in the drive brought Mason and Mia scurrying to the front door. By the time he reached the entrance, Mia chattered at Ellen's side, holding up a new doll his sister had found online and ordered for her. Ellen smiled, enjoying the child's exuberant praise of her new toy, knowing she'd played a part in its arrival.

Mason held a truck in his hand. Not to be outdone by his twin, he handed the machine to Kevin for inspection, lauding its superior qualities.

Kevin smiled, his eyes glimmering as he tried to remain serious. The miniature engineer at his knees touted all the truck's details like a salesman. Kevin needed the coming months to learn about children. Mason wouldn't fail his uncle.

Monty stepped into the midst of the welcoming committee, shook Kevin's hand, and gave Ellen a peck on the cheek. He snorted. "Think you two are ready for this?"

Ellen giggled, lifting her chin in mock indignation. "If you can handle two, we can certainly manage one."

Monty returned her tease with a smirk. "You won't know for sure it's only one for a while." He puckered his lips. "I wouldn't get too confident, if it were me."

Kevin paled. "Bite your tongue, brother."

He knelt down and hugged his kids. "I'll be back sometime tomorrow afternoon. Aunt Ellen and Uncle Kevin will stay here with you today and take you to Sunday school tomorrow. Don't forget to help with the chores."

"We won't, Daddy." The twins chimed.

Mia held up the new doll. "Fallyn will need a friend to stay with her. Will you give this to her? Auntie Ellen said I could share it with her."

Monty glanced up at his sister whose eyes were brimming with tears. She nodded, her mouth struggling to stay in a smile. He touched Mia's face. "That's a generous thing to do."

"I love her. I want her to come home and play dolls with me." Mia's blue eyes puddled at their rims, a single drop inching down her cheek.

Monty rolled his lips inward, his own emotions threatening to erupt. Anyone who didn't believe in a loving God should spend time with a child. They'd not be left unchanged.

When Claire returned to the waiting area, her mother had left. She found the coffee pot and a cup. She fingered the note in her hand, studying each number as if it contained some hidden message she couldn't see. If Nancy, Jamie's mother, hadn't shown markers for a filial connection, Mom wouldn't have latched on to Jamie as a possible donor. She'd rather find ten other candidates than approach him. Ellen, Monty, and Kevin would all have friends and associates to contact. McKenna Taylor and her mother-in-law Livy had friends in the valley. Out there someone must have a matching kidney. But if push came to shove, she'd do it. She'd do anything to save Fallyn. Even begging Jamie.

Of course, she knew the real reason behind their insistence. Mom held unshakable dreams of repairing the relationship. Angie, on the other hand, knew better. But Jamie wouldn't accept the inquiry graciously, nor would he accept the logic of the request without making a scene. A scene Claire would rather avoid.

Her mother's words haunted her. Was her reluctance to ask

him based on buried feelings of betrayal? Was humbling herself before this man who'd broken her an act she refused to perform simply because he was Jamie? Did she carry a grudge so deep she couldn't find a way to let it go? She sank into the chair, wishing she could vanish into the wall. *God, is this message from you? I forgave Jamie. Didn't I? I could ask him for Fallyn's sake. I only know what kind of a man he is. That's all that holds me back. Isn't it?*

She sat in silence for several minutes, fighting the urge to run and hide. She reached for her phone, remembering again she couldn't call from within the hospital walls. She'd have to contact him later. A reprieve of sorts—one she could postpone forever if she stayed with Fallyn. But the child's condition wouldn't improve if Claire allowed her disgust to hold her back. Asking Jamie would break open half a decade of hurts she'd managed to bury. Digging them up would leave her raw and bleeding.

"I can't do this." Claire pounded the arm of the chair with her fist. "You're asking too much." She turned her face toward the window, hiding from others the anguish threatening the remnants of yesterday's mascara. She grabbed both elbows, locking her arms close to disguise the sobs wracking her body. Pain she believed she'd forgotten surfaced. Thoughts of betrayal, humiliation, and pity raged through her. As though she were once again twenty-two, she held a note from Jamie, the one telling her he'd changed his mind.

He'd left for Aspen.

Their wedding was off.

Sorry, Claire.

But not everything could be left at the altar.

CHAPTER THIRTY-SEVEN

THE DRIVE TO EUGENE DRAGGED ON forever. Monty was certain he must have taken a wrong turn somewhere. Ellen told him to allow three hours, and he hadn't believed her, but the holiday traffic after the Fourth crept like a snail on a blade of grass. The congestion reminded him why he'd left Seattle. He could have walked the distance faster.

He hadn't thought of his former home in a while. The busyness of his life in Newport and his relationship with Claire had blocked out the memories that plagued him. The images which surfaced today were happier ones—panoramas of picnics, sailing, and the Seattle night life— with Marissa at his side. They'd lived a good life—one that ended too soon.

His new existence once again held purpose. The children thrived in their changed environment, and they enjoyed a new home. His sister provided family nearby. His job required only a ten-minute commute. In spite of the pain he'd experienced and the conviction he'd never be happy again, he was. And most of his joy he owed to Claire.

Once he reached Eugene, he followed the signs to the hospital. River Bend sat at a juncture of the interstate between two cities, a regional resource with a reputation for excellence. The sprawling pavilion made him blink. The imperious brick buildings appeared to be more like a college campus than a hospital facility. Where would Claire be?

He parked near the main entrance and entered, relieved to find a large reception desk occupied the immediate area inside the door. A white-haired woman with pink-rimmed, owl-like glasses stared up at him, a smile pasted in place. "How may I help you?"

"I'm looking for a little girl named Fallyn, who came in with her aunt, Claire Simpson."

"Last name?"

Monty wracked his brain. Did he know Fallyn's full name? "I'm not sure. But she's either in pediatrics or the intensive care unit. She has kidney problems."

"Mother's name?" The owl eyes studied him, as if wary of a stranger making queries for someone whose name he didn't know. He couldn't blame her.

"I only know her aunt's name, Claire Simpson. That's who came in with her."

The woman sighed, running her mouse down the computer screen, eyeing him from the corner of her glasses. He shifted his weight from one leg to the other as he waited, thinking it might be faster to call Claire's phone.

"Monty?" The familiar voice made him smile. "What are you doing here?"

Feeling rescued, he turned around to discover Claire walking up behind him. He explained his predicament. "I don't know Fallyn's full name, so this kind lady was having trouble finding her room."

"She's asleep." Claire gestured toward the door. "I need some air."

Monty took her elbow and escorted Claire outside. Circles shadowed her eyes, lids now dotted with mascara. Had she been crying? He wondered if he'd arrived at a bad time. She still wore the clothes she'd worn on the Fourth. "Have you slept?"

"Yes. There's a bed in Fallyn's room." She pointed toward a water pool. "I've claimed that bench as my own as well. Quiet, isolated, private."

"Can't you leave?" Monty worried about her being pushed past her limits, her disheveled appearance so unlike the put-together schoolteacher she usually was. He steadied her as they walked to the bench. "Or are you too worried?"

"Angie's plane landed an hour ago." She flopped onto the bench like a sack of dirty laundry. "As soon as she gets here I'm heading to my mother's house for a shower and fresh clothes." She scrunched her nose. "I probably smell as bad as I look."

"You look tired." Monty sat beside her. "Fallyn's stable?"

"Yes." Claire relaxed against the bench seat. "The doctor in Newport suspected a cyst burst and the specialist here confirmed it. That's bad, but there are no signs of other cysts ballooning at present. The disease struck her so young, she has a rocky future ahead." Claire closed her eyes, her mouth straight-lined. "That's why I have to find a donor."

"No one wants to volunteer?"

"Volunteers? Yes. Matches? No." She studied her hands. "I'm looking for one kidney in a world where everyone has two, and I can't seem to find the smallest speck of hope." She turned away from him, her attention seemingly caught in the water display beyond, but the rise and fall of her chest suggested she fought tears.

"Can Fallyn exist without a transplant?" His question made her look at him, the tears he suspected hovering on her lashes.

"For a while. But the treatment will eat up her childhood. All the fun things kids do, she won't." Claire raised a hand and waved. "Angie's here. With my mother. You want to be introduced?" She stood. "I don't think she saw me. We'll have to catch up."

"And you need to sleep." Monty stood and offered an arm. "Once they are installed in Fallyn's room, I'll take you to your mother's house." He patted her hand. "Trust me to deliver you safely there?"

Her smile answered his question.

They followed Claire's mother and sister who'd already reached the elevators. As the door dinged and closed, they punched the button for another. A second door opened, offering them an empty ride to the pediatric floor. Monty wrapped an arm around Claire, who leaned against him in weary silence. He'd meet the family in a minute, but for now he liked the privacy the conveyance provided.

Claire didn't miss the light in Angie's eyes when Monty entered Fallyn's room. As she made introductions, her sister gave the man a discreet once-over before flashing her approval. She returned the look with a grimace, praying her sister wouldn't embarrass her in a bolt of enthusiasm. To her surprise, Fallyn provided the needed reprieve.

"Monty. You came!" Fallyn's head riveted toward Monty, her smile as wide as her eyes. "Did you bring Mia?"

Monty strode to the bedside and touched Fallyn's forehead. "No, princess. Mia and Mason are with their Aunt Ellen. But Mia sent you this." He held up a small cloth doll, eyes embroidered on its face above a crimson mouth of cross-stitched thread. The toy wore a calico print dress beneath a white pinafore apron and hand-sewn slippers. "Mia can't wait for you to come back and play dolls again."

"And fly kites." Fallyn noticed her mother for the first time. "Mom, I flew kites with Mia and Mason on the Fourth of July."

Angie came alive at Fallyn's greeting. "I heard. Did you have fun?"

"I want to do it again." Fallyn's tone grew sober. "Don't take me home until I get to fly kites one more time." She leaned against her pillows, wriggling as if she felt pain.

A nurse entered and recorded information on the monitors, asking Fallyn if she hurt. At her nod, the nurse adjusted a dial with a touch of her finger and patted Fallyn's arm. "Give it a minute or two."

"Kites are fun." Fallyn directed her statement to Angie as the nurse left. "I helped Mason."

"I'd like to see that, sweetheart," Angie seemed visibly shaken. She found a chair near the bed and sat. "We've got to get you well first."

Fallyn nodded. "I got to fly in a helicopter too." She glanced Claire's way. "Noisy."

Everyone chuckled.

Claire laid a hand on Fallyn's shoulder. "I'm going to Grandma's house to take a shower and get some sleep. Will you be okay now that your mommy is here?"

"I'm sleepy again." Fallyn rolled on her side. "I'll sleep too."

Monty lifted a hand first toward her mother and then to Angie. "I'll take Claire to your house so you can stay with Fallyn." They nodded their agreement and he stepped back. "It's nice to have met you."

"How long are you here?" Claire's mother, who'd sat quietly on the couch during the exchange, angled her face toward him, a twinkle in her eye. "If you're here at dinnertime, you're welcome to join us."

Claire smiled. The matchmakers were at it again.

The shower and sleep revived Claire. Monty said he'd be back to pick her up about 4:00. The clock read 3:30 when she heard tires in the drive. She peeked out the window, but it wasn't Monty's truck. She shuddered as the car door swung open. Jamie.

She answered the door without enthusiasm. "What brings you here?"

"The grapevine told me you were in town, and it's not like I don't know my way here, is it?" His mouth held no smile. "Your mom called mine, who called me, and here I am."

"Why?"

"I'm here about that kidney you need." Jamie shoved his hands in his pockets and gestured toward the living room. "May I come in and talk?"

Claire stepped back, and with a sweep of her hand indicated he enter. She followed him to a pair of recliners, where he made himself comfortable on one. She sat on the edge of the other. How different from when they were dating and snuggled into one chair. How foolish she had been.

You have been forgiven, daughter. The unspoken thought gave her courage.

When he met her gaze, his eyes were serious, as if he sought to look through her. She struggled to speak. "You met my niece in Newport. Her condition became acute on the Fourth. The physicians believe the only way she can have a normal childhood is to receive a donor kidney." Claire clasped her hands. "But they seem to be in short supply."

"Go figure." Jamie crossed one knee over another. "I understand the procedure is quite involved for the donor."

"Do you think one of your friends might consider it?"

"That's doubtful." Jamie studied her, the look on his face one that made Claire shudder. She'd seen that look before—calculated, cunning, and conquering. What was he about to spring on her? She braced herself as Jamie continued. "I've done some research of my own. My mother's test showed a filial marker, which made me curious. I asked myself how that could be possible."

Heat crept along Claire's jaw and up her cheeks. She'd vowed she'd never tell Jamie the truth. He'd never know what he'd done to her. She'd spent years hiding her pain. Jamie knew more than he was letting on. She hurried to counter his argument. "Markers help identify people who are possible matches."

"Still, it's strange, don't you think?" He flattened both feet on the floor and leaned forward on his knees, piercing her with his gaze. "Out of a sea of volunteers, my mother turns up with markers for your niece."

Claire lifted her chin. "It gives me hope we'll find someone."

"Well, the coincidence lit a fire in my mother." He picked up a piece of lint from the carpet. "She became convinced I might be a better fit, since she came so close." He rolled the lint in his fingers as if he needed the fuzzy lump to help him think. "I told her I had no reason to donate a kidney to a perfect stranger." Tossing the lint ball over his shoulder, he stood and squared his shoulders. "Unless there's something I don't know." His hazel eyes swept over her, the stare like hardened steel. "Is there?"

In that moment, Claire's resolve faded. The time for truth had come. No matter how many ways she'd tried to hide, the number of smoke shields she'd put up, or the places in which she'd sought cover, she stood exposed. She scanned the room for an exit, a place where she could vanish, and he couldn't find her. The room left her no escape. The words she'd sworn she'd never speak demanded an audience. Jamie wouldn't walk away from this without an answer. She inhaled, forcing the revelation from her lips. "She's your daughter." Claire held her breath, the last five years marching across the panorama of her mind like a panel of judges pointing fingers.

As if she'd clobbered him in the jaw, Jamie's attention jerked back to the carpet, his hands clasped. He didn't speak, his breathing labored like a man biting his tongue to keep from yelling. The movement of air from his lungs became the only sound in the silent room as he continued his fascination with the floor. He lifted his head and fire sparked in his eyes. He spoke through clenched teeth. "I thought we agreed to take care of our problem another way. If I recall, I gave you money for the procedure."

"Which proved you didn't know me at all." Claire's heart raced as she waited for Jamie's temper to flare. Unless he'd changed in the past five years, the violent rage that waited to erupt wouldn't be long in coming. She found her courage. The disclosure she'd prayed would never be made known now laid open and bare, inviting him to seize the information and torment her. She prayed for wisdom. "The last thing in the world I could ever do was abort our child. I used the money for a plane ticket."

"To Pennsylvania." He sank backward, sitting again in the recliner. "I figured out the rest of the story. Especially when I discovered Angela and Brennan O'Brien never adopted a child."

"Of course, they did." The arrogance of this man! Claire's lungs refused to function, her heart pounding against her breastbone. "Angie and Brennan were delighted to have her. I got to be with her for the first six months of her life while I finished school."

"Not according to court records." Jamie smiled at his discovery, knowing he'd surprised her. "They became her guardians."

"No, you're wrong. They adopted Fallyn as soon as the papers could be drawn up." Claire's heart catapulted to her throat. She clawed at the fabric of the recliner to keep her seat. If not for that, she'd bolt and run. Why did this man have to punch all her buttons? Couldn't he walk quietly out the door and leave her alone? "I don't know what court records you consulted, but obviously you didn't find the right file."

A knock at the door interrupted them. Claire stood. "That will be Monty Chandler here to take me back to the hospital."

"What's he doing in town?" Jamie's smirk sidled up his cheek. "Is he a potential donor too?"

"We don't know yet." Claire jumped as Monty knocked again. "At least he's willing."

"Oh, I'll bet he is." Jamie crossed his leg at the knee. "Aren't you going to let him in?"

"Aren't you going to leave?" Claire gestured to the door. *Why had she let him in?*

"I thought you wanted a kidney." Jamie's tone had grown sober. "I came to confirm my suspicions. And to prove to you I've grown up and am capable of taking responsibility for my actions." He leveled her with his gaze. "But now that I know I have a daughter, I would like to meet her."

"Are you planning to file for custody?" Claire's breath stopped in her lungs, her heart frozen in place. "She belongs to Angie and Brennan."

"We'll see." Jamie stood and headed for the kitchen. He stopped at the door. "I'll let myself out."

Claire gripped the edge of the recliner, listening for the click of the back door.

"Claire?" Monty's voice came from the front entrance. "Are you awake yet?"

"In here." She wilted back into the recliner, her lungs screaming for air. What did Jamie mean when he said he'd grown up and wanted to take responsibility for his actions? He couldn't be serious. Could he?

CHAPTER THIRTY-EIGHT

MONTY WALKED IN THE DIRECTION OF Claire's voice, alarmed when he found her crumpled into a recliner, shaking, her face wet with tears. "Claire? What happened? Did the hospital call?" He squeezed into the recliner beside her, grasped her shoulders, and gently pulled her into his arms. The spasms of sobs threatened to break her in two. "Please tell me what happened."

She stopped to catch her breath, the raspy sound like an oversized straw bringing up the last of an iced drink. He wiped her tears with his knuckles, kissing her forehead as she leaned against his shoulder. When at last she could speak, she searched his face as if memorizing the features before she fled. "Jamie was here."

"Jamie. Your ex?" Monty tightened his jaw. "What did he want?"

"To make trouble."

Monty remained quiet for a moment. "You never did tell me about him. Didn't he walk out on you at the last moment?"

"Yes. Three days before the wedding." Claire looked at her fingers before answering him further, the ring finger bare since the day Jamie departed. "He realized he wasn't ready for all the responsibilities our marriage would face." She bit her lip. "I had school to finish."

"Wasn't he willing for you to go on?"

"That would have been fine, if it hadn't interfered with his plans." Claire's attention, as if caught in memory, drifted around the room before she came back to him. "What I'm about to tell you may send you running too."

"No. Claire. I'm not Jamie."

"He wasn't willing to take on family responsibilities." Claire paused, a worried frown across her forehead. "I was pregnant."

"That's why he decided to back out?" Monty resisted the need to say what he was thinking. He caught the sorrow in her eyes. The exposure had cost her. "That's not a man, Claire, that's a coward." He grasped her wrist, pulling her hand to his lips. *A man like that leaving a woman like this carrying his child.* He stopped his mental rambling and looked at her. "What happened to the baby?"

"He gave me money, in his words"—she held up her fingers, forming quotation marks—"to 'take care of it.'" Claire's eyes pooled at the memory.

Monty thought of what Ellen had once said as they toured the house. *"Whatever it is she's hiding, haunts her."* But Claire didn't have a child at her home that he knew of nor did he believe she could have terminated her pregnancy. That only left one option. "You gave your baby away."

Claire drew a deep breath and nodded, her face pinched, tears pooling on her eyelashes. She looked away, breathing deep as her composure struggled to return.

Monty drew her close, holding her against his chest. They sat there together for several moments. When she breathed normally again, he let go of her and she straightened. Her gaze met his and a tiny smile formed on her mouth. He tilted his head, handing her his handkerchief. "Why didn't you share this with me before?"

"I thought you'd walk away. I really wanted to get to know you." Her voice flat, her eyes spoke of regret. "I'm not the kind of woman men go running to find. I fell for Jamie's lines and paid a price I'll never live down."

"Nothing could be further from the truth." Monty took her hand. "You made a mistake. I can't imagine the pain you carry, knowing your child is out there, without you."

"But that's the other part of this. I *do* know where she is." Claire's shy smile warmed her sorrowful face. She studied him, eyes full of questions. "Fallyn is my daughter. I've been able to visit each year to see her and watch her grow."

Monty angled his head, studying Claire as she recovered from her pain, the truth setting her free. Happiness spread across her face.

"I feared I'd run into Jamie here. That's why I finished my schooling in Pennsylvania. I gave birth and Angie and Brennan adopted her." She clenched her jaw. "If Jamie had known I didn't use the money he gave me for the purpose he intended, he would have demanded it back."

Monty ground his teeth, his dislike of Jamie growing by the minute. "That's quite a guy you got rid of."

Claire blanched. "I'm not sure I have. He suspected Fallyn was his daughter, and when I confirmed it, he said he was going to the hospital. I'm afraid of what he might do or say."

"Is he listed on the visitor roster? They don't let just anyone into the pediatric ward, do they?"

"But what if he tells the nurse he's Fallyn's father?" Claire's eyes widened, her skin as white as the handkerchief she held.

"I think we need to go to the hospital." Monty pushed Claire to her feet and then stood himself. "We can catch dinner after we straighten out this troublemaker."

Claire led the way to Fallyn's hospital room, Monty at her side. As they reached the doorway, her mother and Angie were seated on the visitor couch listening to Jamie who stood before them. Fallyn was asleep in her bed.

"I'll wait out here." Monty gave her shoulder a squeeze.

As she entered the room, Jamie turned, his expression unreadable. Behind him, Angie made a face, her eyes wide.

Her mother bridged the silence. "Jamie was just telling us about his real estate adventures. He's had a few sales in your area."

Claire studied him, looking for clues to his mental state. He appeared undisturbed, confident in his surroundings, no sign of earlier turmoil darkening his features. "Do you make enough to justify the three-hour drive over and back?"

"Not always." Jamie assumed a relaxed posture, hands clasped behind him. "I'm not planning to come to the coast as much in the near future."

Claire stared, a fleeting feeling of relief passing over her. "Why? Too far? Inconvenient? Poor accommodations?"

"Change of focus." His hazel eyes looked deep into her own. "I can make a difference here in the valley."

Claire opened her mouth to reply, but in that instant Fallyn awoke, eyes blinking as she looked at all the people in her room. "Aunt Claire? I need a glass of water."

Jamie reached for the water carafe and filled Fallyn's glass, handing it to Claire. She stiffened when he spoke to Fallyn. "Do you need to sit up to drink?"

Fallyn shook her head, taking the proffered glass with the straw poking up. "You're the man we saw at the fish and chips restaurant, aren't you?"

"Yes, I am. What a great memory." He set the container back on the table.

"You and Aunt Claire didn't get married."

Jamie blanched, followed by a rush of red along his cheeks. "No, we didn't." Jamie's eyes held sorrow, as if the child's statement wounded him. "I'm sorry that we didn't."

"Well, you can't marry her now, you know."

Jamie cast Claire a puzzled look before staring at the child. "And why is that?"

"She's in love with Monty."

Claire gasped, her hand going to her throat. Behind her, a muffled laugh sounded in the corridor. She blushed, heat again racing along the edge of her jaw and up her cheeks. "Fallyn, I'm not sure you understand the situation."

"You aren't in love with him?" Fallyn's face sagged, the information bringing sadness to her eyes. "He sure looks at you a lot."

At this, Jamie burst into laughter while another hoot sounded from the hall. "Fallyn, you are one great kid and, I believe, a future prophet."

Claire stood there, speechless, her mother and Angie exchanging giggles. She raised her palms in an act of self-defense. "What can I say to that?"

"Nothing is probably best." Jamie nodded toward the doorway. His eyes, only moments before filled with anger, now twinkled. A smile softened his jaw. "Can I speak to you in private?"

"There's a conference room across the hall." Claire spoke with more confidence than she felt. She strode toward the door, Jamie following on her heels. She shuddered, the showdown she'd feared would happen most certainly now would take place. The people she most cared about would witness it as well. Would this nightmare ever end?

Still waiting in the hallway, Monty leaned against the wall, arms folded across his chest, an amused smile on his face. He winked and mouthed. "I'm right here."

Claire continued to the small room and entered, placing herself on the opposite side of the table to create distance between her and Jamie.

He entered, closed the door, and faced her. "I know saying over and over that I'm sorry isn't going to convince you I'm a man worthy of your respect. But I am sorry, Claire, more than you can ever believe. I was wrong when I walked away. I should never have let you go." He shifted his weight from one leg to the other, his hands in his pockets, attention on the floor beneath him. When he looked up, his jaw was set. "But what I will do, to help you forgive me, is be tested for a kidney match for that little girl." He punched a fist into his palm. "I want to make this right between us."

"You will?" Claire sank in a nearby chair, not sure she'd heard him right. "I never, in my wildest dreams, believed I'd ever hear you say those words."

He stared out the room's window a minute, then heaved a sigh and sat in the other chair. "I've been a complete jerk, Claire. I realized I failed you when you needed me most. I ran because I was afraid. Getting married was one thing. Taking on fatherhood was another." He looked away, head lowered, his shoulders sagged. "But then I started having nightmares. A little girl who looked like you kept calling, "Daddy, Why?" I thought I was going insane." He straightened and faced her. "When I met Fallyn at that restaurant in Newport, I felt so ashamed. I knew what you had done. She is the image of you, except for my eyes. I wanted to fall on my knees and thank you, but I couldn't. I had imposed a death sentence on that child, but you acted upon the courage of your convictions, defied me, and gave her life. All by yourself."

"I didn't believe you'd support me in the decision." Claire pressed back the pain of memories surfacing—those agonizing weeks of not knowing what to do. Of feeling so alone. Abandoned. Ashamed. "The money was a slap in the face."

"You were probably right to think that, then." Jamie's eyes grew moist at the rims. "I can't imagine the anguish you must have suffered making the decision to finish your pregnancy alone. That took courage." He inhaled deeply. "But I meant what I said at your mother's house."

"Which part? Meeting your daughter or challenging custody?"

Jamie raised sorrowful eyes to her. "That I am ready to take responsibility for my actions. I meant it when I said I'd be willing to donate a kidney."

"You will?" Claire gasped for breath, the shock of his words landing like a sledgehammer directly below her sternum. "Thank you! You have completely surprised me."

"Maybe there's hope." Jamie stood straighter, a grin on his face. "I only ask to see Fallyn once in a while, maybe spend a day with her at the zoo, or wherever. Don't tell her who I really am. Give me a title, or something, like crazy Uncle Jamie. And keep me posted on her progress." Jamie took a deep breath. "And maybe you can find a place in your heart to forgive me?"

Claire squeezed her eyes closed, her mouth fighting the hallelujahs on her lips. Like a waterfall at Niagara, a cascade of tears ran down her face. Jamie sought forgiveness, something she thought she'd given five years before, but she'd held back. As the ugly wound within her gave way to God's cleansing, she couldn't speak, so convicted by her behavior. Finally, she spoke. "Thank you." She fought to breathe. "There's no way to describe what I feel, but I do forgive you. I thought I had, five years ago. But I guess a part of me wanted to make you pay for the trauma you put me through." She tried to smile, but the sorrow kept coming in waves, scrunching her face. "We were young, afraid, and stupid."

"The only stupid one was me." Jamie laid a hand on her shoulder. "I should never have walked away." He stroked her cheek. "I am so, so sorry."

"We weren't well suited. It was better that we parted. I see that now." She gazed up at Jamie's handsome, but humbled face. "Please forgive me too. I thought I had forgiven you, but what I really did was allow my disappointment to fester and grow, turning you into a monster from my past. You didn't deserve that. I'm sorry."

"Do you think Fallyn would want to get to know me?"

"If you are a match for a kidney, she'll feel like a part of you forever." Claire looked through the glass of the conference room to the gathering of people in Fallyn's room across the hall. "The problem is that she is going back to Pennsylvania as soon as school starts."

"I think you should talk to your sister."

Monty watched Claire struggle with conflicting emotions, her face a mixture of surprise and frustration as she and Jamie conferred together. Monty ached for the woman, knowing she'd not slept well for two days. Her heart hurt for her daughter, and she had to confront this man from the past who had so terribly failed her. Yet she managed a smile and kept responding with the grace of a saint. He hadn't thought his feelings ran this deep, but seeing Claire weather this storm in her life without so much as a whimper solidified the love that had been growing in his heart for some time. He wanted Claire in his future forever.

When she stood, she and Jamie shook hands as if a business transaction had occurred. But Claire tilted her head, stroked the man's cheek, and gave him a peck where her hand had been. Though Jamie didn't deserve her forgiveness, Monty knew Claire well enough to know she had given it. They exited the room and crossed the hall toward him.

Jamie extended his hand. "You're a lucky man."

Monty grinned. "Thanks. I'm glad you approve."

Jamie studied him for a moment, then turned, and walked toward the elevators.

Monty touched Claire's shoulder, her body trembling beneath his fingers. "Are you all right?"

Claire nodded. "Better than I've been in quite some time." She grabbed both of his hands and squeezed. "Jamie's agreed to be tested as a donor match."

"Think there's a possibility?"

"His mother showed a filial connection. As Fallyn's father, he may be perfect." She clapped a hand over her mouth, face turning red. "As a donor, I mean."

"Let's pray he matches. Fallyn's future depends on it."

"Are you ready for dinner?" Claire checked her watch. "My mother and Angie will want to go before long. I don't like to leave Fallyn alone."

"Why don't I find some take-out, you send your mother and sister home, and we stay with Fallyn until she falls asleep?"

"Sounds like a plan." Claire punched him lightly in the chest, a pensive smile lighting her face. "Thank you for caring so much. It means a lot to me."

"If you haven't figured me out yet, I'm totally at your disposal. You hooked me when you rescued my son in a snowstorm, and you've been reeling me in ever since."

Claire's eyes flashed, her mouth open like a tiny pink circle in her adorable face. "I've never thought of myself as a fisherwoman. Maybe I'm more skilled than I thought."

"As long as you don't apply for a job at NOAA." Monty resisted rolling his eyes. "I can just see you swimming with the sharks."

CHAPTER THIRTY-NINE

ANGIE'S EXPRESSION HELD WARNING WHEN CLAIRE rejoined her and her mother in Fallyn's room. The nurse monitoring the child's medical equipment hovered over a machine writing notes on a chart. Fallyn lay on her pillow, eyes tracking the movements of the nurse as she moved from one set of dials to another.

"Well, this has been an eventful day." Mom sat rigid, arms folded across her chest, mouth straight-lined as if frozen in place. "All this time I thought you and Jamie had broken up over a lover's quarrel. Instead I find out you parted as parents and Angie reaped the benefits." She squared her shoulders. "I don't like being the last to know."

"Who told her?" Claire directed her probe at Angie.

"Jamie." Mom assumed an empirical smile, smug at her news. "From what he said, he was as surprised as I was."

"Well, that's a discussion for another time." Claire resisted being drawn into further dialogue with Fallyn nearby. "Monty went for take-out so we can have dinner here and you two can get home. Monty will bring me by later."

Angie stood and went to Fallyn's bed. She leaned over and gave the child a hug and a kiss goodnight. "I love you, peanut." She straightened, her hand pressed against Fallyn's cheek. "I fly home in the morning, but Claire will stay here with you until you can go home with her."

"But Mommy, I wanted you to see the ocean." Fallyn reached up for her mother's hand. "Have you seen it?"

"Yes, Sweetheart. I grew up here, remember?"

Fallyn's face brightened with the news, then sobered. "I want to play dolls with Mia again."

Angie's eyes held tears as she turned away from the bed and

spoke to her mother. "Mom, why don't you go on to the car? I need to talk to Claire for a few minutes."

"More secrets?" Her mother smiled. "I hope they're not as life-changing as the last one I uncovered."

"Never know." Angie squeezed her mother's shoulder. "I'll fill you in later."

As they watched Mom walk away, Claire worried what her sister would say to her now. Mom knew their secret. Jamie knew as well. What more could be said?

The corridor was busy with attendants pushing dinner carts. The cacophony created by squeaking wheels and sliding trays grew louder. "Not a good place to talk."

Angie made a face. When Fallyn's tray arrived, she scooted inside the door, pulling Claire with her. She looked at Fallyn. "Do you want help with your tray, sweetie?"

The child shook her head as the nurse shoved the tray table over her and adjusted her bed. She picked up her juice and sipped on the straw, moving her plate in a circle. "I get real food today. There's pudding!"

"Do you care if we talk while you eat?" Angie handed Fallyn her napkin. "We'll be across the hall."

"I'll eat slow."

Claire laughed, as did Angie, and they stepped to the conference room. "At least here we can keep an eye on Fallyn." Claire studied her sister. "What do you need to discuss?"

"You better sit down."

Claire frowned. Had something else transpired before she and Monty arrived? Was Angie sick? "What's going on?"

"Fallyn needs you." Angie's smile sagged, as if what she was about to say hurt. "I want her to go home with you." She glanced away for a second, blinking away tears and drawing a deep breath, before she refocused on Claire. "And stay."

"What?" Claire didn't speak, her mouth open, the shock of Angie's words circling the room like gunfire. "For how long?"

"Forever."

Claire sat in stunned silence, the idea of Fallyn living with her indefinitely had been a deep-seated dream she never allowed to take residence in her mind. Now Angie was handing her a gift she had wanted for five long years. "Why?"

"What I am about to tell you may make you angry." Angie glanced away again, her lower lip caught in her teeth. "But I've kept something from you."

Claire frowned. "What?"

"We never adopted Fallyn." Angie's face blanched, the pain of what she needed to say threatening her composure.

"Jamie told me you didn't adopt, but I didn't believe him." Claire's heart raced, reliving the shock of what Jamie had said. "So you aren't her legal parents?"

"No, you are." Angie exhaled, the color returning to her cheeks as she admitted the truth she'd been hiding. "When you first came to us after Jamie deserted you, told us your predicament, and wanted to give your baby to us, we were ecstatic. We believed we were doing you a favor, even though you were making the most difficult decision of your life. Brennan and I discussed it with our attorney." Angie reached for Claire's hand. "Though we were delighted to have a newborn join us, we could see you didn't want to give Fallyn away. You yearned to keep her. We feared the pain would become too great for you when you visited each year, watching your daughter grow, sharing bits of her life, and leaving her behind when you returned home."

Claire didn't speak for a moment. She hadn't expected the secret she shared with her sister to ever be challenged. Angie's declaration tore open a world of forbidden hope inside her, the most precious dream she could ever have imagined, laid at her feet.

"What is she to you, if not your legally adopted daughter?"

"She's our ward. We're her guardians." Angie searched her face, as if seeking Claire's acceptance of the decision she and Brennan had made without telling her. "We would never have said anything if it weren't for the triplets. Fallyn is the most wonderful gift you ever gave me, and to give her back is tearing me apart. But she needs more than I can give her right now. She's sick and vulnerable, and she's said more than once she wishes she could have both of us as her Mom.

"Do you think she knows the truth?" Claire worked to keep the possibilities of Angie's declaration from affecting her ability to reason. Angie had only thought of her feelings when this arrangement developed. Knowing Fallyn wanted Claire as one of her mothers sent shivers down her spine. But Fallyn had lived with Angie and Brennan for five years. They were the only parents the child had ever known. That alone complicated the decision. "Or did you tell her?"

"No. We've never said anything, except her Mommy loved her so much she gave her to us." Angie sat up straighter. "We've cherished every minute we've had with our daughter . . . our niece. Giving her back will be difficult, but she'll need a lot of attention in the days ahead— all the love you have buried inside you."

Claire drew a deep breath, shaking at the thought of what she must do. All she had ever wanted had been laid at her feet, but could she accept the gift? She straightened her shoulders and fixed Angie with her gaze. "My answer is no. This is the wrong decision for Fallyn."

"Wrong decision? I thought you'd be delighted."

"I am. But I have seen what losing a mother does to a child Fallyn's age. Monty's kids came to me last fall emotionally wounded after losing their mother. Mia had reverted to sucking her thumb—the behavior of a two-year-old—and Mason chose to vent his grief in obnoxious behavior."

"But I won't be dead, Claire. Fallyn thinks of you as her favorite aunt and second mother."

"Exactly. *Second mother* is what I am." Claire smiled at her sister. "She misses you, Angie. She cries for you in her sleep. When she's sick, she asks for you. She wanted to come home as soon as the triplets were born so she could see them." Claire brushed away the sudden interference of tears. "I may have delivered her into this world, but you gave her the life she knows."

"Claire, think of what you are saying. How will I get her to all the doctor visits she faces? If she's given a kidney, there'll be a long stay in the hospital. Dividing my time between her needs and those of the triplets will pull me in too many directions." Angie's voice wobbled. "Brennan and I barely keep ahead of the workload now."

"Which is why I've decided to move back to Pennsylvania." Claire lifted her chin. "You still have a spare room. You need help. And I'm not ready to let go of Fallyn."

"Why would you do that?" Angie's cheeks had paled, her mouth slightly open. "What about Monty?"

"That's the piece of this puzzle I haven't figured out." Claire stared at the ceiling, swallowing the lump that had lodged in her throat. "We're only friends. I know he will understand my decision. As difficult as it may be for both of us."

"That man loves you. Every look your way is full of admiration. You'd throw that away?"

"You've never failed me, Angie. I won't fail you now." Claire sniffed. "And Monty is the one man who I think will understand."

"Maybe. But you know you're going to lose him."

"That may have been God's plan all along. Seeing his kids as they were in the beginning helped forge my decision for Fallyn."

"Will you tell her who you really are?"

"Yes. In time. After we've solved her health problems, and she's more stable, we'll tell her together like we always planned." Claire smiled at her sister. "Let her choose who she wants to live with."

Monty stepped from the elevator, the warm food leaving its spicy aroma in a trail behind him. When a male nurse in surgical garb offered to take it off his hands, he laughed. "No, I can manage, thanks."

As he entered Fallyn's room the look on Claire's face made him pause. Something had changed. Had the child taken a turn for the worse? A new diagnosis? "What's happened?"

"Come sit, so we can talk." Claire patted the space beside her. "I need to tell you something."

Monty sat, handed her a clamshell container from the bag, and a fork. "Almond Chicken?"

"How did you know I was wishing for Chinese food?" Claire popped the lid and let the smell of the fresh vegetables waft into the room. "I hope you bought yourself an entrée because I'm hungry enough to devour this entire portion."

"I did." Monty produced his own container. "Let me pray first."

They sat in silence for a few minutes, Monty aware of the tension surrounding Claire since he'd left. Had Jamie returned? Made threats? Or was it something else?

"Angie wants me to keep Fallyn." Her voice had dropped to a whisper.

"Keep her?" Monty resisted the urge to express his opinion. "For how long?"

"Forever." Claire sighed. "But with everything she's facing, Fallyn really needs Angie."

"Kidney surgery?"

Claire nodded. "And recovery." She ran her finger along the edge of the container. "But that's the least of it. Jamie has agreed to be tested as a match. If he doesn't, that means continuing my search. It could be years before we find a kidney. But she's too precious to me to not keep trying."

"True." Monty took another bite. "Ellen could help. But she and Kevin told me last night they expect their own little one soon."

Claire's eyes widened. "That's wonderful news!"

"Ellen probably wanted to tell you herself, so don't mention I told you."

At Claire's nod, he resumed their discussion. "What will you do?"

Claire started to speak, but stopped, her eyes rimmed with tears. "I've decided to return to Pennsylvania."

Monty stared. "What? Why?"

"Fallyn needs the only mother she has ever known. Your kids have shown me what losing a mother can do to one so young. I won't do that to her." Claire touched his arm. "But Angie is overwhelmed. Sending Fallyn back will only complicate her life further. If I go with them, I can provide support on both fronts. Fallyn can know the truth of her birth once she's out of danger."

"Are you sure you want to do this?" Monty stared, disbelief rocking every thought. "What about your career?"

"Careers can wait. People can't. Fallyn needs me to be her advocate. She's young, fragile, and unable to do this for herself." Claire blinked back the moisture gathering on her lids. "Angie is already tired and stretched beyond her ability to cope." She cast him a rueful smile. "I have to do this for them."

Monty looked down at his food, acutely aware of the separation he sensed was coming. Dread coursed through him.

Claire's next words pleaded for understanding. "Angie has

always stood by me. After Jamie's betrayal she stayed at my side when I didn't want to live. She opened her home so I could finish my studies in Pennsylvania while we waited for Fallyn to arrive. She provided answers to friends and others who asked too many questions. She even kept the truth about Fallyn's origins from my mother until I could handle it. Now she's in need. I can't abandon her, either."

Monty stopped eating. The truth in her words hit him like bullets. The depth of her heart made him love her more. Claire couldn't do otherwise. But where did that leave him? "Claire, I—"

"—I will always cherish the friendship you and I have shared. But of all the people I've met, I know you will understand this is something I must do." She touched his shoulder. "I'm sorry."

"Don't be. I do understand." His voice wobbled. "My heart may take time to adjust, but I can't see you doing anything else. I love you."

"Thank you, Monty."

He mustered the largest smile he could find. "Let's leave the door open for the future. Okay?"

Claire nodded, her face awash with tears. "That future may never come."

He reached around her shoulders and drew her close, kissing her on the cheek. A kiss goodbye.

CHAPTER FORTY

MONTY STOOD IN FRONT OF THE Christmas tree, replacing two burned out bulbs on a light string. He heard his telephone ring where he'd left it on the counter in the kitchen and turned, but Mason's voice beat him to the hello.

"Dad, Aunt Ellen wants to know if you want Christmas dinner tomorrow at one o'clock or at four?" Mason stood at the edge of the room, holding out the phone.

"Let me talk to her." Monty took the phone and sat on a winged-back chair near the fireplace. "Hey, Sis, how are you feeling?"

"Like an elephant." Ellen sounded out of breath. "The next few weeks are stretching longer and longer."

"You want me to cook the dinner?" Monty hadn't had any more experience cooking a turkey since he, Ellen, and Claire had joined forces a year ago at Thanksgiving. This Thanksgiving Kevin had taken them all out for dinner at a local restaurant to spare Ellen the work so late in her pregnancy. The kids got their drumsticks, and he enjoyed a day off. "I can pick up a ham."

"No. I can cook a bird." Ellen sounded annoyed. "I want lots of turkey leftovers to feed those two munchkins when you leave on tour in two weeks."

"I don't want you wearing yourself out." Monty worried Ellen took on too much. "Thank goodness Mom and Dad are coming to help with the new baby as well as the twins."

"Thank goodness is right. But Mom was there for you and Marissa when the twins were born, so she knows she has to do the same for me." Ellen chuckled. "I expect to be pampered." She paused. "Anyway, dinner time?"

"Any time you get it done is fine with me."

"Are you still bringing dessert?"

"I picked up a half-gallon of ice cream and a bakery pie."

"Pumpkin?"

"No. Christmas berry."

"See you tomorrow, then. Let's say one o'clock. We can always munch on snacks while we wait."

Monty parked next to Ellen's car the next day, careful to leave room for Kevin's rig, which was missing from the Norse lineup in the drive. He wondered where his brother-in-law might be. Not much was open on Christmas Day in Newport, but Ellen must have needed something. He opened the truck door and Mason scrambled to the ground, followed by Mia who took his hand as she jumped. Not as big as her brother, she didn't trust the distance from the cab.

Both of the children had grown this summer. He'd stopped lifting them down when school started. The booster seats were gone. Mason and Mia had already written long wish lists for their ninth birthdays coming on New Year's Day—lists that reflected the dreams of two happy, healthy third graders. A twinge of regret entered his thoughts remembering the woman who had worked so hard to lead his children back from the loss of their mother onto the path of recovery.

Claire wrote to all of them—a letter for him and colorful notes to the twins. Busy with Angie's triplets and caring for Fallyn, she sounded happy. Jamie's kidney was a match for his daughter, and the surgery happened the end of October. Fallyn bounced back, but Jamie still suffered from the impact on his body.

Monty sighed. Claire's absence left a void he'd not been able to fill. He was happy for her but replacing the emptiness with someone or something else hadn't happened. She loved Pennsylvania, being near her biological daughter, being surrounded by family and former friends from her school stay there. A return to Oregon never made it into her letters. That she planned to come back didn't get even an honorable mention. She signed her missives 'your friend'. Monty and his kids had become part of a past Claire missed, but had left behind. For good. Or so it seemed. It hurt.

He followed the children to Ellen's door, balancing the pie in one hand and the bag with the ice cream in the other. At Mason's exuberant doorbell push—ding, ding, a-ding, ding—Kevin opened the door, surprising Monty. "Hey. Where's your rig?"

"In the street." Kevin pointed across the drive. "Wanted to leave you plenty of room."

Monty studied his brother-in-law. "Has my ticket history become public record?"

"Could be." Kevin teased. "If that's ice cream, we need to get it in the freezer."

Monty stepped into the entry, the unmistakable aroma of cooking food permeating the air. The kids raced ahead to the kitchen while he and Kevin lagged behind, his curious, detail-oriented mind weighing every reason Kevin had parked in the street.

Ellen stood at the sink, a paring knife in her hand. "Merry Christmas, Monty."

"Merry Christmas to you. Anything you want us to do?"

"Why don't you and the kids fill the lazy Susan? There's celery and carrot sticks in the fridge, and the olives and pickles are on the counter."

"Got it." He stuck the ice cream in the freezer and called the twins. "Mia. Mason. Come help with the dinner." The pair popped through the door from the family room where they'd disappeared and stood at his side. "Wash your hands. We're in charge of condiments."

"Condiments?" Mason wrinkled his nose.

"Pickles, olives, vegetables." Monty held up a can. "You can do this."

As the twins hurried away, Monty placed the small containers on their carousel, his mind on another celebration.

"Did you open gifts this morning?"

Ellen's question jarred him from his reverie, and he nodded. "We're back to our traditions. Mason recited the entire second chapter of Luke."

"Marissa taught them well."

Mia returned and darted to Ellen's side, wrapping an arm about her bulging waistline. "Daddy gave me a pair of inline skates."

"Me, too." Mason popped a pickle in his mouth. He made a face. "Sour!"

The doorbell rang, and Mason turned to the living room. "Want me to get it, Auntie Ellen?"

"Take your dad, Mason."

Monty walked behind his son, waiting as Mason opened the door. At Mason's gasp, Monty looked out on the step.

"Claire?"

He hadn't changed. Nor had he shaved, the telltale shadow of a day's growth of beard outlining the sharp contours of his jaw. His deep blue eyes registered surprise at seeing her, the dimple she rarely saw punctuating a smile that said he was glad she was here.

Claire smiled at him as he stood open-mouthed in the doorway. "I understood there was a Christmas dinner here without a pumpkin pie." She held out her package. "I also know there's a pair of munchkins who like oatmeal chocolate chip cookies."

Mason hooted. "I'll take those!" He disappeared inside, his exuberance booming. "Mia! Miss Claire is here. And she brought cookies!"

Monty took the pie and stepped back. "I hope you're here for dinner."

Nearly six months had passed since Claire had said goodbye to this man and his children, choosing to follow a different path and thinking she'd never see him again. She'd steeled herself for the separation. She'd cried tears leaving him, a man who said he wanted to love her and who had never been far from her thoughts. She'd marveled that he'd understood her refusal of Angie's gift of surrendering Fallyn. He'd witnessed her personal torment and having endured the angst of his own children's loss, he'd acknowledged what a similar loss could produce in Fallyn's sunny spirit. This man had given his blessing despite his own unresolved wishes. How her heart had ached at the decision.

He gestured for her to enter and she did, following him as he led the way to the kitchen where Ellen stood beaming, her baby bump protruding beneath her apron.

Claire shook her head at her friend's transformed shape. "You're sure it's only one?"

Monty laughed. "I keep telling her there are twins in the family."

"Yeah, and they're yours!" Ellen wrapped Claire in a hug and added a peck on the cheek. "He's still as smart-mouthed as ever."

To think he might have been hers had circumstances been different. But she'd known Fallyn's future lay in the balance. Claire's sacrifice of her own life's desires insured Fallyn of a better footing as she matured. The child had sidestepped the trauma Mia and Mason had endured. She'd blossomed in the attention of her mother and father as well as in the bonus of having her Aunt Claire at her side. The child knew nothing of the turmoil surrounding her existence, only that she got her wish—two mommies who loved her.

"Did you drive over from the valley?" Monty looked

confused. "You didn't fly into Newport."

"Yes. I drove. I left my car at my mother's when I moved to Pennsylvania." Claire took an apron Ellen handed her and tied it at her waist. "I flew into Eugene two days ago."

"How long are you here?"

"I'm here to help Ellen manage Mia and Mason while you leave for tour. I come highly recommended as a nanny now."

The days in Pennsylvania had stretched endlessly, filled with doctor's visits for Fallyn, hospital stays, and eventually Fallyn's recovery from surgery which had kept Claire at the hospital for nearly two weeks. Angie had come every day, but with Claire on duty she had been free to go home to the triplets as well.

When November brought her sixth birthday, Fallyn had recovered enough that Angie and Claire decided to tell her the truth about her birth.

"We have a surprise for you." Angie had stepped on eggshells as she spoke.

"A surprise?" Fallyn grinned. "Not more babies?"

"No." Claire laughed at the thought. "We thought you'd like to know about *your* birth day. How it happened."

Fallyn surprised them both. "You mean when you gave me to Mommy?"

Claire gasped. "You already knew?"

"I knew you were my mommy when I heard Grandma Simpson talk about it at the hospital." She grinned, two of her front teeth now missing. "When do I get to live back at the ocean?"

Both Claire and Angie had burst into laughter, Claire smiling at her daughter. "Well, I guess that answers that."

"You have to finish the school year here. My leave of absence is up in September, so I'll return to my job."

Claire hadn't minded a single minute of her time in Pennsylvania. Except at night when she thought of Monty and his kids and missed them. Now she was here, with them, with him. Could she hope to pick up where they'd left off?

Ellen handed her a spoon. "Want to taste the gravy for me? My pregnant tongue wants to salt everything too much."

Claire moved to the pan where the gravy bubbled. She dipped the spoon and blew to cool it. She winked at Monty. "Think I'll make a good nanny for your kids?"

Monty grinned. "I can think of a lot of things I can recommend you for."

Claire turned to the sink and rinsed the spoon, the effect of his words sending warm waves along her neck and up her cheeks. "The gravy is perfect, Ellen."

A male voice whispered at her ear. "So is the woman who's blushing."

His hand touched her elbow, and she turned to face him. In his eyes she saw what she had hoped for, the look of a man who had his sights set on her.

"I have two weeks before I set sail."

"Oh?"

"And Ellen doesn't need you yet."

"No."

"Did Fallyn come?"

"No. She has school." Claire smiled. "In the fall, I'll resume teaching. Fallyn plans to live with me."

"We have some serious catching up to do." Monty kissed her cheek. "What do you think?"

Claire smiled. "That can be arranged, Mr. Chandler."

CHAPTER FORTY-ONE

Six months later

THE OCEAN WAVES RIPPLED BEHIND MONTY as he waited for Claire and the rest of the wedding party to join him and the pastor at the water's edge. The metal trellis he'd rented shuddered in the breeze, the ivy and baby's breath fluttering from their niches on the woven arch. The white voile rustled, the thin fabric billowing around the base of the structure. He'd added two potted palms on either side to give a tropical feel to the setting, even though this stretch of beach belonged to their hometown on the north Pacific.

Monty had visited this spot several times in the past week, moving driftwood, arranging it like benches for those like Claire's mother and Angie's nanny, Mrs. Thornton, who would prefer to sit during the ceremony. Most guests would stand. He had come early this morning to attach a kite to each log, making sure the area had been clearly marked for their wedding. As he gazed about him, the warmth of the sun, the blue of the ocean, and the stretch of sand created a wedding picture worthy of a photo shoot.

Angie, Brennan, Fallyn, and the triplets had flown west, the babies now more than a year old. They were squirmy toddlers who had never experienced the beach, ocean water, or trade winds. Keeping them in the stroller built for three would take all of Mrs. Thornton's attention during the service, but she declared she'd be fine.

Fallyn danced in a small circle, her green floral dress accented by a ring of flowers in her hair and her cheeks pink from the press of the wind. Anyone who noticed the lively child with the glowing skin and twinkling eyes would find it difficult to believe she'd received a kidney shortly before Christmas.

Mia and Mason waited by the driftwood, a basket of flowers in Mia's hand and the rings on a pillow assigned to Mason. As if they'd been sisters and brother forever, the three children chattered among themselves. Mason's focus remained on the kites that hovered over them, while Mia and Fallyn discussed their dolls. Mia paused and pointed. "I see Grandma Chandler."

Monty turned his attention to the berm separating the beach from the parking lot. The guests ambled in bunches of twos and threes as they walked down the path to the ocean's shore. His parents had driven in from Seattle, Claire's mother from the valley. His father held the infant carrier with Kevin and Ellen's new baby boy inside. Friends from NOAA came with their spouses. Soon the driftwood seats filled, leaving some to stand behind them. As the pathway emptied, an ensign from the USS Fort Clackamas stood, holding an antique ship's bronze bell. He rang the bell three times and all the guests rose and faced behind them.

Angie appeared at the top of the berm, smiling as she strolled on Brennan's arm toward the ceremony. Ellen came next, accompanied by Kevin.

At last, Claire appeared at the top of the rise, alone. The ensign sounded the bell again five times. She walked unescorted to the altar, a decision she'd made when her father died years before. Her blonde curls whipped around her bridal veil, her form-fitting gown a sea foam green chiffon. She carried white gardenias mixed with a mass of ferns. He'd encouraged her to wear white, but she'd declined, citing her history required honesty, not only in her life but in her marriage. "No more shrinking from the past."

As Claire neared the gathering, Fallyn and Mia stepped in front of her, strewing the flowers from the basket onto the path where she walked. Mason followed, the pillow bouncing as he worked unsuccessfully to contain his eagerness. Claire smiled at her miniature attendants, encouraging them to continue toward their spots on the sand. No orchestra played, only the music of the waves filled the background silence.

He offered his arm when she stood beside him. "You look beautiful."

"Thanks." Her whisper only reached his ears, and she moved closer to him. "Not much warmth in that sun, is there?"

"At least there's no rain."

"For that I'm especially thankful."

The pastor stepped to the middle of the arch. "Dearly beloved, we are here today to witness the vows of Claire Elaine Simpson and Montgomery William Chandler, who wish to be united in the bonds of matrimony. Will you please rise for the opening prayer?"

Claire's heart raced, its wild erratic rhythm making her breathless as the pastor finished the wedding message and she and Monty repeated their vows to each other. Monty's fingers trembled when he placed the gold band on her hand. The diamonds embedded in the circle glittered like stars in the spattering of sun spots that blessed the blustery coastal day. Beside her, Fallyn could scarce stand still, cheeks rosy and eyes twinkling as she waited to embrace a new father. Claire believed any minute she'd awaken and find this day, this moment, these guests to be nothing more than a dream her mind had created while she slept.

"And now by the powers vested in me by Almighty God and according to the laws of the state of Oregon, I pronounce you husband and wife."

Claire blinked. She hadn't awakened. She was here, marrying the man of her dreams, and welcoming his children, embracing a future she never thought could be hers.

Mason jumped up and down beside his father, his whoop making the guests laugh.

Mia grabbed Fallyn's hand and they giggled like sisters, hugging each other. Monty wrapped his arms about Claire and drew her close, kissing her breathless. Behind them the guests clapped. A blast of cold air whipped in off the ocean and rippled the faces of the tethered kites, making them dance as if possessed. The chaos seemed fitting, somehow, because here on this ocean, Claire's heart had been tugged into a web of love as steadfastly as a kite on the wind.

Author Note

This third book in the Mended Hearts series has been fun to write. My heart was in love with the characters from the beginning and as I typed my way into their lives I enjoyed all of their escapades and cried with them through their heartaches.

Because this book took readers back to Newport, Oregon where the first story in the series had begun, I had to find a position for my hero that coordinated with his environment. I had read of the move by the National Oceanic and Atmospheric Administration from its original headquarters in Seattle to Newport and decided that provided the right combination of details upon which to base my novel. Researching NOAA's website and database (open to the public) I discovered the organization is multi-faceted and addresses all sort of challenges dealing with the ocean and weather.

One of those facets was the scientific research teams that track habitats and species in the ocean's depths. Reading blogs written by those scientists gave me the idea for the monitoring of the gray whales. Studying the plight of the gray whale led me to the stories of rescued whales around the world and formed the basis for the fictionalized scene of Monty and his crew freeing the humpback in San Francisco waters.

While writing this novel, news of a fishing tragedy in the Bering Sea made the headlines of my local newspaper. In 2017 a fishing trawler disappeared near the Pribilof Islands and the Coast Guard and NOAA were called in to find the vessel. I fictionalized that account as well as imagining what the emotions of both the rescue crew and the families awaiting answers must be. My heart goes out to those who lost loved ones in this tragedy.

Fimrite, Peter. "Daring Rescue of Whale Off Farallones."
San Francisco Chronicle. 14 December 2005.
Shanks, Anna. "Diver's Extraordinary Encounter with 50ft Humpback Whale."
Metro.co.uk. 19 August 2009.
https://www.seattletimes.com/seattle.../hearings-to-begin-on-why-crab-boat-destination-s... Aug 7, 2017 –

On a lighter note I couldn't resist re-telling the story I heard during a dental exam about the technician's first attempt to cook a turkey for her new husband. She really did cook the turkey long enough to get it crispy brown on the outside and then serve it mostly raw on the interior. He survived though he was sick for three days. Truth is stranger than fiction!

Finally, the lemon and pineapple drink Claire fixed for Mia's sore throat came from a recipe I found on the internet. I have no idea who came up with it to begin with, so I can't give credit to that person, but I've used this, and it does reduce symptoms:

Six lemons squeezed, 1 minced garlic, 3 cups pineapple juice, 2 tbsp. honey. You can also add 2 tsp ginger powder, and 1/4 tsp Cayenne powder, but the juices and the honey work wonders. Thanks to Dave Summers, True Health and Healing.

I love to connect with readers. You can find me at the following places...and if you enjoy any of my books, I'd love if you'd leave a review on Amazon, Goodreads, Barnes and Noble.com or Christianbook.com. Thank you!

BookBub: www.bookbub.com/profile/patricia-lee-5aed9c77-b548-496f-b1b8-8c85e35ff368
Website/blog/newsletter: www.authorpatricialee.net
Twitter: lee_patricia__

Facebook: www.facebook.com/patricialeebooks

All Author https://allauthor.com/profile/authorpatricialee/

Discussion Questions

Have you ever been close to a niece or a nephew, or another child that wasn't yours? What lengths would you go to in order to make that boy or girl happier? Have you known anyone who had to give a child up at birth, and if so, what can you do as a Christian to help that person heal from their loss?

Have you known someone with a life-threatening disease? If you were put in the situation of enduring a deep hurt to help a child, would you be able to put aside your pride to help, even at the cost of your own happiness?

How did you view Angie's plight? Was sending Fallyn home with her aunt a wise choice on Angie's part? Or a mistake for Fallyn? Was Claire justified in saying yes to her sister?

Claire doesn't trust her ability to care for Fallyn. What kinds of things would you have suggested she do to better cope with the child's emergencies?

Jamie Duval wants time to talk with Claire from the beginning of the book until he shows up at her mother's home near the end. Does Claire's view of him color your opinion of Jamie? Do you suppose he might have wanted reconciliation from the beginning had Claire allowed him the opportunity? Do you believe her when she said she'd forgiven Jamie? Why or why not?

Monty's loss of his wife affects his every action. As life begins to flow more smoothly he finds himself attracted to Claire. Do men emotionally heal faster than women? Or is grieving a personal thing for which there is no timeline?

Have you known a woman who became pregnant outside of marriage? How was she treated by friends? Her family? Her church? Does your circle of friends have room for someone who made a mistake and who seeks forgiveness and the opportunity to be restored in a community of believers?

Monty and Claire come into the story as broken people who need mending. At story's end they have found each other, seek a new beginning together, and hope to settle the turmoil of their pasts. What part did God play in their healing? Do you believe God is in the business of Mending Hearts?